## STALKERS

The gurgle returned, along with the moist hiss and the sloshing. Then a different sound worse than all of the others joined in the terrorizing medley—a wet slithering like a bathtub full of eels.

He smelled rotten seafood again. This time the odor was much stronger.

Gavril stopped but could not make himself turn around. The noises from behind him came closer until they seemed to pound on his ears, although he knew they were actually still quite soft. The only other sound he could hear was his own laboring heart.

The gurgle and hiss finally stopped getting louder. At the same moment, the sloshing and slithering ceased altogether. The smell of dead fish remained on the breeze.

Something brushed upward through the hair on the back of his head.

He spun around and fired his pistol twice. "Who's there?" he yelled, firing his Colt .45 once more.

No matter how he squinted into the darkness, he could see nothing but the stars above.

# DEEP CURRENT

**Benjamin E. Miller**

AN ONYX BOOK

ONYX
Published by New American Library, a division of
Penguin Group (USA) Inc., 375 Hudson Street,
New York, New York 10014, U.S.A.
Penguin Books Ltd, 80 Strand,
London WC2R 0RL, England
Penguin Books Australia Ltd, 250 Camberwell Road,
Camberwell, Victoria 3124, Australia
Penguin Books Canada Ltd, 10 Alcorn Avenue,
Toronto, Ontario, Canada M4V 3B2
Penguin Books (N.Z.) Ltd, Cnr Rosedale and Airborne Roads,
Albany, Auckland 1310, New Zealand

Penguin Books Ltd, Registered Offices:
80 Strand, London WC2R 0RL, England

First published by Onyx, an imprint of New American Library,
a division of Penguin Group (USA) Inc.

First Printing, March 2004
10  9  8  7  6  5  4  3  2

For my parents

# ACKNOWLEDGMENTS

Many thanks to my agent, Ethan Ellenberg, whose feedback helped me make this story as exciting, realistic, and suspenseful as it could possibly be. I'm also grateful to my editor, Ron Martirano, for keeping every paragraph on track and making every word count. Lisa R. Lester, copyeditor extraordinaire, helped me keep all the details straight and clear. I'm indebted to Samantha Parker for her encouragement and patience during the long process of polishing the text for maximum readability. Last but most, the foundation of this achievement and all of my others is the unyielding love and support from my parents, Helen Doris Miller and Charles Miller, and from my grandparents, Earl and Juanita Profitt.

# CHAPTER 1

## Fog

*January 10*

The fog was uneven, blowing by in wisps and lumps like a galloping army of phantoms. Todd stopped climbing the stairs from the galley and stared in disbelief. The sky had been clear just a minute before. He slowly stepped onto the deck and turned around in a full circle, eyes wide. The tropical sea was hidden by the opaque blanket in all directions. The stinging afternoon sun had become an area of nebulous glow.

"Dad?" he said.

Todd was fourteen, athletic and tall for his age. He had straight blond hair, blue eyes, and freckles.

Leonard Arlington—Todd's balding, overweight, and wealthy father—was leaning over the port railing. "I can barely see the water," he said, more to himself than to Todd.

Todd joined him and looked for the yacht's bow wave. All he could see through the marbled mist was a fuzzy blur of motion. "Could a cold front . . .?"

Leonard straightened and glared at Todd. "No. There is no fog between French Polynesia and Samoa at this time of year. It doesn't happen."

Yet it was happening, but Todd knew better than to point that out.

The deck had been blazing hot since nine in the morning. When Todd had descended to the galley to stow the fish they'd just caught, every sunlit surface had been painful to touch. Now the air was barely room temperature and cooling fast, and Leonard's new yacht was enshrouded by lumpy white streaks, as if the air had turned to buttermilk.

Leonard turned his glare from Todd to Sophie, Todd's infant sister. Sophie was crying and squirming in her shaded bassinet, which sat on the wooden deck beside Todd's mother. Linda Arlington was dozing on a worn teak tanning chair, one hand holding her place in a closed hardback romance and the other hand drooping above her empty vodka glass.

"The goddamn weather forecast was clear for the next forty-eight hours," Leonard whispered to Todd.

Todd had felt a little queasy before the fog came. His mild seasickness always lingered through the mornings, made worse by the oppressive heat and the smell of fish. He had been steeping in self-pity, pondering how he was also sick of his sister's crying, his mother's drinking, and his father's deep-sea fishing lessons. How in the world was he going to survive the two more weeks of his life that this monotonous, sweltering family cruise was going to claim?

Now the sea had grown strangely calm, with no trace of the gentle swells that normally rolled across the open ocean even in clear weather. And his seasickness was gone, replaced by a new kind of gut-flutter—a chilling sensation of dread.

Todd had spent a large part of his life on boats. His father was a former world-champion big-game fisherman. For as long as Todd could remember, Leonard had been coaching him in the arcane sport, remaining willfully oblivious to the fact that Todd had little interest or aptitude for catching fish. But in all of his short life at sea, Todd had never seen a fog like this. Leonard's expression said that he hadn't either.

It was the stuff of marine folklore, Todd thought. It was the way legends explaining the freak disappearance of crews from their ships started out.

A gust of cold wind blew across the deck. Not just cool, Todd thought—*cold*.

Fog was unexplainable. So was the abrupt drop in temperature. But a *cold* wind on the Tropic of Capricorn in the middle of the austral summer was just plain impossible.

The fog had thickened until they could barely make out the chrome bowsprit.

Leonard cautiously stepped to the bow and peered ahead. "God, what are you doing?" he whispered.

Todd squatted beside Sophie's handheld bassinet and smiled at her. She stopped crying and smiled back, making deep dimples in flushed cheeks that were still streaked with tears. She waved her tiny arms at him and blew bubbles through her toothless gums.

Todd shook his mother's limp hand. "Mom, wake up. Something's wrong with the weather."

She groaned, rolled onto her side, and went back to sleep.

A jarring buzz came from the foghorn on the wheelhouse behind Todd, and a red light on the roof began flashing, turning the fog pink. Leonard ran back to the wheelhouse. Todd joined him, carrying Sophie in her lavender bassinet. He watched his father stare at the video screen and punch buttons on the keyboard of the electronic helm.

"What's the alarm for?" Todd asked. He had no idea what his father was doing. The yacht was brand-new, and Leonard had forbade him to touch the helm computer.

"Shhh. I think it's the navigational radar." Leonard was tapping the Enter key repeatedly, harder and harder, watching menus flash by. Finally he stopped.

"*Proximity?*"

Todd did not like the tone of his father's voice. He sounded confused and scared.

Leonard stepped back from the computer, treading his

son's toes. "It's a land proximity warning, but that's impossible! There are no islands on the charts."

"Maybe it's another ship."

"Couldn't be. We're nowhere near a trade route, and the radar program wouldn't mistake a small boat for land."

"Maybe we should stop," Todd said. The powerful motor yacht was still surging through the calm South Pacific at cruise speed.

Leonard swung out of the wheelhouse and approached the bow again. "It's just this stupid fog screwing up the radar," he said. "I guess I'll have to turn—" He abruptly stopped, looking upward. Todd saw him crouch and thrust out his hands as if to ward off an attacking predator.

"Oh, God, *no!*" Leonard shouted.

A white cliff loomed through the fog, towering so high that Todd thought it was just a few feet ahead. As the vast wall echoed his father's shout, Todd dropped onto his knees and elbows, covering Sophie's bassinet with his torso.

A second elapsed with no collision.

Todd raised his head to look again.

The cliff looked even higher now, and it appeared to be slowly sliding by to the left. Its surface was glistening wet and laced with vertical cracks. Some areas looked rough and irregular. Others were flat and smooth. Some were pure white, others shaded and bluish. It was the strangest kind of rock Todd had ever seen.

As the towering rampart steadily approached, he realized that it was not made of rock at all.

*It was ice.*

"Hey, it's foggy," his mother said. Her words were slurred by drowsiness and alcohol.

Todd glanced back at her. She was sitting up, taking off her sunglasses. He looked forward again, running his gaze up and down the wet ice cliff. Its top was almost straight overhead now. He could not believe its height. The unfamiliar perspective made him dizzy.

Todd heard his mother suck in a deep breath behind him. Then she screamed until her lungs were empty.

"Get below!" Leonard yelled as he hurdled over Todd and Sophie and swung into the wheelhouse. He punched a few keys, then started cursing and slamming his fist on the keyboard.

Todd scrambled down the stairs to the galley, both arms wrapped tightly around Sophie's bassinet. Sophie had started wailing again at the sound of her mother's scream. Todd crouched on the floor with his back against the forward bulkhead by the stairs. He took his shrieking sister from the bassinet and held her tightly against his chest. He placed one of his sneakers behind his head to cushion the blow, then squeezed his eyes shut and whispered, "Please let us live, please let us live," waiting for the collision to splatter his brains all over the hold.

When the impact finally came, sharp pain shot through his head, and he could not breathe. He caught a close-up glimpse of the wood-paneled ceiling before landing hard on the floor. He curled up on his right side, still clutching Sophie to his chest, holding her neck straight with one strong hand. Loud snaps of splintering fiberglass came and went. Then all he could hear was a soft gurgle. The floor began to tilt, rising at the stern.

Leonard shouted down from the deck. His voice was shrill with fear and pain. "Todd! Get the survival gear!"

Now Todd was glad his father had forced them to go through emergency drills before departing. He knew exactly what to do. While Leonard inflated the life raft and got his mother on board, Todd was supposed to gather the first aid kit, a bag of canned rations, and a jug of water. Despite the dizziness and pain in his head, he staggered up the tilting galley floor to the doorway where his backpack hung on a hook.

He discovered that he could not reach for the pack with Sophie in his arms.

The safety drills had not included Sophie. His parents

had not planned to take her on the cruise back then. They were going to leave her with an aunt. But at the last minute, Todd's mother had refused to go if Sophie didn't come too.

The floor was tilting faster. He looked back and saw a pool of water forming against the wall where he'd been sitting. The plan had been to take the rations bag in his left hand, the water jug in his right hand, and the first aid kit in his backpack. Todd tried to think through his headache. He and Sophie would be trapped forever if he hesitated a few more seconds.

He yanked open the tilting cupboard doors, stuffed all of Sophie's clothes into the bottom of his backpack, lay Sophie on top of them, and tucked in her probing hands as he zipped the pack shut, leaving a two-inch gap for air to get in. Then he gently donned the pack, tucked a box of Pampers under his left arm, picked up the bag of dried baby formula in his left hand, grabbed the water jug with his right arm, and splashed through the rising seawater to the tilted stairs.

Sophie screamed in terror as he ran.

# CHAPTER 2

# Marines

The ninety-by-fifty-foot hovercraft bounded over white-capped breakers toward Hawaii's Kaneohe Bay. Corporal Enrica Lopez leaned against the foredeck's blue safety railing and let the warm salty air blow through her thick hair, which was as black as coal and cropped close. Her MEU(SOC)—Marine Expeditionary Unit (Special Operations Capable)—was finally coming home from a six-month tour of sea duty.

Beyond the Mokapu Peninsula's white beach and the dense band of tropical foliage above it, Rica could see the distant blue-green slopes of Koolau Mountain. The slender, vertically corrugated ridge rose from the volcanic island like the upturned edge of a serrated blade.

Private First Class Paz Rodriguez slouched against the railing beside her, as close to her as he could politely get, gazing up at her with his pining brown eyes. "It will feel good to be on land, *sí?*"

Rica nodded halfheartedly.

Paz and Rica were both of Puerto Rican descent, although Paz had grown up in a poor neighborhood of New York City. He was almost two years younger than her and had enlisted a year later. She was the only corporal in their company who could reliably understand his deplorable Spanish accent, so he had been assigned to the four-soldier fire team that she was in charge of.

Rica knew that Paz was in love with her, but the feeling was not mutual. He had the most athletic body she had ever seen and the same smooth, dark complexion as her—part Spanish, part Taino Indian—but he was a brother Marine, and Rica believed in the rule of no fraternization within the ranks. Even if he had been a civilian, Paz was just too young, too short, and worst of all, too religious.

A deep male voice boomed behind them. "Rodriguez! You ain't smiling, devil dog! Don't you like hitting sand?"

The man addressing Paz was Jacob "Gunny" Gavril, the gunnery sergeant assigned to Rica's squad. He was middle-aged, southern, black as tar, and one of the Marine Corps's most decorated noncommissioned officers. He was also six four and built like a bear, dwarfing Paz's gymnastic form.

Normally, a gunnery sergeant in the Marine infantry would have been responsible for managing the logistics of an entire rifle company, a unit with at least two hundred soldiers. Gavril's humiliating assignment to a single twelve-soldier squad—a position usually filled by an ordinary sergeant—had resulted from his open support of childless women who wanted to fight in ground combat units. Gavril's political stance had grown popular in civilian culture but was still career suicide for a male officer or NCO.

"Stogie?" Joan Bledsoe jogged up and handed Paz a cigar the size of a stapler. Only a handful of women had joined the infantry since Congress had repealed the combat exclusion laws prohibiting women in the military from occupying positions that were likely to get them killed in action—or promoted. So far, Rica's fire team was the only one in the MEU with *two* women.

Joan was blond, crew cut, grotesquely lean, and a decade older than Rica and Paz. Rica envied her rippling muscles but not her masculine shape. She also did not envy Joan's face, although she sometimes cursed her own. Rica had the kind of unusual face that induced susceptible young men to offer their souls for a kiss. Joan's face was also unusual, in a different way. With her bulging eyes, scythelike nose, and apparently lipless mouth, she bore a vague resemblance to a snapping turtle.

"For victory," Joan said as she lit another cigar for Sergeant Gavril.

He inhaled and bent over coughing.

Joan laughed. "Sorry, Gunny. They got kind of damp on the ship."

"You mean moldy," Gavril wheezed.

"They might have grown some moss," Joan admitted.

Gavril straightened, rubbed his watering eyes, and spread his huge arms as if to embrace the sparkling breakers and the approaching strip of white sand. "What the hell! For the Corps!" He bestowed a broad, gap-toothed smile on his squad, then puckered up and inhaled a deep drag.

"For God," Paz wheezed between shallow puffs.

Rica was neither surprised nor disappointed that Joan had not offered a cigar to her. Since Rica's early promotion to corporal, Joan had spoken to her only when duty required. Joan had enlisted six months before Rica but was still only a lance corporal, thanks to a battalion level NJP—nonjudicial punishment—that had decreased her rank and pay after her third offense of fighting in the barracks. Rica's promotion had been due to her perfect record and top scores on the ASVAB and advanced training aptitude tests, but she knew that Joan and several others falsely suspected her of sleeping with officers and senior NCOs, a career strategy that was not unheard of in the new coed military.

"You-all don't tell my wife I smoke moss," Gavril wheezed. Then he burst out laughing and coughing.

Joan laughed with him. "I've got one for her too."

Rica returned her gaze to the island. Despite the relief of coming home, she was not in a mood to celebrate like the others. Her four-year enlistment would end in a week, and she had still not participated in a single engagement against a real enemy. Reenlisting would give her hope for an opportunity to prove her courage and capability under fire, but what if *another* term went by with no engagements? She was already twenty-one, so she would be dreadfully behind on finishing her education and starting a professional career at that point.

"Shit, I wish we were heading the other way," Joan said around her cigar. She was now facing the headwind beside Rica, her blond burr sparkling in the tropical sun.

Gavril rolled his eyes. "You're a Section Eight, Bledsoe. Don't you have anybody meeting you on the beach?" Then his big grin collapsed, and Rica knew why. He had realized too late that Joan just might, in fact, have no one. Joan was still single and came from a poor family in Indiana, and it was doubtful that she had a significant other.

"Actually, my parents are here," Joan said. "They're doing the late honeymoon thing. First time they've been off the continent."

"That's great!" Rica said. "My dad will be on the beach too." This was the first time families had been allowed on the beach. In previous years, the Marines had to spend a day unloading, cleaning, and stowing gear before rejoining their loved ones.

For the last decade, Rica's father had been a labor recruiter for sugarcane plantations around the world. He often traveled to Hawaii to mediate between the ethnic Japanese growers and Hispanic workers. His most recent trip to the islands would have ended three days before her arrival, but he had mentioned in his last letter that he could arrange to stay longer to help her celebrate "graduating" from the Corps.

"I'll bet you ten bucks your old man ain't here," Joan said.

Rica whirled toward her sister Marine. She could not feel the wind anymore, or the sun, or gravity. All she could feel was levitating rage. Rica was as strong as Joan, but only because she was big-boned and, at five eleven, nine inches taller. She towered over the wiry blonde, who thrust back her bulging shoulders and also stepped forward, a snarl on her thin, colorless lips.

"*Hey!*" Gavril stepped between them, blocking their views of each other. "None of that shit on my boat! Everybody from the Commandant to Congress is watching you women Marines, and it'll be *my* ass if you fuck up. Even during leave. I swear to God, if I hear about you two raising hell, I'll have you both scraping seaweed off a hull until you drown or desert!" He glared back and forth at them, breathing hard. His eyes were bulging and his thick lips were puckered.

Joan threw down her smoldering cigar at Rica's feet and muttered "whore" as she walked away.

Gavril grabbed the steel railing and pulled so hard that Rica feared he would rip it up from the deck. "God Almighty, my squad is a clusterfuck!" He scowled into the wind, puffing hard to keep his stale cigar lit.

Paz frowned. "We are not, Gunny."

"Especially *you*, Rodriguez!"

Rica hoped the incident with Joan would not spoil Gavril's homecoming. She had learned the hard way that a lot of male NCOs were womanizers. Not only had Gavril never made a pass at her or an obscene joke at her expense; he had gone out of his way to let it be known that any Marine harassing the soldiers in his squad would be eternally sorry when he found out. To her relief, a moment of silence brought back his smile. He nudged Paz. "How about you? You meeting anybody?"

Paz broke his gaze from Rica's profile. "Huh? *Sí*, my sweet girlfriend, Tina. I cannot wait. Without her, I have been sleeping not good."

Gavril chuckled. "Not long now, Rodriguez . . . this is going to be awesome!"

The hovercraft lurched out of the ocean. Its black rubber skirt deflated, and the ninety-ton machine settled onto the wide beach with a soft *whump*. The Marines clapped and cheered. Mission accomplished, a successful amphibious invasion of home base. The Corps never missed a chance to practice a forced landing.

The NCOs barked formation orders, and two squads of ecstatic soldiers marched down the ramp. At the bottom, they joined the troops from the MEU's other five hover-crafts, kicking up sand as they raced toward the line of orange traffic cones that marked the end of the landing zone. When they reached the cones, the river of camouflage flowed into a sea of bathing suits, T-shirts, and tanned skin, and the waters mixed.

Rica stopped running halfway to the cones. While other Marines sped around her, shouting and waving, she shielded her eyes from the low winter sun and gazed into the throng of civilians. She listened for her name, but all she could hear was a jubilant babble of reunion.

When all of the other troops had passed her, she realized she would look like a fool just standing there alone, so she trotted behind the last Marine until he met his wife and children in a collision of hugs. Then she slowed and walked back and forth through the crowd.

And back. And forth.

Rica's father was an ex-Marine, a veteran of the Vietnam War with multiple citations for bravery. He had never let a day slip by without attempting to instill in his children a sense of patriotism and the value of martial glory. Nevertheless, his sons all refused to enlist and none showed an interest in attending one of the military academies. By the time Rica was the only child left at home, his disappointment was profound and overt.

He did not seem to expect much from Rica, even though she made higher grades than her three older brothers while doing more than her share of the chores. He gave her occasional compliments, but only on her beauty or her excellent English, the two virtues that might allow her to marry a well-to-do man from the mainland. When she heard in her high school civics class about Congress repealing the laws excluding women from combat, she finally hit upon what she thought was an infallible way to win her father's admiration. All she had to do was succeed where her brothers had failed in fulfilling his dream of producing another great soldier like himself.

Rica finally stopped searching the beach for her father. "Stupid, *stupid* girl!" she whispered to herself. The exact words in his last letter came back to her. He had said he *could* extend his stay in Hawaii, not that he had actually made plans to.

She borrowed a mobile phone from another Marine and called her father's office in Puerto Rico. He answered. In Spanish, she said, "Hi, Dad. Are you all right?"

"I'm fine," he replied. "How are you?"

"Okay, I guess. I just got back to Hawaii."

"Oh, you did? Did you have a nice trip?"

*Nice trip?*

Rica hung up, returned the phone, and stumbled through the crowd.

Smiling faces, jumping children, tears of happiness, swinging bear hugs—to her relief, no one seemed to notice her, except for the usual suspicious glances from the wives and girlfriends of the male Marines in her unit. She squeezed her forty-pound duffel bag under one arm and sprinted toward the parking lot, ashamed of the tightness in her throat. It wasn't like she was the only Marine in the MEU with no one waiting to greet her when she returned from six grueling months at sea.

As she ran to catch up, the last of the buses taking the single soldiers to the barracks pulled out and sped away.

Rica stopped in a deserted corner of the lot that was hidden from the beach by a row of gently swaying palms. She dropped her duffel bag on the sandy asphalt and walked in a circle around it, catching her breath. Then she snatched up the bag by its shoulder strap and swung it over her head. "Son of a bitch!" she screamed as she slammed it back down on the pavement.

She had seen Joan Bledsoe hugging her fat midwestern

parents on the beach. They had looked so proud. They'd both had tears of joy in their eyes because their daughter was home safe. Rica fantasized about what might happen if Joan should choose this moment to stroll by and call her a whore again.

"Excuse me." She heard a meek female voice behind her.

Rica turned around. A petite Asian girl in a blue dress with red flowers stood by a palm fifty feet away. She was pretty in spite of her thick makeup.

"What do you want?"

"My name is Tina. You know Paz Rodriguez? I'm his girlfriend." Tina paused for a proud giggle. "He asked me to see if you're okay."

Rica scowled. "Why wouldn't I be?"

Tina shrugged, looking away. "Is there anything I can do?"

Rica blinked and wiped her nose on a sleeve. "Can you give me a ride to the barracks?"

"Sure," Tina said. "This way."

Rica followed her. Paz was standing by an old sky-blue pickup at the other end of the lot. When he waved, Tina waved back and blew him a kiss, then grinned over her shoulder at Rica, her eyes twinkling with romantic excitement.

Rica sighed. However confused Paz's feelings might be, he was probably the best friend she had. Actually, he was her *only* friend besides Sergeant Gavril, unless she could also count Tina, whom she had just met.

A car horn blared to her left. Rica turned to look and literally had to jump out of the way as a white Ford Crown Victoria careened into the parking lot and skidded to a halt on loose sand. She glared menacingly at the car as she and Tina walked around it. She could not see through the windows, because they were coated with mirror backing. Antennae bristled from the trunk. The rear bumper had a federal license plate.

A gray-haired man stepped out of the backseat in the blue

dress "C" uniform of a Marine officer—a long-sleeved khaki shirt and tie, light blue trousers with a red "blood line" stripe down each leg, and a white cap. When he turned toward her, Rica stopped smartly and saluted. She could not believe she was face-to-face with Lieutenant General P. J. Greeves, the commanding officer of the entire Marine Forces Pacific. The muggy air suddenly seemed unbearable. A second earlier, she had been making her practiced war face through his window.

"Corporal, do you know Gunnery Sergeant Jacob Gavril?"

"Yes, sir. I'm in his squad, sir."

"Do you know where he is?"

She scanned the beach. "There, with his family."

Two men in identical beige business suits jumped out of the front doors and ran in the direction she was pointing. One of them yelled, "Jacob!" Rica had never heard anyone call Gavril by his first name. Even his wife called him Gavril.

The general got back in the car and shut his door.

Tina led Rica on to her truck.

"What was that all about?" Paz asked.

"Beats me," Rica said. "They wanted Gunny. I hope he's not in some kind of trouble."

Paz was too busy passionately kissing Tina to hear Rica's answer. Rica climbed into the rusty pickup bed, glad that their attention was not on her. The love birds finally got in the cab. They almost made it to the road before they saw Gavril running toward them, waving frantically.

Tina stopped the truck.

Paz stuck his head out. "Holy shit! Look at Gunny!"

Rica had noticed that Gavril seemed extra sweaty and a little unstable on his feet. "If I didn't know him, I'd say he looks scared," she whispered.

"Man, I do not believe in this," Paz said. "This just is not the time." He stared at the white Crown Victoria, running a hand over Tina's right thigh.

Gavril caught up. "Where's Eddy?" he panted. Eddy Brown was the fourth member of Rica's fire team.

"I saw him get on a bus," Rica said.

"Damn it!" Gavril hissed. "They'll have to find him at the barracks. What about Joan?"

Rica pointed. Joan was driving the maroon Nissan sedan her parents must have rented. She had stopped to check out the antennae-covered Crown Victoria.

After Joan trotted over, Gavril motioned them to huddle and lowered his voice. "I have good news and bad news. We have to deploy again, immediately."

"Oh, no," Paz said. "You mean tomorrow, right?"

Gavril shook his head. "This is not just another exercise. It's the real deal."

A spark of excitement ignited inside Rica, making her heart beat hard and fast. *"Awesome,"* she whispered.

"Don't fuck with us, Gunny," Joan warned.

"What's the good news?" Tina asked with tears in her eyes.

Paz said, "Baby, that *was* the good news."

Gavril nodded. "The bad news is the mission *sucks*."

"How so?" Rica asked.

"Can't tell you here," Gavril said. "They'll brief us when we get—"

He was interrupted by a roar as a very strange aircraft swooped overhead, barely clearing the palms. It had two short wings with one enormous propeller mounted at the end of each. The engines were rotating upward as it flew, changing their direction of thrust from backward to downward.

The aircraft zoomed out over the water, then returned, rapidly slowing as it transformed from an airplane into a dual-rotor helicopter. It stopped moving forward precisely over the parking lot, then descended straight downward. Its fuselage was dark blue with huge yellow letters that read U.S. NAVY.

Rica was incredulous. "They sent an Osprey for us?"

"We've got to move fast," Gavril said.

Ospreys were outrageously expensive but ideal for search and rescue missions or incursions of small infantry forces into rugged terrain. They could fly fast and range over long distances like ordinary fixed-wing aircraft, then hover or land vertically to off-load or pick up passengers.

The federal agents pulled their car out of the way just in time as the Osprey made a hasty touchdown, wobbling on its landing gear. The Marines turned their heads and shielded their eyes from the sand blowing against Tina's pickup.

Gavril motioned for them to follow him toward the aircraft.

"Yee-ha!" Rica vaulted from the pickup bed and trotted closely behind Gavril, shielding her face with an arm. "How come it's a Navy bird, not one of our own?" she asked loudly.

"I think everybody's in on this one," Gavril replied.

Paz stared back and forth between Gavril and Tina. His left hand clenched Tina's right thigh. His right foot jiggled up and down on the floor of her truck cab. He let out a low whine. Then he gave Tina a peck on the cheek and jumped out. "Sorry, babe. I will be with you soon."

Gavril shouted just loud enough for his Marines to hear him over the Osprey's roar. "They should use the SEALs or a Force Recon team for this kind of special ops shit. I'll get us out of it if I can."

"You wouldn't!" Rica yelled as she climbed aboard the vibrating machine, but she knew he meant it. She could only hope he would fail, and that this mission would turn out to be as challenging as it sounded.

Hope suffused her like a dose of amphetamine. She was going to get a chance before her enlistment ended after all. It suddenly seemed obvious that her father was still unimpressed because she had only fought and prevailed against the rigors of basic training, sea duty, and a system in which women were still not welcome. After she had participated in a real engagement, and, judging by their reception thus far, maybe even a high-profile operation that would get her on the national news, he would have to acknowledge her achievement.

As the Osprey launched into the clear sky and accelerated along the coast, becoming an airplane again, Rica could hardly feel the thrilling ride. The physical sensations were nothing compared to the thrill of anticipation.

*He will have to*, she thought.

# CHAPTER 3

## Briefing

"What the hell have you gotten me into?" Raymond Price whispered to Clifford Steadman. They were skimming and signing a stack of liability waivers and security affidavits at the Special Warfare Headquarters on Hickam Air Force Base in Hawaii.

"I'm worried about what I've gotten *myself* into," Cliff whispered back.

Dr. Clifford Steadman was a marine biologist. Dr. Raymond Price was a physical oceanographer. Both men taught and conducted research at the Scripps Institution of Oceanography in La Jolla, California. Cliff was thirty-three, tall, lean, divorced, and concealed behind a long mane of curly brown hair and a reddish-brown briar-patch of a beard. He had a large, straight, Roman nose and hazel eyes. Raymond was sixty-two, pudgy, and jowly, with a horseshoe of wispy gray hair around his bald dome. His face was sallow and owl-like, flat and wide with big circles around the eyes, and his teeth pointed inward. Raymond had two grown sons—a doctor and a bus driver—and was still married to their mother. Cliff and Raymond had been close friends for several years.

Raymond resumed reading. "According to this one, our

bodies become government property if we die on the expedition. *Hawaii,* you said."

"And here we are," Cliff said. "I'm having a blast."

"I was going to retire in a year or two," Raymond groused.

"At least we're out of the labs for a while," Cliff said.

"Too late. We're already insane, obviously."

Raymond's expression changed from nervous jocularity to benevolent concern. "Actually, it is good to see you out of your lab, Cliff. I thought the bedroll under the sink was funny at first, but the way you've been working lately, it's . . ."

Cliff was concentrating on a form that would make it an act of treason, punishable by lethal injection, if he ever discussed what he was about to hear with anyone who had not been present at the upcoming briefing.

He loved Raymond, but he hated it when the semielderly oceanographer tried to play father to him.

The grimy bedroll Cliff kept in a sink cabinet in his laboratory was a secret that everyone in the biology department knew about but had chosen to ignore, so far. The institution director had nonchalantly asked him about it once over lunch, and Cliff had explained that some of his experiments required a human operator to record observations once an hour for up to twenty-four hours.

"Isn't that what grad students are for?" the director had asked, then dropped the subject.

Cliff knew that nothing short of attacking a student or dropping his pants during a lecture would bring the administration down on him. He had been the most prolific member of the biology faculty two years in a row, and several universities were trying to steal him from Scripps.

Cliff's explanation for the bedroll was true, but he had gradually started sleeping in his lab just to shorten his commute. Since he always started work before anyone else in the building and was the last one to knock off at night, it was easy to maintain the appearance that he still lived at home.

He could eat breakfast in the cafeteria, shower in the gym, and read a dozen abstracts and conclusions faster than he could drive from home to work through the southern California traffic. His ex-wife had pointed out that he could always move closer to campus. In fact he could not, because an hour from town was as close as he could afford on an assistant professor's salary.

"When was the last time you saw your own house?" Raymond whispered.

"Two weeks," Cliff replied. "No, three."

The young military policeman standing over the two scientists cleared his throat. "Gentlemen, the briefing is about to begin. Do you think you can finish in . . . three minutes?"

"Sorry," Cliff said.

The crew-cut Marine returned to his erect guard posture, hands clasped behind his shiny belt, eyes trained on the outer door of the vestibule where Cliff, Raymond, and two other consultants were signing away their civilian rights. On a table beside the guard was a green plastic tub full of cell phones, pagers, and other gadgets that he had collected from individuals who had already entered the secure briefing room beyond the vestibule.

Cliff began signing the documents without bothering to skim them. Teasing aside, he knew that Raymond was more excited than scared. So was Cliff, but he also knew that the thrill-to-fear ratio might change drastically once they found out exactly why they had been whisked to Hawaii by the Department of Defense. At the moment, they were still as clueless as they had been a few hours ago when a helicopter landed outside Cliff's lab, scattering several graduate students along with their papers and hats.

To Cliff's astonishment, the Marines who jumped out of the helicopter and ran into his building were looking for him. They almost literally dragged him out of his biology lab, claiming—absurdly—that his expertise was needed to deal with a national security threat of utmost urgency. On board the helicopter, they asked if he knew any iceberg experts. "Sure," Cliff replied, pointing to a crowd of spectators in front of the building opposite his. "See that bald guy over there?" A minute later Raymond was sitting beside him, looking utterly bewildered as the helicopter shot into the sky.

Rica glanced around the blue-carpeted, windowless briefing room. The air was cool and dry and smelled of burned coffee. The walls and ceiling were covered with gray foam containing deep, dark hexagonal holes, like a honeycomb. The foam absorbed sound so efficiently that the room felt hushed despite five or six animated conversations going at once. She could identify at least four species in attendance: federal agents in business suits, uniformed military officers of various branches and ranks, her squad of fourteen Marines in their camouflage battle-dress uniforms, and a group of individuals who seemed to have little in common except that they all wore civilian clothing and looked confused.

The dry air was so charged with anticipation that it practically crackled.

Rica and her squadmates were huddled in a rear corner. Sergeant Gavril had spent the last half hour privately conferring with Dale Johnson, the federal agent who had called Gavril by his first name on the beach. Now Gavril was repeating the gist to the other Marines. "The CIA is running this show," he said. "It's a covert reconnaissance mission. They're bringing us along to provide security for the civilians, but we may also get to perform a hostile rescue."

"Wow! Cool," said Private Eddy Brown, whom the feds had rousted from his barracks. Eddy was a thick-featured, dark-freckled redhead. He was five eleven—the same height as Rica—but built like a dwarf. He claimed to weigh even more than Gavril. None of the others knew Eddy well. He was taciturn and incongruously soft-spoken. He spent most of his free time alone, lifting weights or rereading his cherished stash of superhero comics.

"When will we get back home?" Paz asked.

"I thought you said the mission sucks," Joan whispered.

Gavril harrumphed. "It does. We're going in by air to get there fast. Some of us will have to parachute like we're the freakin' Airborne. They said the planes may try to land on an unprepared surface of *wet ice*. After the rescue, the mission may turn into a demo raid."

"No way!" Rica said through a manic grin. She was the squad's demolition expert.

"Meanwhile," Gavril continued, "we'll have to baby-sit a bunch of scientific experts and possibly face enemy forces of—get this—unknown numbers, unknown intentions, *and unknown nature,* whatever the fuck that means."

"So what's wrong with the mission?" Rica asked. "It sounds just like the kind of stuff our SOC training covered."

"Fuckin' A!" Joan whispered.

Gavril looked up at the foam-covered ceiling with a "why me?" expression. "Lopez, your brain is supposed to be more than a counterweight for your jaw. They're sending us lick-ety-split into a weird-ass situation with no intel and no backup. That's not how successful missions operate."

"Gentlemen, it's time," said the stony-faced MP to Cliff and Raymond.

They stood, and the MP frisked them for electronic devices. In a monotone, he said, "The room you are about to enter is equipped with countermeasures against electronic surveillance. If you are carrying any recording devices on or within your persons, they will be detected, and you will be taken into custody."

Cliff said, "Ray's pacemaker won't explode, will it?"

"I don't have a pacemaker," Raymond growled.

The guard stepped aside, and they entered the crowded room. Cliff scanned the diverse audience. His gaze swept across the soldiers in a rear corner, then shot back to one of them, a tall Hispanic young woman with cinnamon-brown eyes. In spite of her unkempt inch-long hair, she struck him as stunningly beautiful. Her peerless face seemed unreal, especially attached to a body that was curvaceous but clad in the field uniform of a rough, tough Marine infantryman. Infantrywoman? Whatever—Cliff would not have believed that such an apparent contradiction existed if he hadn't seen her in the flesh.

The gorgeous woman Marine caught his eye and smiled. Cliff felt a flutter of weightlessness. Then he felt his face flush beneath his bushy beard. He self-consciously glanced down at his wrinkled tie-dyed shirt, stained blue jeans, and Teva sandals.

Raymond gave him a little shove toward an empty seat. "What's the matter, big guy? Got a cramp?"

As they sat down, a middle-aged man with pale skin, blond hair, and a dense mustache broke off his conversation with two Navy admirals, picked up a remote control from the table at the front of the room, and began shouting, "Everyone please take a seat or stand to the side. We only have a few minutes, so this briefing will be abridged. You'll get the details after takeoff. I'm Dale Johnson, Central Intelligence. I'll be leading the mission, although Sergeant Jacob Gavril and Captain Leroy McInnis will be in charge of safety and security. You may be wondering why we've borrowed a squad of Marine regulars instead of a Special Forces unit. They were in the right place at the right time, plus Jacob and I have worked together before. I know I can trust him to help me get this job done and keep it quiet."

Glancing back at the Marines, Cliff saw the big black sergeant lean over and whisper sarcastically to the woman of his dreams, "See what having friends will get you?"

Using the remote control, Agent Johnson dimmed the lights, reeled down a motorized screen from the ceiling, and turned on an overhead projector. The image it threw on the screen showed a boat-shaped, white object against a dark blue background. "That's a satellite photo taken this morning over the equator south of Hawaii," Johnson said. "The object you see is not a ship. It's a tabular iceberg."

Murmurs erupted, but Johnson didn't pause.

"We've been calling it the Floe, although a floe is technically a small raft of frozen seawater, not a large piece of glacial ice that came from land, as we assume this one did. There are no sources of large icebergs in the North Pacific, so we figure the Floe must have broken off from one of the floating glacial shelves around Antarctica, although its lowest areas stand four hundred feet above sea level and the thickest Antarctic ice shelves are barely half that height along their margins. Another unexplained feature is the Floe's topography. Tabular icebergs are normally flat on top, but this one has complex, rugged terrain. The southern quarter is the only flat area extensive enough for us to land on. Lots of planes have landed on dry bergs near the poles, by the way. The only difference on this mission is that the Floe is wet from melting."

*Holy shit,* Cliff thought. *What* have *I gotten us into?*

His beard began to itch.

He forgot all about the gorgeous Latina Marine.

Back in California, he had almost refused to interrupt his work for the mere ten grand plus twenty-four-hour hazard pay that the government had offered. So why hadn't he? A sense of duty? A need to break from his grueling routine? A lemming instinct?

And why the hell did they need a biologist, anyway? When he posed that question to the Marines invading his lab, they said it was part of some standard protocol to hire one expert from each of several disciplines. But why him? They said his name had come up at random. Did the federal government really do things at random? Quite possibly, Cliff thought. But why hadn't they recruited a marine biologist who was already in Hawaii?

*Shit!*

He saw a headline: Naive Academics Bite the Dust.

Maybe landing a plane on wet ice was not as impossible as it sounded. The Air Force wouldn't try a stunt like that unless they were sure it could be done. Right?

He felt a genuine pang of remorse for dragging Raymond into this suicidal junket. Raymond loved nothing better than regaling him with tales of polar expeditions from decades gone by, but the aging oceanographer was obviously no longer in shape for a dangerous mission on which the pace would be set by a bunch of gung-ho Marines. Cliff checked to see if his old friend was giving him an I-told-you-so glare.

Far from upset, Raymond was perched on the edge of his chair, tilting it forward, gazing at the satellite photo with a look of rapt wonder. "How . . . how big is it?" he asked.

"Fifteen miles long and three miles wide," Johnson said, "slightly larger than Manhattan."

"This is poppycock," said the man sitting on Cliff's other side.

Cliff looked at the stranger, wishing he weren't so close to the source of the rude and weird interruption. The man was very tall and bony, with a large Adam's apple, a long pointy nose, and straight blond hair tied back in a ponytail. He was dressed in a light blue double-breasted business suit with an expensive sheen. His posture was that of a bored slouch, as if he were watching reruns while waiting for bedtime. Definitely not an academic, Cliff thought. Not even a dean or provost.

The room remained quiet following the man's outburst, so he kept talking in a distinct British accent. "How could something that bloody huge float around out there without being seen before now? And how could it get to the equator without melting away?"

Agent Johnson said, "Your name, sir?"

"Dr. Chester Wimbledon," the man said.

"Ah, yes, the geneticist from Pherogenics."

*Geneticist?* Cliff thought. It seemed strange enough that they had hired a marine biologist. Why in the world . . . ?

"I am not *from* Pherogenics," said Chester Wimbledon. "I *am* Pherogenics. I built the company from scratch. I—"

"Dr. Wimbledon, the Floe is not actually very big by Antarctic standards," said Agent Johnson.

"It's a baby," Raymond added. "The biggest tabular iceberg on record broke off in 1956. It was sixty by two hundred miles, about twice the size of Connecticut—enough fresh water to give everyone on Earth two glasses a day for six thousand years."

Johnson nodded. "And it has barely begun to melt in the few days it must have taken to travel to the equator from Antarctica at its present speed."

To Cliff's surprise, Raymond did not seem shocked by Johnson's words. "So it's not just drifting," Raymond said. It was a statement, not a question.

"Holy mackerel," whispered the big sergeant at the back of the room.

Agent Johnson flashed them a smile that was wicked with awe and exaggerated by fear. His bushy blond eyebrows were elevated halfway up his forehead. "Ladies and gentlemen, the Floe is sailing due north, crosscurrent, at eight knots—the speed of a cargo freighter. It may be a freak natural phenomenon, but it's headed straight for Hawaii, so we also have to consider the possibility that it's a cover for some kind of attack."

Aha, Cliff thought, so that's how an iceberg can be a risk to national security.

"Even if it's not a military threat," Johnson continued, "a seismologist from the USGS has calculated that it could cause a devastating earthquake if it runs aground at that speed on one of the main islands, so our primary objective is to stop it before it gets here."

Raymond let out a groan and shook his head.

"Dr. Price?" Johnson asked.

"The Navy and Coast Guard have tried bombing Arctic bergs to clear them from shipping lanes," Raymond said. "Also torpedoes and ramming. They've never had any luck. A hunk of solid ice that size is basically indestructible."

"Which is why we won't try to destroy it," Johnson said. "Instead, the Marines will attempt to find and disable its propulsion system. If they fail, my analysts have already told me that nothing short of nuclear bombardment could stop the Floe."

Cliff glanced back at the Marines. They were so young, except for the sergeant. The gorgeous Latina was smiling as if she had just won the lottery, and the others looked almost as excited. Their alien mentality sent a chill through Cliff. Was this really their idea of fun? Overwhelming responsibility, physical torture, and a good chance of premature death?

"Could someone be towing the Floe?" Raymond asked. "Australia and Saudi Arabia have tried towing icebergs to provide fresh water, but it didn't work out."

"I'll let Mr. Panopalous answer that," Johnson said. "Jory is a naval propulsion engineer from Pearl Harbor."

A small man jumped out of his seat and literally dashed to the front of the room. He had gaunt features and dull brown hair with a premature bald spot. He was wearing dirty running shoes, black dress pants, and a white, short-sleeve, snap-front shirt with crisscrossing brown and green stripes. His eyeglass frames were thick black plastic—classic nerd glasses. Despite the conspicuous lack of a pocket protector containing pens of various colors, he would have looked perfectly natural hurrying along a hallway at MIT, circa 1960. In both countenance and stature, Jory Panopalous reminded Cliff of a young Woody Allen.

"I've calculated that it would take about nine *billion* horsepower to move an object of the Floe's size and shape at eight knots," Jory said, bouncing from foot to foot. "That's the equivalent of almost forty thousand Nimitz-class nuclear-powered aircraft carriers, the biggest warships ever built. The Navy has only ten Nimitz-class carriers."

Jory hesitated, wiping sweat from his forehead. Then he swallowed dryly, took a deep breath, and said, "No earthly technology can even come close to matching the Floe's power, so the only logical conclusion is that its drive must be of extraterrestrial origin."

For a few seconds, the only sound in the acoustically

damped chamber was the purring projector fan. Jory Panopalous was obviously not joking. He was breathing fast, his eyes pleading for agreement. Cliff felt embarrassment and dread radiating from the scrawny engineer. It made Cliff's own collar feel hot.

Chester Wimbledon finally broke the silence with a hardy guffaw and muttered to Cliff, "That's what we need, a crackpot alien chaser."

Jory's face turned watermelon red. He clenched his fists, glaring at Dr. Wimbledon. "Extraterrestrial life is *not* impossible," he spat. "It has never been scientifically recorded, but that does not prove it doesn't exist. You call yourselves scientists, but arbitrary skepticism is a form of faith. According to the Drake Equation—"

"Mr. Panopalous," said Agent Johnson, glancing at the clock. "Unless you have more to add about the Floe's propulsion system . . ."

Jory opened his mouth as if to speak. Then he rolled his eyes, aggressively shoved his glasses back up his nose, and stalked back to his seat, shaking his head.

A deep voice with a southern drawl boomed from the back of the room. It was the Marine gunnery sergeant. "Dale, you said something about a search and rescue."

Agent Johnson nodded. "A sport-fishing yacht rammed the Floe and sank yesterday. An American family was on board. They somehow climbed onto the Floe and started broadcasting a distress call that was finally picked up around midnight. Their transmission abruptly stopped after a few minutes, and we haven't heard from them since."

"That's how you discovered the Floe?" Sergeant Gavril asked.

Johnson blushed and grimaced. "Our satellites can see it, obviously, but no one was looking. Our eyes have been fixed on Korea . . . Indonesia too—it's just a matter of time until the population bomb explodes into some kind of bloody purge down there. But Polynesia is pretty dull, so no one monitors it visually."

"So the first thing we'll do is rescue the castaways?" Gavril asked.

"If they're still alive," Johnson said.

"Why shouldn't they be?"

"They said they ran into some kind of . . . trouble."

"Was the distress call recorded?"

Johnson nodded.

"Well, can we listen to it?"

"Sorry, Jacob."

Sergeant Gavril sat back and glared at Dale Johnson, his thick arms crossed over his chest. "What exactly do you spooks call the kind of secrecy protocol where you won't even tell the people you're sending down a rabbit hole what might be on the other side?"

Johnson's left eye began to twitch slightly. Cliff wondered if the expression on the intelligence agent's face was annoyance or fear. "The caller was hysterical and probably suffering from traumatic delusions," Johnson said. "There's no way to know what we'll find until we get there."

"Why have you waited for such a complicated op to get going before trying to rescue the castaways?" Gavril asked. "Surely there was some kind of patrol in the area that could have responded immediately."

Johnson sighed. "The Navy had a helicopter within range. They got there in less than two hours. The ice was covered with fog. They thought their rotor would blow the fog away, but it didn't."

"They crashed?"

"No, the landing went okay. Then they got out to look around, and they never made another report."

Oh, *hell*, Cliff thought. He checked again for a look-what-you've-done glare from Raymond, but the oceanographer appeared lost in thought.

Cliff had not intended to speak, but he heard himself asking, "Are we going to land in the same place?"

"Close," Johnson said. "Before taking off, they would have reported what they found, so we can assume that the helicopter is still sitting there. It shouldn't take us long to find out what happened to its crew."

The door opened and an Air Force officer stepped in. He said, "Mr. Johnson, the planes are almost ready. It's time to issue their clothing and get them over to the hangar."

# CHAPTER 4

## Airlift

The Marines got out of the HUMV beside a vast gray windowless hangar. They were met by an overweight Air Force major who introduced himself as Bert Lazarus. The noisy airfield scene was one of scrambling for combat. No fighters or bombers were in service, but transport planes of all sizes were landing and taking off, along with a swarm of large helicopters — Super Stallions, two-rotor Chinooks, even a few old Hueys.

"Is all of this activity for our mission?" Rica asked.

"Most of it," said Major Lazarus. "Although the pilots don't know it."

Rica had felt physically numb since the briefing. She was struggling to fathom the awesome scientific and historic magnitude of the mystery her humble squad of Marines had been invited to help solve, and the consequences of failure. Not to mention the grand opportunities she might encounter to either demonstrate valor or tragically screw up.

Major Lazarus led them to the hangar's back door. Stenciled red letters on the door read SECURE AREA. AUTHORIZED PERSONNEL ONLY. Rica could smell paint and ozone when they stepped inside.

It was the largest enclosure she had ever seen. The arching roof seemed high enough to house a weather front. Scores of round lights the size of hot tubs hung from the steel framework rafters, yet the hangar seemed gloomy. As they walked away from the corner, the thuds of their hard boot soles on the lacquered concrete made distant echoes.

Occupying most of the hangar was what Rica thought had to be the biggest damn airplane in the world. In fact it was not, but it came close. The airframe was 174 feet long with a 170-foot wingspan. Its maximum gross takeoff weight was almost 300 tons. The first thing that grabbed her attention was the huge stabilizer on the high, pointed tail cone. The horizontal tailplanes atop the vertical fin were more than five stories above the ground and as big as the *wings* on a fighter jet. The cylindrical fuselage reminded her of a fat sausage. The nose was blunt and rounded. The downward-sloping, swept-back wings were attached at the top of the fuselage. Two colossal jet engines hung from pylons that reached far forward from each wing. The wingtips sported winglets that stuck up nine feet at an angle of fifteen degrees from vertical.

Air Force personnel were busy loading pallets of weapons, scientific instruments, and provisions, trotting up and down the cargo ramp or driving forklifts and motorized dollies.

Rica edged close to Gavril and whispered, "You were right, Gunny. They could have easily put together a SEAL team in the time it took to fly in those scientists. Why are they letting our squad do this when they could send a bunch of special ops officers, older guys with combat experience?"

"Beats the hell out of me, Lopez. If you figure it out, let me know."

"Is it really just because Agent Johnson trusts you so much?"

"No way," Gavril said. "He just hasn't told us the real reason."

"This is a C-17 Globemaster III," said Major Lazarus, pointing at the plane. "We'll be taking two of them. The other one is in a different hangar. We'll split you all up in a minute and take half of you over there. Look, they're still welding on skis for the landing."

He pointed under the squat fuselage, where Rica could see the piercingly bright points of several arc welders at work. Their harsh white light flashed on the glistening hangar floor and the dull underside of the plane as the buzzing welding rods were turned on and off. Aluminum body panels had been removed from the plane's belly to expose its framework ribs, and the welders were attaching the ski mounts to structural members above their heads.

"Globemasters have landed on Antarctic pack ice with their normal landing gear," Lazarus said, "but we don't trust rubber tires on *wet* ice."

"Why do we need so much cargo space?" Rica asked.

"We don't," Lazarus said. "Globemasters are the only fast transports with thrust reversers powerful enough to land with no brakes on a runway of the length we have available. We figure it will take at least a mile. And they're the only planes designed to carry a seventy-ton main battle tank."

"We're going in with a *tank*?" Paz asked.

"No, but you guys and the scientists will need ground transportation, so we got General Dynamics to let us fly out one of their prototypes of the Advanced Amphibious Assault Vehicle."

"Really? Is it here?" Rica's excited voice echoed metallically in the vast hangar. She had more experience driving amphibious landers than the others in her squad and had longed for a while to try the new AAAV.

Lazarus nodded and led them around the loading ramp, dodging a speeding forklift.

The prototype AAAV was parked beneath the Globemaster's far wing. It looked like a fat thirty-ton chisel on tank tracks. The body was eight feet high, twelve feet wide, and thirty feet long. The rear and sides were flat vertical panels of lightly armored aluminum. The wedge-shaped front end extended beyond the tracks to form a sharp, high snout.

Atop the snout were two external headlights that seemed incongruously tiny, like the beady eyes of a whale.

The vehicle's original color was slate gray, the color of the sea on a calm overcast day, but two workers wearing white coveralls and filter masks were wielding hoses from an air compressor, spray-painting the aluminum solid white.

"Iceberg camouflage?" Rica asked.

Lazarus nodded.

"Since when does an ALV have a crane on top?" Joan asked. ALV was an acronym for any amphibious landing vehicle.

Along the flat top of the giant chisel, where Rica would have expected to see the revolving turret of a Bushmaster II 30-mm chain gun, lay a steel framework structure resembling the boom of a small construction crane. Several mechanics in hard hats were crawling around it, installing bolts and nuts with whirring pneumatic drills. Their footsteps made hollow *gong*s on the roof. Welders were working on a complex-looking mechanism attached to the rear of the ALV, shooting up a rooster tail of sparks that reflected on the lacquered concrete. Thin blue smoke was meandering upward and collecting beneath the Globemaster's wing.

"That's not a crane," Lazarus said. "It's a drilling rig. The hydraulic hoist they're installing on the back will rotate it up to a vertical position behind the ALV so you can drill blast holes. To make room for the rig, they had to take out the guns and the SATCOM antenna. I just hope—"

Lazarus got a call on the cell phone he was carrying. "Yes . . . uh huh . . . we'll try," he answered. He hung up and shouted to the swarm of mechanics. "That was Dale Johnson! We deploy in fifteen minutes! Get as much done as you can."

Lazarus turned back to the Marines. "I hope this prototype is not full of bugs. It was the only vehicle they could find on such short notice that might do the job. They said it can cross a trench eight feet wide and climb over obstacles three feet high, and it ought to float if you lose control on wet ice and end up in the drink. Or if you have to retreat from enemy forces before we can airlift you out."

"Lopez is a good driver," Gavril said. "She'll be careful."

Rica glanced around at the passengers on her plane. They were all wearing white coveralls with name tags clipped to their bib pockets. They were seated at the front of the cargo hold with their backs to the white plastic walls, which were covered with inset instruments, controls, and compartments.

All of the civilian experts had boarded this Globemaster. The intelligence agents and the other two fire teams in Rica's squad, along with Private Eddy Brown from her fire team, had gone to the other plane. Rica had been surprised to see that three of the six federal agents were women.

The hold was eighteen feet wide and more than fourteen feet high, big enough to contain a full-size mobile home with room to spare. It was well lit by a row of fluorescents at the top of each wall. It looked more like the decor of a futuristic space station than the culvertlike metal tube Rica had expected.

The hangar doors were open and the passengers' seat harnesses were cinched tightly, but the plane's cargo ramp was still down. As they waited for takeoff, Rica noticed that the others' expressions ranged from pure excitement to pure dread. She wondered where her own expression lay on that spectrum. She had felt overwhelmingly more excited than scared until she heard the part about the Navy helicopter's crew disappearing. Now she wasn't so sure which emotion was stronger.

With a gentle hum, the cargo ramp finally began to lift.

One of the passengers abruptly leaned forward. He was a young, slender, Asian man with acne—Kevin somebody, the Navy medic. His face was covered with sweat. For a second he just stared at the closing door, then hysterically threw off his harness and dashed toward it. The ramp was several feet off the floor of the hangar when he leaped from it and tumbled across the lacquered concrete.

"Goddamn it!" said Dale Johnson. He unbuckled his harness and ran after Kevin. Sergeant Gavril joined the chase. The tone of the ramp motor shifted down an octave, and it began to descend.

Johnson grabbed Kevin's arm as he got up from the hangar floor. "Where the hell do you think you're going?"

Even across the length of the hold and ramp, Rica could see Kevin trembling in Johnson's grasp. He was standing on his right foot, bending over to hold his left knee. "I'm—I'm," he stammered. Then he twisted his arm away and yelled, "Fuck you!"

He ran out of sight, limping.

Johnson started after him.

"Let him go," Gavril boomed. "He wouldn't be any use, anyway."

"Fucking deserter!" Johnson yelled. His words echoed in the hangar. He turned to Gavril. "Christ! We can't go without a medic!"

"Call the base infirmary," Gavril said. "Tell them to send whoever they've got . . . whoever's willing to go."

Johnson nodded, pulled out his cell phone, and stepped out of Rica's line of sight. She could not hear the conversation.

Rica felt shaken by the incident. Her own insides were trembling slightly. She wondered if Kevin would be court-martialed. She wondered if he knew something the rest of them didn't.

The four civilian consultants—Steadman, Price, Panopalous, and Wimbledon—looked as if they were struggling to decide whether to follow the medic while they still had a chance. Unlike the federal agents and military personnel, they could probably back out with no repercussions. Rica wondered if they would all jump up and bolt at once, and why they hadn't already, and what would happen to the mission if they did. The longer the planes sat on the ground, the more likely it became that someone else would crack and bail out.

According to her wristwatch, it was a mere twelve minutes before Johnson and Gavril returned to the hold. They were escorting a plain, frail-looking middle-aged woman with sandy blond hair, a red nose, and bloodshot green eyes. She held her new coveralls over one arm and was wearing a long white smock, white pants, and soft blue shoes with thick foam-rubber soles. B. FULCRUM, MD was monogrammed on her coat's breast pocket.

"This is Dr. Bonnie Fulcrum," Johnson said. "She was on loan from Wahiawa Hospital to help train the base emergency room staff. We're very lucky to have her with us." He showed Bernie how to don her seat harness as the twenty-foot cargo ramp cranked upward, its soft yet ominous hum sending a thrill through Rica's abdomen.

Bonnie was seated next to the bearded, long-haired man whose name tag read CLIFFORD STEADMAN, PH.D., MARINE BIOLOGIST. He turned to her and said, "Did they even tell you what this is about?"

Bonnie shrugged and spoke casually around the cigarette hanging from her lips. "I overheard them say we probably wouldn't all make it back."

"*Probably?*" Cliff said. "That's not exactly the way they put it to us!"

Bonnie patted her pockets and frowned. "Anybody got a light?"

It seemed strange to Rica that a doctor would smoke, especially indoors.

Chester Wimbledon passed a gilded lighter from the other end of the civilians. Bonnie grabbed it and lit her cigarette. She inhaled a deep drag, leaned her head back against the wall, closed her eyes, and exhaled a long plume of smoke into the confined cargo hold. "They said they really didn't know," she clarified.

The thrust was hard. The noise was loud. The takeoff was short and steep.

Rica watched the swiveling eyes and clenched jaws of

the civilians. A lifetime of commercial flying can't prepare you for a military takeoff, she thought. In the friendly skies, flight parameters were restricted for the comfort of infirm passengers. Here they were limited only by the capabilities of the aircraft.

Rica looked forward to working with the scientists. If the plane didn't crash or get shot down, she might get a chance to talk to them about the academic life. That might help her decide whether to reenlist or go to college.

Dr. Steadman seemed the most approachable of the civilians. Actually, it was hard to read his expressions behind his thicket of long curly hair and his reddish, nestlike beard. Along with his lean, rangy figure, his ungroomed appearance made him look like he'd been lost in the wilderness for several years. But he was obviously the youngest of the civilian experts. Rica had also noticed how he kept smiling at her and then shyly looking away. During the roaring climb to cruising altitude, she tried to strike up a conversation with him across the wide hold, but they couldn't hear each other.

The Globemaster finally pitched forward to a horizontal angle, and the throbbing engines settled down to the tame hum of cruising flight. Rica was about to ask Dr. Steadman what his research specialty was, but then she noticed that the passenger seated on the other side of him from Bonnie Fulcrum was leering at her. The leering man had a long pointy nose and slick, fine, long blond hair pulled back in a tight ponytail. His name tag read CHESTER WIMBLEDON, PH.D., GENETICIST. A carefully lettered line of smaller print at the bottom added, FOUNDER OF PHEROGENICS.

There was something about Dr. Wimbledon's posture that Rica found vaguely unnerving. His slouch suggested infinite limberness—thin legs twined around each other, head flopped over to one side, arms tangled among his harness straps. The white coveralls seemed to fit everyone else, but Chester Wimbledon was so tall and long-limbed that the arms and legs of his coveralls were several inches too short.

She wondered why he didn't look away, then realized that he was ogling her ample bosom so raptly he had not even noticed that she was returning his gaze.

Finally he saw her scowling. Instead of looking sheepish, he grinned at her with tobacco-stained teeth. In a strong British accent, he shouted loud enough for her—and everyone else—to hear him over the roar of the jet engines, "I think I've seen you before. Did you used to dance at the Platinum Girls Club in Los Angeles?"

Rica felt her face flush as the other passengers stole curious glances at her. She had never been inside a strip club. "Yeah," she yelled, looking cheerfully at Chester Wimbledon. "Your sister and I had a hot double act."

His leering grin turned into a menacing snarl. "Who do you think you are, *girl*?"

Rica resisted the urge to unbuckle her seat harness and lunge across the hold. Instead, she glared at Chester with her war face until he finally looked away.

Chester turned on Clifford Steadman, who was regarding him appraisingly. "What?" Chester said loudly. "Don't tell me even the bloody hippies are turning into prudes nowadays."

"Just out of curiosity," Cliff shouted, "why did you join this expedition, Dr. Wimbledon?"

"It's my duty," Chester said with a haughty snort. "I immigrated from the U.K. twelve years ago, but now I'm an American citizen and a patriot."

Beside Rica, Paz yelled, "Gunny, can we check out the gear now?"

"Go for it," said Sergeant Gavril. "But have your chute on by seventeen-hundred. You and I will make the jump to check the landing site for crevasses."

The Marines walked back to where supplies were stacked along the walls. The loadmaster, a technical sergeant who was the only member of the Air Force crew besides the pilot and copilot, joined them to check the safety of his cargo.

"Where are the guns and ammo?" Paz asked. The gymnastic youth specialized in maintaining the fire team's ordnance and wielding heavy machine guns. As part of the Warrior's Edge initiative to modernize the Army and Marine Corps infantry, their fire team was one of several in which the Corps had recently begun experimenting with weapons specialization even at the lowest ranks. Joan was their sharpshooter and target spotter. Rica was the diving and demolition expert. Eddy Brown carried and operated the squad radio.

The loadmaster pointed along the high stacks of cargo tied down on 463L-type rolling pallets beneath camouflage tarps. "Food, camp gear, weather instruments, weapons, and I don't have a clue what all this crap is. A bunch of federal agents loaded it—told us not to touch." He was pointing to a stack of stainless steel equipment cases with twelve-digit combination locks.

Paz ran his fingers over an ornate seal on one of the cases. Raised gold lines on a light blue background outlined the continents as seen from above the North Pole. The round map included spokes of longitude and concentric rings of latitude and was encircled by two olive branches. "Rica, do you know what this means?"

"That's the United Nations logo," she said. "Look over here. This is weird. All of these cases belong to NASA."

She turned to the other side of the hold and lifted the corner of a tarp. The long row of pallets on that side was occupied entirely by identical rectangular boxes the size and shape of a briefcase—at least a thousand of them, she guessed. "What's in all these crates?"

"Beats me," the loadmaster said. He pulled out a pocketknife and cut open the loose black plastic covering one of the crates. Red letters were stenciled on the wooden box inside.

Rica jumped back, one hand to her mouth. "Oh, holy Jesus God!"

Paz scowled at her for swearing, then patted her on the

back. "Looks like a girl I know is going to have herself a grand old time."

The box was labeled $C_8H_8O_{16}$.

"Which compound is it?" Paz asked.

"Octanitrocubane," she said. "The most powerful high explosive ever synthesized . . . costs a fortune to produce. Twice the energy density of TNT, twenty percent more than HMX, and it detonates at almost twenty thousand meters per second, so no other compound even comes close to its brisance—its shattering power. I could take down the Great Wall of China with a stash this size."

"Oh, yeah, *baby*!" Joan shouted behind them. "Paz, man, you are going to *shit* when you see this."

Paz ran to Joan like a child whose guests have begun unwrapping the presents at his birthday party. She was holding open the lid of a coffinlike case. Rica and Paz leaned to peer over her shoulders, and Paz whistled. The case contained a Vulcan M-134 minigun, a Gatling gun with an electric motor that rotated six barrels around the firing chamber to spray out NATO standard 7.62-mm slugs at six thousand rounds per minute.

In the next case she opened, which was airtight, Joan found something that almost brought tears to her eyes. It was a seven-thousand-dollar Barrett M82A1A antimaterial rifle with a ten-power Unertl scope. The sleek black exotic-looking weapon fired the same fifty-caliber ammunition as a Browning M2 heavy machine gun, slowing the vicious recoil from the thumb-size cartridges to a gentle shove with a system of damper springs in the stock.

While Joan admired the M82, Rica counted the cases of ammunition. They added up to about ten tons, not counting the launchable grenades.

"I don't get it," she said. "Of course they want us to be prepared, but—let's face it—grunts like us are a cheap resource compared to this kind of gear, and two Globemasters could have hauled several platoons. So why did they load enough ordnance to invade North Korea when they sent only fourteen Marines?"

"It's pretty fucking obvious," Joan hissed. "The hardware won't be missed, but the story always comes out when too many troops get killed. Who knows why they think it's so important to keep this op under wraps, but if all fourteen of us buy it out there, they can still cover up the whole fucking mess by just calling it a plane crash."

# CHAPTER 5

# Landing

Jory Panopalous felt ill. He was not airsick, just over-wrought with excitement, as he had been since he'd calculated the minimum power of the Floe's drive and realized that it could not have been designed by human engineers. That realization had been like a shot of some euphoric drug, practically lifting him out of his chair and letting him soar on the wings of awe and wonder and curiosity. After staying high on anticipation for several hours, he was beginning to feel weak from nervous exhaustion, and he hadn't even seen the Floe yet.

Wringing the waist strap of his seat harness in both hands, Jory watched the two male Marines don what looked like hundreds of pounds of gear in addition to their parachutes. Bulging white packs or pockets were attached to their backs, chests, hips, thighs, and calves. Jory's interest in outdoor adventures stopped just short of walking through the city park, so he had never seen anything like the dangerous-looking devices the Marines had strapped onto the soles of their white plastic boots. The devices consisted of heavy steel frames with ten vicious triangular spikes sticking downward. Two more spikes stuck out in front like the teeth of a barracuda. He overheard one of the Marines calling the devices crampons.

"Okay, stay alert," the sergeant yelled. "We don't know who we'll run into down there."

"I do!" Jory shouted. "I just hope you people don't shoot them before they even have a chance to try communicating with us."

The Marines ignored him. They finished checking each other's pack straps and waddled back to the jump doors just aft of the wings.

Jory couldn't stand it any longer. He unbuckled his seat belt and ran up the narrow metal stairs to the flight deck. Squeezing the pilot's headrest in a death grip, he pushed his drooping eyeglasses back into place with a forefinger and leaned forward to stare out the wraparound windows at the vast blue ocean far below them.

The pilot was Bert Lazarus, the Air Force major who had shown the Marines around the hangar. "Hey, what are you doing?" he asked.

"Just looking," Jory said. "We can't see out back there."

He could clearly see the curvature of the horizon, or so it seemed. The sky was clear, and the calm Pacific stretched on for hundreds of miles. The sun was setting on the right, casting a twinkling column of reflection across the water like a golden braid with woven-in diamonds. On the horizon ahead was a brilliant white star that grew more blinding by the second.

The Floe, Jory presumed.

The pilot thumbed a switch and spoke into the radio. "Ten seconds to the drop zone. Are you guys ready?"

Jory heard the southern drawl of the Marine sergeant on the radio. "Ready when you are, Major."

Lazarus counted down. "Five, four, three, two, one, jump!"

Both Marines yelled "Semper Fi!" as their voices faded into the wind roar.

Lazarus adjusted his steering control, and Jory felt the

floor tilt down to the left. The horizon tilted in the opposite direction. They turned away from the setting sun.

Jory pointed over the pilot's shoulder. "There's the other plane!"

Orange sunlight gleamed along the distant Globemaster's fat fuselage and turned its upward-pointing winglets into torch flames. As Jory watched, two infinitesimal specks fell from the open jump door behind its wing. After they plummeted a few hundred feet, rectangular white parafoils appeared above them as if by magic.

"They jumped out too soon!" Jory shouted. "They're going to fall in the ocean."

"Nah, they'll make it," the copilot said. "Those chutes are steerable. They wanted to jump from a lower altitude directly over the Floe, but we have to maintain enough standoff to use chaff and electronic countermeasures if somebody down there fires a SAM at us."

Jory looked for vapor trails against the deep blue ocean. "Your countermeasures won't matter," he said. "If they want to shoot us down, they will."

Lazarus grunted. The heavy, middle-aged man was sweating and frowning, obviously uneasy.

"Have you ever done this before?" Jory asked.

"What? Land a plane?"

"On wet ice," Jory said.

"Nobody has, as far as I know."

"Nobody?"

Lazarus briefly tossed a hand up in exasperation. "Twelve men have landed on the moon!"

"But you can handle it, right? With the thrust reversers?"

"Look, buddy, do you want to do this for me?"

Jory stepped back, vigorously shaking his head.

"Then get the hell out of my cockpit!"

The Globemasters circled the Floe for an hour. Rica began to lose hope, thinking they would have to turn back. Then the pilot's voice came over the cabin speakers:

"Everybody listen up! The team on the Floe has mapped out a runway and given us the go-ahead to land. Secure everything that's loose and tighten your harnesses."

"And say your final prayers!" Clifford Steadman added. A Cheshire grin appeared in his curly beard. His teeth were perfect except for one golden eyetooth. "Now the fun begins," he shouted, winking at Rica.

"Aren't you scared?" she yelled.

"Shitless," Cliff replied. "But I needed a change of scenery. Bad."

Raymond Price chuckled. "When did you finally figure that out, big guy?"

"About ten minutes ago," Cliff said. "This kind of mission impossible isn't like trying to make it as a scientist. This isn't going to drag on for years and years. In a few hours, we'll know whether we've won or lost."

Actually, if we lose, we'll probably never know it, Rica thought. She nodded to Dr. Price. "What about you?"

"This is a unique opportunity for me," Raymond replied.

"Heck, they could have charged Ray a fortune for his ticket," Cliff added. "Before we took off, he said he's been waiting for this his whole life."

"How's that?" Rica asked. "I thought the Floe was a total surprise."

"Not to me," Raymond said. "It's not the first rogue berg, you know. Others have been reported for centuries by ships in the South Pacific, South Atlantic, and Indian Ocean."

"In warm waters?" Rica asked.

Raymond nodded. "Now and then. The tropical sightings were all attributed to sea fog or mirages until 1942, when a whole squadron of Japanese bomber pilots reported flying over one near the equator. That berg was a lot smaller than the Floe. They also saw a streak like the wake of a ship extending south from it."

"Really?" Jory Panopalous shouted from the other end of the civilian seat row. His eyes were alight with fascination.

"I have a personal interest in unexplained phenomena, you know, but I've never heard of that one."

"No surprise," Raymond said. "It was buried in Japanese war records until they were declassified two years ago."

Jory wished Agent Johnson had not confiscated his digital video/still camera. He would give anything to have it if a welcoming party met them on the Floe. Even if the Globemaster crashed, or the party waiting for them turned out to be not so welcoming, he might live long enough to shoot some incontrovertible proof.

Jory kept up with reports of UFO sightings and made annual contributions to SETI, the Search for Extraterrestrial Intelligence, a privately funded team of radio astronomers who monitored the skies for signals. But he was *not* a "crackpot alien chaser." His interest in extraterrestrial life was not based on some pseudoreligious faith or phobia of abduction as it was for so many benighted souls. His curiosity was based on the Drake Equation, an estimation of the density of alien civilizations in the galaxy that was broadly accepted by real scientists as sensible, if not precise. According to the Drake Equation, the Milky Way was probably *teeming* with intelligent life. For as long as he could remember, Jory had fantasized about being the first human to see, to communicate with, to *touch* an extraterrestrial being. That would be the ultimate privilege. No other honor could even begin to compare.

The whine of the jet engines decreased in pitch and increased in volume. The cabin tilted forward and rolled so that Jory was leaning back, looking up at the two women Marines. He took off his heavy eyeglasses and buttoned them into a pocket, then gripped the shoulder straps of his seat harness and squeezed his eyes shut to protect them from flying debris in case the plane crashed. Landing blind would be extra terrifying, but no more than watching the fuzzy blobs everything had become when he removed his glasses.

Like the takeoff, the descent was steeper and shorter than a commercial landing.

"Five seconds to touchdown," the pilot said over the cabin speakers. The plane was now flying straight and pitched slightly upward, vibrating and rolling gently back and forth as it came in just fast enough to avoid stalling. Jory clenched his teeth so he would not bite his tongue. He fought the urge to fling off his seat harness, replace his glasses, and climb back up to the flight deck, where he might see whatever was down there to greet them sooner.

With a gentle bump, the cabin pitched forward to a level angle and began trembling like an old subway car. The throbbing roar of wide-open thrust reversers filled the air, and Jory could feel a mild tug of deceleration. The landing went on for what seemed like way too long, but the shaking and roaring eventually began to subside.

"All right, we're down!" Jory yelled. He opened his eyes, let go of his harness, and reached for his glasses.

His side of the fuselage abruptly lurched upward.

The back of his head banged against the wall.

A scraping sound came from outside.

Someone's cell phone bounced off the floor, then a wall, then the ceiling.

A stack of heavy metal crates broke their restraints and collapsed into the aisle. Jory hoped they wouldn't slide forward and pulverize him.

He was suspended in midair, held back only by his harness. He seemed to be directly above the two women Marines on the other side of the hold, although he knew that was impossible unless the left wing had broken off at the base or the plane was airborne again. How could the Globemaster be airborne again after slowing to a speed too low to generate lift?

Jory threw his arms over his face and screamed.

His side of the plane slammed down and the other side tilted up above him, but not as high as his side had been. When the other side came back down, the floor remained level. A few seconds later, the trembling and roar from the thrust reversers ceased, and the turbines began to spin down.

Jory could hear no splashing, so he assumed they had not overshot their runway and landed in the ocean as he had feared. With a shaking hand, he fished his eyeglasses out of his pocket and put them back on, failing to notice that they were askew.

Raymond swallowed. "Hey, big guy, did you make a mess?"

"I don't think so," Cliff replied. "Why? Did you?"

The loadmaster ran out from his station by the stairs, breathing hard and grinning hysterically. "We made it!"

# CHAPTER 6

# Icescape

"This is Demo One calling Gunny and Weapons One. Come in, ground team." Rica stood behind the flat rear end of the ALV, facing the Globemaster's cargo door with her crampon-clad boots spread wide for balance. Wind swirled into the hold as the eighteen-foot-wide door cranked open. She had grown up in Puerto Rico, trained at Paris Island, and served three years in Hawaii. To her, the wind felt shockingly cold.

Joan stood beside her with the same wide stance, holding her M-16A2 assault rifle at exactly the same angle as Rica's across her flat, muscular chest. Five seconds after Rica's radio call had failed to raise a response, Joan spoke into the microphone beneath the bullet-resistant visor of her white combat helmet. "This is Sniper One calling Gunny and Weapons One. Come in, ground team."

"Can you feel that?" Rica whispered.

"What?"

"The floor is wobbling."

"Yeah. Wind hitting the plane?"

"Maybe."

Rica had never felt a sensation like the strange wobble. At first it felt like trying to stand in an airplane aisle during minor turbulence. Then she realized that the lurching motion was repeating on a regular cycle and that it was only moving her body back and forth—she could feel no vertical acceleration. Each cycle seemed to shift the floor northward for a second, then southward for a second. She decided it felt more like waves from a mild earthquake or standing on a bus that was speeding along a winding road. Whatever its cause, the slight motion made her feel queasy and apprehensive, as if the ice were unstable and might collapse, swallowing the whole Globemaster and all of them with it.

The huge cargo door was composed of two halves. The upper half hinged at the top and swung upward into the hold. The lower half swung down to form the loading ramp with a gentle nine-degree slope. The ramp finally landed on the ice with a soft *thud-crunch,* and its hoist motor kicked off. With dull clangs of steel crampon spikes on aluminum panels, the two Marines stepped out onto the ramp, crouched in the cold breeze, and gazed around, looking for anything suspicious.

"My God," Rica whispered.

"Fucking weird," Joan said.

The wet ice plain stretched out at least a mile behind the Globemaster, as barren as the Moon and still glistening in the last red rays from the sun, which had just set on the opposite horizon. To the right, the plateau ended a quarter mile away at a sharp precipice that hid the sea below it for many miles. The band of bronze water between ice and sky was so distant that Rica could see no waves on it. To the left—inland—the level plain extended much farther, then abruptly shot upward into a surreal cityscape of cliffs, buttes, overhangs, minarets, and arches. The tallest iceforms were still catching the full radiance of the sun, glowing with streaks of crimson like raw antlers that had recently shed their skin. The shadows behind them were a deep azure blue. The other C-17 looked like a dull gray toy sitting sideways in front of the colossal blood-tipped iceforms.

Straight ahead of Joan and Rica, wispy tangerine clouds glowed against a violet sky. The firmament's hue deepened toward the zenith, grading through indigo to cobalt and finally to black, already revealing the brightest stars. The steady breeze generated by the Floe's eight-knot velocity was blowing across the plain from the north, moaning through the bizarre inland terrain.

"This place is awesome," Rica whispered. "It's like landing on another planet."

"You can stay, then," Joan said. "My ass is out of here as soon as we—*back!*"

Joan's harsh voice rang through the fuselage like a gunshot. She and Rica ran up the ramp. Rica was not accustomed to wearing crampons. She nearly punctured one of the civilians who had crept up behind her. She and Joan waved at them frantically. "Get back in the hold! Back!"

The Marines squatted in the shadows behind the sides of the open cargo door, aiming their rifles out at the ice. The Air Force crew fell in behind them with 9-mm Beretta side arms.

"What is it?" Rica hissed. She was not surprised that Joan had seen it first, whatever it was. Joan was the fire team's sniper because of her legendary distance vision. She had won several marksmanship competitions at Quantico.

Joan pointed inland, to the left of the other plane.

Rica squinted into the deepening crimson gloom, hoping her heart would slow down now that she was not moving. She had never anticipated having to face her first real combat engagement while out of touch with her sergeant. The fear that he and Paz had been captured or killed was boiling in her gut.

She wondered if they had tried using the squad radio, a portable but cumbersome box that they had jumped with so they could call the Globemasters. It was probably in one of their packs, turned off.

She finally saw two tiny human figures approaching across the shimmering plain. They lurched from side to side as they walked and glowed a sickly pale pink in the setting sun, like bottles of Pepto-Bismol. They were carrying long black objects that Rica couldn't make out but presumed were rifles.

"This is Demo One calling Squad Leader," Rica said. "Have you heard from the guys we dropped?" Squad Leader was Captain Leroy McInnis, the only Marine officer on the mission. He and the squad's other two fire teams were on the other plane.

A voice came through loud and clear. Rica had never met Captain McInnis, but she assumed it was him. "No. We haven't opened the door yet. We had a rough landing. One of the feds bit off part of his lip, and—"

"*Then I suggest you open it, sir!* Two unidentified mobile units are coming right at you from those . . . mountains."

"Oh, shit—Hey, Brown, drop the ramp!—how fast?"

"Slowly. On foot, I think."

"They're on foot," Joan confirmed. "Carrying small arms."

"Can you identify them?" Rica asked.

"Negative," Joan said.

"Go get your binoculars," Rica ordered.

The cargo ramp of the other Globemaster slammed down. When the echoes from the distant iceforms died away, Rica could hear nothing but the low moan of the wind and her own rapid pulse.

"It's them!" Captain McInnis yelled in her ear.

"All right!" Rica cheered. "Your guys or ours?"

"Yours."

Joan returned with her binoculars. She had heard the radio traffic in her own headset. She covered her microphone wand and whispered, "If that's Paz and Gunny, why aren't they on the radio? They're within range."

"Maybe they're farther away than they look," Rica said. "I'll bet this place plays tricks on you."

"No shit," Joan hissed.

Gavril's deep voice boomed from Rica's headset. " . . . no sign. Not a goddamned trace! I want you to deploy the ALV immediately so we can look for the castaways. Report, Demo One. Are you there?"

Rica keyed her mike with her chin. "I'm here, Gunny. We didn't catch that. Did you guys already look for the Navy helicopter?"

"Affirmative," Gavril said. Even over the radio, the grimness in his voice was clear. "Dale gave us the precise location where they landed, so we went over it inch by inch. Nothing but clean wet ice. Somebody must have hijacked the helo and everyone on it."

# CHAPTER 7

# Dark Descent

Rica let up on the ALV's throttle and shifted the six-speed Allison transmission to neutral. After the tracks ground to a halt, the only sound was the idle of the 12-cylinder, 850-horsepower, turbocharged diesel. She had parked above the end of a trench in the level ice plain that was about twenty feet wide and stretched straight away into the darkness. The bottom of the trench formed a steep ramp that descended toward the edge of the Floe. The stars were bright, but the moon was hidden behind the exotic terrain in the Floe's interior. Rica could see the ice beyond the headlight beams only when she glanced sideways into her periscope's binocular eyepiece.

She leaned aside so Captain McInnis could squint into the periscope. McInnis was skinny and pale with dark hair. He did not look much older than her. Sweat was beaded on his white cheeks and forehead despite the cool air. His terrified expression struck Rica as ghastly in the wan light from her instrument panel. "This must be the place," he said with his Long Island accent. "Mrs. Arlington said she was at the bottom of a ramp that goes down to the ocean. This has to be the place, don't you think?"

Rica nodded. Agent Johnson had finally revealed to the

Marines that the distress call had come from a castaway named Linda Arlington.

"There's no way that trench can be a natural formation," McInnis said. "Its walls are precisely flat and vertical. The ramp at the bottom is perfectly straight. It has to be man-made, don't you think?"

Gavril snapped a thirty-round magazine into his M-16. "Okay, let's check it out!"

Rica lowered the transom flap, which covered the door at the rear of the troop cabin when it was stowed in its upright position. Their crampons clanked on the metal plate as they filed out.

The ice was coated with a thin, distinct layer of opaque fog. It was dense and heavy like the vapor that forms around a thermos of liquid nitrogen or a block of frozen carbon dioxide. The dark trench seemed to be sucking the fog downward like a vacuum, causing the undulating white carpet to flow forward beneath the ALV and across the ice toward the trench from both sides.

"Oh, man, I do not like this," Paz said.

Bonnie Fulcrum, the civilian medic, was soon the only person left on board the ALV. The thin, middle-aged woman sat hunched over, twisting her watch around and around her frail left wrist. Her face was hidden by her unkempt blond hair.

Rica waved at her. "Hey, you coming?"

Bonnie turned to glare at Rica. Her eyes were watery and bloodshot. Puffy gray mice protruded beneath them. "I don't feel like climbing," she snapped.

Gavril looked at her and nodded. "Vicini! Set her up with a radio." Vicini was one of the two privates who would stay behind to guard the ALV. One fire team was guarding the planes, which were three miles away, leaving the squad's other eight Marines to perform the search and rescue.

"Safeties on," Gavril commanded. "Watch your step, and don't get too close to the sides of the trench."

They walked to the top of the ramp beneath the headlight

beams extending from the ALV's high snout. Rica's long calves held her knees above the flowing fog, yet she could not see her boots. She felt her way with her crampons as she neared the steep ramp, hoping she would not step in a hidden crack or trip on a bump and fall.

"Man, I wish the ground would hold still," Paz said. The Floe's mysterious north-south wobble had seemed to lessen since the planes had landed, but Rica suspected that her coordination was just adapting to it. She wondered if the wobble was caused by the Floe's mighty propulsion system.

Gavril peered down the wet ice ramp, which was as steep as the roof of a house and hidden beneath the sluice of undulating fog. "We'll have to use the rope," he said.

McInnis gave the order, and they returned to the ALV for the massive thousand-foot coil of orange climbing rope. The coil was composed of six standard fifty-meter dynamic kernmantle ropes tied together with grapevine knots. Gavril tied one end of the rope to the makeshift drilling boom on top of the ALV, and they began the descent backward, half walking and half rappelling on the steep wet ice. "Headlamps off," he ordered, "and whisper with no hissing sounds. Rely on your headsets. We don't know who might be waiting for us down there."

"What happens if we fall?" Paz whispered.

"You'll probably slide out to sea at a hundred miles an hour," Rica said.

"You know, this would make one heck of an amusement park ride," said Private Eddy Brown.

"Idiot," Joan whispered.

The wind blowing down the ramp grew stronger as they descended. It felt eerily unnatural to Rica that dense fog and strong wind were happening at the same time. The flowing fog seemed to suck the heat from her bones. As they rappelled deeper into the trench, it climbed up her legs and past her waist. Cold sweat poured down her back, and her nipples contracted into throbbing little knobs. The stream of fog finally rose above her head. She knew Gavril was just a few feet below her, but the next time she glanced over her shoulder, his looming bulk had disappeared in the opaque gloom.

Gavril's whisper came through the fog and her headset: "How you doing, Demo?"

"C-cold!" Rica stammered.

She listened for any unexpected noises, surrounded by echoes of meltwater trickling down the walls behind the cascades of fog. The ramp was slightly concave, like a luge track, and the meltwater collected to form a shallow stream running swiftly down its center.

Darkness became total beyond the first knot in the rope. Gavril suggested they turn on their headlamps. McInnis agreed, making a decision that would sacrifice stealth for safety.

Between the second and third knots, the sounds of dripping meltwater disappeared. Rica pulled off a glove and touched the wall. It felt dry and incredibly cold. "Gunny, the walls are frozen solid here."

"Yeah, the floor is too." He made a scratching sound with his crampons that was different from the squeaks and scritches she had grown accustomed to.

According to Rica's knot count, they were about eight hundred feet down the ramp when Gavril whispered, "All stop." After a pause, he said, "The ramp is obstructed. Looks like an avalanche. Everybody form up down here."

Rica cautiously turned to face downhill. A vague pile of jumbled shapes loomed in the fog. As she stepped closer, the shapes resolved into chunks of broken ice with sharp edges and roughly fractured surfaces.

When they were all huddled close, Gavril whispered, "We'll have to climb over. Fire Team One can advance while Fire Team Two waits here to watch our backs. We'll douse our lights when we get to the top. I'll descend the other side with Sniper One, using night vision. The rest of Fire Team One will take up positions on top of the rubble to cover us. Is that okay with you, sir?"

"Sure," said Captain McInnis. "Where do you want me?"

"Do whatever you want, sir. Advance with me or stay behind with the two guys from Fire Team Two."

"I'll stay here," McInnis said.

Gavril began climbing the rubble, testing the stability of each ice block before shifting his weight to it. Rica's fire team followed him, stepping exactly where he did. At the crest, Rica, Paz, and Eddy hunkered down in covered positions where they could aim their rifles into the fog beyond the debris ridge. "Lights out," Gavril said when they were ready.

Rica heard crampons crunching on the ice in the absolute darkness. The sound receded below her on the down-ramp side of the rubble. Through her headset, she could also hear Gavril and Joan breathing hard on their microphone wands. She tried not to shiver as she huddled in the damp and frigid wind, keeping her rifle poised to return fire in the direction of the muzzle bursts if an enemy ambushed them.

"Can you see?" Gavril asked.

"Barely," Joan replied.

"Turn up your gain."

"It's already maxed."

Their AN/PVS-7B night vision goggles were like strap-on monocles that increased the brightness of the image rather than magnifying its size. The large objective lenses collected many times the photons that would pass through the unaided human pupil; then the image was electronically amplified. Gavril and Joan were the only Marines in the squad equipped with these cumbersome devices, which weighed twenty-four ounces and cost six thousand dollars apiece.

Gavril said, "Demo, there's almost no light down here, and we still can't see through the fog. The ramp is not as steep on this side of the avalanche, though. We won't need the rope." A minute later he said, "Look clear to you, Sniper?"

"Yeah," Joan said. "Wait! I see something . . . a dark spot on the ramp." Over the radio, Rica heard more breathing and crunching footsteps. "Shit, I can't tell what it is," Joan said. "Can I turn on a light?"

Gavril said, "Lights on, everybody."

Rica eagerly reached up and flicked on her headlamp.

"Lights off!" Gavril yelled.

Rica smacked her headlamp switch. Once again she was surrounded by total darkness. "Gunny, what's wrong?" she whispered.

"It's fresh blood," Gavril said. "Demo One, try your IR. Tell me what you see."

Rica had practiced this maneuver in the dark many times. Within three seconds, she yanked her infrared goggles from their chest pouch, threw back her hood, slipped the heavy device over her head, and turned the gain all the way up. "Nothing," she said. "It's dark. The ice must be too cold."

"Can you see the guys below you?"

"Yes, bright as day." Each of the Marines appeared as a hazy white trunk and head with red arms and legs. Their hands and feet were blue.

"Count them," Gavril said.

"What? Oh! Just three, plus the two up here with me."

"What about on my side?" Gavril asked.

Rica stood up to get a full view of the ramp on the downhill side of the avalanche debris, and her eyes were blasted by a tall rectangle of white light. "Ow!" she gasped, turning down the gain.

"Demo, report!" Gavril ordered.

"The ocean," Rica whispered. "It's so bright. Looks like it's only about fifty meters on down the ramp. I can see you and Sniper, no one else."

At their sergeant's orders, Fire Team One gathered in a circle, converging their weak headlamp beams on the bright red smear. "It's not fresh like I thought," Gavril said, scraping at the stain with his crampons. "It's frozen. Who knows how long it's been here."

"Let's see if there's more," Rica said. She had removed her infrared goggles.

Joan pointed. "There!"

Paz gasped and crossed himself.

They followed the trail, rifles poised. The left wall became visible through the fog. "Jesus creeping shit!" Gavril whispered. Frozen blood was smeared, dripped, sprayed, and splattered within an area six feet high on the wall and six feet out on the floor. The abstract mural of gore stretched at least ten feet back and forth.

Eddy Brown swallowed dryly. "Gunny, could a human lose that much blood?"

"Oh, yeah," Gavril said.

Paz genuflected again and grabbed Rica's arm, trying to tug her away from the wall. *"Madre de Dios,"* he moaned. *Sweet mother of God!*

Rica was transfixed. For the moment at least, her ever-present yearning for an opportunity to do something heroic was replaced by dread, horror, and a deep suspicion that her squad was following the wake of unnatural, unspeakable violence.

# CHAPTER 8

# Hiders

They searched the vicinity of the macabre residue for clues. There were no footprints, bullet holes, shrapnel, or spent shell casings. "Maybe it was an animal attack," Rica said. "I saw a show on the Learning Channel where a polar bear ate a seal and blood was all over the snow. He even ate the bones."

Eddy looked over his shoulder. "You think it was a polar bear?"

Joan said, "Bless your heart, Eddy."

"Huh? Why?" he asked, frowning.

"Eddy, polar bears live only around the *North* Pole," Rica explained. "And this kind of iceberg came straight from Antarctica."

Some of the blood had collected in a small dip in the floor. Pink hoarfrost covered the frozen puddle's level surface like bread mold. Rica poked at it with her front crampon spikes. They scattered the frost and dug up pink shavings, then big chips of dark crimson ice. She picked up an object her digging had exhumed. It was yellowish-white, roughly cubic, and about a quarter inch across. She held it out on the palm of her glove for the others to see.

"Oh, Lord!" Eddy said.

Rica fingered the object, turning it over. "Looks human. Broken off at the root. A molar from way back in the jaw."

"Come on, Rica, we should be leaving here," Paz pleaded. She wondered why Paz seemed more afraid than the other Marines. Whenever the MEU had been on alert for a possible engagement, Paz had been the coolest of them all.

"Yeah," Gavril said. "Whatever happened here, it doesn't look like anybody survived."

They headed up the ramp.

"Look there!" Joan led them back down a ways. Despite the wind howling down the ramp, Rica could hear surf breaking somewhere in the fog ahead.

A dark round lump lay on the ice at the edge of the area that was wet from waves. Rica stepped toward it, then hesitated as her curiosity tangled with apprehension—the mysterious lump was about the size and shape of a human head.

Rica's curiosity eventually won out. She approached from upwind, just in case, and picked it up. It was firm, heavy, and *sharp*. One of several small shapes protruding from its surface sliced the super-tough Taslan fabric of her glove palm, exposing puffy white fibers of polyester insulation. The sharp projections looked like curved shards of glass and were embedded in a solid black matrix that was coated with frost. The object reminded her of a clinker she had once found after a garbage fire at a dump in Puerto Rico—a puddle of molten plastic had solidified, trapping bits of rock, broken glass, and rusty bolts. Just looking at the sinister orb filled her with dread and revulsion, as if it could somehow contain a pocket of evil in its core.

Joan examined the find and curled her upper lip. "Toss it, Demo. Let's go."

"No way," Rica said. She removed her backpack and carefully inserted the specimen so that none of its sharp projections would stab her.

They marched up the ramp to the avalanche debris. The others began picking their way over the ridge, but Rica stepped sideways to investigate a hole at the corner where the rubble met the wall.

"Rica, what are you doing? Please do not go over that way!" Paz pleaded.

"I'm just looking around," she whispered.

The debris chunks in the corner were the largest. Some were bigger than automobiles. A few of the ominously dark nooks between the chunks looked big enough to be inhabited by fog monsters the size of Eddy Brown and Sergeant Gavril combined.

An ice block only two feet high was wedged between the floor and the two biggest chunks. It stood upright on its edge like a tombstone. Based on the structure of the surrounding rubble, Rica would have expected to see another open cavity there, not a small slab of ice.

She glanced back the way she had come. She could still hear the other Marines climbing, but they were no longer visible through the fog.

Knowing she had fallen behind, she stooped to examine the strangely perched slab, shining her headlamp around its perimeter. It appeared to be welded by melting and refreezing to the floor and to the huge chunks adjacent to it. That's weird, Rica thought. She had seen no other evidence of melting this deep in the trench.

She was attempting to move the welded slab, with no luck, when she noticed a yellow stain extending down the ramp from one of its corners. She also caught a whiff of an unbelievably foul odor, a combination of putrid seafood and a high-traffic outhouse on a hot day. Then she heard a sound coming from behind the slab, an obviously biological medley of gurgling, sucking, and grunting.

Rica sprang back, brandishing her rifle. "Gunny! Something over here is alive!"

"Demo, stand off!" Gavril bellowed. "Go to IR. Everybody else get over there."

Rica heard the others scrambling toward her and saw their headlamps bobbing in the fog. She could still hear the muted *suck-gurgle-grunt* through the low moan of the wind. When her infrared goggles were in place, she looked toward the upright slab. It was glowing an eerie midnight blue against a solid black background. That meant it was warmer than the surrounding ice, although still below freezing.

The approaching Marines appeared in her goggles as spectral figures. There was no way to identify who they were, and she counted seven of them. "Gunny! Is Fire Team Two with you?"

"Affirmative," Gavril said. "So is Captain McInnis."

"It's behind that block," she said, pointing to the upright slab with her rifle.

"Safeties off," Gavril barked. "Check your targets."

Paz moaned, shifting from foot to foot.

"Quiet!" Gavril ordered. He squatted, removed his helmet, and laid his right ear against the slab. His sharp intake of breath made it obvious that he had caught wind of the foul odor as well.

Rica's pulse pounded in her neck. Whatever was lurking in the frigid lair, she could imagine it shoving the door outward, knocking Gavril off his feet, then dragging him into the hole before she could get a read on it.

Gavril stood. "Let's open her up."

Paz said, "Oh, no, Gunny. What if—"

"Would you shut up, you pussy?" Joan snarled, but added, "Gunny, maybe we should back off and use a grenade."

"No way," Gavril said. "No matter what it sounds like and smells like, don't assume you ought to kill whatever's in there until you actually *see* it. I'll try to pry open this ice chunk. The rest of you stay ready, *but check your targets*."

They gathered in a semicircle around the fog monster's lair, as Rica had come to think of it. Five combat rifles and two Heckler & Koch MP-5N submachine guns were aimed at the mysterious piece of ice, which still glowed dark blue through her infrared goggles. Gavril poked the blade of his survival knife into a gap at the slab's upper right corner. He gave them a countdown by holding up one gloved hand with all of the fingers open, then closing the fingers one at a time. When his fist was complete, he shoved the knife handle sideways.

The ice slab popped out of its hole.

Rica gagged when the odor hit her, but she managed not to throw up. She stayed on target with her eyes open.

Joan shook her head as if flinging off mud. "Holy fuck, what a stench!"

They waited. Nothing but the smell of feces and rotten fish emerged from the dark cavity, but the animal noises were louder and more clear.

Gavril cocked his head, listening. "My God," he shouted. "I don't believe it!" He dropped his rifle on the ice and scrambled into the hole on his hands and knees.

"Gunny, stop!" Rica shouted. "We can't cover you in there!" All she could see of him was his broad rear end filling the portal. His hips glowed red and purple in her infrared goggles.

"Sergeant, what's going on?" asked Captain McInnis.

Gavril began backing out of the hole, grunting with exertion. If he was engaged in a tug-of-war with a fog monster, he was winning, Rica thought. She was not surprised.

His head emerged, and the trench was filled with echoes from a sound that was as unmistakable as it was unexpected.

The cry of a baby!

Rica snatched off her goggles and stared. Gavril had dragged two living human beings out of the hole. One was a tall athletic-looking teenage boy. The other was a tiny infant whom the boy was clutching in his arms. Rica put down her rifle and ran to help. The others just gawked as if too shocked to react. "Move your guns," she said. "You're scaring him."

"He's scared of *something*," Joan said, "but it ain't our guns. He's not even looking at us."

The boy was sitting up on the ramp, shivering and hyperventilating. His nostrils flared and his chest heaved with each quick breath. His bloodshot eyes rolled wildly in all directions, mostly down the ramp toward the sea. With trembling arms, he held the baby up to Rica. She grabbed the infant before he could drop it. "Thank you. She's sick," the boy gasped. Then he fainted and collapsed on the ice.

# CHAPTER 9

## Survivors

The children were covered with a thick, translucent, bluish crust. It coated their skin, their hair, and parts of their clothing. The brittle crust had cracked and peeled to form patches that were curled up like roasted pork rinds.

"What is that *stuff*?" Rica asked.

Gavril said, "Some kind of ointment, maybe."

"Even in his hair?"

The baby was swaddled in so many layers that she could barely wriggle her arms and legs. Looking at her flushed pink face, Rica guessed that she was actually too hot, despite having been surrounded by ice for many hours. The boy was also fully clothed, and in an even stranger fashion. He had pulled baby garments of all colors over his arms and legs. These makeshift limb-warmers and his own shorts and T-shirt were stuffed full of disposable diapers for insulation.

The animal noises had come from the baby voraciously sucking her thumb, which she resumed in Rica's arms after a few phlegmy coughs. "Poor thing, she must be starving," Gavril said. "Probably dehydrated too."

"I don't see why they didn't freeze to death," Joan said. She peered at the infant, then recoiled with a smirk of disgust. "Lordy. That can't be just baby shit."

Gavril nodded. "Baby shit stinks, but not like that."

Rica was inclined to agree with them, but she did not actually know what a dirty diaper was supposed to smell like. She had been the youngest child in her family, and no one had ever asked her to baby-sit. Come to think of it, she couldn't even remember ever holding a baby before. The meager weight of the child in her arms gave her an uncomfortably strange feeling. "Didn't the boy say she was sick?" Rica asked. "Maybe that's why it smells so fishy."

Gavril shook his head. "At least one of my three young'uns had everything coming and going by the time they could walk, but they never made poopies that smelled like *that*."

Joan picked up one of the translucent bluish flakes that had fallen from the boy's hair. She held it under her beaklike nose and sniffed. Then she dropped the flake and put a hand over her mouth as her muscular neck bulged in an obvious half retch. She cleared her throat, blinking. "It's the blue stuff . . . the smell . . . rotten fish."

Rica wished someone else would take the baby. She felt her face flush when Joan turned to squint at her suspiciously. "Here," Rica said. "You want to carry her?"

"Uh-uh," Joan replied. "No, ma'am, no way."

It occurred to Rica that someone was going to have to carry the baby up the slippery ramp, and her mouth went dry at the thought of that responsibility. Gavril read her expression. "I'll take her," he said. "I've half raised three of these, and I haven't dropped one yet."

They carried both children up to the ALV.

Captain McInnis decided to post sentries at the top of the ramp, since it was the only place where an enemy could climb onto the Floe from the sea. Everywhere else, the four-hundred-foot ramparts of wet ice formed an unscalable perimeter. Against Gavril's judgment, McInnis chose to be one of the sentries himself. The partner he picked was

Vicini, one of the privates who had guarded the ALV during the rescue.

The adolescent boy came to his senses and insisted on staying in the driver's box with Rica. Halfway back to the planes, he pointed to the electronic periscope's eyepiece. There were no obstacles within miles, so she let him look out at the ripples of opaque fog parting around the ALV's rectangular snout.

He systematically rotated the view field back and forth.

"What are you looking for?" she asked.

The boy whispered his first word since his rescue: "Ghosts."

When everyone but the sentries was safely on board the Globemasters, Bonnie Fulcrum examined the children. She found no major injuries, just some frostnip, but the baby had a respiratory infection, and both children had obviously suffered emotional trauma. "Only time will tell how long it takes them to recover," she reported to Gavril. "*If* they recover."

After they had consumed all of the food and water they wanted, the doctor gave the baby a sponge bath. The boy silently washed himself. Despite determined scrubbing, the odor of marine carrion lingered on the children after they were dry and clothed.

As soon as he was dressed in clean white coveralls, the boy worked his way through the chattering crowd and tugged on Rica's sleeve. "When are we going to leave?" he asked.

The chatter died. Rica glanced at Gavril. He addressed the boy, gently softening his deep voice. "I just talked to the pilots. They said it's not safe to take off at night, but one of the planes will take you and the baby to Hawaii in the morning."

The boy frowned and shook his head. "We should all leave now, even if it's dangerous."

"Why?" Rica asked.

"They don't want us here."

"Who doesn't?"

"The ghosts."

Jory Panopalous pushed his way between two of the Marines. "What did these 'ghosts' look like?" he asked. "Did they talk? What kind of tools did they use?" The gaunt little engineer seemed breathlessly excited. Rica knew it was because he thought the Floe was under the control of extraterrestrials. She wondered if he would still be so eager to meet them if he had seen the splattered gore at the bottom of the ice ramp.

"I couldn't see much through the fog," the boy said. "Can we leave now?"

"Sorry, son. Tomorrow morning," Gavril said.

The boy turned away with a reproachful glare. "You'll all be sorry when they come back."

"Son, wait. At least tell us if there are any other castaways so we can go look for them." Gavril had already tried to debrief the boy, but he had refused to speak.

"There were," the boy said.

"Were?" Gavril asked.

The boy nodded. "We made it into the ice canyon on our life raft. Then the ghosts came, and . . ." The boy's face blanched. His lips began to quiver. He put the fingers of his right hand over his eyes.

"Well, what did these ghosts do?" Gavril asked, exchanging a knowing glance with Rica.

"I can't remember," the boy said.

"But you're sure you and the baby are the only survivors?"

"Oh, yes, I'm sure."

"Do you remember how you got that rancid crud all over yourselves?"

The boy hesitated, then shook his head. He trudged to the sleeping bag that had been prepared for him and crawled into it, facing a wall without another word.

Gavril ordered the Marines who were guarding the planes to continue their duty through the night so those who were tired from the rescue could sleep. Before bedding down, he checked in with Captain McInnis, who had nothing to report. "Sir, if you feel yourself getting tired, tell the sentries here at the planes to get me up so I can relieve you," Gavril said.

McInnis's reply came over the radio with a hint of wry humor. "That won't be necessary, Sergeant. Vicini and I anticipate zero difficulty staying awake tonight."

Rica bedded down between Paz and Joan. After all was quiet except for the constant moaning of the wind among the Floe's inland iceforms, she heard a low snuffling sound and got up to investigate. Everyone else appeared to be asleep.

It was the boy. He was curled up, facing the wall, weeping as quietly as he could. Rica moved her bedroll, lay down behind him, and embraced him with one arm over his shoulder.

"I'm Todd," he whispered. "My sister's name is Sophie."

Rica introduced herself and said, "I'm glad we found you and Sophie when we did, Todd."

"Me too," he said. "But it doesn't matter. When they find us, the ghosts are going to kill us all."

"Todd, whoever attacked your camp, they were not ghosts. They were probably specially trained soldiers who were sent to make sure no one finds out how or why this iceberg is being moved. You're safe now that we're here. We have fourteen U.S. Marines and six Air Force officers with all kinds of weapons."

"The ghosts are very hard to see," Todd said, "but maybe we'll see them coming in time to take off. Maybe."

He sighed and seemed to fall asleep.

Rica knew that two armed sentries were patrolling outside each of the Globemasters, but most of the night had passed before she stopped listening for strange noises and glancing at the pale moonlight shining in through the porthole in the starboard jump door.

# CHAPTER 10

# Wildlife

"Rise and shine, Lopez. We got trouble."

"Huh?" Rica opened her eyes and saw bright sunlight. The crew door, the cargo ramp, and both jump doors were open. Everyone but her and Todd was already up. The Air Force crews were unloading the plane so it could return to Hawaii with the children.

"I can't raise McInnis and Vicini on the radio," Gavril said.

"You want me to go check on them?"

"No, I already sent two troops. I need you and Rodriguez to escort Steadman and Price. They want to go see what's making that noise."

Rica donned her crampons and radio headset. Her knees felt stiff, and her biceps were sore from the rappelling. She descended the fold-down stairs beneath the crew door, then waited for Paz and the two scientists from the Scripps Institution of Oceanography.

Tropical sunshine beat down on her stubby black hair, making her sweat despite the cool breeze. The nighttime fog had burned away, exposing the glittering puddles of meltwater scattered across the plain. The glare was unbelievable.

Raymond Price appeared in the doorway. "Shades and

sunscreen," he said. "Melting glaciers can nuke you to a crisp and give you snow blindness in minutes." He stiffly descended the stairs, then paused with one foot on the ice, looking up at Cliff with his caved-in smile. "That's one small step for a geezer, and—"

"And one giant neck brace for the same geezer, if you aren't careful," Cliff said. "I don't want to spend the next six months pushing you around campus in a wheelchair, Ray."

Raymond did a defiant jumping jack. His paunch jiggled, and the wispy gray hair encircling his bald dome flopped up and down. "I've done this a million times," he wheezed.

"Sure, on *dry* bergs."

"What was the noise you guys wanted to check out?" Rica asked.

"Listen," Cliff said, pulling his curly brown mane away from his right ear. "Creaking, groaning, like an old ship."

Rica could hear cries from the seabirds circling in the clear blue sky, plus a concert of almost subaudible bass notes with a counterpoint of spooky moans. "Isn't it just the wind?"

"I don't think so," Cliff said. He led them toward the nearest edge of the Floe, which was on the stern. Rica watched him, admiring his long confident stride. As best she could tell through his baggy white coveralls, the young biologist's body was very well proportioned.

They forded a meltwater stream that looked a hundred feet wide and less than an inch deep. It was meandering lazily across the plain, reflecting silvery-blue sparkles as if its bed were lined with sapphires. "Why is this stream so shallow?" Rica asked.

"The ice is being eroded only by melting," Raymond said, "which actually happens faster *outside* the stream, because the stream water reflects sunlight and insulates the ice beneath it from the warm air. So the streams are constantly shifting around, keeping this plateau level as it melts."

A new sound came from the sea, a distant *fwoosh-hiss* that sounded like the first gout of spray from a geyser. Cliff gasped and began running toward the precipice. "I knew it!" he shouted.

"Careful, big guy," Raymond yelled. "I'm too old to push *you* around campus in a wheelchair."

Rica ran to keep up with Cliff. Paz stayed behind with Raymond.

As she neared the edge of the Floe, the infinite expanse of sea beyond the bluff grew to include the nearby area previously hidden beneath the towering rampart. Long streaks of greenish-white foam converged in the distance on the Floe's wake, which stretched out straight to the convex southern horizon. Rica would have thought the open ocean was too clean for so much foam. The propulsion system was apparently churning the water like no vessel she had ever been on.

She began to hear a steady rush of falling water and occasional deep thumps followed by splashes, a sound that reminded her of depth charges being detonated near the surface. The strangest sounds of all were the creaks and groans Cliff had pointed out. The symphony grew louder as she ran—eerie and beguiling wails that ranged in pitch from guttural growls to piercing whines.

The flock of soaring and diving seabirds extended as far south as she could see over the Floe's frothy wake. Hundreds more were perched along the precipice, gazing down at the blue ocean with their wind-tousled backs to the explorers. Cliff slowed his dash and cautiously approached the edge, scattering a dozen gray-and-white birds with long beaks that were pink at the base and black at the tip with a yellow band in between.

"Would you look at that!" he exclaimed.

Rica crept up beside him, wary of being pushed off the slippery bluff by the wind.

Dark blue water was welling up at the base of the four-hundred-foot wall in bulging eddies the size of supermarkets. Rica could look down from the dizzying height onto the backs of soaring birds, which were occasionally diving into the sea or swooping up to land on the bluff beside her.

To the left, the cliff curved northward until its surface disappeared. To the right, it stretched on for a quarter mile, then turned out to sea along a sharp promontory at the center of the Floe's stern. Rica counted nine waterfalls spilling over the razor-sharp precipice. The cascades were wide and thin. Halfway down, they exploded into plumes of white spray that continued downward to the ocean in wispy sheets. Most of the wet cliff face was in shade from the noonday sun, appearing dark blue from Rica's oblique perspective, but sunlight was shining on the side of the distant promontory, turning its single waterfall into a dazzling white streak with a vivid rainbow in its spray cloud and a dark downward-rolling shadow on the ice cliff behind it.

The most amazing part of the panorama was also the source of the strange sounds—within the first mile or two of the Floe's wake, hundreds of whales and dolphins were diving, porpoising, frolicking, or just swimming to keep up. The geyser sounds were produced when they exhaled through their blow holes. The depth charge sound was produced when they swam at high speed underwater and then shot straight up into the air, rotating and arching so that they fell on their backs, splitting the water with titanic force. Other whales were floating head-down, slapping the water with their flukes.

Without warning, Cliff whirled around and gave Rica a bear hug. "This place is fantastic!" he said. "Nothing could make me regret coming here." He was shaking her shoulders and smiling. His dark hazel eyes were exultant.

Rica smiled back. "Uh . . . okay, Dr. Steadman."

"Call me Cliff," he said. "You're not one of my students. Say, why the hell did you join the Marines, anyway?" He was looking at her with an expression she could not remember ever seeing before. Rica was all too familiar with the looks of lust that men usually wore when examining her up close. This was something akin but different. Curiosity, she decided. Genuine curiosity.

"I thought it would impress my dad," she said, and her

face flushed as she realized how immature the candid answer sounded.

"Did it work?" Cliff asked.

"Not yet."

"He must be a jerk. Too bad you didn't go to Hollywood. You could have made a lot more money."

"What do you mean?"

"I can imagine you with hair," Cliff said. "You could have been an actress or model."

Rica grimaced. "Yuck! Who'd want to? They don't get to blow things up."

Cliff laughed. His gold eyetooth sparkled in the sun. "Maybe you belong in the Corps after all."

Maybe, Rica thought. She wished there was a way to know for sure.

Paz and Raymond caught up. "Oh, wow!" Raymond panted. "I'll bet you want to stay here, big guy." He turned to Rica. "Cliff has a special thing for whales."

"Look how many different species there are," Cliff said. "Sperm whales, killer whales, Risso's dolphins, short-finned pilot whales . . . Look! There's an hourglass dolphin that must have followed the Floe all the way from Antarctica. But only the Odontoceti are here, the toothed whales—none with baleen. I've never seen anything like this. It must be some kind of cetacean feeding frenzy. Maybe the Floe's cool meltwater is attracting deep-dwelling fish to the surface. Or maybe— Oh, no!"

"What?" Rica asked.

"One of the sperm whale calves is injured. Do you see that marguerite formation? The adults are gathered around him, pointing their heads at him and flailing their tails."

Rica pulled out her miniature binoculars and looked where Cliff was pointing. Several sleek gray bodies the size of train cars were clustered in a tight circle. The whale in the middle was smaller than the others. It listed to the left, and bright red blood flowed over its smooth skin from wounds on its enormous rectangular head.

"May I?" Cliff asked.

Rica handed him the binoculars. He peered down at the Floe's churning wake. He made a low keening sound and handed the binoculars to Raymond.

"He's a goner," Raymond said. "Those lesions are huge."

"They aren't lesions," Cliff said. "They're *incisions*. I'd guess that calf has just tangled with a spinning propeller."

"How did it get cut in so many different places?" Rica asked.

Cliff shrugged, glaring back at the Floe's rugged interior with an angry frown. "You know, sperm whales have the largest brains that have ever existed. Are you still going to blow up the Floe's drive if it keeps heading toward Hawaii?"

"That's the plan," Rica said. "Actually, we'll probably try to disable it without destroying it."

"Good," Cliff said. "The sooner the better."

A jet engine started behind them. As they turned to look, it throttled up from a whine to a roar. A plume of meltwater spray blew backward behind one of the Globemasters like the exhaust from a launching rocket. The huge plane slowly began to inch forward on its skis, turning away to the north.

Paz jumped up. "They're leaving without us!"

Rica keyed her headset mike. "Gunny, what's going on? Are they evacuating the children now?"

"Negative," Gavril replied. "A goddamned river is flowing across the runway—came out of nowhere in the middle of the night. I'm moving the Globemasters inland, as far from that ramp as we can get. The plane that's moving now has all of the civilians on board, except Steadman and Price. The other plane will wait until you and Rodriguez can get your party back here, but move as fast as you can."

"Why?" Rica asked. "What happened?"

"I don't know," Gavril shouted over the jet roar. "But McInnis and Vicini are both dead."

# CHAPTER 11

# Wreck

Gavril chose to park the Globemasters in a level cove tucked back among the tall exotic formations of the Floe's interior. The cove was bordered on one side by a shallow meltwater lake. On the other side was a chasm that was at least two hundred feet wide and apparently bottomless. At the back of the cove, intermittent shade was provided by a row of flat, curving ice spires that stuck up like the fossilized ribs of some extinct leviathan.

Todd invented a makeshift baby bottle by mixing formula in a stretchy latex glove and inserting the full glove into a plastic flashlight case so that one finger protruded from a hole he had bored in the end. A pinhole in the tip of the glove's finger turned it into a floppy nipple. He just hoped that Sophie would not have an allergic reaction to the latex.

Dale Johnson notified headquarters in Hawaii that the two sentries at the ramp had been slain. He typed all of the mission's long-range communications and sent them through a satellite datalink machine so the text strings could be digitally encrypted. As Johnson had explained to the others, this protocol was often used on Special Forces missions because it added an extra level of security beyond that provided by scrambling of the radio signal, which would have been the only protection for voice transmissions. No one but Johnson was cleared to operate the datalink machine. In the event of his death, that responsibility would be inherited by another of the intelligence agents.

"Blood was *everywhere,*" said Private Eddy Brown. Sweat dripped from his copper-wire stubble as he paced back and forth. After a few hours of equatorial sunshine, the cabin was sweltering.

"It was just like what we found at the bottom of the ramp, except the tent was in the sun and it smelled like a slaughterhouse. I swear, it was like a grenade had gone off *inside* somebody."

Eddy tried to light a Camel with his big trembling hands. He dropped it, picked it up, and put it away.

"Blood everywhere," he muttered, "floor, walls, ceiling, slung around like somebody threw it by the handful."

"But you didn't find the bodies," Gavril said, "so there's a chance they could still be alive, captured or hiding somewhere."

Eddy vigorously shook his head. "The bodies must have been dragged away. We found a diluted blood trail outside the tent."

"Where did it go?"

"It faded out after a hundred yards or so."

"In which direction?"

"Toward the middle of the Floe."

"Are you sure?" Joan asked. "Why would the attackers drag their victims inland if they climbed up the ramp from the sea?"

"Maybe they *didn't* come from the sea," Gavril said. "Maybe they're hiding out in the inland terrain. Did you find any bullet holes or spent shell casings this time?"

Eddy nodded. "The tent was riddled, but only on one side."

"So?" Joan asked.

"That means the shots all came from inside the tent,"

Rica said. "If someone had blasted it from the outside, the bullets would have gone through two walls."

"The tent was cut up too," Eddy said, "like they'd had a sword fight inside it. All of the cuts were shaped like this." He held up his forefingers to form a V.

"Maybe the attackers had bayonets," Gavril said. "Did you find the sentries' weapons?"

Eddy nodded. "Both rifles and both forty-fives were on the tent floor, empty, covered with blood."

Gavril's eyes widened. "Who the hell would leave behind two brand-new M-16s?"

"Certainly not pirates or enemy commandos," Rica said.

"Could it be some of our own people?" Eddy asked. "Like, some kind of rogue black ops unit?"

Agent Johnson glanced up from the datalink machine. "Let's not go there," he said. "Not without evidence."

"Easy for him to say," Eddy muttered to Paz.

Gavril was frowning again. "Yeah, any group with more money than manpower wouldn't need to scavenge weapons. Or maybe they left them just to make us *think* they don't need them."

"Dr. Steadman," Rica said, "are there any dangerous animals around Antarctica that could have ridden north on the Floe?"

"Sure," Cliff said. "Leopard seals. When they catch a penguin, they jerk it right out of its skin before eating it. Southern elephant seals also live around Antarctica. The bulls can weigh more than five tons, and they are extremely aggressive. They'll kill a human who strays onto a beach that they consider their territory."

"Oh, come on!" Eddy said. "You really think a *seal* could have done that?"

"It's conceivable," Cliff said. "They can move faster on land than most people think, and any seals that rode north on the Floe would be starving and crazy from the heat by now."

"Elephant seals may be some bad mothers," Gavril said, "but I doubt they eat helicopters whole. Remember the Navy chopper? The one we never found? Unless you know of a seal capable of stealing military property, I suggest we look elsewhere."

Dale Johnson closed the datalink machine, locked it, and cleared his throat. His blond mustache was drenched with sweat, and his fair face was even paler than usual. "I have an announcement," he said.

When everyone was gathered around, he continued. "The Floe has accelerated to eleven knots. Analysis of its GPS trace shows that the increase in speed has been gradual and linear so far, but we have no idea what its drive is capable of at maximum thrust. Considering this and the deaths of two Marines, the mission profile has been updated. We won't have time for any scientific exploration after all."

Raymond Price sighed and frowned. Jory Panopalous spun around with his hands in his sweaty hair, emitting a heartbroken groan.

"From now on," Johnson continued, "all civilians will be confined to the planes for their own safety, unless they feel their area of expertise will be an asset to the remaining mission objective."

"Which is?" Gavril asked.

"Corporal Lopez will immediately attempt to blast off the promontory at the center of the Floe's stern, which is the most likely location of the propulsion system. If that stops the Floe's northward movement, we will all evacuate as soon as the runway clears. If it doesn't, one plane will leave as soon as possible with the castaways and civilian consultants, but all military personnel and federal agents will remain behind until we can locate the Floe's drive and disable it."

*"Now!"*

Rica turned the knob that sent a pulse of electricity along each of the ten red wires stretched across the ice from the ALV. A split second later, the first blast hole erupted two hundred yards away, spewing up a plume of ice chips, meltwater, and steam. The explosion shook the ice beneath Rica's feet harder than she had expected, producing a terrifying feeling that the Floe was collapsing into the ocean. Could such a relatively tiny blast have somehow caused the whole glacial slab to start crumbling?

By the time the second charge detonated, Rica was still on her feet and had recovered her confidence in the solidity of the quaking ice. As the blasts continued and the wind cleared the steam from each new crater, she could see a network of cracks radiating outward across the ice, thankfully stopping before they reached the ALV. Several of the cracks merged between the craters. After the ninth detonation, the sound of blasting was joined by ominous creaks, squeals, snaps, and splashes.

The sounds of splintering ice continued after the blast echoes from the inland terrain had died down. A dark chasm opened along the line of blast holes. It continued to widen until the sharp stern promontory became a separate iceberg.

*Triumph!*

As the squad's demolition expert, Rica had been trained to scuttle ships and demolish oil platforms, not to split icebergs apart. In addition to being unprecedented, the operation had been hasty and understaffed. She had expected failure on the first attempt.

Yet she had succeeded.

Rica beamed as cheers and claps erupted around her, saluting her performance. Even Joan said, "Way to go, Lopez!"

"Thanks to lots of help," Rica replied. She had enlisted most of the Marines and Clifford Steadman, the fittest of the civilians, to aid with the frantic drilling and wiring.

"Aw, shit," Joan said. "Look."

The severed promontory was falling behind the Floe, rotating in the colossal slab's churning wake. Rica closed her eyes. She could still feel the familiar north-south wobble of the ice. It seemed as strong as ever. At least part of the propulsion system was obviously not on the stern promontory, because the rest of the Floe was still motoring northward.

"What do you reckon those spots are?" Joan asked.

Rica looked where she was pointing. The newly fractured face of the receding promontory was covered with tiny black dots. "Beats me," she said. "They're already too far away for me to—"

Gavril's voice crackled in her headset. He had stayed behind to help the Air Force crews guard the planes. "Lopez, report! We felt the blast. Did it work?"

"Negative," she said. "The stern promontory is gone, but the Floe is still moving."

"Haul ass," Gavril said. "Even if we failed to take out the drive, the natives are bound to have taken notice, and my guess is that they'll be mighty pissed."

The half-white and half-gray amphibious lander sped across the glittering plain. The ridges on its metal track shoes crunched into the soft ice and pelted the antimine armor on the vehicle's belly with meltwater spray. Another sunset had tinted the gently undulating ice with streaks of orange and crimson.

"I want you back in the planes before dark," Gavril said over the radio.

Rica glanced up at the fat red sun ball in the cloudless blue-green western sky. "We'll never make it, Gunny."

"You'd better try, Demo. Keep your foot on the floor."

"That might not be safe on wet ice."

"It's bound to be safer than waiting around out there."

"Okay, I'll do my best. Over."

Their course ran alongside the deep chasm that zigzagged across the Floe's stern to the cove where the planes were parked. All Rica had to do was follow the chasm home. She concentrated her skill and reflexes on driving the ALV as fast as the thirty-ton behemoth would go, which was about fifty-five miles per hour. No sounds of conversation came from the troop cabin behind the driver's box. She could imagine her passengers hanging on to their seat harnesses with white knuckles.

The oblique crimson glare created reflections that made some of the meltwater pools look unnervingly like bottomless holes. Rica sped through them with the accelerator on the floor, knowing that she was retracing the safe path they had taken on the way to the stern promontory.

One of the dark pools seemed unusually long. It stretched across perpendicular to her course and to the trend of the great chasm on her left. When she saw how it merged with the chasm, she realized with heart-stopping panic that it was not another meltwater pool after all.

*It was a new crevasse.*

Rica stood up on the brake pedal, adding force to her weight by pulling on the figure-eight steering handles until she could feel her compressed neck bones grinding together.

The tracks locked. The ALV skidded. Its deceleration shoved her forehead painfully against the periscope, giving her a full view of the chasm's new tributary as it approached and appeared to grow wider. The blasting must have opened this new crack, she thought, like a rift in the ground caused by an earthquake.

The ALV slewed to the left until she could no longer see the approaching fissure. Now all she could do was hang on and wait for the sensation of free fall. The right track shoes caught at bumps on the ice, jerking the ALV and threatening to overturn it. At least the resistance was still gradually slowing the out-of-control vehicle.

The apparent sideways motion of the ice in front of her periscope ceased. We've stopped, she thought, probably just in time.

She heard a sequence of pops that started quietly but increased in both frequency and volume until she was sure someone would scream from terror. Then the popping abruptly ceased. After holding her breath for a few more seconds, she let out a sigh of relief.

The right side of the ALV slammed downward several

feet with a resounding thud. The thirty-ton vehicle was tilted at about twenty degrees. It swayed back and forth, creaking. After a few more pops and groans, the swaying stopped.

Joan was the first to break the silence. "Way to go, Lopez."

"Nobody move!" Rica shouted. She could see the sharp precipice that the ALV was clinging to. It was smack in the middle of her periscope's view field, stretching away into the distance. To the left of the precipice was the shimmering crimson ice plain. To the right was a black void.

# CHAPTER 12

# Secrets in the Ice

The burgundy sun flashed green and slipped into the ocean as Jacob Gavril clanked down the Globemaster's cargo ramp on his crampons. He speed-marched toward the rear of the ice cove, holding his shoulder straps to steady the heavy internal-frame pack on his back. The pack contained the hand auger, cable, and hand-levered winch that he would need to pull the ALV off the lip of the crevasse where it was stranded.

He paused before entering the maze of towers, cliffs, arches, and overhangs behind the cove. After unfolding the satellite photo in his pocket, he traced with his finger the zigzagging route he had planned. Based on his best guess at the location of the new crevasse that had nearly swallowed the ALV, this shortcut was the quickest way to get to his squad on foot.

They had not asked him to come. Rica had said they could safely disembark, unless the ALV slipped. The stranded party had camp gear and weapons, so they had offered to spend the night by the new crevasse and wait for rescue in the morning.

Gavril had decided otherwise. His Marines were in trouble—along with one civilian—and he knew that it was his

fault for ordering Rica to drive faster than she had thought
was safe. His intention had been to get them back to the
planes so they could all fight together or try to take off if
nightfall brought some kind of reprisal for Rica's demolition
raid. But Gavril's favorite aphorism was the one about good
intentions and the road to hell. This fiasco was his responsibility—he intended to rectify it as swiftly as possible.

And he had decided to do it alone to avoid reducing the
number of soldiers guarding the planes any more than necessary.

The first zig of his zigzagging shortcut took him down a
long alley between two of the curving, riblike spires. The
alley was about twenty feet wide. It was tilted downward
and had a semicircular cross section like a cement chute or
bobsled track. At the end, he briefly glanced back toward the
two distant planes framed by the chute's entrance. The
Globemasters were silhouetted like toys against a strip of
brick-red sky between iron-gray water and the violet firmament. He silently prayed that they would still be intact when
he returned.

*If* he returned.

At the end of the chute was an arch that was dripping
meltwater. The opening beneath the arch was a nearly perfect circle. Beyond the arch, a vast field of rounded cones
rose from the ground like stalagmites. They ranged from the
size of a man to the size of a small house. Gavril knew it
would be easy to get permanently, fatally lost in such a
labyrinth.

Especially in the dark and the fog.

The first wispy tendrils of the Floe's gravylike mist were
just beginning to form in the chute, but the fog was already
fully developed on the recessed ground of the stalagmite
field, which was protected from the wind by surrounding
ridges. The floor was completely obscured to a depth of two
feet. Despite his haste, Gavril stepped down into the fog
swamp cautiously, fearing that he might plunge into a hidden crevasse or meltwater pool.

He consulted his photo-map again by moonlight, cursing himself for failing to bring along at least one pair of infrared. The moon was bright and had nearly replaced the last glow of dusk. He prayed that no clouds would blow over the moon before he could escape the Floe's confusing interior. If he had to turn his headlamp on, it might give him away to anyone or anything lurking in the shadows.

Finally satisfied that he knew the way, he folded his map and proceeded into the fog swamp among the spectral mounds.

He heard a gurgle behind him and turned around.

The gurgle stopped.

He walked on.

The gurgle resumed. It sounded like someone sucking the last of a milk shake through a straw. No, on second thought, it sounded more like a growling stomach.

This time he turned around faster, and again the gurgle ceased. He decided it had to be a meltwater stream hidden beneath the low fog, somehow casting echoes among the frozen monuments in a way that made the gurgle audible from one direction but not from another. Despite that rational and mundane explanation, he picked up his pace, risking a dangerous fall if he tripped over something hidden beneath the fog.

Finally he climbed the low ridge on the far side of the foggy forest of ice domes. Gasping for breath, he peered out over a level plain. The flat field of fog extending miles in front of him could have been mistaken for deep snow except that its surface reflected no sparkles. Halfway to the Floe's stern edge, the fog blanket was split by two vertical-sided chasms that intersected at a right angle. The fog was gently pouring over their sharp edges and down their walls, disappearing into the blackness below. A tiny white object with the shape of a tilted brick was perched on the near lip of the smaller chasm.

The ALV.

As he stepped down from the ridge, he caught a whiff of marine carrion that was nauseating in the way only rotten things from the sea could be. It was even worse than the weird bluish crust that had covered the children when they were discovered. He supposed some bird with a gullet full of fish had died nearby.

He marched down the gentle slope and out across the plain, briskly wading through the fog, thankful for two decades of hard physical training as the hundred-pound pack bounced against his spine. I'll get to my squad as fast I can, he thought. They're bound to be afraid out there.

He smelled rotting fish again. At least it wasn't human bodies. Gavril had once experienced the unforgettable odor of new mass graves, after an earthquake in Chile.

He fell.

His crampons did not slip. He was sure of that. The ice simply ceased to exist beneath him, and he zoomed straight downward, feet first. Then he felt cold wet ice against his left side, pushing him to the right. The ice rubbed against his face, banging his left ear and cheek. He skidded across an apparently level surface for what seemed like a good fraction of a minute, colliding with several small, cold, wet objects. Some of the objects were hard and some were soft, but they all yielded to his momentum. He finally came to rest in absolute darkness and bitter cold.

He lay still, listening. The stench of dead fish was overpowering despite the cold. It made his eyes water, and his mouth began to salivate in preparation for vomit. He clenched his teeth and breathed through them, shutting off the nasal passage at the back of his throat.

The cold dark air was not only redolent with odor; it was also writhing with sound. The noises were not loud, but they were nightmarishly diverse. The word *bestiary* popped into his mind from the title of a scary poem he had read to his three children. Despite the absolute darkness, he could tell he was in a confined space because all of the sounds echoed.

In fact, the echoes were so clear and loud that he could not distinguish the echoes from the source.

He ran his bare hands over the cold wet surface beneath him, trying not to make sounds of his own. His right hand encountered one of the objects that he had knocked aside as he slid. He picked it up and felt it with his fingers. It was soft, squishy, and slimy at one end, like a raw piece of chicken fresh from the refrigerator. The other end of the object was as hard as stone. The hard part was also slimy and smooth, except for one edge, which was corrugated like . . . like . . .

For the first time in Jacob Gavril's life, fear and revulsion overcame him. He dropped the wet object with a disgusted grunt that nearly became a retch. Ignoring the risk of detection, he flicked on his headlamp. The object was some animal's lower jawbone. The squishy end still had shredded hunks of meat attached. The corrugated surface on the other end was the animal's teeth.

He jumped to his feet, drew his Colt .45 combat pistol, and spun around in a circle. He had left his heavy rifle on the plane so he could make better time getting to the ALV. Now he missed the familiar feel of an M-16 in his arms.

His teeth chattered. His legs and arms trembled from the cold. His breath came out as stout puffs of fog. With each new splash or animal call, he jerked around to face the first echo he heard, grunting in shock and terror.

When he looked up, meltwater dripped in his eyes. He rubbed it away. The ceiling was about twenty feet high and made of bluish glacial ice, as he had expected. The walls and floor were also glistening wet ice, and the floor was strewn with many more bits of carrion. Most of the remains were little more than raw bones, usually broken, their white surfaces streaked with cold-preserved blood and scored with deep grooves as if they had been scraped with a knife. Some of the gore pieces were scattered, but most of them were in distinct conical piles that ranged in size from a bucketful to a grizzly mound that could have filled the bed of a small pickup. The floor was pink from wall to wall with meltwater-diluted blood.

There was no fog. Gavril surmised that the air in this tunnel was so cold that it seldom mixed with the warm, humid, maritime air passing over the entrance.

Despite the clear air, he could see neither end of the level tunnel in the feeble concentric rings of his headlamp beam. For a moment his panic somehow increased, because he could not tell which way he had come from. Then he noticed the scratches on the floor and the path he had cleared through the anatomical detritus as he slid.

He walked swiftly along the path, then stopped when he realized that the animal sounds were coming from the opposite end of the tunnel. His instinct told him to climb back out of the gruesome burrow as fast as possible, if he could. Whoever or whatever had constructed this dripping, reeking, reverberating chamber of horrors *might still be here,* and they might be inclined to add his bones to the collection. On the other hand, the mission's remaining objective was to gather intelligence about the Floe until they knew how to disable its propulsion system, and whatever was at the other end of the tunnel might provide some vital clues.

Gavril clenched his cold-numbed fists in indecision, then checked his gear to make sure it was all intact. Everything was fine except his headset radio, which was thoroughly smashed. Whatever he found down here, he couldn't report it until he got to the ALV.

He pulled back the slide to confirm that a round was chambered in his combat pistol, one of only five hundred Colt .45s that had been specially modified for the MEU(SOC). Then he headed down the tunnel toward the sounds. The echoes grew louder as he walked.

He came to a crossroads. The crossing tunnel was smaller than the one he was following. He turned right, then stopped just in time—reeling his arms for balance—to prevent himself from pitching forward into a vat of chilled carrion the size of a classroom.

The floor of the oval chamber was recessed below the floor of its short access tunnel. There was no way to tell how deep the chamber was, because it was filled to the brim with a macabre gumbo of animal matter. Gavril saw many whole carcasses—penguins, seals, fish, seabirds, crabs, and something with suction cups that he assumed was a squid or an octopus. There were also some large butchered pieces from what looked like dolphins or small whales. The head and tail of a shark protruded from opposite ends of the gruesome stew. Gavril wondered whether the shark ends were severed or still attached to a long body that was buried beneath the other carcasses.

It must be a larder, he realized—a gigantic pantry for some greedy and indiscriminate carnivore that hunted on both land and sea and caught far more than it could eat. But what predator was capable of neatly butchering a whale or landing a shark that big? Only man, as far as Gavril knew. He doubted that any human beings intended to eat the half-rotten carcasses, so he wondered if the tons of animal flesh in this room had been collected for some purpose other than food, perhaps for some bizarre scientific experiment or demented occult ritual.

This could explain the ramp down to the sea, Gavril thought. Perhaps it had been used for hauling the carcasses aboard the Floe. He wondered how many other chambers of death lay hidden within the giant slab of ice.

He turned back and crossed the main tunnel. On the other side he found a chamber identical to the one on the right. It was full of the same types of carcasses.

He walked on down the main corridor, passing several more intersections. Some of the crossing tunnels were smaller than the one he had fallen into, and some were larger. He began to suspect that the interior of the Floe was filled with catacombs.

The sounds of live animals increased to a reverberating din. Gavril sensed from a change in the echoes that he was approaching a larger opening. He cautiously edged forward and discovered that the tunnel ended in the wall of a chamber so vast that his light could not reach the other side. He dropped to all fours and leaned over the precipice to look at the near wall. He could not even discern its curvature.

When he finally worked up the nerve to look down, what he saw filled him with horror and pity. At least fifty feet below him, the bottom of the great chamber contained a pool of murky water encircled by broad ledges of ice. The ledges were stained pink, green, and brown by the feces of the various animals held captive by the high walls of wet ice. Seals and penguins splashed in the filthy water and lounged on the ice ledges. Some of the animals were scratching at the walls of their prison. Some were looking up at his light.

The penguins were scruffy, missing patches of feathers. The afflictions of the seals were worse—swollen lips and eyelids, gangrenous limbs, and raw sores on their backs. Gavril imagined that he could see expressions of misery and despair in their large black eyes.

The pit was also occupied by many seabirds. He wondered why they had not flown out, until he saw that their wings had been broken.

Gavril turned and ran, gagging. His crampons left deep craters where they struck the ice. A thin yarn of vomit trailed down his chin, blown back against his chest by the wind his speed was generating.

At the end of the corridor, his momentum carried him up the curving slope that he had slid down when he fell into the Floe's hellish dungeon. He tripped at the top and sprawled on his belly, sucking down gulps of the blessed fresh air wafting over the plain.

Gavril checked his wristwatch. He had been below for a mere twenty minutes, but the Floe had apparently moved into a dryer air mass, because the fog was completely gone. The moon had descended behind the looming ice formations in the interior, casting sharp elongated shadows halfway across the plain. The area around Gavril was in full shade, but he could see the wet ice glistening faintly in the light of the bright cold stars. Beyond the reaching shadows, the plain glowed with ghostly pale moonlight, starkly outlining the jagged black openings of the two joined chasms. He could clearly make out the precariously perched ALV.

He tried to start running but was too exhausted. Walking would be safer, anyway. Beyond a few yards, the shadowed ice was invisible in the feeble starlight, and he had no desire to find out what horrors lay hidden in the next hole he might fall into.

He had gone about a hundred paces when he heard something gurgle. It was the same sound he had heard in the fog swamp full of ice stalagmites. Only now, it was closer.

# CHAPTER 13

## Stalkers

All of the passengers in the ALV had cautiously crawled out through the roof, managing to vacate the tilted vehicle without tipping it into the new crevasse. While the others pitched camp, Rica had spent fruitless hours trying to think of a way to anchor the ALV so that the melting of the ice beneath it would not allow it to slip off the precipice.

Now she lay awake in her tent. She needed sleep badly after staying up most of the previous night during and after the children's rescue. It was not the fear of fog monsters crawling out of the new crevasse that kept her awake, although that possibility occurred to her every time the wind shifted or she heard a noise in the exposed camp. What robbed her of the inner peace necessary for sleep in even the most comfortable bed was her gut-level awareness of how close she had come to killing everyone on board the ALV. A few seconds of skidding out of control had reduced her from the hero everyone was applauding to a persona non grata with whom no one dared to speak. Self-loathing coursed through her system like a deadly poison.

Now she knew that being killed or taken prisoner by a foreign enemy were not the only mortal risks that soldiers were expected to face. There were even greater risks when the lives of others were directly in her hands. She fought the temptation to cry by concentrating on breathing deeply.

Something stank.

The smell was sweet and sour, with the same trace of fishiness that seemed to attach itself to everything that hung around this frozen hell long enough. Rica knew she needed a bath, but her body odor had never been like that.

She sat up with a start, remembering the vile black lump that she had stuffed into her gear pack at the bottom of the Floe's ramp. She had not opened her pack since then.

She dragged the waterproof pack from a corner of her tent. It was bulging like a bloated carcass. She unzipped the top, and a puff of warm gas hit her face. She recoiled and hastily opened the tent door, sticking her head out for air. The black lump had been frozen solid when she found it. Now it had thawed and released a cubic foot of vapors so ghastly and unfamiliar that she wondered if they were toxic.

She had found the lump at the edge of the surf, and its peculiar odor was somewhat fishy—although not as putrid as that of the bluish crust that had covered the children—so she guessed that the thing had come from the sea. On impulse, she donned her crampons and carried the pack to Clifford Steadman's tent.

To her surprise, his tent was empty. She was trudging back when a whisper startled her: "You can't sleep either?"

She saw Cliff squatting on the ice, looking up at the moon, and walked over to him. "What are you doing out here?"

"Insomnia," he whispered. "Battled it for years. Haven't slept more than an hour since we landed."

"I'm sure Bonnie can give you a sedative when we get back to the planes."

"Won't help," Cliff said. "I'm already desensitized to all the safe ones."

Rica hunkered in the cold breeze beside him. "At least you have a good excuse for not sleeping while you're on the Floe. Everyone is scared."

Cliff shrugged, following a shooting star with his gaze. "It's not that."

"What is it, then? Something physical?"

He sighed and lowered his gaze to the glistening ice, letting his long curly hair fall around his face. "I doubt it. For as long as I can remember, I've put every minute—every breath—into my career. I haven't even paused for a trip to the barber in—let's see—one, two . . . my God, at least three years. I've published a lot of papers, but they've all been dribbles. No breakthroughs. Nothing worth mentioning in *Science* or *Nature*. What most people don't realize is that dumb luck can make or break a researcher's career. In the natural sciences, you get more credit for one big discovery than you do for a lifetime of quality work that doesn't make headlines. The more frustrated I get, the harder I work, but so far it hasn't helped."

"Are you sure you have to make a big discovery?" Rica asked. "Maybe you should try to be happy with ordinary scientific . . . dribbles."

Cliff rolled his eyes. "I never thought I'd give up, but that's what I'm starting to think too. I've only been out of grad school for six years, and I'm already burned out."

"It wouldn't be giving up," Rica said.

Cliff looked at her for a moment. She thought she saw loneliness and longing in his eyes. He gradually leaned toward her until he lost his balance and landed on his left hip. They both had to stifle laughter to avoid waking the others.

"Sorry I'm unloading on you," he whispered. "You can tell I haven't socialized much lately."

"That's okay," Rica said, "I haven't either." She moved a little closer as he hoisted himself back onto his crampons, still squatting with his arms resting on his knees. "What's your specialty?" she asked. "Just general marine biology?"

"Cephalopods," Cliff said. "Octopuses, squid, and cuttlefish—all of the mollusks with suction cups. By the way, the correct English plural of octopus is octopuses, not octopi—everybody asks me about that."

Rica shuddered. "I hate tentacles."

Cliff laughed. "If you're talking about the appendages with suction cups all along them, those are technically called arms. Squid have ten arms and octopuses have eight. Believe it or not, the arms are really elongated lips that have evolved to explore, smell, feel, taste, and . . . strangle. The tentacles are different. Squid and cuttlefish only have two tentacles. Octopuses don't have any. They're about twice the length of the arms and a lot thinner, and they've got suction cups only on the paddles at the ends. The tentacles shoot out like whips to grab prey."

Cliff thrust out his arms in parallel, clasped his hands together, and jerked them back to his chest, as fast as a striking snake. Rica got the feeling he had practiced the illustration many times. She could picture it reviving a groggy student very effectively.

"Cephalopods are the highest form of invertebrate life on Earth," he continued, as if lecturing to a class. "No other animals squirt ink or glowing fluid to confuse predators. Did you know that sepia, the ink from a cephalopod, is so durable that the contents of ink sacks fossilized more than a hundred million years ago can be diluted and used to write with?"

When she was sure he was finished, Rica whispered, "It doesn't sound like you're burned out to me. It sounds like you love your job."

"Yeah . . . I do," he admitted with a shy smile. "Especially the lectures. Mine usually run over until the students start leaving. I love the research too, but not the scrounging for grants. That's getting easier, though. Believe it or not, I'm already . . . most of my colleagues would consider me North America's most knowledgeable teuthologist."

"Tooth what?"

"Teuthologist," Cliff said, pronouncing it slowly. "An expert on squids. There are only about a dozen teuthologists in the world. But I'm interested in everything from the sea."

"Good. Maybe you can tell me what the hell this *thing*

is." She dumped the vile-smelling lump out of her backpack. It landed with a splat in front of him, flattening a little. "Charming, eh?"

He reached out to it.

"Careful!" Rica warned.

She was too late. Cliff cursed and held his thumb up to the moonlight, staring at the drop of blood rolling down it.

"Sorry," Rica said. "I should have told you. It's full of these clear little things that are as sharp as razors." She pointed to one of the projections. "Like pieces of glass, except so thin that they would have broken off if they were really glass."

Cliff leaned over the black lump and sniffed. "Ambergris," he said.

"Huh?"

"A hairball from a whale."

"You're kidding."

"No, ma'am. Sperm whales live mostly on large squid, which are easily digested except for their hard beaks. Up to eighteen thousand beaks have been found in the gut of a single sperm whale. The beaks accumulate in a whale's intestines the way cats get plugged up with hair. This gooey black gunk is a kind of protective wax that the whale secretes to coat the sharp beaks. Believe it or not, this stuff used to be highly valuable because it was the only source of an ingredient in the world's best perfumes." He sniffed and made a disgusted face. "Something is wrong with this specimen. It doesn't smell right."

Rica felt amazed by how much Cliff must know. She had always pictured scientists as unattractive geeks, but Cliff didn't fit that stereotype. He certainly had a nerdy streak, but he also had a sense of humor, broad shoulders, slender hips, and a face that she guessed would be handsome if he shaved.

"So these sharp things are squid beaks?" she asked.

"They have the right shape," he said. "Like the upper half of a parrot beak. But squid beaks are normally black or dark brown. *Do you know what this could mean?*"

With no warning, he embraced her in another bear hug. She wondered if he did that to whoever was closest when the urge struck him, or just to her. "These beaks could be from an unknown species!" he whispered. "Unless they're something man-made that the whale swallowed by accident . . . some kind of plastic container, maybe."

The conversation had distracted Rica from her morose feelings over stranding the ALV, but she was still in a lonely mood. The sensation of Cliff's arms surrounding her felt so good that she wished it could continue. "I have a first aid kit," she said. "Come back to my tent, and I'll patch up your thumb."

He opened his mouth to say something, then closed it. Finally he said, "Okay."

Gavril slowly rotated—gun drawn, nostrils flaring, heart beating fast. He was still shadowed from the moon by the Floe's interior iceforms. When he shined his light on the starlit ice behind him, the mysterious gurgle stopped.

He panned the headlamp in a circle, then reached up to shake it. Its beam was weak and wavering, which meant the batteries were almost exhausted. The darkness surrounding him remained silent.

He caught a familiar whiff of marine carrion and guessed that some air was escaping from the subglacial catacombs.

He started walking toward the distant ALV again, listening for more gurgles. He thought about the animals trapped in that reeking ice pit, starving and dying of disease and injury. Why had he been such a coward? He should have put some of the suffering beasts out of their misery before running from the dripping dungeon. He probably had enough ammunition to put down all of the abscess-ridden seals.

He heard the gurgle again. This time it was accompanied by a faint moist hiss and a sloshing sound as if someone was carrying sacks of water. He had no idea what could be making the noises. All he knew was that he was becoming terrified, overwhelmed by more fear than he had ever experienced during the military engagements for which he had received numerous medals and citations of merit.

Like before, the noises stopped when he turned around. This time, though, he thought he saw a glimmer of movement, a wraithlike shadow passing quickly in front of the lowest stars. He fired his modified Colt .45 toward the movement. There was no reaction except echoes of the report from the Floe's interior iceforms. When the echoes died down, he realized how maddeningly silent the endless ice plain was.

He resumed walking, even faster than before. How could someone be following close enough behind him to make those noises? There was nothing to hide behind within miles, so it seemed like he should be able to see his pursuer even in the feeble starlight. He recalled Todd's creepy warnings about ghosts.

If I could just make it to the moonlight, he thought, surely I'd be able to see the stalker behind me and blow him away.

Gavril considered ditching the pack so he could make better time, but that would invite whoever was stalking him to steal it, leaving the ALV stranded for the duration of the mission.

The gurgle returned, along with the moist hiss and the sloshing. Then a different sound worse than all of the others joined the terrorizing medley—a wet slithering, like a bathtub full of eels.

He smelled rotten seafood again. This time the odor was much stronger.

Gavril stopped but could not make himself turn around. The noises from behind him came closer until they seemed to pound on his ears, although he knew they were actually still quite soft. The only other sound he could hear was his own laboring heart.

The gurgle and hiss finally stopped getting louder. At the same moment, the sloshing and slithering ceased altogether. The smell of dead fish remained on the breeze.

Something brushed upward through the hair on the back of his head.

He spun around and fired his pistol twice. Whatever had touched his head retracted so swiftly that all he saw was a blur of motion receding from the beam of his headlamp. "Who's there?" he yelled, firing his Colt .45 once more. No matter how he squinted into the darkness, he could see nothing but the stars above, the silhouetted iceforms on the horizon, and the starlit ice within a few yards of his feet.

He wondered if anyone at the ALV or the planes could hear the loud pistol shots. Probably, but they would recognize the distant sounds only if they were listening for them, which of course they were not. Gavril had no hope of being rescued, but he wished he could warn the others that someone might be sneaking up on them too.

A second gurgle approached from his left. He fired a shot in its direction, hoping in vain that the bright muzzle blast would reveal his enemy. There was another noise to his right, while the one on his left became as loud as the one in front of him. He heard something immediately behind him and just above the level of his head.

The wet slithers and sloshing abruptly resumed on all four sides, and the sounds began to close in. Gavril dumped the almost empty seven-round clip from his pistol and slapped in a fresh one, twisting around in hopes of glimpsing the invisible pack. "Get away!" he yelled. "I'll shoot."

An indistinct shape finally loomed out of the darkness. It was not as close as he had thought from the sounds.

He fired all seven rounds at it.

The shape paused while he was shooting, then resumed slowly trudging toward him, swaying back and forth in front of the stars. "Oh, God!" Gavril groaned. "Motherfucker!" He knew he could not have missed at such close range, and that any one of those .45-caliber slugs should have stopped a man.

He squinted into the starlit gloom as he reloaded. Why was the shape so damn hard to see?

Sweat was pouring into his eyes, yet the breeze was so cold that he was shivering all over. His trembling hands dropped the loaded clip. It clattered on the ice between his boots. "Fuck!" he shrieked as he bent over to pick it up.

When he straightened, something touched the back of his head again. Before he could spin around, something cold and strong grabbed his gun hand and twisted it in what felt like a full circle, pulling apart the bones of his wrist. He grunted in agony. The three-pound pistol landed on the ice.

He felt something slide beneath his right armpit, from back to front. Something sharp touched his left shoulder, then seemed to trace a line across his torso to his right hip. He felt warm liquid run down his belly and unzipped his coveralls to reach a hand into his shirt. His fingertips slid across his toned midsection, lubricated by the warm fluid. Then they slipped through the incision into his abdominal cavity.

With his right hand inside his bleeding belly, Gavril twisted around in his assailant's cold embrace. At last, he could see the attacker clearly. He tried to scream but could not draw a breath. His face, ears, neck, and scalp exploded with sharp pain as he was lifted off the ice. For a second or two his legs writhed convulsively in the air.

# CHAPTER 14

## Corpse

Rica passed her binoculars to Paz. "About half a mile. You see those two bumps?"

"*Sí*, but neither of them looks like a body. Maybe blobs of ice."

"Let's check it out, just in case." She led him toward the two isolated lumps on the glittering plain.

When Gavril had failed to arrive by dawn, the Marines at the ALV had gone out in pairs to search for him. It was another clear day—hot sun, cool wind, glaring wet ice. The planes were still unable to take off. The runway was now obstructed by three meltwater streams instead of one. The Air Force crews were beginning to wonder if their decision to land on the Floe had doomed two state-of-the-art aircraft with price tags more than six times the construction cost of the Astrodome.

"Whatever happened to Gunny, I hope we're the ones who find him," Rica said.

"I do not," Paz replied.

They marched across the blinding white ice and shallow interlaced streams of sparkling meltwater. With each step, each breath, Rica said a silent prayer that Gavril was still alive. She could eventually forgive herself for wrecking the

ALV, but only if no one—especially Gunny—had died as a result. With any luck, she told herself, he had just gotten lost in the Floe's confusing interior.

As they got closer it became apparent that one of the two white bumps was hundreds of yards farther inland than the other. Through her binoculars, she could see that both objects were covered with fabric that was flapping in the wind. She could also see streaks of red on the white cloth.

Rica walked to the first object with a weakening, nauseating feeling of dread. She hooked her crampons under one side and kicked it over. "It's his pack."

Paz genuflected and began muttering with his eyes closed.

The backpack was smeared with blood, including a huge red handprint. There were several V-shaped incisions in the fabric, and both shoulder straps had been neatly severed at the top.

The nearby meltwater pools were tinted pink and contained several .45-caliber spent cartridges. To Rica's surprise, one of the pools also had a faint bluish tint. When she stooped to examine the blue water, she smelled a fishy odor but saw nothing in the pool that could explain its color or smell.

She checked the pack's contents. It seemed to contain everything they would need to move the ALV. She tried to heft it but could barely lift it off the ice. "Paz, we have to take this stuff with us. We still have to get the ALV unstuck."

Paz stopped mumbling and opened his eyes, then helped her transfer the contents of Gavril's pack to theirs.

They followed the diluted blood trail, which ranged from one to six feet wide and led inland toward the other bloody object.

"What kind of animal or assassin could sneak up on Gunny out here?" Rica asked. "Seems like it would be impossible."

"No animal. No assassin," Paz said. "Something evil.

Todd said a ghost. Maybe not a ghost, but some evil kind of spirit. This place is cursed."

The trail narrowed as they walked. First they came upon a Vibram boot sole—no boot or crampons, just the rubber sole. Then a plain belt buckle, no belt. Then a hunk of dark raw meat in a pool of bloody water. Rica had helped cook many a meal for three growing boys. She knew a piece of liver when she saw one. "Oh, God." She looked away and swallowed.

Paz moaned and stared at the partial organ, biting down on the tips of his left fingers.

Rica walked on. When she noticed that she could hear only her own crampons chinking on the ice, she stopped and looked back. Paz was standing still. His face was tilted upward. His eyes were tightly screwed shut. His hands were clasped beneath his chin. Tears ran down his smooth bronze cheeks, glistening in the harsh equatorial sunlight. His lips were moving, trying to form silent words despite being pulled back by sobs.

Rica felt anger. Whatever they were about to find was at least partly her fault. If she could handle it, considering that, then so could Paz. She swiftly walked back to him, sharpening her tongue as she went.

When she stood in front of the praying, weeping nineteen-year-old, about to give him a direct order to march, she paused to think about what he was feeling. To her, there were two things to fear on the Floe, as on any dangerous mission: death and disgrace. But to Paz, a third item was at stake: his immortal soul. Not only did he believe he could be damned for his sins; he also believed in the old superstition that his soul could be stolen by the devil or the devil's agents, no matter how well he behaved. Paz did not fear death, because he genuinely believed he would live on forever in a better place as long as he died with honor. But he did fear evil.

In order to give him a few minutes to compose himself, Rica waved at his overloaded pack. "There's no point in car-

rying that heavy gear any farther than you have to. I'll check
out the other object and meet you back here."

Paz sharply nodded, his eyes squeezed shut and his lips
clenched between his teeth.

Rica was not surprised to find that the second white object was the upper half of a human body. To examine it, she
had to chase away several scavenging birds that looked like
oversize sea gulls. He was on his back, arms stretched out,
mouth gaping slightly, eyes half open and rolled back in his
head. When she saw the corpse's face and knew for certain
that it was Gavril, she radioed the other teams to call off the
search.

The trailing edge of the corpse was ragged, as if he had
been pulled apart at the waist rather than cut. His coveralls
were missing, but he was still wearing a shirt. The backbone
extended several vertebrae beyond the blood-soaked shirttail, and a loop of intestine stretched out on the ice behind
the collapsed abdominal cavity. The only obvious injuries to
the upper body were a few places where the gulls had
pecked him. Looking closer, Rica saw that his face and neck
were also perforated by hundreds of neat, inch-long, horizontal incisions that seemed to encircle his head in rows.

She wondered if he had been tortured with a knife tip.

At the sound of footsteps, she crouched and raised her
rifle. It was just Paz. He knelt beside the remains, rubbing
the pale gold crucifix he had added to his dog-tag chain.
"They should have sent a chaplain on this mission," he said.

"You'll have to do, Paz." She quietly kept a lookout
while he leaned over what was left of Sergeant Gavril and
prayed in Spanish, bestowing the most sincere, original, and
touching eulogy he could compose.

It was dark by the time Rica drove the ALV up the clanking cargo ramp into one of the Globemasters, wondering if
she would ever be able to eat or sleep again. Wanting to be
alone, she took the next shift as one of the sentries outside

the planes while Agent Johnson reported Gavril's gruesome death over the datalink.

Cliff set up a binocular microscope atop an ammunition crate. He hacked one of the transparent squid beaks—or whatever it was—out of the ambergris lump, ignoring the complaints about the specimen's distinctive fragrance in the sweltering cargo hold. The three-inch half beak would not fit on the microscope's stage, so he tried to cut a sliver from it with a scalpel. When he finally gave up, the stainless steel blade was dull, and the clawlike beak was not even scratched.

Next he tried breaking the beak with a hammer, also to no avail.

Finally he placed the beak in a vise supplied by Paz Rodriguez from his weapon repair kit. The sides of the beak bent inward until they were pressed together by the vise, but the thin transparent object still refused to break.

"Damn it!" Cliff shouted, viciously scratching his long curly beard with both hands. The plane was still insufferably hot from baking in the sun all day. Bert Lazarus and Dale Johnson had nearly come to blows over whether to leave the doors open during the night. Bert had won because he was the pilot, like the captain of a ship, and now his rotund form was slumped in one of the open jump doors, hogging the breeze, silhouetted by the moonlight on the ice outside.

"I'm going to go postal if I don't shave!" Cliff whispered to Raymond, who was sprawled on the floor with his wet, hairy belly protruding from his open shirt. Sweat had pooled beneath the aging oceanographer's neck.

Raymond opened one eye. "I didn't bring my Weed Eater, big guy, but you can borrow the razor in the kit they gave me at Hickam."

"God bless you," Cliff said. He found Raymond's shaving kit and clanked down the cargo ramp to find a meltwater stream.

\*   \*   \*

After Rica bedded down at the end of her sentry shift, the full reality of Gavril's death caught up. Her face contorted, and tears flooded from her tightly closed eyelids. She curled up on her side in a tight ball and bit down on her right forearm, trying in vain to cry silently, until her abdominal muscles cramped and she had to straighten out. Her nose was blocked, and her stomach felt queasy. She was about to crawl out on the windswept cargo ramp, in case she got sick, when something grabbed her left ankle.

She stifled a shriek and reached for her combat pistol.

Joan let go of her leg. "Lopez, what's the matter?"

"What do *you* care?" Rica groaned.

"I don't. I just can't sleep with you squeaking like a rat in a trap."

Rica swallowed and tried to calm down. "It was partly my fault," she whispered. "He wouldn't have been out there if I hadn't wrecked the ALV."

"So what?" Joan replied. "Shit happens."

"That's your explanation for everything, isn't it?"

Joan snorted. "It *is* the reason for most things, babe."

Rica was sitting up now, mashing her wet eyes.

"Good grief, Lopez. If you hadn't hit the brake in time, the ALV would have pitched into that fucking canyon and killed us all. You're going to fuck up now and then just like the rest of us, if you live long enough. So get used to it. You're doing okay."

Rica was speechless. Joan was the last person she would have expected to say such a thing. Despite its harsh tone, that made the message all the more credible and thus more comforting than it would have been if it had come from anyone else.

Rica felt the monster in her gut slinking back to its den.

Joan whispered, "If you tell anybody I said that, I'll cut your fucking tits off."

"Okay," Rica said with a weak laugh. "Same to you."

						*	*	*

Dr. Chester Wimbledon had been perfectly content with the CIA's decision not to let the scientists explore the Floe after all. He knew he would still get paid, and that was all he cared about. Then Clifford Steadman had insisted that he use his portable DNA sequencer and the library of taxonomic gene markers on CD-ROM to help analyze the abominable specimen of ambergris. At first he was not at all interested, but his enthusiasm grew as he observed Cliff's thwarted attempts to damage one of the beaks. He could not believe his luck when Cliff went for a shave, leaving the specimen unattended. Chester pocketed the sharp beak when no one was looking and climbed down the steps from the crew door.

# CHAPTER 15

# Beak

Cliff waved to the Marine sentry patrolling the darkness around the Globemaster. He pointed to Raymond's shaving kit, then to a meltwater stream that was undulating silently from right to left at the limit of the wan radiance from the open cargo door. The sentry nodded, and Cliff marched to the stream, still cursing the heat and scratching his beard.

The stream had no definable edge. The smooth sheet of meltwater that coated the ice just gradually thickened until its depth and direction of flow became discernable. Cliff waded in and knelt on all fours, allowing the frigid water to soak the knees of his coveralls. He pinched Raymond's shaving kit between his thighs to keep it above the stream. In that awkward position, he lathered up and resolutely hacked away at his long thick beard with a safety razor, ignoring the painful coldness of the water and the bleeding from nicks here and there. He was shivering in the breeze, and his shins ached from the icewater soaking his coverall legs, but he knew that the itching would keep him awake all night.

He heard a splash behind him, then several more splashes in rapid succession.

He jerked upright. "Who's there?" he shouted. There was no answer.

He tried to hold his breath and listen. All he could hear was the baby crying. She was still sick and suffering from the heat. Her pitiful wails blared from the cargo door and echoed off the riblike ice spires on the far side of the cove. She had cried often since her rescue, but this was the first time Cliff had wondered who or what might be lured to the planes by her intermittent broadcast.

He resumed shaving as swiftly as he could, swishing the razor in the cold stream and raking his face with abrupt, reckless strokes.

*Gulp. Gurgle. Splash.*

The sounds had come from behind him again, even though he had turned around to face the opposite way after hearing the first splashes. He jerked his head upright, gasping and swiping at his face to clear away the shaving cream. In his haste, he shoved lather into both eyes. "Son of a bitch!" he groaned, blinking and staggering.

The sounds repeated, this time with an additional hiss and a complex slithering noise. He caught a whiff of something that smelled like dead fish.

Cliff stumbled to his feet. He was still trying to clear his stinging eyes when the noise came again. This time it was mostly splashing and slithering, and the sounds seemed to be receding into the distance. He turned toward the noises, but all he could see through his tears and reflexive blinking was a diffuse square of white glow—the Globemaster's open cargo door.

He made for the door, running haphazardly on his crampons. Before he could reach the ramp, a white shape ran toward him from beneath the left wing, heading him off. The tall shape stopped between him and the ramp. He saw a red glowing point in the middle of its head, like a tiny evil eye.

Cliff staggered back. The Marine sentry clad in white camouflage removed the glowing cigarette from his lips and said, "Easy there, Professor. What did you see?"

"See? Shit, I can't see *anything*! I heard . . . I don't know." Cliff leaned over and let the tears drip.

"All right, get on board and I'll— *Hey, what was that?*" The sentry spun around, raising his twenty-inch MP-5N submachine gun. Cliff had heard it too, a clanking as if a heavy man had bounded down the ramp.

Or up it.

Cliff could not see anyone near the ramp. Apparently the sentry couldn't either—his posture relaxed and he waved Cliff on.

Chester Wimbledon strolled up to one of the sentries outside the Globemaster and offered him a cigarette. After they lit up, he asked if he could try shooting the sentry's combat pistol. The young Marine, who looked like a pudgy but strong Pacific Islander, automatically refused.

Chester inhaled deeply through his Lucky Strike, wondering if anyone else on the Floe would recognize the mysterious specimen's potential economic value. Dr. Steadman was the only other life scientist, and he was too wrapped up in his quest for academic stardom to imagine any rewards other than acclaim from his colleagues. Chester knew Steadman's type. His biotechnology company, Pherogenics, employed several of them—otherwise brilliant scientists and engineers who would work seventy hours a week for a blue-collar salary and the all-important pat on the back.

Chester's executive philosophy was "go for broke," and that was exactly where Pherogenics had gone. None of its far-reaching projects had paid off for several years, so Chester had turned to stealing breakthroughs from competitors, and one of his industrial spies had recently been caught red-handed. Now he was facing a lawsuit that was going to take away his savings, his home, his bulletproof Lexus SUV . . . everything. He might even slip so far through the cracks that he would have to cut back on cigarettes. The thought brought tears to his eyes and made his lips quiver, shaking the curl of glowing ash off the tip of his Lucky Strike.

Chester was thirty-one before he owned his first car. He had put himself through college by working as an orderly in a liposuction clinic, where he met an endless stream of people who rode in limousines but could not do arithmetic. After immigrating to the United States, he had expected the land of opportunity to reward him for his intellect and years of effort, but the competition between new Ph.D.'s was so fierce that his only job offer upon graduation came from a college in the boondocks of Idaho, where he actually earned less as an assistant professor than he had as a part-time orderly, shaving patients' heads and scrubbing bedpans.

Then he managed to isolate the gene that produced the chemical mating call of the Caribbean cotton weevil. By splicing the gene into a harmless bacterium that grew on molasses, he could cheaply produce vast quantities of the pheromone, which induced the male weevils to copulate and die at the wrong time of year. He managed to evade his employer's legal claim to this discovery by hiding it until he resigned, and so Pherogenics was born.

But he had never forgotten what poverty was like, or what an unjust fate it was for someone with his intelligence, entrepreneurial spirit, and scientific accomplishments. He would do *anything* to avoid facing it again.

He knew he should be patient and avoid tipping off the others that the razor-sharp enigma in his pocket might turn out to be worth millions of times its weight in gold, but the possibility of reversing his fate at the brink of financial annihilation was so tantalizing that he had to find out immediately whether it was real.

"Okay, you can do the shooting," he said to the sentry in his crisp British accent. He pulled out the transparent squid beak, taking care not to nick himself, and dropped it on the ice. "Dr. Steadman needs a piece of this thing that he can fit under his microscope lens, but his scalpel wouldn't cut it. If you'll just fire one shot . . ."

"Okay," the sentry said. "Stand clear." He keyed his headset mike and told the other Marines what he was about to do so they would know why he was shooting. Then he drew his combat pistol, took aim with both hands, and shot the specimen at about a forty-five-degree angle.

They squatted and stared at the moonlit ice. "What the hell?" the sentry said. The beak had disappeared, which was not so surprising. The amazing thing was that they could find no bullet hole in the ice.

They found the beak about twenty feet away. It had a new white spot near the center of the concave side but was otherwise intact. "Try again!" Chester whispered, breathless with anticipation. "Shoot straight down this time so the bullet won't ricochet."

The sentry stood astraddle the beak and blasted it.

When the mist cleared from the impact point, they saw that the whole beak had been driven two or three inches into the ice. The crater was surrounded by radiating cracks. The sentry dug out the specimen with his survival knife and held it up to the moon. "Goddamn!" he said. In the center of the intact beak was an inch-wide disk of silvery metal, the flattened remains of a .45-caliber slug.

*Yes, yes, yes!* Chester leaned back and shook his fists, nearly swooning with glee.

"It must be made of Kevlar," the sentry said.

Chester knew better. The beak—or whatever it was— weighed nearly nothing and was only a few millimeters thick, yet it had stopped a .45-caliber slug at point-blank range. Kevlar was tough, but not that tough, and he would have heard about it if anyone had started manufacturing a material that was even tougher.

That left only two possibilities. The "beak" might be composed of a new synthetic that was still under secret development. If so, Chester's chemists could probably reverse-engineer it in time to compete with its inventor. The specimen might also be made of a previously undiscovered natural substance. If he could transplant the gene that produced the super-tough compound into a fast-growing microbe, he could patent the recombinant strain. Either way, his lifetime of hard work would finally pay off. His head spun with the potential markets for such a tough biopolymer. Bulletproof windows, light body armor, aircraft parts, prosthetic implants—the possibilities were endless.

The sentry walked toward the plane. "I'd better report this to Mr. Johnson. It might be an important clue."

Chester lunged in front of him. "Wait! I'll give you a thousand dollars to not tell anybody." As soon as he'd said it, he clenched his teeth with regret. Now the sentry knew he had something to hide. But a bribe was all he could think of on the spur of the moment.

The Marine frowned suspiciously and stepped around him, carrying the beak in one hand and his combat pistol in the other.

Chester got in front again, walking backward. He slowed down until they both stopped. "Okay, *ten* thousand. We'll just say you blew the specimen to smithereens. You could buy a car!"

The sentry's frown deepened. "Get out of my way," he said with a menacing glare. He moved to step around the tall geneticist again.

They were in the broad moon-shadow of the Globemaster's wing, perilously close to the glow of the open crew door. Chester thought about promising the Marine a fraction of the profits—he could decide later whether the promise was worth keeping—but he figured the young grunt was probably too stupid to comprehend the value of such an offer. He grabbed the boy's arm and spun him around. "I'll give you a hundred grand, cold cash. Just stop and think about—"

The short blocky Marine pushed Chester away with the hand holding his pistol. "Get off me, you fucking freak!"

Chester stumbled in the darkness. He lost his balance and grabbed the sentry's wrist to avoid falling.

The Marine grunted and tried to pull away.

The loaded Colt .45 waved between them.

Chester hung on.

They both fell.

The Marine banged his head on the ice and dropped his pistol.

Enraged, Chester picked up the gun and aimed it between the young man's eyes, his finger on the trigger. "Goddamn you, you stupid little piece of—"

The Marine grabbed Chester's hand, and the gun went off. The back of the sentry's head exploded, spraying a broad fan of blood across the ice. The spray also included shards of bone, lumps of puddinglike brain matter, and a few tattered strips of meninges that reminded Chester of the placenta he had once seen emerge with a newborn foal. Chester stared at the young soldier's gaping mouth and open eyes, one of which was red from blood draining into it from the neat round hole in his forehead.

*Oh shit, oh fuck, oh shit!*

Chester crouched over the body, looking around. The other sentry was nowhere in sight. Chester tried to swallow but couldn't. His head swam, and his heart thumped painfully as he waited for someone to come running toward the sound of the shot.

# CHAPTER 16

# Orb

Chester squatted by the young Marine's lifeless body, overwhelmed with dread. After several seconds passed and no one had come, it dawned on him that everyone must have thought the sentry was still shooting at the squid beak. Maybe that would give him time to get away. But where could he run? Where could he hide?

A voice crackled in the dead Marine's headset, asking him to respond. Chester numbly stared at the ashen face and the moonlit pool of blood as the request was repeated twice. Then he heard the Marine say, "Okay, Sentry Two, I'm coming over there. If you're just taking a piss, you'd better say so."

Chester was turning to run when the other sentry dashed out from beneath the Globemaster, yelling into his headset mike, "Full alert! Full alert! Sentry Two is down!"

The frantic Marine saw Chester. "Hey, what happened?"

Chester realized belatedly that his fingerprints were all over the weapon. What could he say that would start establishing a credible defense in spite of such damning evidence? "It was . . . it was an accident," he stammered. "He was letting me shoot at the specimen. The bullet must have ricocheted."

Chester felt a rush of relief as the ingenious lie came out. He could just imagine how the dim-witted Marines would react. At first they would not believe him. Then they would test his claim by shooting at one of the beaks. When they discovered that a story as far-fetched as a ricochet from the beak was *possible,* they just might conclude that it was *true.*

"He's lying," Joan whispered. "Charley would never have let the fucker touch his side arm."

Rica nodded. "But why would he have shot Charley on purpose?"

Gavril's death had made Rica the highest ranking Marine on the Floe, even though she was only a corporal. Now she was responsible for the morale and safety of the ten surviving members of her squad, including herself. At twenty-one, with only four years in the Corps, this was her nightmare scenario.

Joan was second in command. She and Rica were privately conferring in a corner of the dark hold.

"Maybe he's a spy," Joan whispered.

"Working for who?"

"For *them*—whoever built the Floe's drive."

"Do you think he could have also killed Gunny? Or McInnis and Vicini?"

"It's possible," Joan said. "The ice made thick fog on both of those nights. He could have snuck away from the plane by crawling under it, then returned before dawn."

Rica glanced toward Chester's bony silhouette, and another monster crawled out of its den in her gut. This time she did not feel like crying; she felt like killing. "What do you think we should do with him?"

Joan pulled back the T-shaped cocking handle to chamber a round in her M-16, then rotated the firing selector switch on the left side of the receiver from the backward safety position to the downward single shot position. "We know he's guilty of at least one murder. I say we waste the motherfucker right now."

"We can't do that!" Rica whispered.

"Watch me." Joan raised the rifle to her shoulder and took aim at the suspect's head.

Rica grabbed her arm.

"Remove that hand or lose it," Joan growled.

Rica stepped into Joan's line of fire, feeling sweat cascade down her back. "Joan, what's wrong with you? You'll be court-martialed!"

Joan stood her ground.

"Besides," Rica whispered, "even an asshole deserves a fair trial."

Joan lowered her weapon, ejected the cartridge she had chambered, and slumped against the wall.

"On the other hand, we can't let a possible traitor run loose in camp," Rica whispered. "Let's lock him in one of the gear cages." The hold of their Globemaster was equipped with three modular chain-link cages designed to secure valuable or dangerous cargo during operations in which civilians or foreign nationals would come aboard.

Joan looked up with a sneer. "You're the boss, *Corporal* Lopez. But if the psycho gets out and kills somebody else, you'll have that on your conscience too."

Chester sat where they had asked him to wait. He could not make out the whispers of the two power-crazed broads, but he could read their body language loud and clear. When they wrapped up their debate and strode purposefully toward him, blind panic took control of his legs.

"Hey! Come back here!" yelled the tall Latina, who was leading the chase. The ugly one yelled, "Demo! He's going back there where the guns are!"

Chester heard pounding footsteps behind him, then a *whoosh* of air.

Two hands gripped the tops of his bony shoulders.

He spun around and swung a punch.

It missed.

He saw a blur of short black hair, a snarl of white teeth,

and a flash of enraged cinnamon-brown eyes. Then something soft but firm plowed into his face like a padded sledgehammer.

He dropped to his knees, grasping his nose. Pain shot back behind his eyes as if his skull had been split down the middle. Warm blood flowed over his fingers.

*"You fuckig bidge! You broge my noldze!"*

Tears poured down his cheeks and mingled with the blood. Blinded by pain, he heard the ugly girl say, "Way to go, Lopez! I didn't think you had it in you."

Before the commotion, Cliff had been tired enough to drift off despite his lingering terror. But after Chester was apprehended and everyone else went back to sleep, leaving the hold as quiet as a tomb, his insomnia kicked in. His exhausted mind began drifting around in that familiar frustrating limbo where he was awake yet not alert enough to concentrate, where whole and worthwhile thoughts—great ideas and long-sought conclusions—seemed perpetually just out of reach.

He had told the sentries about the noises. They had searched but found nothing. Cliff knew something was out there, or he was out of his mind. Either way, he was scared.

He propped himself up with his back against a wall so he could look through the open crew door, which was five feet above the moonlit ice outside.

Raymond rolled onto his back and started snoring.

Cliff thought about Enrica Lopez. She was very attractive, yet a mysteriously dedicated soldier as well. He had a feeling she was destined to do great things, either in the Marine Corps or elsewhere. Whatever happens to me, he thought, I hope she makes it off the Floe alive so she'll at least have a chance to live up to her potential.

The dark hold was strewn with sleeping bodies, but he could easily pick out Rica's. She was lying on her side, facing away from him, her broad hips arching high above her shapely legs and upper body. A desperate desire to go to her struck him. It was so overwhelming that he had to resist the urge to get up at that very moment. Sleep deprivation messing with my mind, he thought—only a lunatic would try to seduce a woman under conditions like these, especially one who was heavily armed.

Even in pleasant circumstances, he doubted she would be interested in a nerdy insomniac. A woman like Rica could have any man she wanted, and for all he knew she was not interested in men at all. The way she had let him hug her and invited him into her tent the night before suggested otherwise, but she had only bandaged his thumb and sent him on his way.

Thinking of Rica had nearly lulled him away when he saw a hint of movement on the gray aluminum floor in front of the crew door. Both his awareness and his vision were slow to react, but he eventually focused on the round shadow that was creeping inward across the sheet metal.

His lethargic brain registered curiosity. What could be making the shadow?

He lifted his somnolent gaze until he saw it—a roughly spherical orb that appeared to be floating in midair just inside the door. The orb was pale blue and about four inches across. It was slowly rotating left and right, left and right, left and right, with mechanical regularity.

Cliff pushed himself backward until his spine was flat against the wall. His eyes were now open as wide as they had ever been in his life. His scooting rear end had made hardly any sound, and he was holding his breath, yet the orb abruptly swung toward him. It stopped halfway between him and the door, hovering over his trembling feet. At the same time, it rotated until he saw a large feature on its surface that was shaped like a flattened W. The W was composed of a black core surrounded by a border of radially striated iridescent bronze. Cliff had no idea what the orb was, but there was something strangely familiar about the black-and-bronze W.

The orb blinked.

And Cliff understood that it was some kind of eye.

He held every muscle rigid against trembling, hoping the gigantic disembodied eyeball would ignore him if he did not move. The eye slowly floated away, examining the other sleepers.

When the W-shaped pupil rotated to the other side of the eye, Cliff had to fight off an urge to shout an alarm and lunge for the farthest corner of the hold.

The eyeball swung back in his direction. The pupil rotated past him. Cliff froze again, and this time the eye continued on into the shadow just inside the aft edge of the door. There it paused above Raymond, who was asleep on his back beneath his old leather motorcycle jacket.

One by one, a set of aqua-blue pinpoint lights appeared beneath the eye. They extended out and down in an arc, curving around the aft facing of the door like a string of glowing pearls.

Before the blue lights had come on, all of Cliff's attention had been focused on the scanning eye, not on the seemingly unoccupied space beneath it. Now that he was looking, he realized he could see more than the cool pinpoints of light under the eye. Surrounding the string of lights, or behind them, was a transparent inch-thick tube. It reminded him of the thick commercial aquarium tubing in his lab, or of the gracefully curving handle of a glass pitcher. He could discern no color or texture—the clear tube was made visible only by the way it bent the moonlight passing through it.

The aqua-blue glow from the tiny lights lit up the white wall beside Raymond. The eerie glow also illuminated the metal floor around him and his leather jacket. Cliff knew the jacket was a reddish-brown color, yet it looked black in the blue light, which also brought out its wrinkled texture.

In a flash of shadow, the eye and the lights were gone.

A faint aroma of dead fish lingered in the hold.

Cliff started to reach over and shake Raymond awake, but he stopped when something else appeared in the doorway. A slender, transparent tendril was creeping across the floor like a hunting snake. It blindly felt its way, touching the floor repeatedly and bending toward Raymond's feet. As it advanced, it rhythmically elongated and contracted, becoming thinner when it stretched and fatter when it shortened.

The elastic tentacle climbed over one of Raymond's boots and up his leg to the edge of the leather jacket. Then it extended through the air above Raymond to his shoulders. The part of the tendril hovering above the jacket flattened to three times its former width. Cliff could barely make out the transparent tendril in the shadows, but he knew it had suction cups when he saw a dozen or so points on the jacket bulge upward to form small rounded cones as if sticks were poking up from beneath the leather.

The tentacle began to drag Raymond's jacket toward his feet. Raymond reached in his sleep to pull the jacket back up, loosely gripping the collar. A tug-of-war ensued, with Raymond gradually losing.

Cliff lunged toward Raymond before the pudgy oceanographer could wake up. He clamped one hand over Raymond's mouth and made him release the collar. Raymond opened his eyes and looked down just in time to see his old leather jacket and the transparent tentacle slither out the door. He shoved Cliff's hand away from his mouth and cautiously crawled toward the door on his hands and knees, briefly pausing before he dared to advance into the beam of pale moonlight shining into the hold.

"Ray . . . don't!" Cliff whispered.

Raymond stuck his head out and looked down toward the ice five feet below the doorstep. "I don't see anything," he whispered.

Then he screamed, and Cliff knew from the volume and the pitch that the scream was not just a reaction to something he had seen.

"Get back!" Cliff shouted, but Raymond remained prone on his belly with his head hanging down from the high doorstep. He screamed again. This time the scream ended with a muted gurgle. His legs began to jerk and thump against the floor. His arms thrashed madly around his half-bald head as if trying to reach something on his back.

Cliff grabbed his old friend's ankles and pulled.

Instead of sliding backward, Raymond's body began to inch forward, dragging Cliff toward the door.

# CHAPTER 17

# Attack

Rica was not asleep, so she was the first Marine on her feet when Raymond's truncated scream echoed back through the hold. She grabbed her rifle, intending to run forward and investigate the new commotion, but then she heard a sequence of three-round bursts from M-16s somewhere far behind her. She turned to look out the open cargo door at the rear of the fuselage. What she saw was so unexpected that she temporarily froze.

The other Globemaster, which was parked a hundred yards away with its right wing pointing toward Rica's plane, was rocking back and forth on its skis. As she watched, muzzle bursts from several M-16s flashed inside its flight deck windows and in the tiny black rectangle of the open jump door. Then the *rat-a-tat-tat* of the combat rifles was joined by the ripsaw buzz of an MP-5N submachine gun.

It was not the rocking of the 134-ton plane or the flashes and bangs of the firefight inside it that gripped Rica's attention. What immobilized her with shock were the *things* she could see crawling all over the huge airframe in the moonlight.

Joan staggered to her feet. Rica grabbed her arm and

pointed toward the other Globemaster. Joan stared alongside her, openmouthed.

From the way they moved, Rica had no doubt that the creatures swarming the other Globemaster were alive. Their most astonishing property was their nearly complete transparency. She could see them only when direct moonlight glinted or shimmered on their smooth wet hide, which had a faint bluish tint and reflected swirls of oily iridescence at certain angles. Their bodies also warped the moonlight passing through them, casting partial shadows on the dull gray aluminum of the plane. The writhing shadows were easier to see than the creatures themselves. Their eyes were the only part of them that was opaque.

"Todd's ghosts," Rica whispered.

The monsters came in various sizes. Most of them seemed to have the mass of a few men, although one leviathan was bigger than a dump truck. It was skittering back and forth atop the fuselage like a thirty-ton spider.

The creatures' complicated shapes were difficult to discern, partly because they were in constant motion. Their movements were complex as well—a ghastly dance of jerks, twists, inchworm contractions, and fluid slithers. It took a few seconds for Rica to realize that the creatures all had the same basic form.

Each body was shaped like an upright wine barrel with eight tapering arms radiating from its top. The arms stretched out at least five times longer than the torso and seemed capable of grasping any surface and contorting into any shape. Above the barrel, where it seemed to Rica that a head should be, two large spherical eyeballs hovered like moths around a candle. The seemingly disembodied eyes moved independently but always remained within a yard of the creature's top.

Both the body and the arms were unbelievably elastic. Two of the creatures appeared to be fighting atop the Globemaster's closest wing. As they flailed and groped at each other with their long arms, their bodies dodged blows

130      *Benjamin E. Miller*

by stretching to twice their usual length and bending in all directions at angles greater than ninety degrees.

They're destroying the plane, Rica realized. One monster had torn loose the end of a wing flap and bent it upward. A cluster of the nimble creatures had climbed atop the towering tailplanes and were dismantling the rudder. The demolition team was working so feverishly that one of them fell off, but the monster whipped up three of its long arms and caught the tailplane above it. In an instant, it had yanked its rotund body back on top of it.

The enormous creature lumbering back and forth atop the fuselage began hammering on the aluminum with some kind of hard object. The blows left deep dents and filled the ice cove with echoes of resounding clangs. Rica noticed that the titanic beast was different from the others in more ways than size—its arms were proportionally thicker and its body was wrinkled from top to bottom, like a pickle.

Another gang of vandals had broken out the cockpit glass, and several of the creatures were simultaneously squeezing inward through the open windscreen frame. One of them pulled something out of the cockpit. The object was round and about the same size as a human's head. The monster swung the plunder above it as if gesturing for the others to look, its eyes weaving back and forth above its body. One of the comrades on the wet ice below reached up its whole bundle of arms like a glass bouquet. The marauder hanging out of the cockpit dropped its prize. The eager creature on the ice caught the object and began tossing it back and forth with another of the glasslike wraiths about a hundred feet away.

Paz was on sentry duty outside Rica's plane. He abruptly rounded the end of the loading ramp and sprinted up it, striking sparks with his crampons. He was swinging his rifle in both hands and yelling as he ran. *"Get . . . your . . . guns!"*

He tossed his M-16 to Rica. She yelled for the loadmaster to close the cargo door. The heavy ramp began to crank upward. Rica and Joan ran to close the jump doors behind the wings. Paz dashed along the narrow corridor between the wall and one track of the parked ALV to the case that housed the M249 squad automatic weapons. He jerked out two of the light machine guns and attached a plastic ammunition box to the left side of each weapon. Each box contained a belt with two hundred rounds of standard M988 5.56-mm rifle ammunition, the same small but powerful cartridges fired by the M-16. He simultaneously flipped up the covers atop the two SAWs and fed the ammunition belts across the receiver trays until the first round was aligned over the feed mechanism. Then he slapped the covers closed, pulled back the cocking handles, released the safeties, and ran forward to the crew door with one SAW slung beneath each arm from its shoulder strap.

Cliff braced his feet on opposite sides of the crew door and pulled backward on Raymond's ankles with all of his strength. Cliff was a tall and big-boned man with a strong grip, but his skinny back was no match for whatever was dragging his best friend out through the door. He was gradually pulled forward until it felt like his arms and legs were about to be ripped off.

He heard a spluttering sound, and a dark wet stain appeared on the seat of Raymond's baggy coveralls. Cliff could smell the feces—just barely—over the reek of dead fish wafting in from outside.

Raymond's pudgy body extended down from the doorstep at a forty-five-degree angle. The oceanographer's arms were stretched out beyond his head, clasped tightly together, torn and bloody. So were his head and neck, as if he had dived into a swimming pool full of broken glass. Cliff's eyes suddenly refocused on the quivering lobes of transparent flesh that encased Raymond's bloody head, and his strong hands began to weaken from sheer horror.

The transparent thing on the ice below the crew door was engulfing Raymond, dragging him into its maw with four tongue-shaped appendages. About once per second, one of the two-foot tongues let go and stretched farther up the victim's body. The reaching organ gripped Raymond's skin with row upon row of inch-long triangular teeth. Then the giant tongue contracted, bunching up at the top of what looked to Cliff like a glass hogshead barrel full of slightly bluish water. The reaching of the four tongues cycled in a clockwise direction around Raymond's body, alternating their extensions and contractions at a precise pace like some kind of machine.

Cliff noticed several loops and curls of blue semishadow dancing on the ice and across Raymond's back. He looked up and saw the creature's many arms, which radiated from the top of the barrel around the ingestion apparatus. Their glassy surfaces shimmered in the moonlight as they writhed like agitated worms.

One of the arms grabbed Cliff's left knee and yanked him off the plane.

"Hey! What's going on?" yelled Chester Wimbledon. His broken nose caused him to speak with a nasal lisp. When Paz zoomed past him, Chester shook his chain-link door, rattling the whole cage.

"The demons are attacking!" Paz replied.

"Demons?" Chester's voice was shrill with panic. He rattled the cage harder. "Let me out! What if they take over the plane? You can't leave me trapped in here!"

When Paz reached the open crew door, Joan and Rica were already standing on opposite sides, steadying their M-16s against the door frame and pumping three-round bursts into one of the monsters on the ice below them. The "demon" seemed to have eaten Dr. Price.

Actually, Paz realized, the moist, many-armed goblin was still ingesting its prey, although Dr. Price was obviously deceased. His body was upside down with his legs flopping limply in the air and the rest of him sticking down inside the demon's transparent, barrel-shaped body. The swallowed parts of the elderly oceanographer had been chewed to a bloody pulp. They were recognizable only by the general shapes of his appendages. His torso and outstretched arms leaned to one side of the barrel and curved around in the beginning of a downward spiral. The demon's bluish body had turned red near the top where its victim's blood had seeped into its tissues.

"You must have missed," Paz yelled to Joan, although he couldn't see how—the horse-size beast was only fifty feet away, and Joan was the best shot he knew. Yet the high-velocity bursts from her M-16 seemed to be having no effect.

"Fuck you," Joan shouted. "I'm hitting it every time."

"Out of the way!" Paz yelled.

Joan and Rica jumped back. Paz brought up the twenty-two-pound loaded SAW under his right arm and let loose a brief burst of ten to fifteen rounds. Then he realized that the demon was retreating and stopped shooting to conserve ammunition.

The creature continued trudging away from the plane with a swinging gait, like a fat old woman with arthritis. Instead of legs, the ungainly imp had four triangular flippers that stuck straight out from the bottom rim of the barrel. The waddling creature reminded Paz of a headless penguin.

A whoosh of cold air that reeked of dead fish blew over Paz as another monster jumped up from below his field of view and lodged itself in the crew door. Its rotund body filled the large portal. Moonlight shining through the living barrel cast quivering waves of bluish half shadow across the floor, the ceiling, and the walls. Rica lunged aside as one of the fiend's arms made a grab for her.

Paz stepped back and started firing from the hip with both SAWs. Each machine gun spat out an arc of hot spent casings that bounced and rolled on the metal floor. With two guns blazing at 725 rounds per minute—12 rounds per second—the report echoes accumulated inside the Globemaster's hold until his unprotected ears felt as if nails were being driven into them. Paz held his breath as hot smoke welled up from the guns and stung his eyes. In spite of his fear and pain, he remembered his training and managed to count the seconds, knowing that his ammunition would be gone in about a quarter of a minute.

The demon's transparent body seemed to pucker or pooch out for a microsecond wherever the slugs hit it, but Paz got the impression that his thundering fusillade was hardly doing any damage. When he let up after a full five-second burst, the demon should have fallen from the door, dead. Any natural being would have, Paz thought. But the rotund beast just shuddered and hung on, dripping gobs of bluish gel onto the floor.

The serpentine arms that were bunched against the door frame began to slither into the hold along the ceiling and walls.

Paz coughed and blinked. He wanted to step back from the encroaching arms, but he knew from experience that the spent shell casings scattered around his feet would roll if he stepped on them, causing him to fall. So he stood his ground and fired another burst, this time concentrating on the arms but being careful not to hit the walls and fill the cabin with ricochets. Rica and Joan joined in behind him, adding to the hail of bullets as fast as they could pull the triggers of their combat rifles.

One by one, the demon's arms were severed. Drops of cold liquid and bits of cold wet flesh hit Paz on the face and hands as he continued firing. Finally the demon's mutilated body fell from the door onto the ice outside with a wet *splat*.

Rica leaned out and pulled the dripping crew door shut, then disgustedly wiped her hand on her pants. The hold reeked of gun smoke and marine carrion. Bluish slime coated the floor, dripped from the ceiling, and slithered down the walls. The severed arms curled and uncurled, writhing on the floor like newborn snakes in the syrupy goop the demon had bled.

Paz ran to reload.

Rica could feel the plane jerking and swaying. She could hear bending metal, popping rivets, and beneath all of it, the baby crying. All of the doors were closed now, but the monsters were obviously still trying to get in. If they broke through the windscreen, the thin interior door between the flight deck and the hold would probably not even slow them down. For all she knew, they might even rip off the crew door or pound their way right through the roof.

She wondered how the nightmarish creatures had managed to sneak past the sentries. They were nearly invisible in shadow, but the planes were surrounded by bright moonlight. Had they dropped right out of the sky?

"Where's Agent Johnson?" she yelled. "We have to let Hawaii know we're under attack."

"I just saw him on the ALV," said Private Eddy Brown. "He's trying to connect with the datalink."

"Help me get everyone together," Rica ordered. "We have to go help the crew on the other plane." She also had a dim hope that Clifford Steadman was still among the living somewhere outside, and if need be, that she could rescue him.

"What about him?" Joan yelled, nodding toward the prisoner. "You want to just leave him on this plane by himself?"

"I'll get him out," Rica said. "You clear the flight deck." While Joan banged on the cockpit door, Rica found the keys to Chester's cage and ran toward it.

The plane lurched forward, and Rica fell in the aisle. The keys slid beneath a stack of cargo that was elevated on pallet rails. Her ears were still ringing so loudly from the enclosed gunfire that she had not heard the jet engines starting.

Lying on her side, she frantically groped for the keys beneath the cargo pallet. She could see them, but they were out of reach. Other passengers hurdled over her to strap themselves into the seats along the walls at the front of the hold. One of them was Todd. He was holding his screaming baby sister tightly in his arms.

The plane made a turn, and the engine noise increased to

a thundering roar that vibrated the whole airframe. Acceleration made the fuselage appear to tilt back as if it were already climbing. "Rica, get on a seat!" Paz yelled. "The pilot is trying to take off!"

Chester rattled his cage, hysterically slinging his head back and forth. "You stupid bitch!" he yelled. "If you leave me in here, I'll kill you!"

The plane jogged a little to one side, and the keys slid farther out of reach. Rica gave up, lunged into a seat, and fastened her harness.

"Roaaaaaa!" Chester screamed, kicking his chain-link door. Rica could see his open mouth and his tongue sticking out as he continued to bellow, but his voice was lost beneath the roaring engines. She noticed that the front of his white coveralls was streaked with dried blood from his broken nose.

Rica could look out through the small window in the starboard jump door from her seat and see the moonlit ice speeding by. The bumpy ride was making the Globemaster's right wing sway up and down. One of the bluish creatures was clinging to the wing above the outer engine. It was a big one, about the size of a compact car. Rica wondered how much its weight was contributing to the bending of the wing. What if it was heavy enough to unbalance the plane during takeoff?

Some of the watery brute's arms were clasping the rounded front edge of the wing. They were stretched taut like the arm of a rodeo rider holding his saddle horn. The bloated creature was leaning back in the wind, letting its other arms whip out behind it. Rica wondered whether the beast was just hanging on for dear life or riding the plane to try and finish what its brethren had started.

As the plane accelerated across the plateau, the creature pulled itself down the pylon against the wind until it stood atop the huge cylindrical engine nacelle. It seemed to be curious about the turbine noise. One of its trailing arms curled forward, holding a small rigid object that was transparent like the rest of the creature and shaped like an oversize yo-yo. When the object reached a certain point in front of the engine, it was abruptly sucked into the intake.

The engine's broad orifice flickered with white light as the blades of the compressor fan devoured the object and spat out sparks. The creature's outstretched arm and then the rest of its elastic body were jerked around the front of the engine and into the intake so swiftly that it seemed to just disappear. Rica felt the thud of an explosion and heard a piercing shriek of shearing metal. The engine nacelle visibly bulged in the middle but did not burst. A horizontal column of orange flame erupted from its rear end.

Someone in the cockpit shouted, "Fire on four! Shut off the fuel!" Someone else yelled, "We don't have room to take off with an engine out!"

The roar of the remaining engines was replaced by the turbulent bellowing of thrust reversers. The Globemaster's acceleration reversed, slinging the passengers sideways in their harnesses. Only the ice close to the plane had appeared to be moving before, but now Rica could see the stars and the Floe's sharp horizon streaking backward as well. She knew that apparent movement of celestial objects meant the plane was turning, not just speeding ahead. It was slewing to the left, and she could guess why—two engines were applying full reverse thrust to the left wing while only one engine was working on the right wing.

The turn grew sharper until the plane was spinning out, rotating counterclockwise around a vertical axis between the wings. The centrifugal force stretched each passenger toward the nearest end of the fuselage, flinging out their hair and arms. Rica feared that Todd would lose his grip on Sophie and the infant would be fatally dashed against a wall.

When the spin finally ceased, Rica stepped out of the harness and crawled to the port jump door for a better view of the new surroundings. She was relieved to see that the plane was not teetering precariously on the Floe's edge, but she was dismayed that many of the creatures had somehow hung on to the airframe through the attempted takeoff.

Paz joined her. Together they watched as the slithering horde climbed down from the roof and assembled in a row in front of the right wing. Reflections of the orange flames rising from engine four flickered over the glassy beings and the wet ice around them.

"What are they doing?" Paz asked.

Each of the creatures had reached up a few of its arms and grabbed hold of the wing's leading edge. The other arms were stretched out forward, gripping the ice with their suction cups. All at once, the creatures tensed, and the plane began sliding forward on its skis at the pace of a brisk walk.

"They're dragging us!" Rica exclaimed.

"To where?" Paz asked.

She pressed her face against the porthole to look ahead of the plane. "Oh, boy, this is not good," she said. They were nowhere near the Floe's edge, but she could see a jagged black band running across the ice about a quarter mile ahead—the deep chasm that bordered one side of the cove where the planes had been parked.

Rica knew that jet engine fires seldom burned for long before a fuel tank ignited. She wondered whether the plane would explode before or after the creatures dragged it into the chasm.

# CHAPTER 18

# Ghost

Rica heard a commotion in the cockpit—breaking glass, screams, thumps, then pistol shots. "They're on the flight deck!" she yelled. "Get everything we need onto the ALV. I'll help the crew."

Paz and Joan ran back through the hold.

Before Rica could climb the stairs to the flight deck, the door flew open and Major Lazarus bounded out. He was sweaty and pale and gasping for breath. His rotund abdomen bounced as he ran. He shoved her aside, opened the crew door, and jumped out. She heard a thud and a howl of pain from outside as she swung the door shut behind him.

Rica grabbed an MP-5N submachine gun, bounded up the stairs, and looked into the cockpit. A whorl of transparent arms was reaching in through the broken windscreen. The arms were whipping around the compartment, wetly smacking against the walls and ceiling and groping for the copilot and loadmaster, who were cringing against the back wall, firing their Beretta M9 side arms.

In the center of the whorl of arms, two large eyes with W-shaped pupils waved around on the ends of snakelike stalks, and four long tongues lined with thin triangular teeth poked rhythmically in and out of a circular opening. When the tongues extended, they curled open like the petals of a flower, exposing their toothed inner surfaces. When they retracted, they snapped together with a moist slap, forming a cone with four snaggletoothed seams converging at its apex, then the cone jerked back into the open top of the barrel-body.

Rica took aim at the grasping maw with the submachine gun. In a little more than two seconds, she fed the ravenous monster a thirty-round clip of 9-mm bullets. While she was reloading, two of its arms reached out and decapitated the copilot and loadmaster.

Todd headed back toward the ALV, carrying Sophie. As he passed Chester's cage, he saw the keys lying in the aisle. The plane's spin had flung them out from under the cargo pallet.

"Come on, kid, let me out," Chester begged. "I promise I won't hurt you." The tall thin geneticist had exhausted himself ranting and shaking his cage. Now he was kneeling on his flexible knees by the door. His forehead was resting against the chain mesh. His long fingers were gripping the mesh halfway up the door, holding his arms suspended above him.

Todd fumbled with the key ring, trying to sort out the keys in one hand while holding Sophie against his shoulder with the other. She had tired of screaming and was now only moaning and coughing. Todd's hands were shaking so hard that he dropped the keys.

"Goddamn it, hurry up!" Chester yelled, his voice cracking.

Todd picked up the key ring and started trying again to figure out which one of the twenty or so keys would fit the lock on Chester's cage.

"Open this door, you stupid little shit!"

"Got it!" Todd said. He tried to insert the key and dropped the ring again. The key he had sorted out disappeared among the rest.

"You fucking retard!" Chester screamed, banging on the door.

It took only a few seconds for Todd to find the right key this time. He reached it toward the lock. Chester screamed and Todd froze, then staggered back from the door. The prisoner clamped one bony hand over his bruised face, peeking out between his long splayed fingers with eyes open so wide they seemed to bulge from their sockets. With the other hand he pointed over Todd's shoulder; all the while he kept screaming.

Chester sucked in a breath, presumably for another scream, and in the momentary quiet Todd heard a noise from behind his head that he had not heard since he and Sophie were hiding in the avalanche debris at the base of the Floe's ramp.

Todd forgot all about Chester's screaming, and the keys, and everything else, as he turned around ever so slowly, enveloping Sophie protectively in his arms. The hold was chilly, yet sweat dribbled from his brow, stinging his eyes. He was so terrified that his diaphragm barely twitched when he tried to breathe.

One of the ghosts was standing in the aisle just inches away. It was as tall as Todd and many times heavier. Its arms were moving independently above its barrel-shaped body, probing the air, the ceiling, and the surrounding stacks of equipment. Four of the arms ended in slender tips, but the other four ended with clubby objects that were hard, smooth, and curved like cowry shells. Two light blue apple-size eyeballs were descending at the ends of arching stalks to examine Todd up close. They blinked as they swayed around his head.

The ghost's lumpy spiraling intestinal tract was easily discernable within the clear body, because the intestine was filled with translucent red fluid. In the middle of the spiral, where the red was strongest, a roughly round object the size of a soccer ball was suspended. As Todd watched, a peristaltic contraction rippled along the thick gut and rotated the object so that Todd could see wispy black hair streaming out from one side of it.

Todd's throat and tongue convulsed, but he was still unable to breathe, much less scream. Even without taking a breath, he could smell the stench of rotten seafood that permeated the cabin. He held a trembling hand over Sophie's eyes so she could not see the ghost. His face began to feel numb. His vision darkened. A flood of hot urine surged down his right leg. He dropped the keys again and stepped backward against Chester's cage, his knees wobbling. Slowly shaking his head, he expended the little breath left in his lungs by sobbing, "No, no, no!"

There was no telling whose head the ghost had swallowed. The face had been scraped away, leaving the bare pink skull pressed against the ghost's transparent intestinal wall. One eye was still in the skull, looking sideways. The other eyeball floated above it. The two upper front teeth were missing, but the rest of them seemed to be grinning. Following the head through the ghost's intestine were two shoes, two socks, a bar of soap, a constellation of lemon cough drops, and a twisted camouflage T-shirt.

Todd could tell he was about to faint. Whether he lost consciousness before or after the ghost attacked him, Chester would be stuck in the cage if he failed to unlock the door first. Without taking his eyes off the ghost, he stooped and picked up the keys yet again, flinging off droplets of piss—they had landed in the puddle surrounding his right foot.

He forced his eyes to focus on the keys long enough to find the right one again. At least he hoped it was the right one—he doubted he would get another chance, although the ghost had just stood there for several seconds now. He wondered why it hadn't killed him. Maybe it wasn't hungry because it had already eaten.

The slithering arms finally began to move toward him, trailing along the ceiling and the camouflage tarpaulins covering the equipment stacks. Todd somehow managed to turn his back on the horrible phantom and insert the key in the lock, watching loops of bluish half shadow writhe across the floor. He hunched over Sophie, shielding her with his back.

The key turned easily, and he yanked on the door. It gave a little but would not open. He looked up. The ghost had curled the tips of three arms through the cage's chain links. One arm encircled both the edge of the door and its frame, preventing them from separating.

"Hey, Mister, hit its arm!" Todd yelled.

Chester remained where he was, squatting sideways against the back wall with his face buried in his quaking arms. His left hand was holding on tight to an aluminum tie-down bar that ran along the wall. His broken nose had resumed bleeding, dribbling blood on the floor.

The blue waves of shadow thickened over Todd. Something cold and moist slid across the back of his neck from right to left.

"Mister! Please!"

Chester did not move or speak. Todd could see his arched back convulsing with sobs.

A cold slimy tendril slid up the back of Todd's right ear, then forward between the top of his ear and his scalp. He smacked it away and turned to face the ghost, sinking to the floor. Now he was face-to-face with the semidigested skull, his nose just inches from its grinning teeth. The reek of rotten fish was unbearable.

He curled into a ball of human armor around Sophie.

The last thing Todd heard before he finally surrendered to merciful unconsciousness was Chester Wimbledon sobbing like a lost toddler.

Bert Lazarus used his elbows to drag himself toward the receding Globemaster. In his panic to escape from the cockpit, he had jumped from the crew door instead of walking down the fold-out stairs, and now an open fracture of his left shin bone was leaving a trail of diluted blood behind him.

His rotund midsection slid across the wet ice easily, but

so did his elbows, making it nearly impossible to inch forward. Sometimes he had to resort to flopping like a seal.

Bert had experienced many nightmares in his forty-four years. This was worse than any of them.

Bitter black smoke wafted over him from the Globemaster's burning engine, stinging his eyes and making him cough. Through his tears, he could see that the plane was getting farther away. He tried to yell "Come back!" but all that came out was a hoarse rattle—his throat was parched from the effort of dragging himself along. Despite the cold wet ice pressing against the front of his body, sweat dripped from his pudgy chin. The exertion and pain and fear were making him so dizzy that the level ice plain appeared to be tilting back and forth. With each forward heave, he could feel the broken bone that was jutting from his leg grate against the ice.

Between his own wheezing gasps, he could hear them behind him.

Something grabbed the ankle of his broken leg and pulled. He tried to dig his fingernails into the wet ice. Most of them just slid across the frictionless surface, but two of them caught hold and ripped loose from his fingertips, leaving bloody streaks as he was dragged backward.

He flopped over onto his back, blinking at the bright moon. The horrible sounds came from all around him now. He twisted his head back and forth in terror. The creatures were trudging toward him on all sides, their glassy wet bodies looming over him. Tangles of transparent arms writhed in the moonlight like nests of blind snakes. Then the arms descended and reached out for him.

He began to sob uncontrollably.

He tried to pray but was unable to form words.

The arm holding his broken leg jerked upward until he was suspended upside down with his head swinging a few inches above the ice. The valve at the base of his esophagus failed, and hot vomit gushed from his mouth and nose, searing his left eye with corrosive hydrochloric acid. He coughed and sputtered and wiped at the burned eye.

Something cold and slimy wrapped around his head like a blindfold and lifted him up to a horizontal position several feet above the ice. Through the transparent arm squeezing against his eyes, he could see the moon and two spires sticking up like white horns in the Floe's interior, but the images were wavy and distorted with a blue tint. Another arm wrapped around his head, lower down, sealing off his mouth and nose. His diaphragm bucked and shuddered as he tried to suck in a breath through the thick cords of cold rubbery flesh covering his face. He madly slapped and clawed at the slimy arms but only managed to scrape up wads of gummy tissue beneath his remaining fingernails.

When the arm had begun to smother him, his mouth had been open for a scream that never had a chance. Desperate for air, he bit down on the arm. His incisors sliced through the cold flesh with surprising ease. A spongy chunk of the constricting arm came away in his mouth. There was nothing he could do with the morsel but swallow it, so he did, and the contractions of his esophagus began squeezing the thick lump toward his empty stomach. His body continued involuntarily gasping for breath, but all it sucked in was cold liquid from the creature's wounded arm.

He began to take another bite, knowing that he would black out from lack of oxygen long before he could chew through the thick arm. Something stung the left side of his throat; then the sharp pain extended across his bobbing larynx to the right side. He felt warm liquid spray onto his chest and chin. He heard splatters on the ice beneath him. Then he was enveloped by darkness, numbness, and silence.

# CHAPTER 19

# Chase

Clifford Steadman limped across the moonlit ice toward the distant Globemaster, groaning with each step. He knew how lucky he was. He had suffered only a bruised chin and a minor ankle sprain when the cephalopoid dragged him off the plane. Fortunately, the predator had been too preoccupied with the chore of eating his best friend to finish him off too. He had escaped its clutches with no other injuries except a double row of tender sucker burns across his right cheek. His right eye had been spared, thank goodness—he knew that attachment of a suction cup to a human eyeball could cause permanent blindness.

*Cephalopoid* was the made-up term that had popped into Cliff's mind when he first saw the creatures. He had no idea what they were or where they'd come from, but they had several anatomical features resembling those of the cephalopods—octopus, squid, and their many-armed relatives. The creatures on the Floe were unlike any earthly animal, and yet their long flexible arms, gelatinous bodies, and suction cups seemed eerily familiar to him.

He frequently looked behind him, trying to maintain his pace without falling. It was not easy, because he had been pulled off the plane without crampons. He didn't even have

boots on, only socks, and the icy meltwater was causing agonizing cramps in his feet. But he could not afford to slow
down or fall. The beast with Raymond in its gut was right
behind him.

At first he had been unsure whether the cephalopoid was
really pursuing him. Now it was obvious that the chase was
on, but it was an absurdly slow chase. The creature's four
bloated flippers—each resembled the prehensile upper lip
of a black rhinoceros—could propel it no faster than a slow
walk.

Nevertheless, it was gradually gaining on him. Every
time Cliff looked over his shoulder, it seemed a little closer,
reaching toward him with four of its arms. Instead of tapering to slender points like the other four arms, those that were
grasping for him each ended in some kind of bulbous device
that was moving too fast for him to see clearly. The
cephalopoid gulped and sloshed as it waddled after him. He
could also hear an ominous frenzy of *scrape-snap* sounds,
like someone was swiftly opening and closing a set of hedge
shears. When he realized that the shearing sounds were
coming from the devices at the ends of the cephalopoid's
arms, it dawned on him that these must be the same as the
incredibly tough transparent "beaks" he had found in the
ambergris.

Cliff was too busy putting one foot in front of the other
to feel much of anything except the icewater in his socks,
but beneath his concentration was a dizzying whirlpool of
emotions. Mostly fear, but also grief and remorse over Raymond's death, along with an early sprout of excited professional curiosity about the creatures.

The Globemaster was hard to see through the thick trail
of black smoke that the wind was blowing back at him from
the burning engine. The smoke stung his eyes, nose, and
throat. He realized after a while that the plane was gliding
forward at about his own pace and wondered if the pilots
were dead at their controls.

He glanced behind him again. The moonlit cephalopoid

was closer than ever. Its entire body and most of its arms were opaque crimson from Raymond's diffused blood. Cliff gave it the finger, coughing and blinking from the smoke, and yelled, "Why haven't you suffocated already?"

The predator trudged on, still snapping at him with the beaklike pincers at the ends of four long arms.

Cliff looked up at the full moon through the passing clouds of black smoke. In the unlikely event that he survived to see land again, what was he going to tell Raymond's wife and two grown sons? The CIA would probably try to cover up this whole fiasco. It wouldn't be hard. All they had to do was make up a plausible accident to explain the deaths. If he came forward with the truth, they could simply deny it, and he would be laughed out of academia.

Cliff saw a tight pack of the transparent creatures a hundred yards or so to his right. They were twisting, lunging, and contorting in what looked to him like some kind of pagan ritual—a frenzied dance fueled by drugs and spiritual fervor. Then he realized that they were actually fighting over possession of several dark objects. Peering closer, he saw that one of the objects was a human leg. Another was an arm. The creatures' glistening bodies and the ice around them were stained with blood. He wondered who they had butchered.

Suddenly the creatures ceased their brawl and trudged away, leaving the body parts behind. Cliff looked in the direction opposite their flight and saw why. The titanic beast that had been hammering dents into the roof of the other Globemaster was approaching the kill. Cliff recognized its extra-thick arms and wrinkled body. Unlike the other cephalopoids, the thirty-ton leviathan used its arms to help it walk, leaning forward on four stiffened arms like a gorilla walking on its knuckles.

When it reached the kill, the monster picked up the scattered body parts, one in each arm, and lifted them above its headless top. The victim's blood flowed down its wet arms and body in dark streaks. The house-size beast pumped the prizes up and down in the night sky and waved its basket-ball-size eyes back and forth. Its wrinkled barrel-body contracted three times, pumping out a loud *gulp-boom* noise with each spasm.

When it was done celebrating, Cliff expected the monster to eat the scavenged parts and then come after him. It seemed to be looking right at him, following his slow progress across the ice with its eye stalks. But instead of heading his way, it abruptly trudged after the smaller cephalopoids that it had routed, carrying the body parts and not looking back.

Cliff heard an electric motor and peered through the smoke. The moving Globemaster's cargo ramp was descending. It thunked down on the ice and began to drag, making a low scraping noise. One of the cephalopoids swinging from the plane's tail dropped onto the ramp and started to climb into the dark cargo hold. Cliff saw strobing star-shaped flashes inside the dark hold and heard machine gun fire echoing across the plateau. The invader fell and rolled off the ramp. Then it got up and waddled after the plane.

At least Cliff knew now that someone was still alive on the Globemaster. Wondering why they had opened the cargo door, he looked in front of the sliding plane and realized that its nose was jutting over the rim of the great chasm.

A bright light came on inside the hold, silhouetting a large black rectangle. As Cliff realized that the rectangle must be the flat rear end of the ALV, the plane's fuselage pitched forward a few degrees and slewed to the left. The hinge of the cargo door was lifted so high that the ramp hung down on the ice at a forty-five-degree angle.

The roar of a piston engine reverberated from the hold. The plane pitched forward a few more degrees. Then the thirty-ton ALV surged backward out of the hold and down the ramp. The rear end of its tracks hit the ice with a resounding crunch. When the lander's weight was no longer holding down the rear end of the fuselage, the plane tilted up vertically, swiveled to the left, and fell into the chasm. Cliff watched the broad left wing and tailplanes slide downward behind the ALV. Their enormous size and distance made them appear to descend in slow motion.

The ALV stood poised on its rear end for a moment. It looked like a rocket with its chisel-like nose pointed toward the stars. Its beady headlights lanced upward into the coal-black sky, as if beaming a defiant message to alien worlds. Cliff wondered which way the vehicle would fall. When he saw that it was toppling toward the chasm, he feared that it was close enough to pitch over the edge and follow the Globemaster to its doom.

After a second or two, the heavy machine finally slammed down on its tracks. It did not disappear into the chasm. The engine growled with maximum acceleration, and the ALV swung away from the precipice. Its headlights pierced the smoke trail left by the burning jet engine.

At first the approaching headlights seemed dazzlingly bright. Cliff raised a hand to shield his eyes. Then the thin sliver of the chasm's far wall that he could see from his low elevation began to glow with orange light for hundreds of yards in both directions. A moment later a blinding orange fireball hundreds of feet wide erupted from the chasm. The harsh orange light beamed all around the dark ALV, even between its spinning tracks, silhouetting the thirty-ton vehicle as if it were a Tonka toy. In front of the great mushroom cloud of combusting jet fuel, its headlights seemed to dwindle to candle flames.

Thunder from the explosion shook the ice beneath Cliff's feet and rolled across the desolate white plateau.

As the fireball climbed into the night sky amid swirling eddies of black smoke, its image was reflected in the thousands of meltwater pools dotting the wet plain. Cliff could feel the heat from the infrared rays it emitted. The ascending mushroom of hydrocarbon vapor finally consumed itself high overhead, and the ALV's headlights seemed blinding again, stabbing into Cliff's eyes whenever the machine hit a bump that tilted the beams upward.

He glanced over his shoulder. The cephalopoid had fallen behind. It lurched and quivered with each step, as if it could barely muster the energy to lift its flippers. Its eye stalks drooped beneath the top of the barrel-body, and its long arms dragged on the ice behind it.

The ALV skidded to a halt beside him. He climbed aboard and saw Rica in the driver's box. When he stuck his head in to thank her, she grabbed his arms and pulled him toward her until they lost their balance and leaned against the wall. "Thank God you're alive!" she said as she hugged him. Then she jumped back into her seat, pressed her face to the periscope, and shifted into gear.

Cliff was stunned by her affection.

"Can I drive?" he asked. "There's something I really want to run over."

"Not now," she said, keeping the throttle on the floor and the periscope locked on the remaining Globemaster.

As she drove past it, Rica watched the creature that had chased Cliff across the plateau. The thing plodded methodically onward, dragging its arms behind it, giving no indication that it had even noticed the huge ALV. She saw several more creatures scattered across the ice plain where the Globemaster had slung them during its aborted takeoff. Some were missing an arm or two. Some were tainted red with human blood. All of them were plodding in the same direction.

No one else could see out of the ALV, so she told her passengers how the scattered army was trudging away. "Where do you think they're going?" she asked.

"Back to hell, I hope," Paz said.

Cliff said, "My guess would be the ocean." He was thinking of the transparent beaks in the ambergris. Wherever the eight-armed marauders had come from, some of them had apparently been eaten by a whale.

"They're probably returning to their landing ship for medical treatment," said Jory Panopalous. "Maybe we should not have defended ourselves. Their choice of first-contact mode may have dire implications, you know—dire implications indeed."

# CHAPTER 20

# Marooned

The remaining Globemaster was ransacked and deserted. There were no monsters, no living humans, and no bodies— only smears and puddles of blood and bluish slime that reeked of dead fish. That meant all of the Air Force personnel had perished, because none of those on the other plane had made it onto the ALV.

Five Marines had also died in the battle, leaving only Rica's four-soldier fire team and Private Chris Gerard from one of the other two fire teams.

Except for Raymond Price and Chester Wimbledon, all the civilian consultants had survived.

All but one of the CIA agents had apparently been killed on the remaining Globemaster.

The surviving agent was Dale Johnson, who now lay unconscious while Bonnie Fulcrum bandaged his head. They had found him sprawled in the troop cabin of the ALV with a deep crater in his skull above his left eye. They knew he had been trying to get through to headquarters on the datalink machine when the pilots had attempted to take off, so they surmised that the plane's violent spinout had flung him against a wall.

After retreating from the besieged cockpit, Rica had

found Todd unconscious, still clutching Sophie in his arms, lying in front of what was left of Chester's cage. There were no signs of Chester, except smears of blood on the cage's floor. The children were physically unharmed, but Sophie's worsening bronchitis was still a concern. Todd had woken on the ALV and told Rica how he'd unlocked the cage and then fainted when a "ghost" began touching him. They concluded that the creature had devoured Chester and departed the plane satisfied. Perhaps the prisoner had even sacrificed himself to divert the monster's attention from the children.

They expected the datalink machine to be on the ALV, but it wasn't.

"Does this mean we can't call for help?" Todd asked.

Rica nodded, staring at the tangle of bullet-riddled plastic and hanging wires that had once been the surviving Globemaster's cockpit radio. "Our headsets and the radio on the ALV are only for short-range communication, and the squad radio was on the other plane. But don't worry, Todd—Mr. Johnson is supposed to check in with headquarters every twelve hours, so they'll know we're in trouble when they don't hear from us in the morning."

Todd began to whimper. He was hunched over Sophie, rocking her. "I'm sorry," he moaned. "I'm still not used to seeing people die."

Rica gently put her arm around him. "Maybe you won't have to get used to it, Todd."

At the same time, Joan said, "Don't worry, kid, you'll get more practice. Unless you're next."

"Maybe the aliens won't come back," Jory said. Blood had just dripped onto one of his eyeglass lenses from the ceiling, and he was attempting to wipe it off with a sleeve. "If they wanted to finish us off, they would have done it before they left."

"What makes you so sure they're aliens?" Cliff asked.

Joan said, "Jesus, Steadman! Did you see the fucking things? What else could they be?"

"Yeah, they weren't only weird," Todd said. "They were

*humongous.* If they were just animals, somebody would have discovered them before now."

"No earthly animal could take so many bullets and keep on coming," Paz added.

"They may look like sea creatures, but they can breathe and walk on land," Bonnie said.

"And you can't see through animals," Todd continued. "The aliens don't even have blood. All Earth animals need blood. I guess they aren't ghosts, but they are a whole different kind of life."

"Yeah. The alien kind," Joan said with conviction. She was gazing up at the bright stars through the open crew door, which hung cockeyed from one hinge. "Panopalous was right all along. I wonder where they came from."

Jory joined her at the door. "Still, we have no proof," he said, staring out at the moonlit ice. Then he abruptly turned around. "Yes, we do! The alien that Todd saw on the other plane must have stolen the datalink machine! Only intelligent beings with an understanding of our technology would know how to cut off our communication with headquarters."

"Maybe they accidentally ate the datalink," Cliff said.

Joan rolled her eyes at him. "Steadman, it was a metal box the size of a briefcase with sharp corners."

Cliff shrugged. "If they are technological beings, why didn't they use weapons when they attacked us? Or space suits? Surely they would have used *some* kind of tools."

"How do you know they didn't?" Jory asked, leaning out of the crew door to look both ways. "Maybe their tools are invisible, or microscopic. Maybe they use controlled energy fields instead of matter. Maybe those monsters *are* the tools of an alien race. Their technology could be biological instead of electromechanical, or some combination. The bottom line is they must be controlled by some form of higher intelligence, either their own or—"

Cliff interrupted him. "They didn't *act* very intelligent, or controlled. They just ate or destroyed everything in sight.

Half the time, they seemed to be playing or fighting with each other."

Jory glared at Cliff. "They were obviously communicating and cooperating in their own way . . . don't try to judge an alien intelligence by your own Earth-centric paradigm of intelligent behavior, Dr. Steadman."

"Satan is the higher intelligence," Paz muttered. "The demons are just his servants."

"Didn't you see those tongues?" Joan asked Cliff. "What kind of Earth animal has teeth on its tongue?"

Cliff shrugged. "A mollusk. Snails, slugs, cephalopods— almost all of them except the bivalves. The toothed tongue is called the *radula*. The chiton is a mollusk that scrapes algae off coral reefs with a radula that contains teeth made of magnetite, the naturally magnetic iron oxide mineral. It's the hardest substance generated by any living creature. No one knows how they do it; man-made magnetite is highly inferior to the chiton's. The cephids' radulas have four separate lobes, but that's a minor adaptation. So are the claw-beaks. They're shaped just like the beak of a squid. They have a different function and location on the body, but a single mutation could account—"

"Hey, you said they didn't use any tools," Joan said. "What about those little blue lightbulbs under their eyes?"

"I doubt they were lightbulbs," Cliff said. "The blue glow could be from bioluminescence. Most sea creatures that live below the euphotic zone have evolved to use bioluminescence for communication, finding mates, attracting prey, confusing predators . . . Bacteria inside a gland called a photophore produce two chemicals, luciferin and luciferase. An exothermic reaction between them gives off almost all of its energy as light. It's the most efficient source of—"

"Whatever," Jory said. "As I was saying, *some form* of high intelligence must be responsible for this invasion, because there's no way it could be coincidental that a huge but unknown species has shown up for the first time on the Floe."

Cliff groaned, mashing his eyes. "You're right about that. The cephids must be associated with the Floe's advanced propulsion system in some way."

"And whoever built the Floe's drive came from out *there*," Jory said, pointing up at the stars. "Because no one down *here* could build a drive that generates one hundredth of the Floe's thrust. Case closed."

Todd said, "What did you just call the monsters, Dr. Steadman?"

"Cephids," Cliff said. "Short for cephalopoids, because they have several anatomical features that resemble those of the cephalopods—the mollusks with suction cups."

"And you think that means they're terrestrial," Jory accused.

"Well . . . not necessarily," Cliff replied. "They could just have analogous organs due to convergent evolution."

"Say what?" asked Eddy Brown. The stocky, taciturn, redheaded private was kneeling to scrape slime off his combat boots with his knife.

Cliff explained. "Convergent evolution is when two unrelated species share common features because they have adapted to the same ecological niche. Birds and bats, for example. Bats are mammals and birds are descendents of the dinosaurs, so their wings must have evolved independently."

"You think the aliens look like cephalopods because they evolved in a similar environment on their planet?" Jory asked.

"It's possible," Cliff said. "It stands to reason that the most advanced aquatic invertebrates from all terrestrial planets would have similar morphology, regardless of their underlying chemistry—DNA, RNA, silicon, or whatever. Vertebrates won out on Earth, but invertebrates are better off in some ways . . . more flexible, less vulnerable to injury. Maybe the invertebrates took over on the world of the cephids, or maybe organisms analogous to vertebrates never even made an appearance there."

Jory smiled. "So now you agree that they must be extra-terrestrial."

"Actually, no," Cliff replied.

"I see," Jory said.

"Look, Jory, I know an alien invasion wouldn't defy any laws of nature. And it stands to reason that extraterrestrial life probably exists out there somewhere. But I can't help it if my knee-jerk intuition says we don't need such a far-fetched explanation for the cephids."

Jory glanced up at Rica, who was slumped alone at the top of the bloody stairs leading up to the flight deck. Then he looked back at Cliff with a sarcastic smile. "So your judgment is based on knee-jerk intuition rather than the facts. What kind of scientist does that make you, Dr. Stead-man?"

Cliff flushed and also glanced at Rica. She was leaning against a bloody, bullet-riddled wall, facing the floor with her clenched fists covering her forehead. She gave no indication that she had heard Jory's insult.

"Maybe Wimbledon was right," Cliff muttered, and he could tell from the dilation of Jory's nostrils that the little engineer knew he was referring to the "crackpot alien chaser" comment. He added, "You think they're aliens because you *want* them to be aliens."

"Like you want them to be cephalopods?" Jory retorted. "Wouldn't it be sweet if you could claim the discovery of a major new species, publish a bunch of papers . . . your career would turn onto easy street."

Cliff nodded and tried to relax. "It would if we survive." He leaned out the crew door and looked around with a trace of a smile. "I guess I should try to forget about it until backup arrives or we get off the Floe, but I can't wait to get my hands on a specimen . . . so many things I want to check."

"Me too!" Jory said. He joined Cliff, gazing out in the opposite direction. "Me too."

"You know, this could be the biggest discovery of the

century in marine biology," Cliff said. "I just wish Ray were still alive so he could share—"

"The century?" Jory scoffed. "Good grief, Steadman, first contact with an alien civilization is the greatest scientific moment of all time!"

Behind them, Bonnie snorted and spoke around her cigarette. "Whatever they are, they aren't civilized."

"Maybe they ain't sea monsters or aliens either one," said Eddy Brown.

All heads turned to him except Rica's. Eddy was so large and spoke so seldom that he easily got attention when he did.

Joan let out a derisive grunt. "What do *you* think they are, Brown?"

Eddy shot her a brief scowl, then self-consciously glanced up at Rica, who still showed no signs of even hearing the nervous chattering of the other survivors. "Maybe . . . maybe they're man-made," Eddy said, "like some kind of robots or mutant clones or something. Maybe, like, a genetically engineered thing that's designed to be a weapon . . . or guard dogs."

"Good grief," Jory said, rolling his eyes.

Eddy glared at Jory and Jory looked away. "I'll good your grief, little dude! I'll bet you a hundred bucks the Army is trying to use genetic engineering to create . . . monsters. If they aren't, you can bet somebody else is."

During this exchange, Joan's derisive expression gradually relaxed, and her eyes opened wide, staring at Eddy. "Goddamn, Brown, you just had an idea! I'm sure that shit came from one of your comic books, but it's no crazier than aliens or sea monsters." She looked around at the others. "The Floe could be a . . . a Trojan horse meant to land thousands of these bulletproof, man-eating motherfuckers on an enemy beach. Maybe they really sent us out here just to test the new system!"

Rica was vaguely aware of the debate, but her mind was on other things until Todd cautiously climbed the cockpit stairs and whispered in her ear: "Sophie and I want to thank you for getting us off that other plane."

She tried to smile at him. The boy's gratitude was more comforting than he could know.

She had been thinking about Chester Wimbledon. It seemed obvious now that Gavril, McInnis, and Vicini had all been slain by the horrible marauders. Had Chester told the truth about Charley as well? Had the shot that killed her brother Marine been nothing but a freak accident? If so, she had doomed an innocent man to the most horrifying death imaginable by leaving him locked up when the monsters attacked.

After Todd interrupted her morbid reverie, she looked up and saw Cliff and Jory glaring at each other while Joan and Eddy talked. She stumbled down the stairs, taking care not to slip on the bright red blood and bluish slime.

Bonnie and Eddy were smoking cigarettes inside the hold. For the first time in her life, Rica did not mind the smoke, because its smell partially masked the other odors.

"Bedtime!" she announced.

They all looked at her. She clenched her jaws, hoping she didn't look as scared as everyone else did. Before Gavril's death, not looking scared had been vital to her for personal reasons. Now that she was in charge of getting the survivors off the Floe alive, it was also her professional duty.

"We're all behind on sleep, so we might as well try to catch up," she explained.

"Yeah, right," Joan sneered.

Rica ignored her. "We don't have enough information to determine for certain what the . . . the cephids are. Besides, we shouldn't trust our logic right now . . . the state we're in. Let's just focus on staying alive until backup gets here. Bledsoe and I will take the first watch. Rodriguez, Brown, and Gerard will relieve us at oh-two-hundred. We'll all work out a plan tomorrow, as soon as we have enough light to see."

She took a deep breath and stood up straight. "Everyone should be bedded down, as best you can, in ten minutes. I don't want to hear any more talking until daylight unless there's an emergency. Understood?"

To Rica's profound amazement, everyone obeyed her orders—the three male Marines, the civilians, Joan—all of them.

# CHAPTER 21

# Retreat

At dawn, the survivors crowded into the ALV along with all of the camp gear and weapons they could fit.

They could find no food. It had all been on the plane that exploded.

Their destination was a flat-topped mesa that stood above the surrounding terrain at the center of the Floe. The mesa would be as good a place as any to make a stand. It would have perfect visibility on all sides and was not near any chasms or edges of the Floe.

They had discussed alternative plans. They couldn't stay on the disabled Globemaster, because the doors could not be closed. There wasn't enough room to await rescue in the ALV. The fastest way to leave the Floe would be to cast off and motor away with the ALV's twenty-six-hundred-horse-power water jets, but even if they could somehow lower the thirty-ton vehicle down a sheer cliff four hundred feet high—the ramp where the children were found was far too steep — they had no way to alert rescuers of their location. The ALV was specifically designed to be nearly invisible from the air, so it could drift undetected for years in the middle of an ocean that covered a third of the Earth.

Rica did not slow down for bumps or dips. They had to

make the most of daylight in case the following night brought another attack, and the ALV was already being held back by the several tons of ammunition in the hold. There was no guarantee that the transparent marauders would wait until dark, but all four of the previous attacks had occurred late at night. Cliff had conjectured that the cephids were instinctively nocturnal, like the octopuses in his lab.

Rica worried about her passengers. They were packed like sardines, standing front to back along a central aisle between secured stacks of equipment. At least the ALV's twists and jerks couldn't sling them very far.

Agent Johnson was still unconscious but medically stable. He lay atop the cargo, his chest nearly touching the roof, strapped down on the heavy crew door they had removed from the Globemaster to use as a stretcher.

Paz and Joan opened the roof hatch and stood on the ladder below it so that their upper bodies protruded above the ALV. Joan faced forward and Paz faced backward. Each of them held a squad automatic weapon, the standard light machine gun of the Marine infantry. Private Chris Gerard stood ready to hand fresh ammunition boxes up to them.

Rica drove upstream through a rapid sluice of meltwater in the bottom of a narrow canyon. The gurgling stream reached above the ALV's tracks in the tightest segments, nearly floating the amphibious vehicle. The sky was bright blue with wispy pink cirrus clouds, but the horizontal rays of sunrise left the canyon's bottom in deep azure shade. Driving up a stream guaranteed that the ALV would not skid down a slope or fall into a crevasse, but it also made them vulnerable to ambush from above, so Paz and Joan kept a careful watch on the walls of bluish ice towering over them.

Cliff's sprained ankle ached as the ALV leaned and jerked and slipped, grinding its way up the stream. At least his tightly laced boot added support—he had found his boots on the ALV where someone must have thrown them before evacuating the doomed Globemaster.

His expeditions at sea had taught him how to handle motion sickness, but his neighbors, Jory Panopalous and Bonnie Fulcrum, both looked dangerously nauseous. The stale sweat, body heat, and dirty-diaper fumes trapped in the gloomy troop cabin were undoubtedly contributing to their misery, not to mention the smell of dead fish that still clung to both children. Cliff was resigned to the fact that he would catch the brunt of it if Jory lost control of his stomach—the cabin was too cramped for a sick passenger to even turn away from the others.

No one spoke until several minutes into the ride, when Private Eddy Brown released a loud "I wish we knew what the fuck they want!"

Todd was standing between Cliff and Eddy, holding Sophie tightly as usual. He shrugged and said, "They want to kill us. And eat us."

"I doubt they came all the way from another solar system just for that," Jory said.

"I agree," Cliff said. "I still don't think they came from outer space, but I suspect what we saw last night was strictly opportunistic feeding."

"What's that?" Todd asked.

"It means they attacked for some other reason and just happened to eat a few people because it was convenient."

"Maybe they weren't really eating at all," Jory said. "They could have been collecting specimens to take back to their ship for analysis."

Todd said, "Why do you think they attacked us, Dr. Steadman?"

Jory answered the question for Cliff with apparent certainty. "They stole the datalink machine, remember? And they disabled both planes so we couldn't fly away. They obviously wanted to prevent us from reporting them to headquarters."

"But why are they invading Earth?" Todd asked.

"They aren't," Jory said, again with a tone of certainty that irritated Cliff. "If they wanted to take over, they would have brought a military force that could defeat all of our defenses. This group must have come just to gather intelligence, but they still want to keep their mission secret."

"Bullshit!" Joan's harsh voice descended through the open roof hatch and rang in the aluminum box. "Maybe you know a lot about aliens, Panopalous, but you obviously don't know squat about military operations. If they were on a covert op, they wouldn't be moving the Floe—it's not exactly a stealth vehicle. You guys ought to be figuring out how we can kill those fuckers without using up so many bullets, not wasting time solving the mysteries of the universe."

"Amen," Paz said.

The ALV lurched, shuddered, and tilted back as it climbed over a high ledge. Rushing water drummed against the floor. Bonnie stuck a bent cigarette between her lips and tried to light the trembling tip.

"Oh, hell no," Jory said. He grabbed the cigarette, twisted it apart, and dropped it.

Bonnie bared her teeth at him, then looked like she was going to cry.

"How many shots did it take to bring one down?" Cliff asked.

"About four hundred for the one Paz shredded with his SAWs," Joan said. "I think that's the only one we killed."

"Maybe incredibly elastic tissues is another thing they have in common with mollusks," Cliff said. "Did you notice how they can extend and retract their eyes like a snail? You might think their softness would make them more vulnerable—it probably *would* make them easier to cut with a knife—but I'll bet it lets bullets pass through without causing much harm. In all vertebrates, including humans, most of the damage in a gunshot wound doesn't come from the puncture. It comes from the bullet slowing down and transferring its energy to a shock wave that tears and crushes surrounding tissue. I'll bet cephid flesh stretches instead of tearing and doesn't slow bullets enough to absorb much energy. A slug passing through may only leave the kind of pinhole that a hypodermic needle makes in human flesh."

"So what should we do next time?" Joan asked. "Charge them with bayonets?"

"We do not have bayonets," Paz informed her. "Only our survival knives."

"Where do you reckon their spaceship is?" Todd asked.

"It's probably a submarine," Jory said. "Deep in the ocean would be the ideal place to hide an alien spacecraft. As long as it's quiet, it could be huge and move all over the world without being detected by humans."

"If they're really aliens, I'd bet their ship is inside the Floe," Cliff said. "That could be why they've moved the Floe north from Antarctica—to melt the ice and free their ship so they can go home."

Jory's eyes lit up. "Steadman, you're a genius! We have to look for it! Maybe we can establish communication and strike a truce."

"Panoplous?" Joan shouted, her voice rising in alarm. "If you deliberately go and rile those things up . . . so help me God, I'll shoot you dead if you make it back."

Jory scowled and swallowed, staring up at the seemingly lifeless form of Dale Johnson. "Maybe he can give us some answers, if he ever wakes up."

"Do you think the CIA knew about the cephids?" Cliff asked. "I've been wondering why they picked me, among all the marine biologists. They must have already known what the cephids look like."

"The castaways probably described one," Joan said. "Johnson refused to play the recording of their distress call for us."

"If the CIA thought the cephids might be aliens, that would explain why they spent so much money on this mission," Cliff said. "It could also explain why they hired Jory instead of some other naval engineer."

"Hey, that's right!" Jory said. "I'm only an amateur . . . enthusiast, but there is no such thing as a professional expert on extraterrestrials. The CIA has an unofficial protocol for situations that might turn into first encounters, you know. It calls for the utmost secrecy. That could explain why this mission was so hush-hush. If we did encounter aliens, the CIA would want to prevent other nations from finding out about the contact for as long as possible so the U.S. could have an exclusive information exchange with the alien civilization . . . maybe pick up some of their advanced technology."

"And if the cephids didn't turn out to be aliens?" Cliff asked.

"Then they wouldn't want the public to find out they'd spent millions preparing for a possible encounter," Jory said. "Most voting taxpayers know so little science that they think extraterrestrial life is impossible. Johnson didn't tell us what they suspected because he knew if we came home alive, one of us would eventually let it leak."

"How did you come to know about the CIA's first contact protocol?" Joan asked.

"Ha!" Jory replied.

"Okay. What does it require besides secrecy?"

"Women, for one thing."

"Women?"

"It was drafted by a bunch of liberals," Jory said.

"Why do you say that?"

"It specifies that the first contact party must include a representative proportion of women and minorities."

"Holy shit!" Joan said. "I wondered why three of the CIA agents were women. One of them was Asian, too."

"What about us?" Paz asked.

"Yeah," Joan said. "Gavril was black, you and Rica are Hispanic, and our squad is the only one in the company with two women. They probably couldn't find any civilian experts in the specialties they wanted who weren't white males, so they had to meet their diversity quota with the agents and soldiers. A special forces team would have been all male and mostly white, so they sent us Marines instead. They must have already been about convinced the cephids were aliens to make such a big priority out of following the protocol. Who would have guessed!"

When they arrived at the mesa, Rica was relieved to see that it had not melted away since the satellite photographs she was using to navigate had been taken. The mesa looked like a round stage a thousand feet across. The problem was getting onto it. The steep scarp at its edge was more than forty feet high, and even with its metal tracks the ALV could not climb wet ice at a significant grade.

She backed away, warned her passengers, accelerated on the level approach, and hit the scarp at top speed. The thirty-ton vehicle surged up the steepening slope and launched into the sky. Sophie and Jory began screaming when weightlessness hit. The engine whined and the tracks buzzed, spinning faster than normal when they were freed from the ground.

The white-and-gray behemoth crashed down on the mesa's top, landing squarely on its tracks. It had no suspension springs or shock absorbers, so it did not bounce. The impact hit its passengers with a terrible jolt. After Rica's warning, Paz and Joan had climbed down from the hatch and wedged themselves in among the human cargo. Everyone fell, but no one was seriously hurt.

Rica parked the ALV on the Floe's flat summit and rested her forehead on the figure-eight steering control with her eyes closed. "We made it," she sighed. With everyone on board, she had been so afraid of wrecking that she had thought of nothing else throughout the harrowing drive.

Joan took the first sentry shift because of her superior distance vision. She stood atop the ALV with dark sunglasses and binoculars in the wind and blazing sunshine.

Todd and Bonnie remained aboard the ALV to care for Sophie and Agent Johnson. Sophie's miserable cries and barklike coughs resounded in the aluminum box. According to Bonnie, the infant's bronchitis had progressed to pneumonia.

Jory Panopalous worked on the depth-imaging sonar scanner that had belonged to Raymond Price. He wanted to use the instrument for its intended purpose, to image the Floe's interior the way doctors take sonograms of a developing fetus. But when Rica saw the gadget, she asked if he could modify it to work in air instead of ice. "We need a portable device that can detect solid objects sticking up above the surface of the mesa," she said. "The weather's fine now, but imagine trying to shoot an army of transparent cephids before they can overrun the camp on a stormy night."

The other survivors worked feverishly to erect fortifications before dark. They discovered a pair of chain saws among the camping gear. The saws were a mystery until Rica found a diagram in one of their orange plastic cases showing how to build an igloo. Now the ever-present breeze was filled with the revving of nine-horsepower engines and the odor of the bluish exhaust as Cliff and Rica wielded the two-foot saw bars to cut rectangular blocks from the ice.

Paz, Eddy, and Chris placed the hundred-pound ice blocks in a spiral according to the diagram. Each new block instantly fused to the others it was touching. Deeper than a few inches, the Floe's interior was still cold enough to refreeze the thin film of meltwater between two recently excavated blocks. Watching the blocks fuse together, Rica finally figured out why the ice had been dry and the wind had been so cold at the bottom of the ramp where they'd found Todd and Sophie. The melting walls were chilling the air as it poured down the ramp, preventing it from delivering enough heat to warm the shaded ice at the bottom above freezing.

The first two igloos came out crooked, but by late afternoon, the camp was surrounded by a ring of five gleaming domes. Each igloo was ten feet in external diameter and six feet high at the center, with a six-foot tunnel-foyer pointing toward the center of camp and, in the opposite wall, a vertical slot that was just big enough for a gun barrel. With a gunner in each igloo, they could defend the exposed camp from all directions. Eventually the igloos would melt under the tropical sun, but hopefully the foot-thick walls would remain strong enough to protect their inhabitants until a rescue arrived.

Cliff, Eddy, and Chris erected an eight-by-fourteen-foot cabin tent so Bonnie would have adequate room to treat her patients. Since meltwater dripped constantly inside the igloos, Paz and Rica also set up one-person dome tents for sleeping. All of the camp gear they needed had been salvaged, except for one tent pole that was somehow lost in transit. Rica could have rigged a substitute by taping spare backpack staves together, but she couldn't find the duct tape either.

The igloos, the ALV, and the jungle-green camouflage tents were the only objects besides humans that protruded more than an inch above the glittering white stage in the clear blue sky. Rica surveyed their handiwork and spoke to Paz with a wry smile. "All we need now is an Eat Here sign."

A minute later, she smelled dead fish and felt something tap her shoulder. She whirled around, holding her breath, prepared to draw her sidearm.

It was only Todd. The bluish crust had long since been washed away, but its tenacious stench still followed both children wherever they went.

Todd was standing with his back to the sun, shielding Sophie from its brutal rays. He was able to walk on the wet ice because Rica had given him one of several extra pairs of boots and crampons that the team had brought in case they found survivors. "Rica, I'm really hungry," he said.

She put an arm around his back, resisting the temptation to lean on him—she felt barely able to stand herself. "I'm sorry, Todd. I'm hungry too. I wish—"

"I didn't come out to complain," he said. "I want you to take care of Sophie while I go fishing."

"You know how?" she asked.

"I'm supposed to," Todd said.

"Do we have any tackle?"

Todd shook his head. "But Paz said he could make some hooks with the stuff in his gun repair kit. I'll bet I could catch some really big fish if I just had some bait."

"What kind of bait do you need?"

"Any kind of meat," Todd said. He swallowed dryly and looked away. "What did you do with the . . . with Mr. Gavril and the sentry who got shot in the head?"

Rica's eyes began to burn. Her throat felt tight, and her head started throbbing. Thanks to nervous exhaustion and low blood sugar, she was closer to the limit of her emotional control than she had ever been. She was not angry at Todd, just reminded of Gunny's face and the role she had played in his death, and in Chester Wimbledon's.

"We buried them in the ice," she said.

Todd sighed. "I guess there's no bait, then."

"Wait," Rica said. "Hey, Joan! Could you shoot down one of those birds?"

Joan was still standing guard atop the ALV. She gazed at the flock of seabirds following the Floe. "Not from here, but I could go hunting. Yo, Rodriguez! You got enough balls to eat a raw seagull?"

Todd handed Sophie to Rica.

"Todd, I'm busy. Can't Bonnie watch her?"

Todd shook his head, looking down. "She's taking a break."

"What?" Rica shouted. "There are no breaks here!"

Irritably, Todd said, "Bonnie is just like my mom, okay? But you would be a *good* mother. I want you to watch Sophie, and don't let anybody else." He trotted to the ALV, which Joan had already started up.

Rica walked to the medical tent, holding Sophie tightly beneath her breasts and taking baby steps to make absolutely certain she did not trip over her own crampons and fall. She couldn't imagine why Todd thought she would be a good mother. She had no motherly experience at all. And she didn't have time to start practicing now.

As she approached the tent, she heard a spooky noise over the perpetual flutter of the wind. It sounded a little like singing. By the time she got to the door, it had stopped.

She removed her sunglasses and peeked into the greenish gloom. "Bonnie?"

There was no response.

Rica lay Sophie on the dry tent floor, then sat inside the door to remove her crampons. As she leaned over to reach her boots, she saw a small curved piece of broken glass beneath the folding worktable they had brought from the surviving Globemaster. She grabbed Sophie and scanned the floor, afraid there would be more glass lying around.

She saw the upper half of a broken glass medicine vial.

She also saw Bonnie's legs protruding from behind a stack of floodlight cases.

Rica yelled for help and scrambled into the tent on her knees. She shook Bonnie but got no response. The frail doctor's mouth hung open, drooling a little. Holding Sophie in one arm, Rica laid two fingers against the carotid artery in Bonnie's neck. Her pulse was strong but slow.

Still wondering what could have happened, Rica stood back up on her knees and scanned the tent again. On the table was a syringe with no cap on the needle.

She carefully picked the broken vial off the floor. Letters were printed on its side. All that remained were an M, an O, and part of what looked like an R.

Morphine.

Everyone was afraid. Bonnie had chosen to treat her fear with medication.

# CHAPTER 22

# Fort

Even with no infant care experience, Rica could tell that Sophie's health was deteriorating fast. The baby's coughs had become pitifully weak grunts. Her wheezing had become quick and rasping. Her tiny pink forehead was frightfully hot; her nose was clogged with mucus; and her eyes were brimming with yellowish pus, which Rica carefully wiped away with her shirttail. The infection seemed to be raging throughout the tiny child's body, blitzing her immature immune system despite the cocktail of antibiotics Bonnie had prescribed.

Rica wondered if Sophie had come down with a killer case of the flu because of her frigid ordeal in the avalanche debris, or if she had contracted some exotic disease. Was the disease carried by the cephids? How contagious was it? Had Bonnie given her the right medication? Or had the pathetic drug abuser doomed Sophie by giving her something that was useless or even harmful?

As Rica rocked the sick child in her own tent, it occurred to her that she had not heard Sophie cry all day. Apparently the infant was no longer *able* to cry.

Cliff said, "Knock-knock" and stuck his shaggy but

beardless head through her tent door, letting in a crimson beam from the sunset. "Got a minute?" he asked.

Rica nodded, wondering if this visit was personal. She regretted not enjoying more of his company after patching him up that night in her tent. Her desire to know more about him had not diminished since then, but there had been no privacy and no time for intimate conversation.

"Jory and I need a live specimen to study," Cliff said. "If the cephids return, we want you to let a small one into camp so we can trap it in the pit where we dug up the igloo blocks. We've already tested the trap. Agent Johnson doesn't need the Globemaster's crew door anymore, so we'll use it for a lid. We'll park the ALV on top of it to hold it down."

"No," Rica said.

Cliff sighed. "I told him that's what you'd say." He peeked out at the sunset, his expression grim. "No one is coming to get us, are they?"

Rica felt dread wash over her. If the others started thinking they were not going to be rescued, they might give up or start fighting over what to do next. She'd been wondering how and when it would begin.

"It's been ten hours since we failed to check in," Cliff said. "If they ever intended to send backup, they would have gotten another team ready as soon as we took off and kept them on standby, right?"

Rica sighed and nodded. "And I know of at least one fleet with Ospreys that could have gotten here by now. Cliff, please don't tell anyone else just yet."

She was still holding Sophie, but one of her hands was free. Cliff reached out and clasped it in both of his. "They can't just abandon us here," he said.

She curled her fingers around his hand, which felt strong and warm. "Sure they can. Standard government procedure. It's happened to prisoners of war all over the world. Maybe they can't launch a rescue without compromising our mission's secrecy. Maybe they think we're all dead already. There could be any number of reasons. At this point, the

Floe is so close to Hawaii that they're probably thinking about only one thing."

"What?" Cliff asked.

"Stopping it."

"How *can* they stop it?"

"Remember what Agent Johnson said at the briefing?" she asked. "If we don't disable the drive, the only option left will be nuclear bombardment."

As darkness fell, Paz set up the camp stove on the lee side of the ALV so the massive vehicle would shelter its flame from the steady breeze. Meanwhile, Eddy stood guard on the roof, and Todd plucked the birds Joan had shot. Bonnie was still sleeping off the morphine in the medical tent. Except for Sophie and Dale Johnson, who was still unconscious, the other survivors all squatted around the stove. Thanks to the reflective ice, the circular blue flame from the white-gas burner provided enough light even after the stars came out.

Using dead birds for bait, Todd had caught enough fish to feed the camp for a week, but most of the castaways had chosen the remaining birds for what they knew might be their last dinner. Each of them roasted a plucked carcass by skewering it on a spare gun barrel and holding the hot steel tube with an insulating item of clothing.

Todd roasted one bird for himself and one for Eddy while Sophie slept snugly beside him in the bassinet he had just constructed. The bassinet's handle was a piece of string. Its bottom was a bowl-shaped segment of rubber that Todd had cut from one of the tires in the Globemaster's landing gear fairing while Joan was shooting birds.

Joan was the first to eat. She pulled her bird off when it was still half raw and began noisily chomping and slurping.

"Is it just me," Cliff asked, "or is anybody else here scared stiff?"

"I'm scared limp," Jory said.

"I am not afraid to die," Paz mumbled, gazing into the

blue stove flame as he absently gnawed a petrel's stringy thigh. "I just pray to God to not let me fuck up."

"Same here," Rica said.

"Amen," Joan said.

"Or wimp out," said Private Gerard, the sole survivor of the other two fire teams in Gavril's squad. Unlike Eddy Brown, Gerard had not been taciturn by nature before this mission, but he had kept to himself and hardly said a word since the attack. His apparent detachment worried Rica, but so far he had done his share and obeyed all of her orders.

Paz shook his head, gnawing his charred dinner and staring at the stove flame. "I have no fear of cowardice because I have control of that. But no matter how brave I am, no matter how much in control, I could still fuck up."

Joan said, "Good grief, Rodriguez, now you've got *me* afraid you're going to fuck up."

Private Gerard laughed at that.

"Maybe the cephids won't bother us here," Todd said.

Cliff grunted. "When they attacked the planes, their behavior looked like territorial aggression to me. Predators will back off from prey that poses a danger to them—no meal is worth dying for—but they'll die in droves to defend territory."

"So what?" Jory said. "Your experience with earthly predators does not apply to the aliens."

"Maybe," Cliff said, "but once they figure out we're still on the Floe, I'd bet they'll keep on coming until the last one dies."

"The last one of them, or the last one of us?" Todd asked.

"Whichever," Cliff said.

"Lopez, something's wrong!" Eddy yelled from atop the ALV.

Rica jumped up and grabbed her rifle. Her hot second course sizzled when it landed on the ice. "You see them?"

"No," Eddy said. "The wind has stopped blowing."

She reached up her hands, and the bulky private swung her onto the ALV's roof. Sure enough, the humid air seemed stagnant, an ominously unfamiliar sensation. "The Floe must have stopped!" she said.

"Can you see the ocean?" Cliff asked.

The moon had just come up. It looked close and huge hovering above the horizon. Most of the sea was too dark for Rica to make out any details, but she could see the moonlight glinting on wave crests up and down a column beneath the glowing orb. "Yeah," she said. "There are lots of waves, and they're bigger than before."

"Damn it!" Cliff said. "Give me a boost?"

Eddy pulled him onto the roof.

"Long-distance swells from the northwest," he muttered, looking out over the Floe's western flank. "See how they appear to bend southward as they get closer? That can mean only one thing: a tailwind is compensating for the Floe's speed. The Floe is still moving, and we're sailing right into a tropical storm."

"Oh, that's just fucking *perfect*!" Joan shouted. "Who wants to bet on what gets us first? Cephids, a typhoon, the crud that's killing the baby, *or a goddamned nuclear missile*!"

Rica was not listening to her sister Marine's tirade. She was looking out at the flat top of the mesa. In the oblique moonlight, movement was becoming detectable all around the camp. Without the steady breeze, the Floe had once again become the ultimate fog generator. The movement Rica saw was the random dance of mist tendrils rising from the ice. Soon, she knew, the wisps of fog would coalesce into an opaque white cloak.

# CHAPTER 23

## Siege

They waited, watched, and listened as the fog grew denser and deeper. At first the swirls of mist seemed to meander around the tents and igloos at random. Then the fog began to flow radially outward from the camp, which was at the exact center of the stagelike mesa. The dense fluid poured off the mesa on all sides, accelerating as it cascaded down the steep scarp. At the mesa's edges, the fog was low and flowed at the pace of a walk, but closer to camp its motion was so sluggish that it mounded to a depth exceeding six feet.

Joan stood on the roof of the ALV, above the fog, scanning the mesa with binoculars. The undulating plateau was clearly visible in the moonlight. She had a stomachache from eating too much half-roasted seagull, but she did not let it distract her.

For what seemed like the tenth time, Paz whispered up at her from the fog, asking what she could see. She replied, "What are you afraid of, Rodriguez? Snakes? The fog is less than a foot deep at the perimeter."

Paz's questions stopped. Joan resumed scanning the creeping white carpet. "Come on, you ugly motherfuckers," she whispered. "This time we're ready for you."

"It can only detect objects that pass through the horizontal plane where the mikes are positioned," Jory said. He was pointing to a ring of chrome microphones radiating from the top of a tripod. "How high do you want them?"

"As low as possible without interference from the ice," Rica said.

Jory adjusted the tripod. "About a foot should be okay."

The modified sonar equipment had been too heavy to build a portable cephid detector, so Jory had set up his contraption in the center of camp. He led Cliff and Rica to his tent, following a wire stretched across the ice. "Come on, I'll show you the image."

"You mean it's working now?" Rica asked. She could hear no pinging. In fact, the camp was eerily quiet with everyone whispering and creeping around on tiptoes.

"I don't know if the aliens can hear," Jory said, "but I didn't want to take a chance on luring them, so I set the system to use an ultrasonic frequency."

"The fact that we can't hear it doesn't mean they can't hear it," Cliff said. "And they *can* hear, by the way." He told them about the hovering eyeball that had investigated the Globemaster's hold before the cephid attacked Raymond Price—how it had turned to look at him when he scooted back against the wall. He chose not to add the fact that earthly cephalopods could not hear, at least not as mammals did, because they had no ears.

A blue dashed circle filled the screen of the laptop attached to the sonar. The background was black except for several white rays that began near the center of the circle and extended straight outward. The rays were thin to begin with but grew thicker toward the edges of the screen. One of them was much thicker than the rest. The next thickest were five identical rays spaced evenly around the circle. There were also several thinner rays. All of the white rays blinked at one-second intervals, and some of the smaller rays were moving around.

Jory pointed to the blue dashed circle. "I digitized this

line for reference. It represents the edges of the mesa. Each of the white rays is a sound shadow cast by an object on the ice. You can see some moving—those are people. The big one is the ALV. The five symmetrical rays are the igloos. To watch for intruders, all you have to do is check for new rays popping up near the blue circle. And keep everyone away from the microphone stand so they won't cast a huge shadow that could hide incoming aliens. Who's going to sit in here and watch this thing?"

"Do you know how to shoot?" Rica asked.

Jory shook his head.

"Then you are," she said. "The rest of us will be busy manning the guns in the igloos."

Bonnie staggered from the medical tent, stooped with her hands on her knees, and spat on the ice.

"Bad hangover?" Eddy asked, grinning.

"No, bad smell."

"What is it?" Rica asked. "Gangrene? Did Johnson—?"

"Not in the tent," Bonnie moaned. "Out here."

Rica sniffed the air, feeling her pulse quicken. "Probably just the latrine."

"It's not shit," Bonnie said. "It's dead fish. I've only been smoking for a few years, and I still have a *very keen sense of smell*."

Rica caught a whiff of the odor. "Battle stations!" she yelled.

The camp burst into activity. Cliff dived into his assigned igloo. Paz powered up the tripod-mounted minigun. Todd ran into the ALV with Sophie and locked the door behind him. Joan rotated on the roof with her binoculars. Rica heard her harsh voice whispering through the headset radio: "I don't see anything, Demo."

Rica ran to Jory's tent and stuck her head in. "What have you got?"

"Nothing," Jory said, keeping his eyes on the laptop screen.

Rica crouched by the tent indecisively. Her heart was pounding. Was it a false alarm? Was Bonnie just having a drug-induced olfactory hallucination? Not unless it was contagious—Rica thought she could smell dead fish too, and it seemed to be getting stronger.

She keyed her headset mike. "Sniper, Weapons, are you picking up a bad smell?"

"Affirmative," Paz said. "Stale seafood."

"Chinese fish market," Joan said, sounding nauseous.

Damn it, Rica thought. It has to be the cephids, but where are they?

She remembered how flexible the monsters attacking the planes had seemed. She keyed her headset mike. "Fire team! They must be crawling under the fog, too low for Jory's sonar."

*"Fuck!"* Joan replied. "What do you want us to do?"

"I—I—" Rica stammered. Her mouth was dry. Her head hurt, spinning with adrenaline.

Joan hissed, "Spit it out, Demo. We have to do *something!*"

"Everybody get down!" Rica yelled. She pulled back the tarp covering the small mound of fish in which she had embedded M67 fragmentation grenades—Todd had managed to catch more fish than they could possibly eat. Each grenade contained six and a half ounces of Composition B high explosive and had a wounding blast radius of fifty feet. With any luck, the ravenous cephids would snatch up the baited grenades and swallow them before they exploded, making good use of the grenades, even in a situation like this where she could not see her targets.

She gripped a squishy carcass and released the hand grenade's spoon, feeling cold fish blood trickle down her forearm. She hurled it with all her might. The baited bomb zoomed away in the fog. She hunkered down, covered her ears, and waited.

The grenade exploded with a painfully loud concussion. The flash of light was diffused throughout the fog.

Immediately after the blast, she heard a roar coming from behind her—a smooth and continuous but deafening sound, like an unmuffled drag racer being revved up to the red line. It was accompanied by a flickering orange light.

It was the Vulcan M-134 minigun. Its six barrels were spewing the most rapid automatic fire Rica had ever heard, along with a ten-foot gout of flame and a plume of smoke that ascended above the fog. Rica had never seen such a powerful weapon in action. Miniguns were normally mounted on helicopters because they required so much power and ammunition.

The blurred rotation of the barrels around the firing mechanism was powered by a rectangular Army-green battery that sat beneath the waist-high tripod with thick cables snaking up to the gun motor. Paz had told her that the minigun battery was equivalent to three heavy-duty truck batteries.

Paz was holding the plastic handgrip sticking up from the rear end of the minigun. Every muscle in his body was flexed and vibrating. He was swinging the heavy weapon left and right as fast as he could.

Through the minigun's thunder, Rica heard the deeper booms of Joan's semiautomatic fifty-caliber rifle. The shots were coming at regular intervals only a second or two apart. When the shooting from both weapons finally paused, Rica shouted into her headset mike. "Sniper, report! What did you see?"

"Son of a bitch motherfucker!" Joan replied. She fired the heavy Barrett M82 again.

"Sniper! What are you shooting at?"

"Their eyes!" Joan yelled. "When the grenade blew, they stuck their eyes up out of the fog. They're everywhere, Lopez, like a field of weeds . . . must be hundreds of them!"

Rica noticed that Joan had used her real name on the radio. It probably didn't matter, and now was not the time to mention it. "Weapons One, can you see them?"

"Negative," Paz replied. "But the stink is worse. Stay down, Demo. I will clear the other side of camp."

Rica flattened herself on the ice as he swung the minigun around and began blasting away at the fog, firing brief bursts between the igloos.

Something grabbed the back of Rica's shirt collar. She reached for her combat pistol as she rolled over.

It was Jory. He was yelling in her face, but she could not hear him over the minigun. Paz finally stopped shooting, and Jory yelled, "I can see them now. They all stood up at once. They're still coming."

"How close?"

"Eighty meters, maybe seventy now."

Rica keyed her headset mike. "Hold your fire."

She ran back to Jory's tent with him. Cliff was already there. "I couldn't see shit from my igloo in this fog," he explained.

They hunched over the laptop screen. Less than halfway between the camp and the blue dashed line, the white rays representing sound shadows cast by the cephids were closing in on all sides. The rays were so thick that the image became entirely white toward the edges of the mesa.

Joan's voice came over the radio: "I see one that's just trudging in circles. I think I shot both of its eyes out. You want me to keep shooting the eyes?"

"Go for it," Rica ordered. "Rifles One and Two, get up there with Sniper One so you can see. I'll join you in a second."

Rifle One was Eddy's handle. Rifle Two was Gerard's. As far as Rica knew, they were both still in their igloos staring out their gun ports at the fog.

"Weapons One, start strafing the mesa again. They're all around us, from sixty meters out."

The minigun's roar resumed. So did the booms from Joan's rifle.

Rica watched Jory's scanner. Three of the sound-shadow

rays cast by cephids had stopped advancing. "Those must be casualties," she yelled in Cliff's ear.

As they watched, an advancing cephid shifted sideways until its ray merged with one of the motionless rays and stopped. A moment later, the combined ray began to retreat.

"Look!" Jory yelled. "I told you they're a civilized race. They're dragging their wounded off the battlefield."

"I doubt that," Cliff said.

"Then how do *you* explain what we're seeing?"

Cliff shrugged. "My guess is they're eating their wounded and going home to digest."

Rica ran to the ALV, climbed onto the roof, and gazed out across the vast plateau of moonlit fog. Only then did she fully understand the edge of panic she had heard in Joan's voice. Hundreds of glassy cephids were methodically trudging toward the camp from all directions, wading against the current of low fog. They had stopped removing their casualties. Now they were crawling over their fallen comrades as fast as Paz could mow them down with the minigun.

Shimmers of oily iridescence swirled over their barrel-shaped bodies as they swayed from side to side. Their writhing transparent arms glistened in the moonlight like icicles come to life. It took all of Rica's will to resist giving the order to board the ALV and flee the camp, but she knew the vehicle could become their collective coffin if they attempted to drive out through the concentric waves of headless marauders.

She tried shooting a few bursts from a squad automatic weapon. Despite their bulk, the cephids were hard to hit because of their constant motion and the fog hiding most of their bodies. She started targeting the ones that had recently eaten. Their spiraling intestines were full of opaque animal parts—flesh, bone, scales, hair, feathers—that were easy to spot against the white fog and the moonlight. "Rifles One and Two, go for the ones with full guts!" she yelled.

Eddy and Gerard had finally joined Joan and Rica atop the ALV. The four Marines stood back to back, projecting fire in all directions. Rica and Eddy fired aimed bursts of 5.56-mm rifle ammunition from their SAWs at 725 rounds per minute. Gerard held an H & K MP-5N submachine gun in each hand, placing 9-mm pistol rounds in the general vicinity of the closest cephids at 800 shots per minute. Joan disabled one cephid for every two shots with her excessively powerful antimaterial rifle, pausing only to reload its ten-round magazine. Paz blindly blasted away down in the fog, spraying out 6,000 rounds per minute with the minigun.

Rica wondered who was racking up the most kills.

One of the cephids towered above all the rest. It was way out near the mesa's edge. As it trudged closer, Rica recognized its thick arms and the deep wrinkles running up and down its massive body. This was the beast that had crawled back and forth atop the remaining Globemaster, clubbing the roof with one of its closed claw-beaks. A few seconds after she spotted the waddling leviathan, its glassy body was illuminated by four distinct rings of aqua-blue light encircling its torso. The rings were like fluorescent bulbs, making the mammoth creature's whole body glow with diffracted light. At first the rings glowed continuously; then they flashed on and off in a brief pattern that seemed to repeat several times.

Rica watched incredulously as the full cephid intestines began to quiver all across the mesa. The dark spirals of jumbled animal matter appeared to rotate downward, as if they were corkscrews being twisted into the ice. Soon they had all disappeared, and the stench of marine carrion grew a thousand times worse, causing Rica's mouth to fill with saliva. As incredible as it seemed, she could think of only one explanation: the leader of the cephids had used his body lights to signal the others, telling them to purge themselves so they would be more difficult to shoot.

Rica carefully took aim at the distant king cephid, who was still flashing his four light rings. A split second after she fired, a fountain of aqua-blue sparks erupted from the top ring. The ring's glow faded as the liquid sparks spewed onto the ice, splattered outward, and continued glowing beneath the fog.

The house-size monster thrust its eight arms straight up in the air, as if signaling surrender. Then its body collapsed straight downward. With a wink of moonlight on glassy wet hide, it disappeared beneath the opaque fog.

"You got it!" Eddy cheered.

"No, I just made it mad," Rica yelled.

She could no longer see the king cephid, but a broad disturbance in the fog was retreating from the king's former position toward the edge of the mesa, leaving a wake of churning eddies and producing ripples that spread out in a V like a bow wave. Rica had no doubt that the disturbance was caused by the king cephid's flattened form slithering beneath the fog.

Meanwhile, the rest of the ghastly invaders were still closing in.

# CHAPTER 24

# Hostage

Rica heard voices and rolled over. Her nose plunged into a pool of icy meltwater that had leaked into her tent and collected around her sleeping pad. She sat up sputtering. Her whole body ached, her stomach felt queasy from dehydration, and her ears were still ringing from the prolonged gunfire.

The invaders had finally given up sometime after midnight. According to Jory's sonar, none of them had gotten within ten yards of the camp. They had dragged away every scrap of their fallen comrades as they retreated.

She peeked out the door. The dawn sky was overcast, a mercy to tired eyes but a harbinger of the storm to come. The wind from the south had grown stronger, dispersing the fog. It was blowing across the high mesa as fast as it had when the weather was clear, but in the opposite direction.

Rica had never felt so thirsty. Finding both of her canteens empty, she stooped and sucked up the cold water that had pooled in her tent. Then she stiffly climbed out and stumbled toward the latrine, noticing that the formerly smooth surface of the mesa now had the texture of a plowed field outside the camp. She could see thousands of lead slugs imbedded in the chipped ice, remnants of the tons of ammunition fired during the seige.

Paz was relieving himself, standing at the latrine with his back to the camp, when he heard her scream. He had never heard Rica scream like that. He had never heard *anyone* scream like that.

He spun around and watched with the greatest terror he had ever felt as the slender glassy rope surrounding Rica's ankles dragged her into the dark opening of an igloo's narrow foyer. She caught hold of the entrance with both hands. Her compressed white fingers were all he could see, but she was still yelling for help.

Paz dashed toward the igloo. He dived forward and skidded the last twenty feet across the wet ice like a batter sliding into home. Joan and Cliff lunged from their tents. Together they grabbed one of Rica's hands and managed to match the force with which Paz was pulling on the other. Eddy jumped down from the ALV, where he was standing watch, and reached in for Rica's head. "No!" Paz yelled at the muscle-bound private. "You will break her neck!"

Instead of pulling Rica free of the cephid, they pulled both her and her captor out of the igloo. Its gelatinous body discharged from the foyer with a sucking pop.

Before any of them could reach for a gun, the transparent beast jerked itself upright and held Rica in front of it. Two glassy arms slid around her narrow waist several times, and the powerful brute lifted her off the ice, waving her back and forth like a doll. Two open claw-beaks hovered around her head. Their edges looked razor sharp to Paz. The cephid's vulnerable eyes were retracted within its body behind its hostage.

Joan knelt on one knee, using the other to steady the SAW she had brought from her tent. "I can't get a shot!"

The cephid began backing away, leaving the camp.

Paz drew his survival knife and charged, yelling Rica's name. A few feet from the cephid, he jumped like a pouncing tiger. He twisted in midair to dodge a whipping arm and landed with his inch-long crampon spikes planted firmly in the cephid's torso. The slimy beast quivered and gulped but maintained its grip on Rica. Still riding on the cephoid's side, Paz saw one of the opaque eyeballs inside the bulky barrel of bluish jelly. He stabbed at it, sinking his knife in to the hilt. The eye jerked sideways, and the blade missed it.

The other eye popped up from the opposite side of the barrel top, stretching away from Paz at the end of a two-foot stalk. He reached across the barrel and grabbed the stalk at its base with his left hand. Apparently realizing its mistake, the cephid attempted to retract the light blue eye but could not pull the rigid, apple-size organ through Paz's clenched fist. Paz reached with his knife to sever the eye stalk.

The cephid's cone of toothed tongues shot up out of the barrel top. The four radula lobes parted, then slapped back together around Paz's left forearm. His fist opened involuntarily and he bellowed in agony as the inch-long teeth sliced through his flesh and scraped along his bones. The closed radula cone retracted, dragging his bloody appendage down into the transparent gullet.

Paz had never felt such pain. For a moment it seemed to take away his breath and all of his strength. The overcast but still bright daylight seemed to grow dark. Yet he maintained his grip on the knife. He also began stomping the cephid's side with his crampons, as fast and hard as he could pump his legs, allowing the creature's grip on his arm to hold him upright. Groaning in agony, he hacked at the arms encircling Rica's waist. The spongy flesh was surprisingly easy to cut.

Before Paz could sever any of its arms, the cephid released him. The radula popped up and opened wide, and Paz fell backward onto the ice, banging his head.

Cliff had neither a knife nor a gun. He had never felt so helpless. He watched in horror as the cephid backed away, still holding Rica above the ice. The constricting arms had prevented her from breathing for so long that her normally bronze face had turned a splotchy beige color.

Blood from Paz's arm was diffusing down into the cephid's gullet.

Joan ran to Paz and fell to her knees beside him, cradling his mutilated arm. Paz was squirming on his back, trembling and whimpering, trying to get his bearings. For a moment Cliff could not take his eyes off the nineteen-year-old's horrible injury. The thumb and forefinger were gone. The remaining three fingers had no flesh on the tips. The forearm was shredded from the elbow down, the skin hanging in loose strips. When Joan splashed cold meltwater on the limb in an attempt to dull the pain, it washed away blood and Cliff saw a long swath of pale bone.

Joan looked up. Her thin lips were constricted into a white ring around her front teeth.

Paz spun his knife across the ice to Cliff. "Help her!" he commanded.

Cliff grabbed the knife and sprinted toward Rica, realizing that he would crawl down the brute's gullet and cut out its heart from the inside if that was what it took to free her. Joan and Eddy were also converging on the beast, obviously eager to take over where Paz had left off.

Before he could reach the cephid, its arms loosened and Rica dropped to the ice on all fours. She weakly crawled toward Cliff, gasping for air and slipping on the wet ice. The cephid staggered back and forth a few times on its stubby flippers, then stood still. Its arms hung limply on the ice all around it.

Cliff ran to Rica and helped her up, keeping an eye on the cephid. "I guess . . . the igloos . . . were a bad idea," she gasped.

They held each other and watched the cephid's strange behavior. Rica continued gulping air. "Paz must have . . . stabbed it . . . in the brain," she said.

"I don't think so," Cliff said. "Something else is wrong." After the physical punishment he had seen other cephids take in stride, he doubted that this one had been mortally wounded by Paz's knife or crampons. Yet it seemed to have lost either its will or its stamina.

The cephid was standing almost still when a flood of clear water erupted from beneath it, surging out in all directions. The tide washed over their boots and dispersed on the ice. Cliff held his breath to avoid gagging on the reek of dead fish until the wind blew it away.

As the flood surged out, the cephid's barrel-body collapsed straight downward, getting shorter and fatter until it became an eight-foot-wide pancake. The arms rose up into rigid arches and quivered for a moment. Then the arches began spasmodically straightening, slapping the wet ice, and becoming arches again.

"It's seizing!" Cliff exclaimed.

The cephid began trembling all over. Its skin quivered and puckered, alternately clenching into a wrinkled and warty texture, then stretching out smooth. Waves of color rippled across the transparent pancake—maroon, tan, sea green, periwinkle. Even its vile smell had changed, becoming less like dead fish and more like pig manure.

"What's happening to it?" Jory asked from a safe distance.

Bonnie had also emerged to see what was causing the wet slaps. She and Joan helped Paz walk to the medical tent. His destroyed arm left a trail of diluted blood on the ice.

Cliff cautiously circled the creature. Its eyes followed him, apparently stretching upward as far as they could. He imagined a pleading expression in the W-shaped irises, which were constricted so tightly that the pupils were barely discernable hairlines. A pinkish-beige color had become permanent and was growing stronger, not on the cephid's skin but somewhere inside its pancake-shaped body. Daring to step closer, Cliff saw that the opaque color followed the spiraling gut.

Rica went to check on Paz. Her face was still pale and her legs wobbled as she walked, but she had caught her breath.

A minute later the cephid's arms stopped thrashing. The creature lay still except for some twitching at the tips of the arms. The lumpy intestinal tract had become an opaque dirty pink mottled with purplish splotches.

"Now we know why they only attack at night," Cliff said. "They must have evolved in total darkness. Five minutes of sunlight just killed this one . . . on a cloudy day!"

"Are you saying it died of *sunburn*?" Jory asked.

"Exactly," Cliff said. "I think."

"Good Lord," Jory said. "Just like vampires." Then he bent over coughing. During the night he had developed a sore throat. "Maybe their home star doesn't radiate in the UV range," he said. "Or their planet doesn't rotate, and they come from the dark side."

"Along with the gonads, brain, and lymph glands, the gastrointestinal tract is also the most radiation-sensitive part of a human," Cliff said. "Death of the GI tract is what actually kills people with radiation sickness, unless the dose was high enough to cause rapid brain death. This makes me wonder what the sun would do to *our* intestines if they absorbed ultraviolet better than our other tissues."

"If they come from a place with no sunlight, why do they have eyes?" asked Private Gerard. He had slept through most of the commotion but had arrived in time to see the cephid's death throes.

"Their eyes are very large," Cliff said. "Adapted for low intensities. They can probably see quite well by starlight."

Rica had returned from the medical tent.

"How's Paz?" Cliff asked her.

She grimly shook her head. "Bonnie says he probably won't bleed to death. At least we know now that we're safe during the day, and you guys have your specimen to dissect. After the price Rodriguez just paid, I sure hope you learn something from it."

"Oh, we will," Cliff said. He had already started planning the autopsy.

# CHAPTER 25

# Autopsy

Cliff and Jory dragged the carcass to the pit in the center of camp. They could not get a grip on its slimy flesh, but they managed to lock their hands around its claw-beaks. They kicked its limp arms into the pit, one by one, until its center of gravity shifted over the edge and the rest of the creature slid in.

"Like a wheelbarrow full of Jell-O," Jory said. "Hard to believe they're so tough."

"And strong," Rica said with a shudder. She turned to Cliff. "It'll freeze solid at the bottom of the pit, won't it?"

"I hope so," Cliff said. "There's no other way to preserve it. I'll do what I can before it's frozen. Then I'll saw off parts and thaw them one at a time for examination."

"How do you think it got into the igloo?" Rica asked. "Did it sneak up in the sound shadow of the dome and then crawl around to the entrance when nobody was close enough to see it through the fog?"

"Impossible," Jory said. "I would have seen a bump on the side of the igloo's sound shadow. It must have crawled *over* the dome."

"Hey, Eddy," Rica shouted. "Take a flashlight and check all the igloos for cephids."

*"Pardon?"* said the bulky private.

"You don't have to crawl into them," she said. "Just shine a light in through the gun ports. And tell Joan I want her to go with you. Dr. Steadman needs my help with the autopsy." She glanced at Cliff, who was laying out what looked like surgical instruments beside the pit. "Right?" she said.

Cliff stopped counting something on his fingers and looked up. "Huh? Yeah. Sure."

Eddy left.

Jory cleared his scratchy throat and said, "Why do you want to help?"

"Why do you think?" Rica said. "You guys are not the only ones who want to see what this thing is made of."

Cliff smiled and winked at her. "Normally I would dictate into a recorder while I'm dissecting, since I can't use my hands to take notes. But we don't have a recorder, so you can be my stenographer." He nodded toward the black garbage bag he had brought to the pit.

Rica looked in the bag and found an orange hardcover field notebook with a number-five pencil attached on a string. "Okay," she said, "shoot."

Cliff jumped down into the pit. His waterproof boots landed on a tangle of the cephid's arms, and he sank into the morass of transparent flesh up to the ankles.

"Hey, shouldn't you wear a mask and gloves?" Jory asked. "I'll bet we have some."

Cliff shrugged. "It would slow me down. If this thing is carrying any diseases that are contagious to humans, we're probably infected already."

Jory blanched, grasped his sore throat, and shivered.

"The igloos are clear," Eddy reported.

Rica saw that he was standing alone. "Did you check them by yourself?" she yelled.

He shrugged. "Joan wouldn't leave Paz."

Cliff stuck one bare hand down into the tangle of cephid arms and began to feel around. "This may be a futile exercise," he said. "This thing is so transparent and squishy that

I may not be able to separate its organs. Even if I can, I probably won't recognize any of them if it's really from another planet. An extraterrestrial might resemble Earth animals on the outside because of adaptation to a similar environment, but—ouch!"

He withdrew his hand and looked at it. The tip of his forefinger had a cut that was just deep enough to bleed.

"Boy, that was dumb," he said. "I guess you can't even see their claw-beaks when they're mixed in with the other parts. Anyway, no matter what environment it's adapted to, an alien's internal organs would be a legacy from millions of years of evolution that could not have taken the same twists and turns as the lineage of invertebrates I'm familiar with. I wish I had some kind of dye that I could inject into the tissue to make the structures more visible. I thought I could see some of the organs inside the one that ate Raymond, after his blood diffused into them."

Jory abruptly dashed to the medical tent. Rica presumed he had found the autopsy too disgusting to bear.

He returned a few minutes later. His left sleeve was rolled up, and he was mashing a wad of gauze against the inside of his exposed elbow. He handed Cliff a small graduated beaker that contained a large-bore syringe and about a cup of dark red liquid.

Cliff stared at the beaker, then at Jory's arm. "Jesus Christ," he said. "Thanks, Panopalous."

"That's it. I'm done," Cliff said.

Rica had expected the dissection to take longer. He had only spent half an hour cutting into the cephid, retracting its layers, suctioning bluish slime, removing bits of meat, and palpating them in his hands, making various noises and expressions of curiosity and frustration. Nevertheless, the carcass was beginning to freeze and Cliff was shivering and groaning from the cold. He could barely bend his wet fingers.

Jory's blood had been sufficient to stain the cephid's tissues a dark translucent red. Crimson streaks were smeared all over Cliff's coveralls and the pit's frosty walls. As Cliff had hoped, the blood made the specimen's internal structures vaguely discernable.

So far, the autopsy had failed to confirm or refute his hypothesis that the cephid had died of intestinal sunburn.

"Now it's time to prepare microscope slides and fire up the DNA sequencer they sent for Dr. Wimbledon," Cliff said. "I hope we can figure out how to work it."

"Won't do any good," Jory said. "The experts think most extraterrestrials probably have a genetic code based on a nucleic acid similar to DNA, but the odds of it being composed of exactly the same nucleotides as the good old double helix are practically nil. It's almost certain that a sequencer built for terrestrial DNA won't work on alien genes."

Cliff climbed out of the reeking pit, stretched his legs, and began pacing back and forth beside the grizzly buffet of parts he had removed. The organs were laid out in a row on one side of the pit, all fourteen of them, tinting the surrounding meltwater with Jory's blood.

"Very interesting," Cliff muttered. "But about what I expected."

"You can't identify any of the organs?" Rica asked. She could see variations in size, shape, and texture among the watery hunks of meat, but they bore no resemblance to the human organs she had learned about in biology or the organs she had removed from the animals she had cooked in Puerto Rico.

"None of those things look familiar to me either," she said.

Cliff squatted to stare at the cephid parts. "They wouldn't," he said. "You've only seen the organs of vertebrates. Probably only the higher mammals."

"So you do know what some of them are?"

"Not *some* of them," he said. "*All* of them." He pointed to the organs, one at a time. "Liver, kidneys, spleen, pancreas, brain, stomach, and intestine of course."

"Are you sure that thing is its brain?" Rica asked. The gnarled lump of bloody gelatin looked more like a uterus to her, and it had a large tube running through it lengthwise.

"Quite sure," Cliff said.

"Come on, that can't be a brain," Jory said. "What's that hose thingy sticking out both ends?"

"The esophagus," Cliff said, as if it were nothing unusual.

Rica stared at the organ. *Its esophagus runs through its brain?*

"Where are the lungs?" Jory asked.

"It doesn't have any," Cliff said. "I double-checked."

"Then how can it breathe on land?"

Cliff shrugged and held his hands up in the air.

"What are those things?" Rica asked, pointing to the next two body parts. They looked like stacks of matted feathers. "Something it ate?"

"No, gills," Cliff said.

"So the aliens can still breathe underwater?" Jory asked.

"I'd guess they can," Cliff said, "although the gills could be vestigial. They were on the inside of the mantle cavity."

"Mantle?" Jory asked.

"That's what the central body of a cephalopod is called."

Rica pointed to the next item. "What's that?"

"Guess," Cliff said.

She walked around the pit and prodded the conical donut of tissue. Several words came to mind—*hole, orifice, sphincter*. "I wouldn't dare," she said.

Cliff laughed. "It's the funnel. Only mollusks have them, on Earth anyway. It's a muscular tube used to expel water for propulsion. I found it at the bottom of the mantle between the flippers. This specimen also has a valve in its throat that looks like it can direct ingested material either down the esophagus to the stomach or directly into the mantle cavity."

Cliff marched away from the pit, looking at the ground.

Jory and Rica followed him. "Where are you going?" she asked.

"I'm following the trail of blood from Paz's arm back to the spot where the cephid crashed."

"What were those last three organs?" Jory asked, coughing as he jogged to keep up.

"Hearts," Cliff said.

"All of them?"

"It has three *hearts*?" Rica asked. "I thought they didn't even have blood."

"They do," Cliff said. "And they have three hearts, just like plain old earthly cephalopods."

"How can they be transparent if they have blood?" Jory asked. "Wouldn't they at least be reddish?"

"Actually," Cliff said, "their blood is probably what gives them a bluish tint, if it's like the blood of cephalopods, which is a thin blue color instead of opaque red because the molecule that carries oxygen—hemocyanin—has a copper atom at the center instead of an iron atom like hemoglobin, and the hemocyanin is not confined within circulating cells."

They arrived at the place where the cephid had died. Cliff got down on all fours, sniffed a puddle, and made a disgusted face. Then he puckered his lips and sucked up a mouthful of the water the cephid had released.

"Oh, Lord," Jory said, looking away.

Cliff spat out the water, then hacked and spat several more times. "Salty," he said. "The cephids are big, living barrels of seawater."

# CHAPTER 26

# Dive

Rica assembled the survivors in the medical tent, which rippled and swayed in the growing southerly wind. The group was silent, subdued, exhausted. Besides the flapping fabric, all she could hear was Dale Johnson's wheezing inhalations. According to Bonnie, the federal agent was still medically stable, comatose but breathing on his own. During the night, though, he had come down with a sudden and severe respiratory infection with the same symptoms as Sophie's and Jory's.

While they waited for Eddy to return from the latrine—he had woken up with a serious case of diarrhea—Bonnie pulled Rica aside, glaring daggers at her. "I understand why you hid the morphine," Bonnie said in a hissing whisper. "But you didn't have to hide the syringes, *and you didn't have to take my fucking cigarettes!*"

"I didn't!" Rica was bewildered—she hadn't removed anything from the medical tent. She hoped the way her stomach was clenched didn't show on her face. Bonnie had problems, but she held a medical degree and was old enough to be Rica's mother, so her wrath stung.

Bonnie's squint narrowed. "You're lying, or there's a thief in this camp."

"Are all the syringes and morphine gone?" Rica asked anxiously.

Bonnie hesitated, eyeing her suspiciously. "No, the backup supply is still there."

Rica had to admit that the apparent supply shortage was serious, but she had no time to deal with it now. With any luck, Bonnie had just misplaced a few items in her drug-induced fugue and they would turn up later.

"It's almost noon," Rica announced to the group. "We have to decide what to do with the daylight we have left. We could try to prepare for another siege tonight, but we'll probably have to take refuge in the ALV and hope the cephids don't break in or wreck us."

"Why can't you just shoot them all like you did last night?" Jory asked.

"Paz?" Rica said. "How's our ammunition doing?"

The gymnastic youth lay beside Agent Johnson on a blue foam sleeping pad, his left arm wrapped in bloody bandages. His words were slurred by morphine.

"We started with . . . with almost two hundred thousand rounds. Now we have about a hundred."

"A hundred thousand?"

"No, a hundred."

"There is one thing we can do," Rica said. "Our biggest problem last night was seeing through the fog. Believe it or not, we have floodlights and a generator. Jory, you're the engineer—I'll leave it to you to figure out how to elevate the lights above camp while Cliff and I are diving. That would help us aim grenades. We still have plenty of those."

"Diving?" Bonnie said. "We're all about to die here, and you want to go diving?"

Rica had already discussed it with Cliff while he was exchanging his bloody coveralls for a pair that had belonged to Dr. Wimbledon. Cliff was the only other survivor with deep scuba diving experience. He had seemed eager to help her attempt to complete the Marines' primary mission objective.

"The Floe is still heading north and still accelerating,"

Rica said. "And they told us it will cause a major earthquake if it plows into Hawaii. There are plenty of explosives back on the Globemaster, but my only hope of knocking out the drive is to get down in the water where I can locate the propellers by homing in on the sound."

Bonnie scowled at Rica reproachfully. "I can't believe you're still thinking about that after all that's happened to us. We should all stick together and wait here for a rescue."

Rica sighed. "At this point, we have to face the possibility that no one is coming to rescue us. Besides, U.S. Marines fight to their objective no matter what. We don't give up just because we've suffered heavy casualties."

"Not all of us are Marines," Bonnie muttered.

"But you *are* a United States citizen," Rica said. "That makes you responsible for national defense if the military needs your help. If you still aren't convinced, consider this. We still don't know a damn thing about the Floe. It could be an invasion platform with one hell of a biological defense system, and it's now close enough to launch a cruise missile strike on Hawaii. If we don't stop it, our government may resort to other means, and the slight possibility of survival that we've been clinging to will be eliminated entirely."

Jory grabbed Bonnie's shoulder. "Okay. She's convinced."

Bonnie flung Jory's hand away. Then she nodded, and an expression of concern replaced the crease of anger between her bloodshot eyes. "What if you run into the cephids down there?"

Rica shrugged. "Then Cliff and I will die a few hours sooner than the rest of you."

Four of the survivors drove west to the closest edge of the Floe. The wind was strong, the overcast had thickened, and the sea was choppy—not the best diving weather. Rica and Cliff dressed in cold-water wet suits inside the ALV's troop cabin while Joan and Eddy prepared to lower them over the side with the which. With her back to Cliff, Rica stripped

down to her underwear and pulled on the tight black neoprene.

When she turned to face him, Cliff looked into her eyes
and gently gripped her shoulders. "Rica, if by some miracle
we get home alive, I'd love to take you out for a big steak
and a bottle of champagne."

She half smiled and reached up to touch his stubbly face.
"I'll take the steak. You can have the champagne."

"It's a date, then," he said. "We'll go as soon as they turn
us loose . . . and after a long sudsy bath."

Rica almost said, "Maybe we could share that, too." The
thought made her blush.

Cliff also blushed, apparently reading her mind. "You
sure know how to kick-start a man's will to live, don't you?"

"I'm trying." She gripped his face and kissed him hard on
the lips. "We'd better get started. Turn on your keypad." She
pointed to his waterproof dive computer, a bright yellow
box strapped to his left forearm. It was the size and shape of
a VHS videotape. It included a miniature keyboard with all
of the letters and numbers, enabling the diver to program it
underwater or send messages to the surface along a wire.

Joan had driven the ALV this time so Rica could show
Cliff how to use the computer and the other military equipment that he had never seen on his research dives. Rica
hoped she had not left anything out. She knew that insuffi-
cient familiarity with the equipment was a leading cause of
death on scuba dives.

They exited the ALV and strapped on tanks, valves,
masks, fins, and various other high-tech gadgets that the
CIA had borrowed from the Fourth Marine Force Reconnaissance Company in Hawaii. Rica tied on a bag beneath
her breasts that contained a waterproof canister with a timer,
detonator, and twenty pounds of octanitrocubane. Then they
donned climbing harnesses, clamped on to the ALV's winch
cable, and put their weight belts on over top of everything
else so the belts could be easily jettisoned for an emergency
ascent. Rica cinched her belt up until she could hardly

breathe, knowing that the pressure would eventually loosen it by compressing the air bubbles in her thick neoprene wet suit.

Her underwater demolition training had covered every nuance of swimming and setting shaped charges, but nothing had prepared her for this. She hoped the dive was not going to be another tactical disaster like the igloos, and that it would not cost Cliff his life, making him another casualty of her inexperience along with Sergeant Gavril and Dr. Wimbledon.

To conserve their strength, they let the winch motor lower them rather than rappelling down the wall. The wind swung them back and forth. They held the slippery ice away with their arms and legs to avoid spinning and banging their heads. Their frog fins didn't help. Rica feared that the long rigid flippers might fall off and flap away in the wind.

The descent seemed to go on forever. When she looked down, the tiny streaks of whitecaps on the dark gray ocean appeared to be as far away as they were when they started. Above her, the looming white cliff and the two silhouetted heads peering over it—Joan and Eddy—did not seem to be receding either. The only apparent motion between the chaotic waves and the rolling gray clouds was the smooth wet ice sliding upward a few inches in front of her face, until a flock of black cormorants flew by below her. When she glanced over her shoulder, she saw wide open space bounded only by the junction of light gray sky and dark gray water at the horizon. The contrast between a solid wall in front and open space behind made her reel with vertigo. Or maybe it was the pain her harness was causing in her lower ribs, which had been bruised by her encounter with the cephid hiding in the igloo.

When they finally hit water, she ducked her mask below the surface and saw the ice wall extending on downward, reflecting blue wave shadows, until it disappeared in the black abyss. The wall's surface was covered with shallow pits and bumps, but no protrusions that could house some kind of thrusters.

At first they drifted free, the cable angling back as the Floe pulled ahead of them. Then the cable snapped taut, dragging them forward. The parting waves squeezed Rica's harness against her bruised ribs with even more force than her weight had applied during the descent. The water adjacent to the wall was being dragged along with the ice, but was not moving quite as fast. If they had been exposed to a full eleven-knot current, the Floe's present velocity, it would have torn them apart.

Rica's skin prickled all over with fear sweat. She kept imagining that she could feel the turbulence from radula lobes or claw-beaks snapping shut near her body. She had been experiencing recurring tremors since the cephid in the igloo had taken her hostage, and the symptoms of post-traumatic stress could be life-threatening now that a delayed reaction or an uncoordinated movement could cause her to drown.

Swimming with the Floe to lessen the drag, she yelled, "Todd didn't catch any sharks, did he?"

"I think he did," Cliff replied. "Why?"

He was armed with a tranquilizer pistol and a six-foot pole with a cup at the end that held a twelve-gauge shotgun shell. When the shell was thrust forcefully at a firm target, a pin at the base of the cup would detonate it. The "boom stick" was a formidable weapon. It was currently loaded with a magnum charge and fifteen balls of 00 buckshot, each equivalent to a .33-caliber bullet. Unfortunately, the boom stick was also awkward to reload and dangerous to other divers.

Rica was equipped with the latest innovation in portable harpoons. The slender gun fired an arrowlike shaft that trailed a thin polymer cable spooled on a reel in the stock. It was even more awkward to reload than the boom stick, but a quiver strapped to her thigh contained five spare harpoon-and-reel combinations.

The heaviest piece of equipment Rica carried was a battery-powered spool with five hundred feet of insulated line that could transmit a signal between the dive computers and the surface crew. The reel could also pull a diver through still water at several knots. The end of the reel's line was connected to a similar line running alongside the ALV's winch cable and to the winch cable itself, allowing the divers to remain tethered to the ALV while swimming beyond the reach of its cable.

She and Cliff were connected to each other by a separate ten-meter tether.

Rica shouted over the water rushing around them. "The deadliest things down there won't be sharks or cephids. They'll be the current, the gas, and the cold." She paused to blow salt water away from her lips. "The wind on our way down was nothing compared to what the Floe's slipstream may do to us underwater."

"I know all that," Cliff shouted. "Let's go!"

Rica unsnapped her breathing hose and regulator from its storage position on the shoulder strap of her tank pack. She ran a wet finger around the mouthpiece to moisten it, then opened the tank and tried a breath of the oxygen-nitrogen-helium mixture. The gas felt cool and thin as it filled her lungs.

With her mouthpiece in place, she rolled onto her belly and plunged her head beneath the waves, descending with a jackknife dive. She hoped Cliff could keep up, and that he would not be too preoccupied with the unfamiliar equipment to look out for trouble.

The turbulent eddies near the corner between ice, ocean, and atmosphere were strong enough to give Rica whiplash. She angled away from the wall to avoid a collision, swimming downward as hard as she could. The tether between her and Cliff pulled taut, and she looked up at his rangy silhouette.

He was just beginning his dive.

Fifty feet down, the noise of the surf was not so loud, and the Floe's wake was less turbulent. She stopped swimming for a moment to listen. To her surprise, she could not hear the familiar sound of ship screws. The only noise besides some distant whale song was a faint *whoosh* that repeated about once per second.

That must be the drive, she thought. Maybe the Floe was an experiment being conducted by humans after all, a test of some new super-quiet propulsion technology for submarines. But if that was the case, how did the cephids fit in?

HEAR IT? she typed on her dive computer. When she hit the SEND button, Cliff's computer beeped. He looked at it and nodded, releasing a cascade of bubbles.

They resumed the descent until the ice wall was barely discernible in the dim azure twilight.

When the tether pulled taut again, Rica looked up and saw that Cliff had stopped above her and a few yards astern. He was punching keys on his dive computer.

Her computer beeped. It read, HOLE.

Cliff was pointing to the wall beside him.

Rica held the harpoon gun in both hands as she was trained to hold her rifle and swam toward Cliff at full throttle, churning the water with her long rigid fins. When she got close, she saw a dark round opening about fifteen feet wide in the ice wall. She waved frantically for him to swim away from it. After her experience with the cephid in the igloo, she would never trust dark holes again. This one could be a cephid lair or an engine intake or something just as deadly that she could not even imagine.

Again Cliff pointed to the undersea ice cave.

Rica emphatically shook her head.

Simply pointing was the divers' signal for "Let's go that way." If he had just wanted her to look at the hole, he should have pointed to his eyes first. Surely he was just being lazy with his hand signals, she thought. Surely he didn't really intend to swim in there.

Cliff punched more keys on his dive computer.

Her computer beeped, and she glanced at it. The message was, DON'T GRAB. I KICK.

She looked up just in time to catch a glimpse of his flutter-kicking fin tips as they disappeared into the cavern. Two seconds later, she could see nothing within the dark cavity except the dim glows from his high-tech equipment—the green luminous dials of the watch and compass on his right wrist, the amber screen of the dive computer on his left forearm, and the twin blue buddy lights atop his shoulders.

Rica held out her open palm, the divers' sign for "Stop!" but Cliff was not looking back.

Seeing no other option, she followed him into the Floe.

# CHAPTER 27

# Tunnel

Rica had often wondered why so many recreational scuba divers wanted to swim into submerged caves. Cave diving was probably the most dangerous sport in the world, second to serious mountain climbing. She knew that a significant percentage of cave dives ended in tragedy when a diver got trapped, tangled, or disoriented in a confusing and confined space.

Now she understood.

Cliff turned on his headlamp soon after entering the dark tunnel. Rica was so transfixed by the beauty of the ice that she forgot to turn hers on as well. His lamp illuminated a narrow band of the cylindrical passage that surrounded him but was in front of her. The middle of the band was bright and yellowish, the color of the lamplight. A few feet fore and aft, the glow faded to pale sea green, then to increasingly deep shades of blue. The edges of the lamp-lit band undulated as he swam, shadows becoming pockets of light and then shadows again.

The passage curved, seemingly at random—first right, then left, then over a brief hump followed by a long plunge. Rica's teeth hurt, her ears popped constantly, and she could not seem to get enough air. Her legs were aching and she was gasping the trimix as fast as she could get it from the regulator when her dive computer began an alternating two-tone beep, like a European police car.

DEPTH, it read.

She spread her legs out straight and extended her fins sideways—a frog kick in reverse. The drag quickly stopped her descent. Cliff had stopped at the same time in response to his own computer's alarm. On the surface, they had input a total desired time for the dive. The computer had then monitored their depth, sounding an alarm when it was time to ascend, provided they came up slowly enough to decompress safely.

Her gauge indicated that they had reached 220 feet, a dangerous depth that put them in league with expert divers.

As she recovered from the exertion, breathing got easier, but only a little. The mixture she was dragging into her lungs was so dense that it felt more like a liquid than a gas.

BUMPS AHEAD, Cliff typed.

TIME TO GO, she replied.

CAME THIS FAR, he typed. FIVE MIN.

She turned on her headlamp and swam on with him. They still had plenty of oxygen, and the deadline they had programmed into the dive computers was a conservative estimate, leaving ample time for them to return to the camp before dusk and prepare for the cephids as best they could.

Dark stripes appeared on the walls ahead, parallel to the tunnel's axis. As she got closer, Rica realized that the stripes were shadows cast by their headlamps shining against objects protruding from the walls. Closer still, the foot-long objects began to take form.

They were fish.

She could see both heads and tails sticking out of the ice. The silvery scales shimmered with iridescence. The mouths gaped open. The eyes either stared straight out or were covered by murky membranes. All of the dead fish were roughly the size and shape of a man's forearm, but Rica could not tell if they all belonged to the same species. She wondered how they had come to be stuffed into round holes in the walls of the tunnel.

Rica shivered. Her limbs were starting to feel stiff with cold despite the vigorous swimming. Like a pump, her movement had been rapidly exchanging the warm water inside her wet suit with the icewater outside it. The expedition was equipped with dry suits, and she would have worn one if she had known they would be diving *inside* the Floe where the tropical water had been chilled to freezing.

She hoped the shivering would not get worse. If it did, she would be in danger of losing the regulator from her mouth and gasping in water.

Cliff grabbed one of the fish tails and pulled the carcass out of the wall. It drifted away, upside down. He peered into the hole he had unplugged, placing his face mask less than six inches from it.

Rica tugged on his shoulder, vocalizing a hum of alarm into her regulator. She had no idea what might be in the holes besides dead fish, and she was pretty sure Cliff didn't either.

When he pulled his head back, she was relieved, thinking he was ready to go. Then he yanked off the tight elastic band of his headlamp and aimed the beam with his hand, placing his face even closer to the hole. Before she could protest, he thrust his right hand in to the wrist.

Then to the elbow.

Then to the shoulder.

Rica grabbed his other arm and pulled him out. She didn't care if he kicked her.

Cliff held his headlamp over the hand he had stuck into the hole. Between his neoprene-clad thumb and forefinger, he was holding a flexible translucent object the size and shape of a small Bartlett pear. Rica paddled until her mask was a few inches from the strange orb, which had a smooth, white, iridescent surface. She saw motion inside the object, a swirling shadow, and realized that the thing was a transparent shell filled with milky circulating fluid.

And something else—whatever had made the moving shadow.

She poked the flexible orb. It rebounded like a water balloon. She reflexively jerked her head back and grunted in surprise when a complex alien shape lunged against the orb's transparent skin from the inside. Eight tiny arms curled, kinked, and wriggled against the curving membrane as if trying to reach through it and grab her mask. The cylindrical body between the writhing arms jerked back and forth like a spastic finger.

Her computer beeped with another message from Cliff: MAMA.

She replied, GO NOW.

He typed, OPENING AHEAD 10 M. Then he zipped the egg into his dive pouch and launched down the tunnel with a mighty frog kick.

Rica followed. What else could she do? Harpoon him? At least they still had enough trimix to stay down a little while longer.

She was about to type a firm order to abort the dive when the tunnel's walls abruptly disappeared and they were launched like torpedoes into a dark and infinite void. A current dragged them away from the tunnel's opening, and Rica realized that they must have emerged beneath the Floe.

She glanced at her depth gauge. They were only 430 feet down, an unusually great depth for divers but inexplicably shallow for the Floe's bottom, which they had not expected to reach.

Cliff was the first to twist around and look up at the bottom of the Floe. His mask turned toward her, flashing a reflection from her headlamp, and she saw his whole body jerk. His limbs stuck straight out in a gesture of shock and fright. He pointed to his eyes and then at something behind her. Before she could turn around, he began kicking toward the tunnel, flailing the water as if a whole school of hammerheads were nipping at his fins.

There were thousands of them. Maybe millions. *Maybe even tens or hundreds of millions.*

Rica lay suspended in the amniotic stillness of the deep equatorial Pacific Ocean, disoriented except for her knowledge that the infinite surface sliding by was above her. The flat slab of ice extended in all directions as far as her head-lamp could penetrate the clear water. It loomed out of the darkness beyond her feet, slid over her like the belly of a landing alien city ship, and disappeared into the gloom above her head.

The Floe's bottom was completely covered with cephids. The transparent creatures were hard to discern underwater, but she could tell they came in all sizes, from squirts no bigger than a dog up to monsters that could swallow a full-grown steer. They were gripping the ice with the suction cups along their arms, holding themselves rigid. All of the barrel-shaped bodies were oriented in the same direction, parallel to the Floe's movement, with their arms pointing forward. The fat cylindrical bodies absurdly reminded Rica of jet engines suspended beneath a wing.

Then she realized what the cephids were doing, and the analogy did not seem so absurd.

Waves of aqua-blue bioluminescence were rippling across the inverted field of glassy wraiths. Each wave meandered as far as she could see to the east and west and was propagating from north to south at high speed—about a hundred miles per hour, she guessed. She could see three or four waves at the same time. They passed over her about once per second. The waves were about twenty feet thick and spaced at least 150 feet apart, so each animal was flashing light from its four glowing belts for only a tiny fraction of a second.

The passing of each wave was accompanied by a swift and powerful muscular contraction. Between waves, the cephids swelled with seawater until their bodies were distended into spheres, like ticks engorged with blood. When the wave of aqua-blue light arrived, the bloated barrels flashed and contracted. The force of the water rushing out between their flippers caused the cephids to shudder and sway at the ends of their rigidly flexed arms. The four radula lobes were open while sucking in water, but they closed and protruded to form hydrodynamic cones when the cephids were thrusting forward.

The dull rhythmic whooshing Rica had heard in the water beside the Floe was much louder here. It was obviously being caused by the synchronized contractions of the cephids' funnel jets. Even the Floe's constant north-south wobble made sense now—it could be caused by the slight ebb and flow of power as new ripples of thrust began at the bow and swept backward across the bottom.

Rica felt numb with disbelief as she realized that this was the secret of the great iceberg's propulsion. It was not a self-propelled vehicle, nor a test of some new submarine technology. It was being carried on the backs of millions of swimming cephids.

But why?

She heard what sounded like a low growl. None of the cephids toiling beneath the Floe had seemed to notice her or Cliff, so she turned to look elsewhere for the source of the sound.

An enormous dark shape was approaching from the south. It seemed to be coming right at them. She waved for Cliff's attention. When he stopped swimming toward the tunnel and looked her way, she could tell that he had seen it too.

The surrounding water was surprisingly full of fish. Occasionally a cephid would detach from the Floe, zoom down to catch one, and return to its place. But there was no way the long shadow approaching from the south could be a fish. It looked more like a submarine. Rica wondered if she was about to witness the first solid evidence of alien technology.

She didn't bother trying to swim away. The huge shape was approaching too fast for her and Cliff to escape. It emitted another deep growl that she seemed to feel more than hear. The actual direction of the sound was impossible to discern underwater, but the growl was much louder than before.

The leviathan finally came close enough to her headlamp that she could make out its broad tail swishing up and down. She realized that it was a whale, and it was not coming straight at them after all. It was swimming on a horizontal bearing that would pass at least a hundred feet below them.

Rica resumed breathing, feeling her tense muscles relax.

The whale abruptly angled up toward them, opening its mouth. Rica could see hundreds of conical teeth the size of drinking cups in its long, straight, narrow lower jaw. As it came closer, she could see its tongue and a network of light scars crisscrossing its enormous gray head.

She had no time to react to the realization that she was about to die after all. The remaining second of her life was not even long enough to type a message to the surface so Joan and Eddy would know what had happened. The whale was so close now that she could tell it was going for her instead of Cliff. She hoped her death would buy him enough time to escape.

The leviathan's intention was unmistakable as its jaws opened wider to engulf her. The current of water being forced aside by its massive head shoved her backward. She could see deep into its throat.

The jaws clamped shut with a thud and zoomed past her. The surge of water expelled from the whale's empty mouth twisted her upside down, and a bump from its lips spun her around. She caught a glimpse of its incongruously small black eye staring back at her. One of the winglike tail flukes swished over her head as the whale arched downward and descended as rapidly as it had charged upward.

Cliff swam over to her side and gripped her arm, frantically pointing upward.

She rolled over and looked up at the Floe. At least a dozen cephids had detached from its surface. They were descending at high speed, like incoming aerial bombs, using their funnel jets for propulsion and letting their long arms stream out behind them.

She assumed they intended to attack her and Cliff.

When they passed by just fifty feet away and kept going, she realized they were pursuing the whale.

Cliff began typing on his dive computer.

Rica noticed a cephid that appeared to be dead. It was far below and off to the west, drifting upside down. Its arms waved lazily in the weak eddies at the outer edge of the Floe's influence on the currents. No sooner had she spotted the drifting cephid than an even larger whale appeared out of the depths and snatched it.

The cephid was not dead after all. Its four belts of aqua blue light came on, but their glow was flickering and feeble, and it made no moves to defend itself. The whale performed a quick about-face and descended with its prey's limp arms streaming back from both sides of its clenched jaws.

The armada of cephids chasing the other whale broke off their pursuit at a depth somewhat shallower than the depth where the paralyzed cephid had been drifting. Instead of gradually slowing down, they abruptly flared out their arms, reversed their orientation, and came to a halt with a frantic series of thrusts from their funnels. Then they ascended at a more leisurely pace on a trajectory that was angled to the north so they could catch up with their former positions on the Floe.

Rica's dive computer beeped. The message from Cliff read, SHE MISTOOK YOU FOR CEPHID. She wondered how he knew the whale that had almost eaten her was female.

The retreating group of cephids stopped swimming. Their eye stalks extended, pointing toward Cliff and Rica. They were less than two hundred feet away and at the same depth as the divers. Some of their light belts flashed rapid signals.

Rica glanced at Cliff's mask and saw the alarm in his eyes.

The cephids were charging straight for them.

She kicked upward toward the opening of the tunnel.

Cliff grabbed her arm and stopped her. His other hand was pointing downward.

She grunted a tone of protest into her regulator and strained to free her arm, watching the cephids accelerate.

He maintained his grip while typing another message with his free hand.

Her computer beeped again, but she ignored it. The cephids had already closed half the distance. All she could think about was getting back to the tunnel. Her struggle to break free had turned into fight-or-flight panic.

Cliff grabbed her left wrist and held it up in front of her mask so she could see nothing but the glowing amber computer screen. It read, TUST.

*Tust?*

Trust!

She stopped struggling and looked at Cliff. He was jabbing a finger at the abyss again. He let go of her arm and dolphin kicked downward, streamlining his body by pressing his arms to his sides.

Rica glanced back at the cephids. The one in the lead was pulling forward two of its claw-beaks, and its radula was beginning to open.

She looked up at the tunnel entrance. Even if she cut the tether between her and Cliff, it was too late to outrun them.

She jackknifed and followed Cliff's descent, dolphin kicking with all her might.

# CHAPTER 28

# Predator

Rica willed all of the energy in her body into the powerful muscles of her back and legs, thinking of nothing but speed. The water rushed by her face so fast that she feared it would rip her mask off. She barely noticed when she zoomed downward past Cliff.

A moment later, the thirty-foot tether between them jerked taut. She tried to drag him along for a few seconds, but then her body gave out. All she could do was gulp down painfully deep breaths of trimix and wait upside down for the cold embrace of the cephids.

To her surprise, several seconds passed without the sensations of constricting tentacles or slicing claw-beaks. She used her arms to turn over and look up.

Cliff had not been caught, as she'd expected, but he wasn't even trying to swim. He was stretched out, facing upward, with his ankles crossed and his hands tucked leisurely behind his head, as if he were relaxing on a beach. At first Rica thought his strange posture must be some trick of the light, but then she realized that he really was affecting a position of repose.

She looked above him.

The cephids had stopped. They were hovering together,

just out of reach, flashing signals to one another with their aqua-blue light belts. She noticed that they had halted at the same depth where they had broken off their pursuit of the whale.

To her amazement, Cliff waved at them, then gave them the finger.

She typed a question mark on her dive computer and sent it to Cliff.

He typed a response. Instead of sending it to her computer, he swam over and held his own computer up where she could read its screen. It read, NO MORE MESSAGES. THEY HEARD THE BEEP.

That much she understood. The cephids had seemed oblivious to their presence until he had sent her the message about the whale. But why had the cephids just aborted their chase?

Before she could type the question, Cliff pointed to the thermometer on his wrist. Behind his mask, his eyes were smiling. She looked at his water temperature readout, then at her own, and she finally understood.

She gazed all around, still catching her breath from the narrow escape. It was the first time she had really tried to see as far as she could into the darkness beneath the Floe. She could discern at least five or six cephids that were drifting alone and inert like the one the second whale had caught. All of them were at depths below her and Cliff. She could also see dozens of healthy cephids zooming down from the Floe to catch fish. None of them were descending beyond her depth, although the fish were just as abundant below her.

WHAT NOW? she typed.

WE WAIT, he replied.

Rica checked her trimix reserves, then his. She returned her wrist to a position where he could read her computer and typed, NO TIME.

NO CHOICE was his response.

They waited. Watching her chronometer, Rica concentrated on breathing slowly and relaxing her muscles to minimize her rate of oxygen consumption.

One by one, the hovering cephids returned to their positions beneath the Floe. Some of them kept their eye stalks extended for a while, bending them to look down at the divers. When the last of the eyes retracted, Rica pointed to the tunnel and showed Cliff the word she had already typed: FAST.

They jettisoned their weight belts. Rica hung on to Cliff and depressed the trigger of her motorized cable reel. They kicked to boost their acceleration as the reel pulled them up the cable toward the tunnel.

They had almost made it when a single eye sprouted from one of the millions of transparent cephids covering the Floe's bottom. The other eye joined it, and the stalks curved, pointing toward the ascending divers. The cephid detached and sliced through the water, making twice their speed with a single squirt from its funnel. Rica prayed that it would not announce their presence and none of the closer cephids would notice them.

Cliff saw the ghostly predator bearing down on them and fumbled with his boom stick. Rica held on to the cable reel with one hand and aimed her harpoon gun with the other. The cephid was almost upon them. It flared out its eight arms, slowing its charge and preparing to envelop Cliff in a thin membrane that stretched between its arms like an umbrella—a part of cephid anatomy that Rica had not noticed before.

She fired.

The harpoon passed through the cephid as easily as her headlamp beam and sped on into the darkness. She depressed the lever that released the harpoon line. The line spun off the reel and zipped through the cephid, disappearing beyond her light. She could see no signs of injury on the attacking predator, but it was obviously hurt. It closed its arms into a tight, quivering ball and tumbled past them, spinning end over end.

She grabbed Cliff's hand, and they dolphin kicked as the motorized cable reel pulled them into the tunnel.

As they rounded the first bend, Rica looked back and saw that the wounded cephid had regained control. It was whipping back and forth, its eye stalks weaving like angry cobras. Then it stopped, looked at the tunnel, and launched toward them with its arms streaming behind.

Rica pointed to the motorized reel, then to the harpoon quiver on her thigh.

Cliff seemed to understand. He grabbed the reel in one hand and held on to her gear harness with the other, freeing both of her hands so she could load another harpoon. Trying to concentrate on her task, Rica reminded herself that the cephid was not as close as the distortion from her mask made it appear.

The reel dragged their bodies against the smooth ice when they rounded bends in the tunnel.

Rica knew they were ascending way faster than sixty feet per minute, the maximum safe rate.

She frantically fumbled with the harpoon gun, glancing behind her. At first she could see the cephid only when the tunnel was straight for several yards, but the enraged predator steadily gained on them until it was close enough to remain visible even around the curves. Its first four arms reached out in front of it, snapping at them with claw-beaks the size of dinner plates. Rica had no doubt that the beaks could sever a human ankle with one bite. When she felt something gently tug at her left foot, she looked down and saw a neat triangular gap in the tip of her neon-green flipper.

She felt a sharp pain in her chest.

She abruptly exhaled, and silvery bubbles exploded from her valve. For a moment Rica forgot about the predator nipping at her fins, because she knew that she had just come within a second of dying from a ruptured lung. She had made the most dangerous mistake a diver can make. She had forgotten to breathe while ascending, allowing the gas that was confined within her lungs to expand as the pressure around her decreased.

Cliff shook her arm and pointed ahead. She looked up just in time to see the cylindrical forest of dead fish—sharp fins, frowning mouths, leering eyes—approaching at high speed.

She instinctively closed her eyes as she and Cliff plowed a furrow through the scaly bodies, which pummeled her head and arms. She held the harpoon gun in front of her like a shield, fearing that one of the heavy fish would knock the regulator out of her mouth. When they emerged from the section with egg tubes, she looked back and saw that several of the fish had been torn from their tubes or had broken apart, spilling their guts into the water. The pursuing cephid had paused to scavenge the drifting bits of carrion.

The two-tone alarms in their dive computers started beeping simultaneously.

Rica looked at her screen. It read, N2 PARTIAL CRIT, which meant that the partial pressure of nitrogen dissolved in their bodies had reached a critical level according to the computer's calculations. She knew that those calculations were based on several uncertain input parameters. Perhaps she and Cliff could survive climbing a little farther before stopping to let the nitrogen diffuse from their blood back into the gas in their lungs. Or perhaps it was already too late, unless they quickly descended to recompress.

She toggled to another screen showing their schedule of decompression stops. They had already missed two. The chances of injury would still be small if they stopped here for a while, but if they didn't . . . within hours after leaving the water, they would die one of the most painful deaths imaginable as nitrogen boiled from their blood to form obstructing bubbles in their joints, hearts, and brains.

Cliff stopped the reel motor. They both splayed their flippers to halt their ascent. Swallowing to adjust the pressure in her ears, Rica turned to face back down the tunnel.

They had no choice but to make a stand.

Cliff held the boom stick like a spear while Rica worked frantically, still trying to reload the harpoon gun. Her fingers were numb and stiff from the cold.

Once the gun was ready, she pulled the loaded harpoon's line off the reel and tied the line to the base of another harpoon so that the two projectiles were joined by a tether about thirty feet long. If she shot the cephid when it first came into view, she might have time to reload again, but only once. And she was sure that just launching two more shafts through the predator's body would not stop it.

Rica knew that her rapid breathing from fear and exertion was using up oxygen too fast, but there was nothing she could do about it. She did not dare pause to check her gauge.

As she tied the final knot in the harpoon lines, Cliff shook her arm. She looked down the tunnel, which was a vertical shaft at the moment. The cephid materialized out of the dark depths—first its snapping claw-beaks, then its long glassy arms, then its extended eye stalks, and finally its rotund body. It swarmed up at them, the beak-tipped arms lunging like striking snakes.

Rica fired. Again she hit her mark, and the shaft passed through the cephid as if the monster were as ethereal as it looked. The harpoon continued on with no apparent loss of speed until it embedded itself firmly in the wall. The cephid flinched but kept coming after them, letting the thin harpoon line slide through it. Rica jerked open the gun's breech and shoved in the second harpoon, forcing herself to concentrate on the gun instead of watching the monster that was almost upon them.

When the gun was finally loaded, she did not pause to look up, much less aim—she just fired. This harpoon went nowhere near the cephid. It embedded itself in the ice right in front of her.

She grabbed Cliff's arm in one hand and the cable reel in the other, letting the harpoon gun swing from its neck strap. She depressed the reel's trigger and kicked upward to give the motor a boost, dragging Cliff behind her.

The cephid continued its charge, ignoring the line between anchored harpoons that was sliding through its body.

Rica was suddenly surrounded by bubbles as their accelerating ascent caught up with the air they had released a few seconds before.

One of the lunging claw-beaks bit a hunk out of Cliff's right flipper. He pulled his knees up to his chest, grunting with fright.

The cephid halted with an abrupt jerk and swung sideways against the wall, its arms flung out in front of it. The tether between the anchored harpoons had jerked taut.

Rica released the reel's trigger and splayed her flippers to stop her ascent, wondering if fatal nitrogen bubbles had already formed in her blood.

Cliff also stopped, then jackknifed and swam back down the shaft until he was just beyond the flailing cephid's reach. He fired his tranquilizer pistol, and the dart injected its contents into one of the cephid's extended radula lobes. The effect was immediate but minor—the two-ton predator merely seemed a little less determined to get free and dice its prey.

Cliff poked one of its arms with the boom stick, but its spongy flesh was too soft to detonate the shotgun shell.

The cephid twisted around, reached for the narrow filament passing through its body, and snipped itself loose with one claw-beak.

Rica triggered the cable reel and kicked upward, hoping the tether between her and Cliff was short enough to pull taut and jerk him away from the predator. She wondered why Cliff was not also kicking upward. He appeared to be too close to outswim the freed cephid. Had he given up?

She watched in agonizing dread as the cephid swarmed up at him. Cliff was not moving except for one foot, which was lifting its long frog flipper up in front of him. When the cephid was upon him, half a second from snipping off his legs, he jabbed the end of the boom stick against the rigid plastic flipper about an inch beyond his toes.

The twelve-gauge shell detonated with a thud that felt heart-stoppingly loud underwater. White light flashed, a bubble the size of a beach ball briefly appeared around Cliff's foot, and the broad spray of pellets ripped through both of the cephid's grapefruit-size eyes, leaving nothing but bronze and sky-blue tatters. Rica saw a neat round hole in Cliff's flipper as he kicked away from the mortally wounded beast, which was hysterically swiping at its truncated eye stalks with all of its arms.

They waited for the dive computers to tell them they had decompressed long enough. Divers who had worked for several hours at such depths had to endure *weeks* of gradual decompression in a hyperbaric chamber, but Rica and Cliff had not stayed down long enough for that much nitrogen to enter their bodies. The computers said they could ascend to the next stop in an hour. Rica checked her chronometer. It was already after 2:00 P.M.

SHOTGUNS WORK, Cliff typed.

Rica typed, MORE MAY COME.

Cliff nodded and reloaded the boom stick.

Ten minutes later, their dive computers beeped simultaneously.

They looked down at their forearms.

The message was from Joan and Eddy on the surface: STORM IS BAD. DARK UP HERE. CEPHIDS R COMING.

# CHAPTER 29

# Climbers

Rica let the motorized reel pull them up through the tunnel at top speed. They had barely begun the first of three decompression stops, but the implications of the message from Joan and Eddy were clear: if they did not ascend now, no one would be left on the surface to hoist them up the Floe's side.

When they reached the tunnel's entrance, the water outside was completely dark. Rica saw a dim flash followed by muted thunder. The arc of electricity had to be close for its flash to be visible at the tunnel's depth. She pictured the elevated igloo camp on its exposed stage and wondered if it was about to be struck by lightning. Maybe it already had been.

The next flash was brighter. It illuminated a continuous swarm of transparent cephids blocking the tunnel's entrance. They were purposefully climbing the submerged wall, gliding upward past the entrance with rhythmic extensions and contractions of their arms, gripping the smooth ice with their suction cups. How are we going to get through *that*? she wondered.

At least the climbing cephids seemed to take no notice of the two shivering divers drifting just inside the tunnel.

Cliff tapped her mask and pointed behind him.

She glanced backward.

A cephid with both eyes intact was jetting through the tunnel toward them. Behind it she saw two more, then four, then many.

Rica typed a message to Joan and Eddy: PULL FAST. Then she depressed the reel's trigger, held on to Cliff, and closed her eyes as they accelerated.

Rica knew her request had reached the surface when she felt the drag increase threefold. She and Cliff bumped along the ice tunnel and shot out into the Floe's turbulent wake, knocking a rubbery cephid aside. Then they were out of the water—dripping, swinging, slamming against the cold wet side of the Floe.

The unfamiliar force of gravity pulled down on Rica and her heavy gear, causing her climbing harness to bite painfully into her groin and armpits. She held her breath to lessen the pain around her bruised lower ribs.

It felt like the ocean was still surrounding her, even after she could see its raging surface below her feet. It filled her eyes, and when she spat out her mouthpiece and gasped for fresh air, she drew water into her lungs. Choking, she swiped at her face and realized that she was being pelted by dense rain.

It was hours before sunset, yet the sky was almost completely dark. When lightning flashed, she saw dense black clouds rolling overhead. The waves leaped and growled and rammed against the Floe as if reaching up to drag her back down.

She found the presence of mind to clamp herself and Cliff securely on to the ALV's winch cable so they no longer had to rely on the thinner cable from the motorized reel.

By the time she stopped coughing enough to take in her surroundings, the cable had pulled her and Cliff above the climbing horde of cephids. Lightning strobed on the glassy wet bodies covering the wall beneath her, making their smooth, coordinated, boneless movements appear choppy.

More cephids were emerging by the hundreds from the crashing black waves. They seemed oblivious to the driving rain and turbulent wind.

When Rica looked up, she saw that not all of the cephids were below her and Cliff after all. One slithering creature about the size of a pony was right above them, gliding up the ice as if by magic. Cliff saw it too. They both kicked away from the wall, trying to avoid a collision.

Cliff's shoulder slammed against the creature's dangling rear end.

The cephid leaned out from the wall, eye stalks extended, apparently wondering what had hit it. Since the impact had come from below, it kept looking downward while they ascended above it. Rica resumed breathing when she thought they were beyond the monster's reach.

Something wrapped around her left leg and constricted. She cried out in pain. It felt like the two thin bones in her calf were being squeezed together, crushing the tender layers of flesh caught between them. The harness dug into her groin as if she had jumped from the roof of a house and landed astraddle a sawhorse. Something popped in her hip. It felt like her left leg was being pulled off.

Rica shrieked in agony again and again.

The winch cable had stopped ascending.

Cliff frantically tried to twist around so he could use his boom stick, but his harness was holding him in a position facing away from her.

The cable began to descend, jerking.

Rica heard distant shouts through the wind and rain and crashing surf. A powerful floodlight beam hit her from above. She looked up and could see nothing but the blinding light.

A dark, ragged-edged shape rushed down at her out of the radiance. She lowered her face just in time as a chunk of ice the size of a shoe slammed into the top of her head. It sliced through the wet suit's hood and lacerated her scalp.

She looked up again, shielding her eyes with an arm and

weeping from the pain in her leg and hip. This time she could see a small black square protruding over the edge of the Floe, silhouetted against the lightning-streaked clouds. The square could only be the snout of the ALV. She realized that the cephid was pulling down on her leg hard enough to drag the thirty-ton machine off the Floe.

She drew her diving knife from the sheath on her thigh, trying to think through the haze of pain and panic. The cephid applied an abrupt tug. Rica screamed and dropped the knife.

She reached out to Cliff, who was loading his tranquilizer pistol. "Give me!" she yelled, grasping at his knife.

He was still facing away, but he managed to hand the knife to her.

She bent over sideways toward her bound calf.

The cephid had climbed until its extended eyes were level with her foot, which had lost its frog flipper. The creature's conical radula was slowly opening. The interlocking triangular teeth quivered and stood erect as they pulled apart, draping long strings of gummy saliva that melted away in the rain.

Rica jabbed and swung at the constricting arm. She managed to stab it once. Then she cut a deep gash in her own leg.

It was impossible for her to reach far enough in such an awkward position. In desperation, she held the knife by the very tip of its handle and slashed again at the arm, which was now stained red by the rain-diluted blood running down from her cut. A long incision appeared in the glassy coil. The incision was pulled open by the tension on the arm, but the cephid's flesh did not tear and its grip remained strong.

The monster's waving eyes apparently saw what Rica was trying to do. It reached up another arm, grabbed her wrist, and pulled her over to the left.

She felt something spring apart up and down the right side of her spine. The pain in her back blew away every other sensation her brain was receiving. It was deep and sharp and so intense that her vision shrank to a small disk.

A gunshot rang out, the distinctive boom of Joan's fifty-caliber rifle. The cephid's left eyeball exploded at the end of its stalk, leaving a ragged stump. Both the stump and the other eye instantly retracted into the barrel-body. The cephid slithered across the wall until it was shielded beneath Cliff and Rica.

The arm wrapped around her wrist was squeezing so tightly that she could not feel her hand, so she knew she had dropped Cliff's knife only when she saw it fall. The bloody knife bounced off one of the cephid's tongues and fell past the beast, glinting in the floodlight beam as it tumbled away through the downpour. The cephid shot down a free arm and caught the knife in midair, then lifted it back toward Rica. She feared that the fiend intended to stab her, but it just held the knife with the squirming suction cups of another arm and sniffed at her blood on its blade.

The cephid dropped the knife into its maw, retracted its radula, and swallowed the blood-dipped delicacy.

A second elapsed.

The cephid's grip on Rica loosened. She heard a spluttering gurgle and saw at least two hundred pounds of water and dead fish eject from its bottom. The load of waste tumbled down the ice wall onto the rest of the cephid army, which had almost caught up.

Her attacker let go of both her and the wall. It fell sideways, its limp arms swinging outward as its body spun around. It plowed into the throng below, knocking three of its comrades loose.

The three detached cephids extended their arms to form rigid arches like the spokes of an umbrella. Rica could barely see the thin membrane stretched between the arms, catching air as they fell. The cephids drifted on the southerly wind, away from the Floe and to the north. Their heavy barrel-bodies swung to and fro beneath their built-in parachutes. Just above the crashing waves, they whipped their arms upward and clamped them together to form a long rigid cone. Each cephid split the water with its bottom end, trailing the cone of arms like the tail of a comet.

Several other cephids were now close enough to reach up and grab Rica's ankles. She tried to untangle the harpoon gun, but her right hand could not reach it and her left shoulder had been dislocated when the cephid grabbed her wrist.

The cable lurched, then pulled them up the wall faster than the winch could possibly reel it in. Eddy and Joan were evidently backing up the ALV. Cliff shouted something, but a thunderclap obliterated his words.

He repeated the shout. "Are you all right?"

This time she heard him and yelled, "No!"


Joan relocated Rica's left shoulder and bandaged her lacerated calf while the ALV lunged across bumps and skidded through meltwater streams. Eddy was driving recklessly, trying to put as much distance as possible between them and the cephids by the time they reached camp.

No lightning was visible in the windowless troop cabin, but thunder reverberated through the LIBA ceramic armor and Kevlar spall lining that covered the aluminum walls. Tropical rain hammered the roof like a thousand kettle drums.

Cliff repeatedly wiped his bloody nose. The blood was draining from his aching sinuses, which had filled with fluid as water pressure squeezed them during the rapid descent.

Rica was prone on her back, gasping and groaning. The cut on her scalp was still bleeding, but not severely. Perspiration dripped from her smooth bronze face. Her lips were drawn back from her clenched white teeth in a grimace of agony, and a spasm was arching her spine off the floor as if she were in labor. Cliff wondered if her symptoms were being exacerbated by the bends, which were liable to strike them both at any moment.

"Back hurts . . . so bad . . . can't feel my leg," she moaned, gripping his arm with one trembling hand.

Oh, God, she's paralyzed, he thought. "Rica, can you move your toes?"

She nodded and wriggled her toes. He realized that she was talking about the pain from the oozing gash on her calf.

The ALV skidded to a halt. "Joan, could you come up here?" Eddy shouted.

Cliff heard some whispering; then Joan yelled, "What do you mean, we're lost?"

Cliff joined her at the door of the driver's box.

"Look," Eddy pleaded, shaking the frayed and water-stained satellite photo that Rica had been using to navigate when she drove the ALV. "When I line this up with the compass, the landmarks out there don't make any sense."

Joan rolled her eyes. "Bless your heart, Eddy. Let me drive."

Eddy swung his bulk from the driver's seat and stepped out beside Cliff, looking hurt.

Joan sat and looked into the periscope, then at the photo, then back at the periscope.

"Fuck," she said.

"Maybe the rain is melting the Floe and it doesn't look like the picture anymore," Eddy said.

"Not just since we drove down here," Cliff said. "Up till now, we could still recognize the landmarks after three days of tropical sunshine. Joan, try rotating the photo away from alignment with the compass."

Joan slowly twisted the photo to the left, then to the right. She abruptly stopped and looked into the periscope. "I'll be damned. You're right, Steadman!"

"What?" Eddy said. "What's going on?"

Cliff looked back at Rica, trying to think in spite of his exhaustion and depleted nerves. "The Floe has changed course," he said.

# CHAPTER 30

# Sea Monsters

The thunder and lightning had stopped by the time they reached camp, but the tropical downpour still roared on the hard ice like highway traffic. It also pounded on the roof of the medical tent, where the survivors gathered to exchange news and plan for the army of cephids that they presumed was on its way.

Dale Johnson had died while the divers were gone, but Sophie was better. She was crying again.

Paz was sleeping, drugged with morphine. His mutilated arm had continued to bleed but so far showed no signs of gangrene.

Jory was much sicker. He talked in a whisper, his eyes were red and watery, and he walked like an old man with rheumatism. Despite his illness, as soon as the ALV arrived, he went out in the rain with Joan, Eddy, and Gerard to drill a hole in the ice and erect a light pole. The pole was actually a twenty-foot drilling stem that he had removed from the vehicle's roof where several like it were stored alongside the framework boom. While the ALV was gone on the diving expedition, he had attached four floodlights to one end of the stem.

Gerard settled in atop the ALV to watch out for cephids approaching in the rain.

Bonnie helped Rica out of her wetsuit and examined her back by the dim light of a fluorescent lantern.

"Could the Floe resume a collision course with Hawaii?" Rica asked through clenched teeth.

"It would have to double back at this point," Cliff said.

She let out a shuddering sigh. "Then we don't have to worry about stopping it anymore, which is good because— Ow! Stop! I can't bend that way."

"Actually . . ." Cliff began, but he could see that she was in too much pain to listen.

Bonnie dropped Rica's shirttail. "No vertebrae broken or dislocated, but the muscles and ligaments are all fucked up from your neck to your ass. You should be immobilized for a while."

"Fat chance of that," Rica groaned.

Jory returned to the tent, coughing and dripping rainwater. His heavy eyeglasses had slid down to the tip of his nose and were covered with raindrops. Cliff summarized the dive for him. Afterward, Jory spoke in a rasping whisper: "How can the Floe's bottom be so shallow?"

"Beats me," Cliff said. "Raymond said about seven eighths of the Floe should be submerged, but it's actually floating like a cork, half in the water and half out."

Jory nodded contemplatively. "At least it makes sense that the Floe has been accelerating at a steady rate. The thrust from all of the aliens swimming flat out is probably constant, whereas the drag is linearly decreasing as the Floe melts and its draft becomes shallower. *Millions* of them, you say . . . they must be invading Earth after all. Or they have been here for many generations, long enough to multiply."

Damn it! Cliff thought. Jory had completely missed the revelation that seemed so apparent to him after learning the secret of the Floe's propulsion.

"If Hawaii is not their target, where do you think they're going?" Jory asked.

"Let's check the GPS trace." Cliff walked around the worktable and opened a laptop computer that was connected to a portable GPS receiver. On the first night, Raymond Price had set up the computer to record the GPS receiver's exact coordinates at ten-minute intervals. The result was a set of red dots plotted on a map of the world. Most of the line of overlapping dots ran straight north toward Hawaii, but the top of it was a squiggle curving generally to the northeast. "They're not holding a straight course anymore, that's for sure," Cliff said. "I wonder if they've lost control."

He zoomed in on the squiggle, then opened a laminated bathymetric chart showing the depths of the ocean floor around Hawaii. "I'll be damned! They're following the seabed contours between five hundred and six hundred meters."

"Why?" Jory asked.

Cliff shrugged. "For an explorer who has no charts and doesn't know the area, that would be one way to search for a deep passage to the north."

"So they're just trying to get through the islands?"

"That's what it looks like to me," Cliff said.

"Where's the next land?"

"If they resume their former course north of Hawaii, they'll end up in . . . Alaska."

"Alaska? Why would they want to go there?"

"Maybe they don't. I'd bet their destination is the fiftieth parallel."

Jory coughed and wiped his nose. "What's there?"

"Cold water," Cliff said. "That's where the thermocline rises to the surface in the North Pacific. It makes a sudden transition from temperate to polar temperature in the surface layer."

"You really think they can't survive in warm waters?"

"If they could, I wouldn't be here." Cliff had told Jory how he'd saved himself and Rica by descending when the cephid pack charged them beneath the Floe. "Most polar creatures could not survive in temperate waters, and vice versa," he added. "When we swam out of the envelope of partial meltwater, the temperature increase was abrupt. And as I expected, that was exactly where they stopped. Salinity may also be important. Warm, salty water might not kill the cephids, but it definitely immobilizes them, which has the same end result in an ocean full of other predators. So they *have* to head for one of the poles before the Floe melts away."

"But why the North Pole?" Jory asked. "It's closer now, but the Floe must have been near the South Pole to start with. If they can't handle warm water, why'd they drag the Floe into the tropics in the first place?"

"Why did the chicken cross the road?" Cliff asked.

Jory scowled. "This is no time for jokes, Steadman."

"To get to the other side," Cliff said. He did not mean it to be funny.

"You're saying their objective is to reach Arctic waters, and it has been all along?"

"We can't be certain," Cliff said, "but I can't think of anything else that fits the facts. Unless they left Antarctica to commit mass suicide."

Jory grimaced. "Mass homicide is more their style. So they're just dragging the Floe along for a source of fresh or cold water during the journey."

"Or both," Cliff said.

Jory slumped with his head in his hands, staring at the laptop screen. "But *why*? Why land on Earth at the South Pole and then travel to the Northern Hemisphere this way? It still doesn't fit into any of the confrontational first-contact scenarios I've seen."

Cliff sat on a folding camp chair, too tired to stand any longer. He hoped the debate he was about to initiate would not be a waste of time. If he was right, what he had to say was of paramount importance, and he would need Jory's support. Besides, the survivors were too exhausted to do anything at the moment except talk and wait for the cephids.

He glanced at Rica, who was prone on her rigidly tense

back. She was still awake in spite of Bonnie's morphine. She had not spoken for half an hour, but her cinnamon-brown eyes seemed to be watching him and Jory attentively. Bonnie had nodded off beside her.

Cliff gently laid a hand on the sick engineer's shoulder. "Jory, the cephids are not extraterrestrials. I'm sorry."

Jory tensed and shrugged off the hand. He clenched his fists and skewered Cliff with a reproachful glare.

Go ahead, Cliff thought. Behead the messenger. See where it gets you.

Jory slumped with a morose sigh. "Oh, who cares what we conclude anymore. Right or wrong, we're all going to die here tonight, so we'll never get a chance to tell anybody."

Cliff said, "You first decided they must be aliens because no human technology could propel the Floe, right?"

Jory nodded, palpating his sore throat.

"But there is no technology!" Cliff said. "The cephids are just using brute force."

Jory shrugged. "They stole the datalink machine."

"Jory, the internal organs of the cephid I dissected looked exactly like those of the higher cephalopods. Trust me— that's an unlikely coincidence if they evolved on another planet."

"Big deal," said Joan. She and Eddy were sitting on the cold floor, wiping off rainwater. "Is that really less likely than unknown squidlike things growing as big as elephants without anyone discovering them before now?"

"Actually," Cliff said, "giant squid reach a length of at least sixty feet, probably more. That's twice the length of an elephant and longer than any of the cephids I've seen."

"You mean giant squids are *real*?" Joan asked.

Cliff groaned in frustration. "Most scientists thought they were mythical until 1873, when the first complete specimen was described in Newfoundland. Scientists just recently photographed *Archeteuthis dux* in its natural habitat for the first time. I should have been on that expedition, by the way.

I was scheduled to go. I would have been the principal investigator! But I'd been working such long hours in the lab that I came down with bronchitis and had to bail out. Anyhow, there's also the 'colossal squid,' which is even bigger. *Mesonychoteuthis hamiltoni*. It lives in the abyss around Antarctica. The first complete specimen was caught in 2003. We probably still haven't discovered the biggest species of squid out there."

Cliff paused for a ragged breath, grinding his teeth.

"Anyway, a live one has never been captured, but hundreds of carcasses have washed ashore or come up in nets around Newfoundland, New Zealand, and Norway."

Jory said, "Okay, how do the cephids walk around on the Floe without suffocating? No sea creature would leave the water voluntarily, right?"

"Wrong," Cliff said. "Octopuses crawl out on beaches to hunt. I've heard that Polynesian natives catch them with lures that look like rats. Giant Pacific octopuses like to hide under rocks that stick out of the water and grab seagulls when they land."

"An octopus might survive out of water for a while," Jory said, "but the cephids are so energetic! They must be able to breathe air."

Cliff shook his head. "No lungs, remember? I think they breathe by circulating the seawater stored inside their mantle cavities through their gills. I'd bet anything that the gurgle I heard before our first encounter with them was a cephid bubbling air through its water supply to oxygenate it. Their bursts of energy probably can't last very long. The one that chased me seemed to suddenly run out of steam after a few minutes. The same thing happens to all of the cephalopods I know, because their hemocyphin is less than half as efficient as our hemoglobin at carrying oxygen."

"No other large Earth animals are transparent," Jory said.

Cliff smiled. "Below the depth where sunlight can penetrate, transparent animals are the rule, not the exception. The only natural source of light down there is bioluminescence, which is so weak that transparent creatures are nearly invisible to predators and prey. And several of them have eyes that extend on long stalks to distance the opaque retinas from the body. I know of two species of transparent squid—*Toxeuma belone* and *Bathothauma lyromma*—that have stalked eyes with bright bioluminescent photophores right on the eyeballs that function like headlights."

Jory tried to pull a facial tissue from a full pocket-size pack. When the tissue tore, he hurled the pack across the tent and wiped his nose on his sleeve. "When they attacked the planes, they were like . . . like gremlins! Don't tell me a *mollusk* could be intelligent enough to have that kind of attitude."

"Octopuses are!" Cliff said. "They have distinct personalities, like cats. If you reach for them, some will consistently swim away, some will fight, and some will close their eyes and let you pet them. They tend to be curious, playful, peevish . . . One of my octopuses squirts me in the eye with his funnel if I forget to say hello before I feed him."

"Bullshit," Joan said.

"I swear," Cliff said earnestly. "They are tool users, even in the wild. Where there are no available dens, I've seen them build lean-tos by propping up flat rocks with round ones. They also use rocks as shields against predators, and when they find a tasty-looking bivalve they can't open, they wait motionless until it opens on its own. Then they pop a stone in between the shells to prevent it from closing. Considering that our closest common ancestor is probably a microscopic worm, it's amazing how many subtle things humans and octopuses have in common. For example, several species blanche white when they're afraid and turn blood red when they're angry."

"Really?" Todd said. "They can change colors just like a chameleon?" He was rocking his sleeping sister in his arms, sitting on the floor close to Cliff's feet so he could hear the debate over the rain pounding on the tent roof.

"Better," Cliff said. "Chameleons change colors by secreting hormones, so the changes are drab and slow. Cephalopods can instantly select precise colors and patterns by flexing microscopic muscles that open and close pigment cells called chromatophores. Some can even change the texture of their skin to mimic rocks or coral. Cuttlefish can show sexy gray to a mate on one side while flashing warning zebra stripes to a rival male on the other side, then switch the patterns in a blink. Several species of octopus are normally opaque but can close their chromatophores to turn nearly transparent when threatened."

"How can their brains control millions of individual cells at the same time?" Todd asked. "Humans can't do that."

"Part of their solution is distributed processing," Cliff said. "Two thirds of their nerves are in their arms. Each sucker has its own ganglion. As best we can tell—I'm working on this now—the brain sends a general order, and the local ganglia take care of the details. Local control allows each arm to function somewhat autonomously, and that makes cephalopod reflexes very fast."

Joan scowled up at Cliff. Her bulging eyes had dark half-moons under them. "Are octopuses as hard to kill as the cephids?"

"Not quite," Cliff said. "In fact, it's hard to keep them alive in aquariums because they're so sensitive to water chemistry and temperature. But they regrow ripped-off arms all the time. When an arm is severed, there's hardly any blood loss, and the skin immediately contracts and closes over the stump. In forty-eight hours they can heal wounds that would bleed a human to death.

"A Tahitian was showing me how to hunt a giant Pacific octopus with a spear one time. He impaled the thing dead center. Ran it clean through—we thought it was dead for sure. So help me, that son of a bitch dragged itself up the spear handle, wrapped the hunter's head in its arms, and nearly strangled him before I could cut it off. And that wasn't even a big one! They're incredibly strong—an octopus the size of a house cat can pull with the same force as a man. Most of the time they're gentle toward people, but they've been known to grab a diver with one arm, anchor themselves to the seabed with another arm, and hold the diver under until he drowns."

Cliff paused and looked around the tent at the remaining survivors, then continued. "And they have an unbelievable tolerance for pain. If you build a bonfire on the beach between an octopus and the sea, it will walk right through the fire to get home, or so I've been told."

"Fuck," Joan said. "That does sound like the cephids."

# CHAPTER 31

# Colonizers

Jory hung his head and shook it, mashing his sore throat. For a second Cliff thought he was finally convinced. Then he said, "The cephids are adapted to walking on land. If they had evolved that capability anywhere on Earth, someone would have seen them before now."

"Not in Antarctica," Cliff said. "The continent is nearly as barren as outer space above water, but below the floating sea ice, the ocean floor is home to all kinds of bizarre life forms, including the largest known invertebrates . . . more than three hundred varieties of sponges, some bigger than bears and hundreds of years old . . . orange sea spiders six inches across . . . the giant isopod, creepiest-looking thing you'll ever see, basically a foot-long marine wood louse. The cephids would fit right in."

"Come on, Steadman! Even in Antarctica there have been sealers and scientists and bored rich people crawling all over the continent for centuries."

Joan and Eddy nodded. So did Todd.

Cliff took a deep breath and responded. "Actually, there are no records of anyone even landing on the continent, except the tip of the peninsula, until the Norwegian whaler Henrich Bull put ashore in 1895. Antarctica has been thoroughly *explored* since then, but only a few research stations have been continuously *inhabited*."

"What about all those mines and oil fields they started up a little while ago?" Jory asked.

"That only lasted a few years," Cliff said. "Remember the monster storm that killed a bunch of people and destroyed all the infrastructure? Nobody except the scientists has wanted to touch the continent since that happened, and even they don't get out much in the winter—it's too cold and dark. What if that's the only time the cephids emerge? Millions of them could have been swarming over the ice shelves all along, hunting seals and penguins, and no one would have noticed, especially since they're so hard to see in low light."

"Carcasses would have been found," Jory said.

"You'd think," Cliff said, "but you've seen how they always remove their dead, whether they're eating them or whatever."

Jory paused for a wracking cough, then played his ace in the hole. "The cephids are cold-blooded. If they crawled out of the water in Antarctica, what would prevent them from freezing solid?"

"I think I know," Todd said.

All eyes turned to Todd. Cliff was astonished. This was the point that made him most doubtful of his own theory that the cephids had evolved in Antarctica.

Hesitantly, Todd said, "Do you remember the stinky stuff that was on me and Sophie when you found us?"

"God, who could forget!" Joan said.

"Well, I did that," Todd confessed. "My dad killed a small cephid with his knife, and I noticed that its body stayed wet even though it was below freezing down there. The stinky stuff came from its skin. I thought it was ecto . . . ectoplasm. Sorry I didn't tell before—I didn't want anybody to find out I'd smeared that stuff on Sophie because I thought that's what made her sick. But I had to! We were freezing!" Todd's face contorted as if he were going to cry. He was rocking Sophie vigorously.

"The slime was warm?" Cliff asked.

"No, it was cold," Todd said, "but we would have had frostbite without it."

"Some kind of antifreeze?" Joan asked.

"Couldn't be," Cliff said. "Some Antarctic fish have antifreeze in their blood, but antifreeze can only depress the freezing point a few degrees. Cephids walking around in Antarctica would be exposed to air a *hundred* degrees below freezing. Their exudate must actively produce heat somehow. Maybe an exothermic reaction takes place when it comes in contact with air, like those little hand-warmer packets you can get."

Todd said, "Octopuses get around on land by just slithering on their arms, right?"

Cliff nodded.

Todd said, "Do you think the cephids learned to walk upright on flippers so the rest of their bodies wouldn't have to touch the cold ice?"

"Could be!" Cliff said. "It would also help them conserve slime. If the stuff really releases that much heat, it must take a zillion calories a day to produce it."

"You know what I think?" Eddy asked.

A sadistic glint flickered in Joan's eyes, but she was too exhausted for a snide reply.

Eddy said, "I still think the cephids are somebody's clusterfucked secret science experiment."

Rica sat up with a groan. The tent grew silent, all eyes on her. "Cliff, why have you been telling us all of this stuff instead of resting?" she asked.

He squatted in front of her, wobbling with exhaustion. She noticed that he was bruised all over from the harrowing dive. *"Because we still have to stop the Floe,"* he said. "And everyone needs to understand why, and that means understanding what the cephids really are. Even if the Floe is not headed for Hawaii . . . even if the cephids are not aliens or biological weapons . . . even if it means sacrificing ourselves, stopping the Floe is more important now than we ever thought it was. If I'm right, the cephids will be able to leave the Floe once it reaches the fiftieth parallel or thereabouts. Then it will be too late to prevent them from colonizing the Northern Hemisphere. They may have been trying for millions of years—Ray said rogue icebergs have sailed north from Antarctica before—but they've obviously never succeeded, or they definitely would have been seen before now."

"How could animals be smart enough to try something like . . . colonization?" Joan asked.

"They don't have to be," Cliff replied. "They could be following a blind instinct to explore new territory. It doesn't matter whether they have a conscious plan. The end result will be the same."

"With so many of them down there, are you sure it's a good idea to go on the offensive?" Joan asked.

"Of course," Cliff said. "What have we got to lose? We obviously can't fight off all the cephids one by one."

"If they're really just sea creatures," Eddy said, "why's it such a big deal if they get loose in the Northern Hemisphere?"

"Because the vicious sons of bitches will *take over*!" Cliff shouted. "They aren't invaders from Mars, but they might as well be. They'll wipe out prey species and drive northern predators extinct by outcompeting them."

"I'm not going to do anything suicidal just to save a bunch of fish," Eddy grumbled.

"Then what about people?" Cliff asked. "The cephids beneath the Floe are swimming in water that's almost fresh. That means they can probably live in rivers and lakes. Even if they can't, they'll be a threat to oceangoing vessels and coastal communities. Try to picture them, Eddy—swarming up the sides of cruise ships, lurking in the bilges of freighters, attacking swimmers on the beach . . . imagine hunting packs slinking inland at night, taking pets and live-stock and people. We could prevent all of that, here and now."

"How?" Rica asked. "The Floe doesn't have an engine we can blow up. And how can you be so sure the cephids will spread through the north if we just leave the Floe alone?"

"I'm not," Cliff said. "We have to stop it just in case."

"Why can't we let somebody else deal with them later?"

"Because introduction of foreign species into new habi-tats is a genie you can't put back in the bottle," Cliff said. "No matter how hard we tried to exterminate them, the scourge would remain until the end of time."

"What if the cephids are a rare species themselves?" Rica asked. "You wouldn't want to drive *them* extinct, would you?"

"I'd worry about that if I thought it was likely," he said, "but the incredible number of them under the Floe suggests that they're thriving back in their natural habitat."

"Jory, what do you think?" Rica asked.

A wicked glint had entered the engineer's watery eyes. "I agree with Cliff one hundred percent."

Cliff stared at him, astonished. "You're finally convinced that the cephids are not aliens?"

"Hell, no," Jory said. "But I agree that we should try to stop the Floe at all costs, because it's harboring about a bil-lion extraterrestrials who obviously have not come in peace. I say it's time to invoke the standard protocol for the hostile invasion scenario: kill them all and ask questions later."

"Wonderful," Rica said. "I'm glad we all agree on what we *wish* we could do."

Cliff stood up, staggering for balance. "Rica, how much octanitro do you have here in camp?"

"About four hundred pounds."

He groaned. "That's not enough."

"What do you want to do? Blow up the whole Floe?"

He nodded emphatically. "How much is back on the Globemaster?"

"I don't know. Tons. But not enough to blast a berg this size out of existence."

"It wouldn't have to," Cliff said. "We just need to break it into pieces that are small enough to melt before they could reach cold waters."

Joan said, "Where do you plan to park the ALV while you demolish the Floe, Einstein?"

"We'll figure that out later," Cliff said.

Rica sighed. She knew she was too tired, injured, and drugged to think clearly. "It would take a month to drill enough blast holes," she said. "And a surface blast would just leave a crater. But glacial ice is brittle—we might have a chance if we could detonate all of the octanitro at once beneath the center of the Floe."

*"Beneath?"* Cliff asked. "How the hell are we going to do that?"

"I don't know! We obviously can't carry tons of explosives on our backs while we dive. I'm not able to dive again, anyway."

Cliff glanced at his wristwatch. "Do you have everything else you would need? Wires? Timer? Do you even know how to build such a huge bomb?"

"Plenty of wire and batteries," Rica said. "And I know how. Check the timer in my dive pouch."

Cliff picked up the black pouch, unzipped it, and removed the heavy metal cylinder containing the octanitrocubane Rica had taken on the dive in case they located the Floe's engines. He began unscrewing the lid.

"How long until the Floe is too far north?" she asked.

"I did some calculations a minute ago," he grunted, straining at the canister's lid. "If we can break the Floe into pieces no larger than one tenth of its present dimensions, and assuming . . . erggg! . . . that I didn't screw up any of—"

"Cliff, I trust your math. When's the goddamned deadline?"

"The sooner the better, before the cephids can finish us off! At the latest, we have to blast the Floe before tomorrow morning, or we don't stand—"

A paper-thin sheet of water sprayed outward in all directions from the base of the cylinder cap. It poofed up the tent's roof and hit Cliff's arm so hard that he yelped from the sting. When the pressure dissipated, he poured out the rest of the water, the plug of black octanitrocubane, and the timer, then handed the timer to Rica. "Please tell me that's not the only one we have left," he said.

She tried to set the timer. "It is, and it's trashed. We went deeper than the canister was designed for."

Cliff hesitated. His haggard face took on an expression that Rica found strangely chilling—he looked mournful and thrilled at the same time.

He shook Jory, who had fallen asleep. "Hey, Panopalous, did you record your sonar video during the battle last night?"

Jory coughed and nodded.

"Get it," Cliff said. "I need to know how fast the cephids were walking—their top speed."

"Why?" Jory asked.

"So I'll know how long I can spend fetching the rest of the octanitro before they could get here."

Rica tensed. If the cephids overran their defenses while the ALV was gone, their only hope would be to get away from the besieged camp on foot. "I'm surprised they haven't shown up already," she said.

Cliff shook his head. "It got light enough just after we got back to zap all the ones that crawled out during the storm. All we have to worry about now is more of them emerging after dark."

"How can you be sure?" Rica asked.

He shrugged. "You said it yourself—they'd be here by now if they hadn't died or turned back."

Jory and Cliff worked with the laptop and a calculator

for a moment, confirming that they had time to get the octanitro.

"Cliff, don't go," Rica pleaded. "It's no use. I could build another timer from an alarm clock, but nobody has one."

"That won't stop us," he said. "Besides, the explosives could help us survive tonight."

Rica tried to stand up, then sat back down. The gloomy tent seemed to spin around her.

"Take someone with you," she said.

Cliff looked at Jory, who nodded. Then he started rummaging around the tent, recklessly tossing items aside. "Where's my heavy fleece outfit?"

"What color is it?" Jory asked.

"Black," Cliff said.

"Haven't seen it."

"I could have sworn I left it in here when we set up camp."

Cliff gave up the search and settled for a Gore-Tex raincoat.

"I want to take the DNA sequencer and a sample from the dead cephid," Jory said in his rasping whisper. "I've been studying the manual. I can try an analysis on the way."

With characteristic abruptness, Cliff dropped to his knees, clasped one of Rica's hands, and kissed her. "I'll be back soon," he promised. "One way or another, we are going to end this tonight. If you can't fix the timer, you can get everyone else off the Floe once we figure out how, and I'll stay behind to detonate the bomb."

Before she could draw a breath, much less argue, he was out the door and gone in the rain. Jory followed with his arms full of scientific equipment.

An hour later, the ALV was out of radio range and the exhausted survivors remaining in camp had dispersed from the medical tent.

It should not have been totally dark yet, but the storm

clouds had thickened again until not a glimmer of twilight remained in the sky.

Joan stood watch atop one of the igloos. Her binoculars had somehow disappeared from her tent, so she had borrowed Rica's. Bonnie had injected her with a concoction of caffeine, ephedrine, and nicotine that had made her nauseous and jumpy but wide awake with razor-sharp senses. Not that they did her any good—the gurgles and slithers of cephids would be impossible to hear through the roaring rain, and even the bright floodlights shining down from the twenty-foot pole behind her could not penetrate the downpour all the way out to the mesa's edge. The harsh light just glared on the wet ice around Joan's long shadow, hurting her weary eyes.

The jury-rigged sonar was also useless in the rain, which turned its screen into a solid white sound shadow.

Rica was inside the igloo beneath Joan, sitting on one of the orange plastic chainsaw cases with her injured back propped against the minigun's battery. She was prepared to operate the Mark 19 MOD3 machine gun, which could fire 40-mm grenades through the igloo's gun port at a rate of 375 per minute.

In case it would help her stay awake, she allowed a trickle of icy meltwater to drip on her head and run down the back of her neck. She too had taken a risky dose of Bonnie's alertness potion. It had elevated her metabolism so much that sweat was dripping from her eyebrows despite the cold air in the igloo. Nevertheless, she did not trust the stimulants to overcome her exhaustion coupled with the morphine she had already taken.

Eddy Brown's diarrhea was worse than ever, and he could feel himself coming down with the same pulmonary syndrome as Sophie and Jory. His nose was clogged, and his chest felt like he had just been revived from near drowning. He lay down in his private tent and was snoring loudly before he could close his sleeping bag.

Twenty feet beneath the tent in which Todd was rocking

his crying sister, a glassy bluish cephid clung to the walls of a vertical shaft with its suction cups while digging at the ice above it with all four claw-beaks. The upraised arms swished back and forth like the legs of an Olympic sprinter, scraping the open beaks across the ceiling with all of the speed and power the slimy brute could muster. Each stroke gouged out a furrow of white ice shavings that swiftly melted when they fell onto the digging cephid and the others waiting below it.

After two minutes of continuous cutting, the cephid flashed one aqua-blue ring at the bottom of its barrel-body to signal the others that it needed to rest. Then it flattened against one wall and glided downward like a blob of bluish Jell-O stuck to a windowpane.

Another cephid hoisted itself up near the top of the shaft and raised its open claw-beaks. It paused for a moment to make sure the faint keening sound coming from above was still distinguishable through the dull rain-roar. Then it picked up where its exhausted comrade had left off, scraping at the roof with the uniquely violent fervor of an enraged predator defending its nest.

# CHAPTER 32

# Diggers

"Man, I'm glad that damn baby finally shut up," said Private Gerard. He was pacing in the medical tent with a squad automatic weapon. It was just after dark. The external floodlights glaring down through the camouflage tent fly projected dim greenish blobs onto his white coveralls.

After the previous night's successful defense against the cephid siege, Gerard had snapped out of his funk and started talking more. For the last hour he had seemed compelled to speak at least every five minutes, usually just to remind everyone of how screwed they were, as if they might have forgotten.

Bonnie put down the full morphine vial she had been turning end over end between her fingers. It was the last one. She had no idea whether Rica was lying or someone had stolen the rest of the morphine supply.

Bonnie leaned away from Paz, who was feebly writhing and moaning incoherent prayers in Spanish. Sure enough, she could no longer hear Sophie crying. She thought about going out to check on the infant, but the rain was pouring harder than ever—accompanied by some distant thunder—and she knew that Todd would bring Sophie back to the medical tent if her condition worsened again. With any luck,

Sophie's silence meant she had gone to sleep and was resting peacefully.

"You know what?" Gerard said. He was peering out the tent door, rifle poised, squinting left and right through the rain.

"No, what?" Bonnie said with a weary sigh.

"We're screwed," Gerard said.

Eddy Brown opened his eyes with a snort. What could have woken him? Surely not his own snoring, although it had been quite loud judging by that last *snerrreck!* as he came awake. Maybe it was the thunder, which was now far away but continuous, like the sound of a distant artillery barrage.

He coughed, rolled over, and closed his eyes.

A tremor from the ice nudged his back. It was different from the mild vibrations caused by the pounding rain. Must be some hail mixed in, he thought as he returned to slumber.

The big private's difficulty breathing woke him again and again. Each time, the continuous rumble of thunder was louder and the tremor in the ice seemed a little stronger than before.

When he heard a dull knocking, he lifted his head and listened, suppressing a cough. Nothing but the downpour and approaching thunder, not a peep from the other tents. Must be the generator, he thought. Probably rainwater in the fuel tank.

The next time Eddy woke, he heard a scraping, chopping sound, as if beavers were felling a whole forest. His feet and hands got clammy. His heart thumped like the wings of a grouse taking flight. "Who's there?" he whispered, fumbling for his headlamp.

He felt a thump from below.

Eddy sat up, fighting the phlegm in his sore throat to get enough breath for a yell. He heard a cracking sound, followed by a faint chorus of alternating squeaks and pops.

The sleeping pad beneath him abruptly tilted back and to

the right. He heard a snipping noise, like scissors, then the sound of tough tent fabric being ripped.

He fell through his torn tent floor into the ice.

His back landed on something soft. He sprang up, and his sock-clad feet sank into the cold, wet, squishy surface. The thing he was standing on lurched, throwing him off balance. He reached out both hands, unable to see beneath the dark tent, and felt the cold walls of the shaft he had fallen into. Its top was at the level of his shoulders. He placed his hands on the edges and hoisted himself out with his powerful arms.

He crawled around the tent on his hands and knees, feeling for the door zipper, taking care not to fall back into the pit. The search would have been easy if he had only known which wall was which.

He heard a wet slithering behind him, then more sounds like scissors being snapped shut. He could smell dead fish in spite of his clogged nose. He began coughing so hard that he could barely control his movements.

He finally found the door zipper and tugged at its slide. The swift yank caused the slide to catch a wad of fabric in its left groove, binding it firmly in place. Eddy grasped the fabric in his big round hands and tore the zipper open.

As he lunged from the tent, something cold and wet slid along his back, then looped around his neck. It pulled him over backward and dragged him to the hole in the floor. He grasped the cephid's arm with both hands as it constricted around his throat, squeezing off his breath.

They must have homed in on my snoring, he realized, certain that it would be his last thought.

Eddy twisted onto his back so that the thick cephid arm reaching out of the hole was between his knees. He did not want to go down headfirst. The pain would be briefer that way, but he wanted every second of life he could get, even if the final seconds were hellish beyond his worst nightmares. Maybe he would get a chance to warn the others with a shout if the arm let go of his throat once the cephid started eating him.

When his feet dangled into the hole, he balanced briefly on his arms, stuck his legs out sideways, and found himself squatting upright with one foot on each side of the pit. The cephid arm contracted, pulling his torso downward. He grasped it with his hands again and pushed upward with his massive legs, which had once lifted more than five hundred pounds in a squat rack.

Eddy strained as hard as he could, feeling the searing pain of all-out contraction in his gluteus and quadriceps muscles. He was determined to resist until he blacked out. His body moved upward a few inches, then downward when the cephid pulled harder, then upward again. He saw aqua-blue light flashing in the pit and heard popping noises. Then he heard a wet ripping sound, and suddenly he was standing upright.

Before his mind could even interpret what was happening, he was outside in the rain, crawling on his hands and knees—he knew better than to try standing up on the ice in his wet socks.

The reflected floodlights glared in his eyes. Blinking and squinting through the rain, he managed to make out the dark rectangle of the medical tent and scrambled toward it.

The cephid arm was still cinched around his neck but had loosened enough for him to drag in a slow breath. He had obviously torn it from the creature's gelatinous body. He stood on his knees and tried to pull the arm off, but he could not untangle its many slippery loops. The cold appendage was still slithering and writhing like a wounded snake, attaching and detaching suction cups on his face and neck.

His frantic twisting and tugging caused one of his knees to slip, and he fell sideways. His shoulder hit something hard and hot. As he struggled to get up, he heard a metallic crash and the sputter of a dying gasoline motor. Then the floodlights went out.

He had knocked over the generator.

The performance of Eddy's brain was hindered by a lethal mix of fatigue, illness, pain, and terror—never mind that it had never been the fittest part of his body. So when he saw what his blundering had done, his immediate reaction was to correct it. He let go of the cephid arm to heft the two-hundred-pound generator upright. Intending to restart it, he was feeling around for the pull cord when the slimy arm constricted so tightly about his neck that he could feel the pulse in his carotid artery grind to a halt.

He could hear Joan and Rica shouting about the lights, but by the time they figured out what had happened, it would probably be too late. Somehow he had to let them know that the cephids had begun their attack earlier than expected. He finally managed to draw enough breath for a shout, but when he opened his mouth, a mass of cold rubbery tissue surged into it, completely filling his oral cavity.

He felt pain inside his right ear. He tried to reach it, but his hand was blocked by a loop of the cephid arm. One of the suction cups had attached over his ear canal and was applying vacuum.

The pain in his ear abruptly changed from pressure to a sharp sting. When he lost all sense of orientation, he knew that his eardrum had ruptured. Something cold slammed into his right side, and he realized that he must have fallen again. It felt as if the world were spinning around him, although he could still see nothing in the darkness but a long arc of lightning on the horizon. The streak of flickering light appeared to be below him, producing the terrifying sensation that he was falling into the storm-swept sky.

Nausea and violent shivers wracked Eddy's body. He regretted tearing off the cephid's arm. If he had succumbed in his tent, the cephids would have given him a relatively painless death with their claw-beaks. Not every second of life was worth living after all.

The cold arm tip inside his mouth gathered protoplasm and surged in deeper, breaking out his front teeth. The squirming tendril probed at the back of his throat and the base of his tongue, bending his uvula and epiglottis. His stomach heaved, but he could not vomit because his esophagus was blocked by the cold, rubbery mass.

Eddy began to black out, not from strangulation but from sheer revulsion. He wondered why no one could hear him struggling, why no one came to help. Perhaps they were all asleep, or deafened by the thunder and downpour, or already dead.

The dismembered arm slid around his head, gathered slack, and pushed into his left lung, splitting his inflamed trachea all the way down. Belatedly, he tried to bite down on the arm. Without his incisors, all he could do was gnaw at its sides with his jaw teeth.

Thrashing and retching in a dark and directionless void, Eddy felt the cephid arm pull something loose inside his chest.

His brain gave in to the hypoxia and horror, and he slipped into merciful oblivion.

Joan stuck her head into the medical tent, blinking as rivulets of rainwater drained from her blond burr. "It's just the generator," she sputtered. "Probably out of gas. I'll get it restarted in a minute."

Bonnie's headlamp was the only source of light in the tent. She had positioned it on the worktable where it would shine through the last morphine vial, projecting on the wall a fuzzy image of the meniscus at the top of the clear solution. The fragile vial contained enough morphine to numb Paz's mangled arm for several more days. Bonnie figured it was also just enough to provide one fatal dose for someone of about her own weight.

Apparently Joan was having trouble starting the generator. Bonnie could hear a faint but continuous stream of obscenities drifting through the downpour from the Marine.

Gerard was still pacing up and down the rectangular tent with his light machine gun. He saw Bonnie pick up the full morphine vial and start twirling it in her fingers again. "I

swear to God," he said, "if you don't put that thing down,
I'm going to throw it outside."

Bonnie watched his eyes. He was not looking at her now.
His fearful gaze was rolling around the gloomy enclosure,
even up at the low fabric roof, which shimmied and rippled
in the growing wind.

The Floe had almost reached the region of the storm with
intense lightning. Occasional close flashes were casting
green light with camouflage-shaped shadows into the
translucent tent. Bonnie could see the silhouettes of raindrops dribbling down the northern wall. Projected shadows
of the same drops seemed to be trickling down Gerard's
soiled white coveralls.

"What was that?" Gerard asked.

"What?" Bonnie whispered. She twisted toward the door,
accidentally knocking off the morphine vial.

All she could hear was the rain and the suddenly surging
pulse in her ears. Her stomach was clenched like a bear trap.

"Don't know," Gerard said. "Probably just a sheet of rain
hitting the ice."

Bonnie sighed and picked up the vial, which had landed
safely on the wadded jacket that Paz was using for a pillow.
"I hope Eddy and the baby are getting some rest," she said.
"They have an MDR strain of bacterial pneumonia, you
know. So does Jory."

"MDR?"

"Multiple drug resistant," Bonnie said. "None of my antibiotics will kill it. Sophie seemed better tonight, but it
probably won't last. And Jory's lungs are filling up with
fluid. Cliff may already have a dead man for a partner on the
ALV."

Gerard took a deep breath as if testing his own lungs,
then went back to pacing. He was at the other end of the tent,
looking at something on the floor, when Bonnie saw the silhouette on the northern wall. It had a simple shape at first,
an eight-foot dome projected against the translucent fabric

by the flickering lightning, as if a haystack had suddenly appeared on the ice outside.

As the lightning winked out, the silhouette began to move.

# CHAPTER 33

# Storm

Bonnie sat rigidly still in the flickering semidarkness, breathing only through her mouth so her deep breaths would make no noise. She could hear nothing but the rain on the roof and the tent fabric rustling in the wind. Her neck seemed paralyzed, so she rolled her eyes as far as she could to the right and gazed at the northern wall, waiting for another flash of lightning that was bright enough to cast shadows.

The flash came, and the tall silhouette was still there. In fact, it was closer, and this time she saw eight arms writhing above its top like Medusa's hair. Bonnie carefully regulated her quavering breath and followed the cephid's shadow with her eyes as it trudged along the wall toward the far corner of the tent. She mouthed Gerard's name. All that came out was a tiny squeak that was too low for him to hear over the rain.

The cephid paused by the pad where Paz was sleeping. The nineteen-year-old's wounded arm, wrapped in bloody gauze, was adjacent to the wall. Bonnie saw three prehensile suction cups press against the fabric from outside, creating round indentations and causing the wall to bulge inward.

Gerard was facing the opposite side of the tent. Just before he turned around, the suction cups withdrew from the wall and the nearby lightning winked out. After scanning the northern wall, where nothing seemed amiss, Gerard turned back to the south again.

Bonnie tried to get up, but her legs would not move. Neither would her arms.

She willed Gerard to turn around and see the moving shadow the next time lightning flashed, or to notice the subtle way the cephid's huge body was changing the sound of the rain.

Gerard was playing with Jory's Hewlett-Packard scientific calculator, which he had found on the floor. "How do you turn this thing on?" he asked.

Bonnie wondered how the cephid was casting a solid shadow. The light should have passed right through its transparent body. It must have already eaten someone, she realized, engorging its tissues with opaque human blood.

"Ger-Gerard."

"Yeah, what?" he said. "Damn it, I found the On button, but when I try to add two plus two, the screen just beeps and says, 'Error: Too Few Arguments.'"

"Be-behind you."

He whipped around, dropping the calculator and raising his SAW. The last flash of lightning was gone. He was staring at a seemingly opaque wall.

Gerard slumped and exhaled. "Lady, you got it bad. You're seeing things." He gave her a hard look, then dropped his gaze to her trembling white hands.

Lightning flashed. "Look!" Bonnie squealed, jerking her head to the right.

Gerard looked up. Streaks from falling raindrops were the only silhouettes on the glowing wall. He glared at her, breathing hard, angry at her for scaring him.

Bonnie stammered, "I . . . I saw—"

Gerard whipped left toward the western wall. *"Did you hear that?"*

Bonnie managed to jerk her head up and down a half inch. She had heard the loose wall and floor of the tent rustle against each other right where Gerard was standing. Unlike the one-piece dome tents, the floor of the medical tent was a separate sheet of nylon that was attached to the walls with hooks so that it angled upward on all sides to keep water out.

As Gerard turned his head back around to look at the wall, Bonnie saw motion between his feet. Something red, wet, and glistening slid swiftly into the tent between the floor and wall. It reached up between Gerard's widespread legs, and his whole body suddenly went rigid.

Bonnie lurched and fell from her chair in response to the private's scream. It sounded as if he were trying to tear his lungs out. Spasms in his calves bounced his rigid body up and down. She could see his tongue sticking out when his head tilted back. A foot-wide claw-beak had seized his crotch, gripping his genital area and half of his ass cheeks within the razor-sharp edges of the beak. His blood flowed down both legs of his dirty white coveralls and dribbled on the tent floor between his feet.

Gerard's trigger finger flexed, and the camp's last magazine of rifle shells was expended in automatic fire that blasted a row of holes in the ceiling.

The cephid arm retracted, attempting to drag its prey from the tent, but Gerard's body refused to fit through the gap between the hooks holding up the edge of the floor. The cephid responded with brute force, tugging the whole tent southward.

The tent collapsed around Bonnie and Paz, knocking the worktable over. The morphine vial and a rack of other medicine bottles shattered on the floor. The broken bottles had contained all of the remaining antibiotics and painkillers.

Bonnie's headlamp was lost among the rustling folds of fabric. In almost total darkness, she felt the lumpy ice sliding by beneath the thin floor and realized that the cephid was dragging the tent and everything in it across the mesa.

She finally managed to scream.

Then she started searching through the folds of slick nylon with her hands, hoping to encounter the headlamp. Instead, her fingers raked across something sharp. At first she thought it was broken glass. Then she realized it was her bone saw.

Amputation was still the only treatment to prevent gangrene or fatal blood loss from hopelessly mangled limbs. Bonnie had taken out the saw to amputate Paz's moribund arm but had lost her nerve to carry out the operation.

She grabbed the saw, twisted some of the tent floor into a roll, and hacked her way out.

The wet ice was painfully cold. The raindrops were warm, but they stung her face in the wind.

Her crampons had been lost in the tent, so she crawled on all fours toward an igloo, holding on to the saw. The wind and rain made her fall on the slippery ice again and again.

Her palms and kneecaps were numb with cold by the time she crawled into the igloo's narrow foyer. She crept to the main dome and huddled just inside it, peering back out, shivering in the cold damp air. Icy meltwater dripped on her head and ran down her temples to her chin. As she began to calm down and stopped heaving for breath, she closed her mouth and resumed breathing through her nose.

The igloo reeked of dead fish.

Bonnie heard a noise that sounded like someone slugging down a beer, and the inside of the dome gradually lit up with aqua-blue light. She could see the seams between igloo blocks and drops of meltwater hanging from the ceiling. A moist slithering began behind her and oozed forward around her on both sides.

Grunting with panic, Bonnie scrambled against the slippery floor and walls of the foyer. She had made it to the entrance when a cephid arm whipped around her left ankle and dragged her back in.

She screamed with all her might.

A tall dark figure ran toward her, staggering like a drunk. It knelt in front of the foyer with a groan, and Bonnie knew from the feminine silhouette that it was Rica. "It's got my foot!" Bonnie wailed.

Rica grabbed her wrists and pulled, bracing her crampons on the sides of the entrance.

Bonnie felt her spine stretching. "Let go," she groaned.

"What?" Rica shouted.

"Let go! Let go!" Bonnie tried to shake off Rica's vise-like grip.

With a sudden contraction, the cephid pulled the two women apart.

Bonnie had realized she was still holding the bone saw in the crook of one finger. She grabbed its handle, curled into the dome, and hacked through the cephid's arm with two swift strokes. Then she dragged herself forward, holding the back of the saw and digging its blade into the ice for traction. Another lunge using the saw like an ice axe brought her back to the entrance.

Rica grabbed her shirt and dragged her out, then produced and prepared a grenade in one motion before heaving it into the igloo. "Come on!" she shouted.

Bonnie dropped the saw and tried to crawl, but her arms and legs were trembling too much for the delicate control needed to balance on wet ice. Rica saw her flouncing and dragged her away by one arm.

The igloo exploded behind them.

In spite of the morphine, every step shot a bolt of pain up and down Rica's back as she dragged Bonnie to the base of the light pole. The leaning pole was in an open part of camp with good visibility on all sides. Joan was already there with Todd and Sophie, patrolling around them with an MP-5N submachine gun in one hand and her M-16 in the other. The

rifle ammunition was all gone, but she could still fire
grenades from the M203 clip-on launcher attached beneath
the M-16's barrel.

The continuous thunder was so close now that the roaring rain was quiet by comparison.

"Where's Eddy?" Rica yelled.

"I saw most of him inside a big cephid," Joan said.

"What about Gerard?"

"Dead," Bonnie gasped, blinking rain from her eyes.

"Paz?" Rica asked.

"He was in the tent," Bonnie said.

*"Lopez!"*

Rica turned toward Joan's shriek but saw no cephids.

"Look!" Joan yelled, pointing north.

They ran to the igloo dome that was blocking their view.
Joan leaped to its summit and helped Rica up. Holding each
other for balance, they gazed down from the mesa at the
dark inland terrain.

The prow of the Floe had entered the edge of the intense
electrical storm, which was sharply bounded by some invisible front in the sky. About once every two seconds, a white-
hot arc flashed between the clouds and the Floe, striking the
tallest of the fanciful iceforms within the storm's tight
perimeter. Bolts were even striking at an angle from the east
and west, drawn across the flat expanse of dark ocean to the
Floe's high topography.

As the Floe sailed into the storm, the ridges, spires, and
arches being struck by lightning were getting closer to the
mesa. Rica saw a zigzagging arc hit a tall minaret about a
mile away, shattering its upper half, leaving a cloud of steam
and falling debris.

"Rica!" This time it was Todd yelling.

She forced her stiff back to twist around. A pale blue
flame of prelightning plasma—St. Elmo's fire—was dancing atop the light pole. Bonnie was gazing up at it, but Todd
was not yelling about the deadly buildup of electrical
charge. He was hunched over Sophie's makeshift bassinet,

gazing out at the solid ring of cephids that was flowing inward around the igloos like a flood of viscous slime.

"We have to abandon the camp," Rica said.

"No fucking shit!" Joan replied. She fired a burst from her MP-5N into the glittering, slithering horde. The slow and tiny 9-mm pistol bullets had no apparent effect.

Rica slid off the igloo, lurched to the pole, and resumed dragging Bonnie, who still had no crampons. "Clear us a path to the south, Sniper."

Joan fired several grenades into the cephids on the side of camp opposite the approaching lightning. Before the cephids that had survived the blasts could close in, the surviving humans huddled close and stumbled across the resulting morass of steaming slime and twitching arms. When they had made it beyond the contracting gauntlet, Rica could see their strobing shadows getting shorter as the lightning strikes behind them came closer.

Joan ran in front of her and stopped. "We can't leave Rodriguez here."

Rica glanced back at the blue flame atop the light pole. It had grown brighter and doubled in height. "We have to get these kids off the mesa," she yelled over the thunder.

"There!" Joan ran toward a crumpled pile of dark fabric.

Rica followed when she saw that something was moving inside the collapsed tent. "Careful!" she warned.

Joan cut into the tough fabric with her survival knife, and Paz's good arm thrust up through the incision. Rica heard him gasping for air.

"Find your crampons so I won't have to drag you," she said to Bonnie. "And hurry!"

"I'll help," Todd said.

Paz blinked and sputtered when the rain began pounding his pale face. Rica and Joan knelt on opposite sides of his head. "Get away," Joan said, shoving Rica back. She pulled Paz upright by his armpits, embracing him a second longer than necessary. "Time to go, Rodriguez." She maneuvered his center of gravity over her shoulder and heaved upward.

"Put down," he groaned. "I . . . walk."

Rica looked back at the flaming pole, to which they were still electrically connected by a continuous sheet of rainwater. "Actually, Paz, you'll have to run."

# CHAPTER 34

# Pack Hunters

They ran as fast as they could across the dark mesa. Bonnie had found her crampons. Paz was weak from blood loss, but once he got going he was able to keep up. Only Rica lagged behind, unable to maintain a symmetrical gait because the constant spasm in her back was pulling her over to the right.

A blinding flash lit up the others' backs. For an instant Rica could see the whole white surface of the mesa through the rain. At the same time, a thunderclap hit her from behind with the force of a head-high breaking wave, and she felt a painful jolt of muscular contraction throughout her body. She sprawled facedown on the cold ice, tingling all over.

Looking back, she saw the abandoned camp a hundred yards away. A cloud of steam was wafting downwind through the rain. Dozens of dead cephids lay scattered on the ice, their arms flung out away from the light pole like trees felled by a volcanic eruption. Live ones were already moving in to scavenge.

Before she could get up, another bolt of lightning struck the pole. The discharge shocked her body and blasted a hundred-foot-wide disk of steam, spray, and cephid parts straight up from the ice like the plume from a shallow depth charge.

"We're next!" Joan yelled, grabbing Rica's arm and dragging her away.

They slid down the mesa's steep scarp on their backs and landed in a shallow stream bordered by high banks. Rica hoped the banks would protect them from lightning when the edge of the electrical storm passed over in a few seconds.

She tried to call the ALV. Her radio had shorted out in the rain. Joan's appeared to work, but she got no response.

"They're right . . . behind us," Todd gasped, still catching his breath.

A row of cephids was perched along the rim of the mesa. They were waving their eye stalks and gesticulating with their arms. "Keep moving," Rica said. "We'll stay on the ALV's route and hope we meet it before they can catch us."

"When are Cliff and Jory supposed to come back?" Todd asked.

Rica looked at her watch. "Forty minutes from now, but we don't even know if they're still alive."

After a few more minutes on the run, it became apparent that Joan, Todd, and Bonnie could outpace the cephids but Paz and Rica could not. Paz was now barely stumbling forward with Joan's help, gingerly cradling his destroyed left arm and wincing with every step. Rica was not as close to collapsing, but her lopsided posture and lurching gait prevented her from keeping up.

Joan used their last launcher grenade to blast the closest cephid. While the rest of the pack paused to scavenge the scattered remains, Rica made a decision and announced it: "We have to split up."

Todd gasped. "No, Rica!"

"Todd, I'm sorry. I just can't go fast enough."

"I am . . . also done," Paz groaned.

Rica said, "Joan, I want you to take off with the kids. Pull ahead of us. Paz and I will wait until you're out of sight; then we'll try to lead the cephids off your trail. If you meet the ALV, come look for us. Maybe we'll still be ahead of them."

"Fuck you, Lopez! Keep walking. I've seen the way you and Steadman look at each other. He'd knife me in my sleep if I let you fall behind."

"Tell him I'm sorry," Rica said.

"Who's going to blow up the Floe if you buy it now?" Joan asked.

Rica hesitated, blinking in the rain. She hadn't thought about that. "I don't know. But you have a duty to get Todd and Sophie out of here alive."

Joan gazed forlornly back and forth between Paz and the cephids, who were almost finished eating. "Fuck! All right."

Rica handed Joan the small backpack she was wearing. "Take this. It's a bomb. I put it together while we were waiting for the cephids tonight, but I didn't have time to rig a switch." She pointed out two naked wires protruding from opposite sides of the lid flap. "Just pull these wires out and touch them together, and *boom!*"

Weakly, Paz said, "*Adiós,* Bledsoe. *Adiós,* Todd and Sophie. God be with you."

Todd hugged Rica, then ran to keep up with Joan, glancing back through the rain. When lightning struck a high ridge to the left, Rica saw that he was crying. She wondered if she would ever find out whether he and Sophie had made it off the Floe alive.

"Are you going with Joan and the kids or staying with us?" she asked Bonnie. "Your best chance is with them."

Bonnie sighed. "I'll stay with my patients."

"Look!" Joan pointed to the dark, round, twenty-foot opening she had spotted ahead of them in the steep right bank of the valley.

"I'll bet it's drier in there," Todd said. He was hunched over Sophie, attempting to shield her upturned face from the rain. "We could hide and wait for the ALV."

"We better keep moving," Joan said.

The next time lightning flashed, Todd looked over his shoulder and saw a pack of cephids. About twenty of them were gathered in the stream, standing still, watching them. Either Rica's plan to lead them away had failed, or she and Paz had already been caught, or this was a different pack from the one that had been pursuing them before. "Joan," he squeaked.

"Go faster," Joan said, dousing her headlamp.

"I can't run," Todd whispered. "We might fall."

They speed-marched around a bend, sloshing loudly. Between lightning flashes, they were surrounded by total darkness. Sophie sounded off like an ambulance siren as her bassinet swung back and forth on its handle of string. Todd tried to keep going straight during the blackouts between flashes, correcting his course when the next flash came.

After a long hiatus, lightning raced overhead and the cephids appeared in front of them like evil apparitions. Again the transparent creatures were standing still in the shallow current, this time downstream, forming a biological barricade across the valley.

"How did they do that?" Todd gasped, trying to whisper. "They were behind us a minute ago."

Joan halted and slowly stepped backward. "Must be a different pack." She whirled back and forth, crouching indecisively. The walls of the valley were too steep to climb. "We're trapped," she sputtered, wiping rain from her eyes.

"The cave!" Todd whispered. Its entrance was behind them now. If the strobe-lit snapshots of the valley's twists and turns stored in his memory were accurate, they could run back and duck into the opening without either pack of cephids seeing where they'd gone.

Joan drew her knife and ran back upstream, splashing. "Come on. At least we can get our backs to a wall if they come in after us."

The air in the ice cave was much colder. Todd could see his breath. Frigid meltwater dripped from the high ceiling.

They crested a hump and then walked downhill. When

they got too deep for the flickering lightning to illuminate the floor, Joan turned her headlamp back on. The air got even colder, and the drips of meltwater ceased.

Todd heard a crunch beneath his feet and looked down. The floor was covered with dry hoarfrost that was like nothing he had ever seen. The coarse crystals looked razor sharp and sparkled with rainbow spectra in Joan's headlamp beam. They came in all shapes—hexagonal plates, swordlike spikes, furry snowballs, multiarmed crystal cactuses. Some of the delicate growths were unbelievably huge and complex, rising several inches from the floor like plants in an alien desert. Todd felt as if he was destroying something priceless with each step.

"Great," Joan said. "Now they can follow our tracks."

Todd looked back. The cave entrance was far away, but he could make out the glistening cephids standing just outside it.

"Oh, no," Joan whispered. She was scanning a sparkling wall in front of them with her headlamp. The cavern had dead-ended. "Here's where we stop and fight. Let's look for a corner."

They found a dark opening in the wall, a vertical crevice less than a foot wide. "Jesus, something must have died in there," Joan said. Todd could smell it too—a stench even worse than the slime from a dead cephid.

Joan shined her light into the crevice. "Shit. It's not very deep. I can see the back." She looked Todd up and down. "You can't fit in there, can you?"

Todd eyed the stinking crevice. "I'm pretty flexible."

"Do it," Joan said. "Try to keep the baby quiet. I'll hold them off as long as I can."

Todd held Sophie's bassinet in front of him and easily stepped into the crevice sideways.

He fell.

He slid down a cold wet chute on his side, shrieking and clutching Sophie to his chest.

His feet plunged into a surface that seemed liquid and

solid at the same time, like Jell-O with chunks of fruit. Their
momentum submerged them. The liquid was so cold that
Todd gasped reflexively, drawing it into his lungs.

He kicked against something semifirm, and his head
breached the surface. He coughed and spat between continued gasps of cold shock. Sophie emerged crying and coughing.

Todd swiped his free hand through the stuff surrounding
them and revised his analogy. The stuff was not really like
Jell-O. Too watery and lumpy. More like chunky stew.

And despite the cold, it stank worse than he could have
imagined. The stench filled his lungs, making him gag and
belch. He could feel Sophie retching. He selected one of the
larger, firmer lumps and explored it with his free hand until
he was certain that he knew what it was: a dead bird. Both
wings and most of its feathers were missing.

Shivering violently, Todd realized that he and Sophie
were immersed in a totally dark chamber along with hundreds of dead animals. He held his sister above his head and
screamed for Rica. Then he remembered how they had gotten there and screamed for Joan.

Rica led Paz and Bonnie in a circle. By the time they returned to the ransacked camp, the cephid pack behind them
had almost caught up.

She stumbled to the nearest igloo and shined her headlamp into its gun port. The dome was unoccupied but clut-
tered with several items of equipment, including the
minigun battery and both chainsaw cases.

They crawled in. Paz lay his head on one of the cases and
passed out.

Rica noticed that Paz's belt holster still contained his
heavy pistol. She had discarded hers once the ammunition
ran out. She checked the gun and found that he had saved a
single cartridge in the chamber. She could guess what the
bullet was for. It made her wonder if she had overestimated

her devout brother Marine's confidence that he would live on in a better world if he only died honorably in this one.

She got out one of the chain saws and made sure it had gas. Then she sat cross-legged, facing the foyer with the saw on her lap and Bonnie behind her. She had no trouble staying awake—the morphine was beginning to fade, allowing the ache in her back to wake up.

Joan heard Todd's echoing yelp when he fell into the crevice. Then she heard a splash. Then—after a pause—his fit of coughing, gagging, and cries for help.

The cephids were upon her. Before closing in, they surrounded her in a semicircle and weaved their arms together to form a continuous slithering barricade. There was obviously no use in trying to fight them. She turned and dived headfirst into the reeking crevice.

What she encountered at the bottom of the wet chute made Joan forget who she was for a moment. When she stopped screaming obscenities and sucked in a sickening breath, Todd was looking at her in a way that made her feel ashamed. He was shielding his eyes from her headlamp with one arm and holding Sophie above the carrion stew with the other.

Joan averted her headlamp beam. If an adolescent boy could handle bathing among long-dead animal carcasses, so could she, by God.

She heard a moist swishing sound. It seemed to come from the hole that had just disgorged her from the low ceiling. As she shined her light up at the opening, a spinning mass of transparent flesh launched from the chute and splashed down between her and Todd.

# CHAPTER 35

# King

Rica kept thinking she had just heard the familiar moist scuffle of a walking cephid outside the igloo, but she knew it could have been the wind or her imagination. Then she saw a vague shadow pass by the foyer's entrance, and the sound of the rain splatter was blocked for a moment.

She revved up the chain saw. Bluish smoke billowed around her head, forming a layer of haze beneath the dripping dome. Paz did not wake up, despite the painful din of the tiny combustion engine in the hard-walled enclosure.

"Hey, check his pulse," Rica shouted to Bonnie.

A transparent arm with a claw-beak at the tip tentatively slithered along the foyer like a curious python. Rica waited until it reached the main dome, then triggered the saw up to ten thousand revolutions per minute and severed the beak with a quick jab.

The arm stump withdrew like a cracking whip.

Rica shut down the saw, coughing.

"Lean over to breathe," Bonnie said. "Small motors produce carbon monoxide when they're cold."

Rica took the medic's advice and found a few inches of fresh air adjacent to the floor.

They waited again, listening. Paz remained asleep. Rica watched the foyer, but all was quiet.

"Are they gone?" Bonnie whispered.

"I think so," Rica said. "I wonder why. It's not like them to give up so fast."

She heard a chorus of drips and felt several cold droplets of meltwater strike her face simultaneously. She looked up at the arching ceiling and saw that many more droplets were still hanging on. Suddenly the droplets quivered and the largest ones fell, making another round of echoing drips.

When drops rained down in unison for the third time, Bonnie was looking up too. She wiped the meltwater from her eyes and whispered, "Why . . . why is that happening?"

Rica slowly shook her head, still watching the drops.

The largest drops fell again. This time she felt a mild tremor in the ice at the instant they let go.

The tremor preceding the next round of drips was stronger and accompanied by a dull thud.

Rica concentrated on listening. Her whole body felt as tense as a piano wire.

Bonnie's breathing accelerated until she began to wheeze with panic.

*Thud. Plink-plunk-bloop.*

"Is it the ALV?" Bonnie squeaked.

Rica shook her head. "We would hear the engine."

*Thud! Drip-drip-drip.*

The sound of the rain had changed. It was muted, as if many of the raindrops falling close to the igloo were landing on something soft. Rica snapped off her headlamp and listened, but all she could hear was the rain and Bonnie's quavering wheezes. The thuds and tremors had ceased.

"We have to get out of here!" Bonnie hissed. She crawled across Rica's lap toward the foyer. Rica heard her gasp in the darkness when she cut herself on the fanglike chain-saw blades.

Bonnie let go of the saw bar and fell against Rica, who toppled backward. When Rica's shoulders hit the wall, Bonnie's weight pressed down on her midriff, bending and stretching her back. She was unable to stifle a long shriek of pain.

Rica wrapped her arms around the medic's stringy thighs and held on. "You can't go out there," she whispered. "It's right outside!"

"Let go!" Bonnie grunted.

"No! It'll grab you the second you crawl out!"

Bonnie was hyperventilating, emitting a sharp whimper after each inhalation. Then she stopped struggling, and her breathing abruptly slowed. A second later her light body went completely limp. Realizing she had fainted, Rica carefully dragged her away from the chain saw.

Rica was looking up when lightning flashed outside. Some of the bright light penetrated the walls of the igloo, causing them to glow a dingy blue. Two round shadows were hovering over the dome, about three feet apart. Each shadow was the size of a dinner plate.

Rica knew what the shadows were. She held her breath and watched them. When lightning flashed again, they had moved to a different part of the dome.

The roar of rain on the roof was replaced by muted sloshing and slithering. Then an eerie, lingering groan filled the enclosure. Rica was not surprised when she heard a loud crack and felt a jolt from the wall behind her. The next flash revealed a broken seam zigzagging up one side of the dome.

She wondered if Bonnie's instinct to flee had been right after all. She shook Paz. He stirred but remained unconscious. So did Bonnie.

The noises ceased. Had the monstrous cephid abandoned its attempt to crush the sturdy igloo?

A hard thunk resounded through the top of the dome, and Rica realized that the beast had merely switched tactics.

A few seconds later, the igloo imploded with a deafening crash. A falling block slammed against Rica's right shoulder and tumbled to the floor. Rain and warm air hit her face. A forking bolt of lightning raced overhead, blasting her dark-adapted retinas. Then a gentler flash revealed the cephid's giant eyes above the hole it had bashed in the top of the dome. They were the size of basketballs.

The eyes lunged down at her, their narrow stalks stretching through the jagged hole in the roof. The orbs hovered on opposite sides of Rica's head and rotated so that the wide-open, W-shaped pupils were facing inward to examine her. She could clearly smell the dripping organs.

With an involuntary snarl, Rica twisted her head and snapped at one of the stalks. Her incisors grazed it. The huge eyes retracted so fast that they seemed to disappear.

She heard a moan and looked down. Paz was feebly squirming beneath several of the hundred-pound igloo blocks. Bonnie lay against the wall, untouched by the debris. Rica frantically tried to dig Paz out but could not get a grip on the heavy chunks of wet ice.

Before long, the huge cephid was bound to pluck them out of the rubble and make a meal of them, unless she could somehow divert its attention. She crawled through the foyer with the chain saw, stood up in the rain outside, flicked on her headlamp, and yanked the saw's starter cord with all her might.

The engine sputtered and revved. Blue smoke belched in her face. She stood with her feet wide apart, swaying with pain and drug-induced vertigo.

"Hey, you!" she screamed at the transparent behemoth stooping over the broken igloo.

The cephid straightened up and looked her way, blinking at her headlamp beam. It seemed to be the size of several elephants. Rain flowed over it in glistening waves, making its transparent form easily visible.

The ponderous brute took a step toward her, and she recognized it. The extra-thick arms, the long vertical wrinkles on the barrel-body—this was the king cephid, the beast that had led the attack on the planes and the following night's siege in the fog. Cliff had also told her how he'd seen the

lumbering giant carry off pieces of whom they surmised to
be Bert Lazarus.

The king cephid flashed its aqua-blue belts of bioluminescence, squinting at her through the rain, and Rica got the
creepy feeling that it had recognized her as well. Her last
doubts about its identity were eliminated when only the bottom three belts lit up—she remembered shooting out the top
belt during the battle in the fog.

Rica held the idling saw behind her back, carefully angling the bar away from her legs. She kept an eye on the
monster's tire-size claw-beaks, wondering if she was within
their reach. "Here, doggy," she called. "I've got a special
treat!"

She revved the saw to feel its reassuring vibration.

Am I really as brave as I sound? she wondered. When
those huge arms reach out for me, will I wade into them
swinging the saw? Or will I drop it and run?

She did not get a chance to find out.

She saw a light beyond the edge of the mesa, hundreds of
yards behind the king cephid. It was a wavering beam that
reached up through the rain. A second later, the spinning
tracks and gray belly of the ALV launched into the sky from
the mesa's steep scarp. The thirty-ton vehicle tilted forward
in midair and landed on its tracks, splashing runoff.

The thud and jolt got the king cephid's attention. The
monster turned around.

Holding the chain saw in one hand, Rica used her other
arm to shield her eyes from the ALV's headlights, which
were beaming directly at her through the king cephid's
transparent body. She could hear the engine now. The driver
appeared to be shifting up.

The king cephid twisted around and lashed out with one
of its beakless arms. The arm hit the back of her knees. Before she could react, her stiff back landed on the cold wet ice
hard enough to knock the wind out of her. Fortunately, her
sudden fall had prevented the arm from wrapping around
her legs. The chain saw spun several yards across the ice and

came to rest on its side. The chain ground against the ice for a second or two before the idling motor sputtered and died.

She had thought she was beyond the king cephid's reach. Evidently its arms could stretch farther than she'd guessed.

A closed claw-beak that probably weighed more than Rica came swinging straight down out of the rain. She rolled over as it slammed down where she had been sprawling. The impact pelted her with spray and ice chips.

The beak opened and snapped at her head, but she twisted away, gasping at the pain in her back.

Before the beak could make another pass, she pushed herself up into a squatting position, groaning with pain.

The open beak whizzed over her head like a scythe. Before it could return, she lunged away from the cephid, grabbed the chain saw, and sprinted away.

The spasm in her back jerked her sideways with each stride. She had only gone a few paces when the jerking caused her to lose her balance and fall again. This time she kept her grip on the saw as she skidded across the ice.

When she looked up, she saw that the king cephid had turned to face the ALV again. The vehicle was close. Its headlights lit up the falling raindrops and made dazzling reflections on the ice. It seemed to be going faster than Rica had thought it could, even at full throttle. There was no way it could stop before hitting the camp, and if Cliff and Jory had succeeded in their mission, it was loaded with several tons of the world's most powerful explosive.

She saw a hint of motion inside the king cephid. Its spiraling intestine had suddenly clenched into a tight coil. At the same time, she realized the ALV driver's intention.

She scrambled on the wet ice, trying to right herself so she could run.

The ALV's right track clipped the edge of an igloo. The dome seemed to explode. Broken ice chunks were hurled in all directions. The ALV reared up on its other track for a moment, then slammed back down and kept coming.

Rica's crampons finally caught hold, but she was almost

out of time. After three powerful strides to build speed, she lunged forward and sailed through the rain, holding the saw out in front of her. She was still falling when the ALV plunged into the king cephid.

The driver was going for a direct hit, but the beast apparently realized the danger and tried to step aside. The ALV's sharp snout struck its body a glancing blow, ripping a deep gouge in the gelatinous flesh. The left track also ran over one of its ten-foot flippers. The appendage seemed to disintegrate beneath the metal track shoes.

The impact twisted the ALV sideways. The driver braked, locking the tracks. The long vehicle spun counterclockwise through the camp, flinging aside two dome tents that had survived the last battle. Its rear end swung past Rica, close enough for the wind to ruffle her soggy coveralls.

She got up and lurched after the ALV, carrying the chain saw. The king cephid gave chase, gulping and flashing its bottom three light belts. Limping on its remaining three flippers with the aid of its arms, the giant beast was still faster than Rica.

The ALV stopped skidding and accelerated toward her. Joan must be driving, she thought. Who else would have the nerve to try ramming the king cephid at full speed?

If Joan was driving, it meant Cliff had picked her up on his way back with the explosives, which meant he too was still alive, and so were the children—probably. Knowing they had survived redoubled Rica's will to reach the safety of the fast machine before the king cephid could catch her.

As the ALV rolled past her, she ran to the open troop door at its rear. Someone pulled her in and slammed the door. To her surprise, it was Jory.

"Where's Cliff?" she asked.

Jory was unable to answer. He was having a coughing fit.

The ALV was accelerating.

She made her way around high stacks of explosives to the driver's box. Her heart leaped when she saw Cliff hunched over the figure-eight steering control, his forehead pressed to the periscope. He was covered with sweat.

"We have to get Paz and Bonnie," she said. "They're still in one of the igloos."

Cliff had stopped accelerating but was still driving at a low speed.

Surely we've left the camp by now, Rica thought. "Why aren't you stopping?" she asked. "You're not going to try ramming it again, are you?"

"Hell, no," Cliff said. "That thing could wreck us. Or tear the roof off if it gets a hold."

"So where are you going?"

"It's chasing us," Cliff said. "I'll go slow and lead it away from camp, then double back for Paz and Bonnie. We don't want that monster around when we stop to pick them up."

# CHAPTER 36

# Joan

Todd spun around to put himself between Sophie and the cephid that had just plunged into the underground pool of carcasses. He frantically waded away through the chest-high sludge, shoving aside floating bits of carrion and stumbling over squishy bodies that had sunk to the bottom. Joan was screaming obscenities behind him. He heard a lot of splashing and saw chaotically moving shadows projected onto the wall and ceiling by her bobbing headlamp.

He reached the wall and huddled with Sophie between him and the wet ice. The carrion chamber was warm enough for the walls to be melting, even though they had been frozen solid back in the ice cave.

The chamber grew quiet, except for low moans from Sophie and blooping drips of meltwater. Joan's light was still on but no longer moving. Todd wanted to look behind him but was too afraid.

"Hey, kid, what the hell are you doing?"

He dared to look back.

Joan was shining her light up the chute again. The cephid floated nearby, an inert dollop of clear jelly.

"All right! You killed it!"

"Nah, it was already dead. The others must have thrown it in here to add it to their . . . stash."

Joan's teeth were chattering so hard she could barely speak.

"Sophie is sh-shivering," Todd gasped.

"If we can't get . . . out of this water," Joan stammered, "we'll be dead of hypothermia in a few minutes."

They had donned several layers of puffy polyester fleece beneath their filthy white coveralls when the rain had begun. The hydrophobic material could insulate them from cold air even when wet, but it was not adequate protection from immersion in icewater.

The nearly vertical chute was too steep to climb. Joan explored with her headlamp and spied a ledge on the opposite side of the pool. Above the ledge was the dark entrance of a hallway-size tunnel.

"Where does it go?" Todd asked.

"Beats me, kid."

Joan climbed out and helped them into the passage. Todd paused to pour the fetid water out of Sophie's bassinet and wring out her clothing.

They came to a crossroads. Joan started to turn right. "The other way slopes upward," Todd observed. They decided to go left.

The floor was dry again. Their breath made sparkling fog. Todd could feel stiff ice freezing in the outer layers of his wet clothing, but he stopped shivering and started sweating after they had walked at top speed for a while.

After a mile or so, Todd said, "Maybe we should try the other—"

Joan clamped a cold hand over his mouth. "I hear something! Stay here." She drew her survival knife and ran down the passage.

Todd stood and watched, wishing he had his own headlamp. The tunnel curved to the right about eighty feet ahead. When Joan reached the bend, she abruptly stopped and began to back up in a low crouch with her arms upraised.

Todd could hear nothing, probably because his ears were still full of putrid water, but he began to see subtle shifts of shadow in the curving tunnel beyond Joan.

As if arriving from another dimension, a swarm of cephids materialized in the dark tunnel at the limit of Joan's lamplight. They approached at the pace of a slow run, slithering along the floor, the walls, and even the ceiling with such haste that their movements were jerky. Todd began to hear echoing pops, like someone walking on bubble wrap, as they tore their suction cups loose from the ice without bothering to release the vacuum. He wondered why they were not walking on their flippers.

"Run!" Joan yelled. She turned toward him, leaning forward to sprint. As she took the first step, a cephid arm uncurled from the ceiling and grabbed her right knee.

The king cephid chased the ALV as Cliff drove away from camp. The injured leviathan hobbled along as fast as it could, which was about eight miles per hour. Cliff concentrated on keeping the ALV just beyond its reach.

Rica tapped his shoulder. "Cliff, where's Joan? Where are the kids?"

*"What?"* he said. "They're not in the camp?" He briefly glanced at her. She was stooping in the narrow doorway, breathing hard and trembling all over, soaked to the skin with rainwater, still holding the chain saw in a white-knuckle grip.

"No," she said with an expression of incredulous grief. "We split up. They were supposed to meet you on your way back."

A loud clang resounded through the vehicle, and they felt a jolt from the rear. Cliff stomped the accelerator. Rica kept quiet so he could concentrate on driving.

A few minutes later they sped back to camp. The king cephid was still limping toward them, but they had lured it all the way to the edge of the mesa before turning around.

Paz was conscious but delirious. One of the igloo blocks

had hit his forehead, and the deep gash was weakly bleeding.

Bonnie was shivering, drooling, and babbling nonsense. The way her gaze darted around reminded Cliff of how Todd had looked just after the boy's rescue.

After loading Paz and Bonnie, they collected any equipment that could be useful from the igloos, including the baited grenades left over from last night's battle. When they finished tossing the stale fish into the ALV, Cliff felt like his chest had imploded, but not from exertion. He glanced at his wristwatch, trying to breathe. It was still earlier than any cephids should have been able to reach the mesa.

"Rica, I'm—I'm so sorry," he stammered.

"It wouldn't have mattered," she said. "We didn't have time to evacuate, anyway. They must have come up through the ice. We saw a big hole where Eddy's tent used to be."

*"Through the ice?"* Cliff said. "My God, of course! That explains the hole under the Globemaster too."

"It's getting close," Jory called. He'd been keeping an eye on the king cephid while Cliff and Rica loaded the bait-bombs.

Rica lurched toward the driver's box, but Cliff beat her to it. "Where to?" he asked.

"Back toward the plane," she said. "Maybe you just missed Joan and the kids and they're still out there."

After Cliff had put some distance between the ALV and the king cephid, he said, "I hope we've seen the last of that bastard."

"Me too," Rica said with a shudder. "What did you mean about a hole under the Globemaster?"

"It was like an open manhole," Cliff said. "Kind of hidden behind one of the skis. When we were loading the explosives, Jory almost fell into it."

"That must be how they got past the sentries when they attacked the planes," Rica said.

"Yeah, and I'll bet the Floe is so light because it's riddled with tunnels! Subzero glacial ice could be like a self-sealing hull—seawater intruding a crack would freeze and plug it up."

They hadn't had time to discuss how the underwater passage they'd discovered during the dive could have been produced. Now it seemed obvious.

"The arches and chutes and overhangs," Rica said, "could they be tunnels that have partially melted away?"

"No doubt," Cliff said, keeping his face pressed to the periscope. "Hey, Jory! I think we just figured out why the Floe is floating so high in the water. About half of its volume must be air-filled tunnels. Why do you think it hasn't just fallen apart?"

Jory lifted his head. "Huh?" He had fallen asleep, slumped atop a stack of octanitro crates.

Cliff wished he could consult Raymond Price. In the rare peaceful moments since Raymond's death, Cliff had missed his old friend so much that the oceanographer's absence felt like a ghost haunting him, an anti-presence that followed his every move. Now he also longed for the deceased scientist's expertise.

He repeated his question before Jory could fall back to sleep.

"Ice is weak," Jory replied. "The Floe must be holding together like a house of cards, every beam and column reinforcing the others . . . just barely."

"So what would happen if we took out a column or two in the middle?"

"Maybe nothing. Maybe *kashoomp!*—the whole thing crumbles. Let's all jump up and down at the same time and see what happens." Jory tried to snicker and bent over with a wracking cough.

"I have a better idea," Cliff said. "Rica, would a blast inside the Floe be as effective as one beneath it?"

"Better," she said.

"Then let's try to find an entrance! The tunnel we swam through was big enough for the ALV. Maybe we could drive down into the Floe."

Rica nodded contemplatively, her eyelids drooping from exhaustion. She was sitting beside Jory with the chain saw across her lap. Her injured back would not allow her to slump, and it kept her shoulders twisted over to the right. "If the Floe is really like Swiss cheese, the blast might set off a chain reaction of cave-ins that could spread a long way from ground zero."

"Yeah," Jory said, "so where are we going to be standing when we push the button?"

"Rica, are you positive you can't fix the timer?" Cliff asked.

"Not a chance," she said. "Sorry."

"Then I'll stay behind to detonate the bomb," Cliff said. "But everyone else can cast off in the ALV if we can just get it into the ocean. I thought about lowering it with the winch, but I don't know how we could anchor the cable in the ice securely enough to hold up thirty— Hang on, here we go!"

The ALV pitched forward and zoomed down the mesa's steep scarp, filling its passengers with the sensation of free fall.

Rica took over the driver's seat so Cliff could climb up to the roof hatch and look out for cephids, Joan, or the children, not to mention holes in the ice.

The thunder and rain had stopped.

As she drove slowly southward, Rica thought about Cliff's plan to sacrifice himself. As a Marine, it was her duty to complete the mission, whatever the cost. Cliff was just a civilian. Furthermore, she was the demolition expert. If anything went wrong with the bomb at the time of detonation, she could fix it. He couldn't. So she had no intention of letting him be the one who stayed behind. She would knock him out and set him adrift unconscious if it came to that.

On his way to get the explosives, Cliff had been driving as fast as he could, and his view field had been limited by the periscope. This time he could see much better. When he spotted the huge cave entrance, he banged on the roof.

Rica stopped.

He told her which way to go.

The cave looked big enough for the ALV. She twisted the steering control hard to the right and hit the gas. Cliff ducked down and closed the roof hatch as the thirty-ton vehicle surged into the dark aperture.

The passage ended after a hundred yards. As soon as they stepped out on the crystalline frost, Cliff pointed and whispered, "Footprints!"

"Todd! Joan!" Rica called.

Echoes were the only answer.

Cliff shined his headlamp around the rainbow-sparkling cavern. "Where could they have gone? Their tracks only lead *into* the cave."

"Look!" Rica whispered. She was stooping to examine several rows of alternating triangular scuff marks. "These must be cephid tracks."

"A lot of them," Cliff said.

They looked at each other, thinking the same thing: this is where Joan, Todd, and Sophie were cornered and killed.

Todd heard Joan's command to run, but he disobeyed. He started toward her, to somehow free her from the cephid that was hoisting her up toward the ceiling by one leg.

Joan bent upward and scraped at the cephid's slimy arm with her fingernails—she had dropped her knife when the cephid grabbed her. The struggling made her swing and bounce. When she rotated to face Todd, she paused to wave him away. "Kid, *please*!" she panted, in a begging tone that Todd would have never expected from her. "Get the fuck out of here!"

Todd stopped and looked down at Sophie. For the first time in days she was awake but not crying or coughing. She was raptly watching the cephids, which glistened with swirls of oily iridescence as they slithered around Joan's swaying headlamp. Some of them had passed by Joan and were closing in toward Todd. He could see their writhing reflections glittering in Sophie's big attentive eyes.

Joan threw her headlamp at him. It clattered on the ice. "Go on!" she yelled. "I can stop them, but you have to get far enough away."

When her boots touched the upside-down cephid's open maw, which was dripping strings of gummy saliva onto Joan and the ice below her, the four toothed lobes of the radula began to close. She pulled a thin wire from each corner of the backpack Rica had given her, and Todd finally understood. He scooped up the headlamp, turned, and bolted, clutching Sophie's bassinet in both arms.

He had rounded the first bend when the tunnel lit up. The overgrown frost crystals turned into sparkling, blinding, multicolored stars. Then a blow from behind knocked his breath out and threw him forward.

Todd twisted around in midair so he would land on his back. He had learned the maneuver to prevent his snorkeling mask from being torn off by the water when he dived from the yacht. This time its purpose was to protect his sister and Joan's headlamp. He squeezed the top of her bassinet against his chest so that she was completely encased as he slammed down on his shoulders and skidded, plowing up frost.

A tide of orange flame rolled around the bend toward him, clinging to the ceiling. The flames dissipated as they passed overhead.

Meltwater dripped on his face as he put the headlamp on.

His ears hurt from the explosion. He could feel Sophie squirming but could not hear her cries.

Todd wondered what had caused the flames. He remembered his chemistry teacher saying that high explosives released no combustible gases the way fuel-and-oxidant mixtures like gunpowder could. He concluded that the pits of decaying carrion had released combustible and possibly toxic gases into the tunnels.

A second after the shock from the blast had subsided,

Todd felt a new vibration in the ice. Had the explosion set off a delayed cave-in?

He watched the ceiling. It was already refreezing. Dull patches of fine-grained frost were growing on the glistening wet surface like a speeded-up film of proliferating bread mold, but he saw no cracks or falling chunks.

Despite his damaged ears, he heard a deep rumble. The rumble became a roar. Then he heard splashing, like a heavy surf.

And Todd knew what was shaking the ice.

He got his trembling legs under him and sprinted on down the tunnel. His left hip hurt from the fall, forcing him to limp, but he ran as fast as he could. The roar and splashes echoed louder behind him. Then he heard something else, something familiar yet so out of context that it took him a moment to recognize it.

*Barking.*

It was the barking of seals, not dogs.

He also heard chirping and squawking. All the sounds were echoing down the tunnel like a funhouse cacophony.

The flood swept him off his feet. He mashed a hand over Sophie's mouth and nose as they were submerged. The water was so cold it seemed to sting him all over. It also stank even worse than the water in the carcass pool had, but this smell was different. It was a reek of sickness rather than death. He bobbed to the surface and held Sophie above him, floating on his back.

Something furry bumped his cheek.

"Haaeee!" Todd yelled in horror and confusion when the hairy thing squirmed left and right in the crook of his neck and then kicked off from his left jaw. Only then did his mind accept the incredible reality that he and Sophie were caught up in a subglacial flood with a menagerie of live animals.

"Let's look at the back wall," Rica said. As she and Cliff edged around the ALV, she recalled the splatters of blood and the tooth they had found at the bottom of the Floe's ramp. She hesitated at the final step, almost too scared to look.

They found the stinking crevice and the footprints leading into it. Rica tried to squeeze into the dark opening sideways but couldn't fit.

"Can I try?" Cliff asked.

She stepped aside. "Okay. I guess I'm not thinking so well at this point. Maybe Bonnie could—"

Something knocked her down. Then the sound hit—a boom that was deep and sharp at the same time, rattling loose parts in the ALV. The dark crevice widened and propagated across the floor between her and Cliff. Glittering crystals began falling from the walls and ceiling, followed by huge chunks of ice.

"Cave-in!" Cliff yelled.

They dashed to the ALV.

Rica dived into the driver's seat and mashed her forehead against the periscope's eyepiece. She jammed the transmission into reverse. The ALV sped backward, climbing at a moderate grade. Its rear end slammed into the right wall and bounced off. Then it caromed off the left wall, still accelerating.

Debris was no longer falling from the ceiling, but now the cave's floor was collapsing. A slab about the size of a tennis court dropped out of Rica's view field near the back wall, leaving a black void beneath the headlight beams. Then more slabs cracked and fell, one after another. The front of the collapsed portion of the floor kept up with the retreating ALV, the edge of the dark hole remaining less than three yards in front of the vehicle's snout.

Rica knew that her backpack bomb must have been detonated. Feeling the unstable ground quaking beneath the thirty-ton ALV, she wondered if the explosion had set off the chain reaction of tunnel collapses that she had predicted. If so, she and the other survivors were about to be swallowed up in a gravity-driven maelstrom of crumbling, crushing, disintegrating ice.

*    *    *

Todd managed to hold Sophie above the fetid deluge until they were swept over a low waterfall. When they plunged into the pool at the bottom, swirling eddies tore her bassinet from his hands. His headlamp was also pulled off.

He groped blindly through the ice-cold sewage, yelling Sophie's name. All he found was a feebly flapping penguin.

The headlamp was still shining. He could see it bobbing on the surface, sometimes pointing into the murky water and sometimes at the frosty ceiling.

Downstream of the waterfall, the flood subsided. Todd found himself crawling on wet ice, gasping and shivering, knocking dead or dying animals out of his way as he scrambled toward the light. He had to retrieve the headlamp first, or he would never find Sophie.

He could not hear Sophie crying. She's dead, he thought—I've lost her forever.

The cold made Todd so dizzy that the floor seemed to tilt back and forth like a seesaw. It would be so easy to lie down and surrender, he thought. I could just go to sleep on the ice in these wet clothes and it would all be over in a few minutes.

But he and Sophie had endured too much together for him to give up now. Since her birth, he had managed to protect her from all kinds of horrors. If there was a force in the universe that could compel him to abandon her, he still did not know what it was.

He made it to the headlamp. His fingers were too numb from cold to untwist its elastic strap, so he settled for carrying it like a flashlight. He scanned the floor with its beam, starting at the scarp that had formed the waterfall and working his way downstream. He saw nothing but feathers and hair and drowned animals.

As Todd went farther without seeing or hearing his infant sister, panic grew in his gut like fast-acting gangrene. Tears blurred his vision, flooding his eyes faster than they could drain down his cheeks. His breaths came fast and deep, further obscuring his view with plumes of fog.

Several times he started to run but forced himself to slow down. He had to search carefully, to make sure he did not overlook her. If he got to the end of the tunnel without finding Sophie and there might be even the tiniest spot that he had not checked, he would have to start the search all over again. That was what he would do anyway, of course, even if he *had* checked every spot.

A feeble cry echoed through the passage.

Todd spun around. Where was she? It sounded like the cry had come from behind him, but that was impossible— he had searched the floor thoroughly.

He ran forward a few paces.

"Wa-wa-wa-wa-wa!"

She *was* behind him. He ran back, and the cry got louder. Then softer. He had passed her somehow.

He turned around, frantically sweeping the headlamp beam.

The cry repeated.

He snapped his head up. It sounded like she was *above* him, but how could that be? He remembered the cephid that had pulled Joan up to its maw as it hung from the ceiling. He slowly lifted his gaze, hardly daring to look.

The flood had deposited the bassinet on a ledge. Todd ran to the wall and lifted his arms.

He could not reach her.

He jumped, just an inch or two at first, afraid his crampons would slip. Then he jumped harder, as if he were trying to make a slam dunk—a move that he had practiced a lot back home and was good at. He repeatedly jumped higher than he had ever jumped in his life, in spite of his fatigue and thick wet clothing, until his crampons finally did slip, and he fell.

Todd wondered how long it would take for Sophie to freeze to death. Before the storm, he had wrapped her in several thick layers of polyester fleece that would insulate her even when wet, but he knew that no infant could last long in this deep freeze, no matter what she was wearing. I'll probably outlive her, he thought, but I'm not going to leave her. He tossed his headlamp up on the ledge, hoping the light would help calm her fears during these last minutes of life.

Todd huddled and shivered with his back to the wall. Sophie continued to cry and squirm above him. After a while, he put his hands over his cold-numbed ears to block out her wails.

He was beginning to give in to the cold when he saw a dim light bobbing along the dark tunnel toward him. As far as he knew, the cephids could produce only aqua-blue light by bioluminescence. This light was yellowish-white.

It has to be a headlamp, Todd thought. But who else could possibly be down here?

# CHAPTER 37

# Hideout

"Hey! Help! Over here!" Todd yelled. He saw the silhouette of a tall thin man beneath the bobbing headlamp. The man walked with long limber strides as if accustomed to strolling the tunnels.

"Who are you?" Todd shouted, shielding his eyes from the headlamp beam.

The man did not answer. He was holding something behind his back with his right hand.

Todd knew that besides the injured Paz, Cliff and Jory were the only male members of the expedition who could still be alive. The approaching silhouette did not look like either of them. Maybe he's part of a team sent to rescue us, Todd thought. Or maybe he's here to protect the Floe or the cephids by killing us!

Todd tried to get up, hoping to lead the man away from Sophie until his intentions became clear, but his coveralls constricted around his chest and pulled him back down. He tried again, harder, with the same painful result. His rear end was frozen fast to the subzero ice, trapping him at the silent stranger's mercy.

The man stopped a few yards away. "Who else is down

here?" His voice was unfamiliar—nasal, hoarse, and muddled as if he were chewing a huge wad of bubble gum.

"Who are you?" Todd repeated.

"I asked you who else is here, boy."

"Nobody," Todd said.

"Nobody but you and the baby?"

Todd nodded, still shielding his eyes from the headlamp.

The stranger did something with his back turned to Todd. Then he came closer and removed his headlamp. He was wearing a black polyester fleece anorak and black fleece pants. He reeked of rotten fish and stale cigarette smoke. Todd saw that his skin, clothing, and hair were caked with translucent bluish gunk. Apparently the man had discovered a dead cephid and had smeared himself with its slime to avoid frostbite, as Todd had done on the night of his shipwreck.

The stranger shined the headlamp beam up at his own face, and Todd recoiled in shock. The face was pale and dirty, the jaws covered with scraggly stubble. The long, fine, light-colored hair was slicked back with a thick layer of cephid slime. The lips were chapped and shriveled, indented with several blood-scabbed cracks. The eyes were darkly bloodshot, and one had yellow pus in the corner. Puffy purple bruises hung beneath both eyes. The nose was flattened and bent to the left. Its tip was an unnatural gray, like cement.

"Don't look so good, do I?" said Dr. Chester Wimbledon.

Todd stammered, "You . . . you . . . How did—"

"Later," Chester said. "Hurts to talk. Let's get the baby down before she freezes."

Todd knew that Rica had arrested Chester, broken his nose, and locked him up, but she had never explained why. Todd's intuition told him not to trust the escaped prisoner, but Chester apparently intended to help, and Todd saw no other choice.

Chester pulled Todd loose from the floor. Then he looped a rope around Sophie's bassinet and dragged her off the ledge. Todd caught the bassinet, plucked her out, and held her close beneath his chin. "Thank you," he said.

After Chester retrieved his headlamp from the ledge, Todd drained the cold sewage from the bassinet. He wrung out the many layers of fleece in which Sophie was swaddled, then replaced them. She seemed to be all right, although chilly and still sick.

Chester reached for Sophie. "I'll take her."

"No!" Todd staggered back a step, shivering wildly.

"You're too cold," Chester said. "You might drop her."

Todd knew that Chester was right. He could barely stand. Hesitantly, he handed Sophie over. "Where are we going?"

"Back to my camp," Chester said. He briskly led them through the tunnels, turning at several intersections. His breaths accelerated with exertion and began to whistle through his broken nose. Todd was hopelessly lost but assumed that Chester was not.

At first they were climbing. Then they began to descend. The farther down they went, the more suspicious and apprehensive Todd became. He was about to snatch Sophie's bassinet and run back the way they had come when Chester turned into a cul-de-sac and stopped. The escaped prisoner pointed to a grimy sleeping bag and said, "Get warm."

Todd was incredulous. "You've been *down here* all this time? With the cephids?"

"The what?" Chester asked.

Todd explained the name Cliff had given to the Floe's transparent monsters.

"They never go into this chamber," Chester wheezed. "They've already eaten all the carcasses that were stored in here." He started to touch the frostbitten tip of his lopsided nose, then forced his hand back down with a tormented grimace.

"But weren't you scared down here?" Todd asked.

Chester stared at him. "What do you think? But they're not such bad fellows once you learn their ways. If one of them bothers you, just smack its eyeball like this." He cuffed

Todd's jaw with a chapped open palm. Todd staggered back, frightened and confused. "Just like that," Chester said. "That's how they establish the pecking order down here. I'm the *boss* in this neighborhood. They don't fuck with me anymore."

"How did you survive the attack on the planes?" Todd asked. "We thought you were killed by the cephid that made me faint."

"No, it jumped off before the plane fell into the chasm," Chester said. "You had unlocked my cage door, so I jumped off too, and I hit my head on the ice. By the time I came around, everyone was gone. I've been looking for other survivors ever since. Where did you go after you abandoned the other plane?"

Todd looked around at the cul-de-sac while telling Chester about the igloo camp. The frost on the floor had been thoroughly trampled, and bits of junk were scattered about. Todd saw a canteen, a pair of dirty underwear, and a box about the size of a briefcase with a white jacket thrown over it. Broken morphine vials were piled at the base of one wall. Crushed cigarette butts were everywhere, and the odor of stale tobacco smoke lingered in the tight enclosure. Todd wondered if that was the real reason the cephids had not come in here to eat Chester in his sleep.

There were several frosty brown bumps on the floor. Todd peered closer at one and realized with disgust that it was a frozen pile of human feces. He could also guess what had made the frozen yellow streaks on the walls.

The most horrific part of Chester's abode was a midden of frozen cephid parts in one corner. The pile included eyeballs, toothed radula lobes, claw-beaks, and intestines. Todd swallowed and said, "Mr. Wimbledon, have you had anything to eat since you came down here?"

"*Dr.* Wimbledon," Chester said. "I've had three meals a day."

"What have you been eating?" Todd asked.

Chester pointed one long finger at the pile of cephid parts

with a wry smirk. "What do you think? Sushi from hell, of
course. A pack goes by in the tunnel outside twice a day.
There's usually a straggler at the rear that none of the others
seem to miss. I just reach out and snip off its eyes with that."

He pointed to a long fiberglass tent pole leaning against
a wall. Half of a cephid's claw-beak was duct-taped to one
end of the pole.

"Then I drag the bugger back in here. They snap and
whip a lot, but you can dodge them once they're blind. Too
tough to chew . . . you have to cut it up and swallow the
pieces whole . . . tastes like old chewing gum dipped in shit,
but it has kept me going."

Todd felt sick, and more than a little uneasy. He found it
hard to believe that the cephids would go to so much trouble to rid the Floe of survivors camped on its surface while
ignoring an intruder in their subglacial warren. There had to
be something Chester was not telling him, something in addition to the escaped prisoner's body odor and personality
that he had used to ward off the cephids.

"I still don't see why you came down here," Todd said.
"Why didn't you just stay on the other plane?"

Chester handed Sophie back and stared at Todd. "Boy,
you must be even dumber than you look. That bloody plane
was baking in the sun, and there was no telling when they
would attack it again. Down here I'm out of the weather and
there's plenty to eat. Now go get in that bag until you stop
shivering. I'll head back up and find the others so we can all
stick together from now on. You have to tell me who's still
alive and where you last saw them."

Todd was still suspicious. "Why did Rica arrest you?"

Chester waved a long bony hand dismissively. "All a big
mistake. We'll clear that up later."

Todd reluctantly told Chester everything he knew as he
crawled into the filthy bag and removed Sophie from her
bassinet, tucking her against his chest. He saw a pair of
grimy gloves and put them on his miserably cold hands.

"Mr. . . . Dr. Wimbledon? I know it's been bad down here. I'm sorry we didn't come looking for you."

"Yeah, well, at least you finally unlocked that fucking cage," Chester said through one side of his mouth. He was lighting a cigarette in the other corner of his chapped lips. "So you and the baby have nothing to worry about. But that Lopez girl . . ."

Chester was crushing the half-empty cigarette pack in the long fingers of his right hand. His fist was contracted so tightly that it was shaking. He suddenly realized what he was doing and examined the remaining cigarettes with concern, pulling them out one by one to make sure they weren't broken.

He extended one toward Todd. "Want a smoke?"

Todd shook his head. He had been dozing with his eyes open, paying no attention to Chester's words. He fell soundly asleep as the escaped prisoner left his revolting hideout.

Rica, Cliff, Bonnie, and Jory picked their way over the fresh rubble in the cave where Joan and the children had disappeared. They had left Paz alone on the ALV. Motes of glittering ice dust swirled in their headlamp beams and made them cough. The floor's collapse had opened another large passage. Since someone had been alive just minutes before to detonate the backpack bomb, Rica hoped that Todd and Sophie might *still* be alive, and that the remaining adults could find them by splitting up and searching the labyrinth.

But rescuing the children was now a secondary objective. The primary objective was to find an entrance that the ALV could drive into. They were running out of time to destroy the Floe—only seven hours left until dawn—and it could take weeks to find a passable entrance, if one existed, by driving around on the surface. Rica's solution was to search on foot from inside the labyrinth. They planned to take the largest tunnel at each intersection until they found a main artery, then follow it upward.

At the first crossroads, all four tunnels were equal in size. Rica leaned against a wall and kneaded her twisted back, taking care not to impale herself with the huge glittering frost crystals that had grown from every surface like cactus spines. "Okay, it's time to split up. Bonnie, you can come with me. Do you understand what we're doing?"

Bonnie nodded, leaning her head to one side with her mouth hanging open and her twitching eyes tilted up at the ceiling.

Rica briefly laid her cheek against Cliff's, then drew her knife and hobbled as fast as she could along the right tunnel, yelling Todd's name.

Todd woke slowly to the sound of Sophie crying. It was not her hunger cry. It was not the cry that meant she was too hot or too cold or needed to be changed. Nor was it the lonely cry, the sick cry, or the nap-time cry. So what was her damn problem?

There was another sound besides the echoing cries—a medley of gurgles, like a babbling brook. Meltwater, Todd decided. The Floe's rapid thawing must have allowed a trickle to descend through a crack and invade Chester's cul-de-sac.

Todd took a deep breath, still dozing. The smell of dead fish was much stronger than it had been before, overwhelming the odors of shit and stale cigarette smoke.

It was so hard to wake up. It seemed like only seconds had passed since Chester had left, and now Todd had to get up and take care of Sophie. He managed to open one sticky eye, and through that frost-framed slit he saw a light.

The light was a diffuse glow that twinkled on the frost crystals covering the ceiling.

Its color was pale aqua blue.

Todd heard a wet slither and instantly became wide awake, twisting his head back and forth in terror. He saw hoops of blue light flashing all around him, but a dark round object that was too close to focus on was blocking most of his view. A string of aqua-blue pearls lit up above it, and he realized that the dark sphere was an eyeball.

Todd was too petrified to think. All he could do was stare back at the hovering eye.

After several seconds passed and the cephids had still not touched him, he remembered Chester's instructions. He reared back his right arm, then hesitated, wondering if Chester had lied. It doesn't matter, he thought. I'm cephid food anyway. Still, he couldn't work up the nerve to slap the cephid's eyeball.

Todd had expected to feel Sophie squirming against his chest, but he couldn't. He reached into the bag and could not detect her with his hand either. Could she have wormed her way down next to his legs? Trembling with panic, he swished both hands back and forth inside the bag.

Then on top of it.

Then all around it.

Now he knew what Sophie's unfamiliar cry meant. It meant that the cephids had finally taken her away.

# CHAPTER 38

# Murder

Chester Wimbledon stood on the edge of the mesa and scanned the Floe with binoculars. The storm was over, and the moon was high, bathing the bone-white icescape in its spectral glow. He finally spotted a corner of the ALV sitting motionless in a deep valley. Before sliding down the mesa's scarp, he checked the 9-mm Beretta M9 in his belt to make sure the safety was on.

The pistol had once been the side arm of an Air Force officer. Chester had taken it from the doomed Globemaster, which he had exited by safely descending the crew stairs, not by jumping off as he had told Todd. Unlike the Marines, Chester had been wise enough to save his bullets since then. The gun had a full clip, and from what Todd had told him, he was fairly certain that it was the only live ammunition left on the Floe.

He had tried several times to set his nose straight. Each time he had failed and nearly lost consciousness from pain. One tiny piece of bone was offset above another. Whenever he moved, the two fragments dug their sharp edges into a sensitive membrane between them. For two days and nights he had felt a stab of agony with every breath, every footstep, every pulse of blood through his face. Desperate for relief, he had deliberately allowed his nose to get numb with cold, and that had led to the frostbite that might require the whole appendage to be amputated—if his plan worked out and he managed to get home alive.

In spite of the unrelenting pain and cold and fear of being caught, Chester was still sane enough to know his options. He was going to die on the Floe, or in the ocean after the Floe melted, or he was going to be rescued by another military operation. If any other adults remained alive on the Floe when a rescue arrived, they would testify against him, and he might be convicted of the Marine sentry's murder. Even if he was acquitted, the investigation would make the incredible toughness of the cephids' claw-beaks common knowledge, and his bankrupt company would stand no chance of beating its well-funded competitors to a gene or patentable process that would generate royalties from the manufacture of goods containing the wondrous material.

Therefore, his only hope for salvaging a life worth living was to eliminate the other adults and dispose of the evidence before summoning a rescue.

Chester was not optimistic, but whether he won or lost, he planned to enjoy the next few hours. Without any due process, Rica Lopez had brutally injured and permanently disfigured him. Then she had locked him in a cage without treatment and left him there when the cephids attacked the planes. He had cried like a baby and begged God for mercy, something he had formerly taken great pride in believing he could always forbear. There had been times in the cephids' frozen dungeon when the hell-heat of unfulfilled vengeance was all that had kept him from freezing to death.

Now, at last, it was time to make her pay.

"Help! Mister! Help!" Todd's words echoed away through the frigid labyrinth.

There was no response.

The stinking cephids loomed over him on all sides, like gawkers watching a run-over pedestrian. They blinked their extended eyes, flashed bioluminescent codes to one another, and intertwined their arms, scratching and rubbing themselves.

When he tilted his head back and looked above him, he finally saw Sophie. One cephid was holding her out on three arms as if offering a sacrifice to some pagan god. Others were examining her closely, their eyes extended to hover all around her. Beakless tentacle tips were probing her swaddling and slithering across her contorted red face.

"Get away from her!" Todd screamed, kicking off the sleeping bag. He jumped up with his headlamp strap around one elbow, pulled several cephid arms aside with his hands, and snatched his little sister back. The cephids did not resist. He gripped her in both arms, shouldered his way through the slimy horde like a rushing tailback, and ran for the entrance of the cul-de-sac.

He had barely cleared the cephids when he tripped over something heavy and pitched forward, just managing to execute his rotating dive maneuver so he would fall on his back and not crush his sister. He sat up and tried to dig his crampon spikes into the ice, but his feet were tangled in a white jacket. He had tripped over the square box that the jacket had been covering. Now the box was exposed, and Todd recognized it.

It was Agent Johnson's datalink machine.

The cephids were trudging toward him. Sophie was still crying, so he assumed she was okay. He got to his feet and ran up the curving corridor outside, following Chester's freshest tracks.

Chester limped in front of the ALV, dragging his right leg with the foot turned outward. He waved his arms and yelled. Surely they would let him in if he appeared to be injured. His handgun was tucked into a hip pocket where the person manning the periscope could not see it.

When no one responded, he hobbled to the vehicle, still feigning a dislocated knee, and banged on the door with his fist. A few seconds later he concluded that the ALV was deserted and climbed in through the roof hatch. With any luck, the cephids had finished off the other survivors, but he had to make sure.

On the driver's seat he found a note for Todd:  *"We went to look for you in tunnels. Stay here, hatches closed, no matter what."*

"Bugger!" Chester hissed. He crumpled the note and tossed it into a corner. If the cephids didn't get them all, the searchers would eventually find his hideout and the datalink machine. Then they could piece together what he had done and call for a rescue.

After Todd had fainted outside Chester's unlocked cage, the cephid had hovered over the children for a moment and then moved on. It was from this display of atypical self-restraint that Chester had figured out the true secret of surviving among the cold-blooded brutes, a secret he had not told Todd.

He had looked on the ALV and found no one except Dale Johnson, who was waiting for his datalink machine to establish a satellite connection. It was then that Chester had thought of hiding out away from the others and postponing rescue until the cephids killed everyone but him. It took him only a few seconds to bash Dale Johnson's head against the wall until the agent was bound to be dead.

Over the next two days, he'd checked in with headquarters at the prearranged times, pretending to be Agent Johnson. He convinced them that the mission had proceeded smoothly since Sergeant Gavril's death. He told them that all of the deaths had been caused by heat-crazed elephant seals, which the Marines had subsequently shot. He said the Navy helicopter had been found in a crevasse, apparently pushed there across the wet ice by the wind.

Meanwhile, Raymond Price had used his depth-imaging sonar to determine that the Floe was a natural phenomenon. A long spur of ice was sticking down beneath the Floe into a deep, narrow, and previously unknown current that swept straight up the Pacific like an undersea jet stream. The spur was catching the current like a sail, dragging the Floe along. The current broke up when it reached the Hawaiian islands, explaining the Floe's recent change to an irregular course.

Since the Floe was not a national security threat after all and had passed by Hawaii, there was no need for another military operation except to extract the survivors, all of whom—according to Chester—had voted to stay on and study the Floe, now that they had learned to look out for elephant seals. The Marine Corps still wanted to send an Osprey to evacuate the children as soon as possible, but Chester managed to convince them that both children were doing fine and there was no longer any danger on the Floe, so it would be an unnecessary expense.

Chester knew his ruse was wearing thin. So were his nerves. He was tired of waiting for the cephids to do the dirty work. At the last check-in, the CIA had asked why only one of the two Globemasters had shown up on the latest satellite photos of the Floe. Chester had said one plane was on a brief flight for aerial reconnaissance at that time. They had seemed to believe him, but if they updated the satellite photos before he checked in tomorrow morning, he was sure they would send another team to investigate.

Swearing to himself, he turned to climb out of the ALV. He did not notice Paz Rodriguez stretched out on the floor, the only reason the marine had survived the near encounter.

Sophie was too young to remember anything about the Floe, so Chester planned to let her live. The media would portray him as a hero for saving her. He'd make at least a million from the talk show circuit and the rights to his memoirs.

Regrettably, Todd would eventually have to go, but not until Chester no longer needed him to look after Sophie.

The first thing Chester had to do was hunt down the other adults and kill them before they could find the datalink machine.

Todd emerged from the shadows beneath a dripping arch and crept to the ALV when he was certain that Chester was gone. Still following footprints, he had nearly caught up to the escaped prisoner, but the implications of finding the datalink machine had finally dawned on him, and he'd pulled back before Chester could hear Sophie.

In all of his fourteen years, Todd had never felt such rage.

He found the ALV dark and quiet. The temptation to rest nearly overwhelmed him, but he could guess what Chester was planning—he had seen the escaped prisoner checking and concealing his gun. Somehow, he had to stop Chester or warn whoever else was left before the killer could find them.

But how could he overtake Chester while carrying Sophie? The very idea was ludicrous. Not only was she a physical burden and a potential hostage; she would announce his presence to anyone within earshot. His only option was to leave her on the ALV and pray that the cephids would not break into the vehicle before he returned. He placed her on the floor beside Paz, hoping the Marine's body heat would help keep her warm, and began searching for a weapon.

All he could find was a one-liter MSR fuel bottle. The red steel cylinder was full of gasoline, so it would pack a hefty wallop. He hooked a finger through the black plastic ring in its screw-in cap and gave the soft driver's seat a couple of practice whacks.

Satisfied, he bounded up the ladder to the roof hatch.

Before closing the ALV's hexagonal lid, he took a last look at Sophie. She was staring up at him with her big trusting eyes. Todd nearly lost his nerve. He had never dreamed that he would someday have to leave her by herself in so much danger.

Todd scrambled over the shattered floor of the ice cave, following the others' footprints back into the labyrinth. He was afraid that Chester would ambush him, but he was not as scared of the cephids as he had once been. Retrieving Sophie from their clutches had bolstered his confidence. But how had he managed it? The cephids must have let us go, he thought, but why?

At the first crossroads, the footprints split up three ways. One person had turned left, and one had gone ahead. It looked like *three* people had turned right, so Todd turned right too. He figured there had to be at least two sets of prints in the tunnel Chester had taken—one set from Chester and one from his quarry.

One of the three sets of boot prints was huge. The other prints were smaller. Thinking of who could be left alive, Todd deduced that Chester was stalking Bonnie and Rica.

The tunnel forked after several minutes. One set of prints went right and two sets went left. Todd turned left, jogging as fast as he could. A minute later he heard someone ahead calling his name. The echoes were eerie and shrill.

Bonnie.

Todd felt relieved that Rica was not the killer's first intended victim. It had been obvious to Todd from the start that Rica cared about him and Sophie, so he felt the same way about her. Then he thought about how unfair to Bonnie his relief was, especially considering all she had done to care for his sister, and he redoubled his efforts to catch up. If he could hear her shouts, so could Chester.

He saw her headlamp. She was a long way ahead on a straight stretch that contained the dark round entrances of several crossing tunnels at regular intervals. Todd swerved back and forth, trying to catch a glimpse of Chester's silhouette in front of the sparkling tunnel segment surrounding her light. He wanted to warn her by yelling, but he knew that would ruin his chances of sneaking up on the armed killer, who would probably just shoot Bonnie and then come after him.

Todd stopped when he realized that Chester's footprints had disappeared. He swiftly backtracked until he saw where they turned right into one of the many passages intersecting the long corridor. He could guess what Chester was up to, and it meant that he probably had only seconds left to act.

Todd hesitated, trying not to panic. He wondered if his quick breaths had already given him away. Between Bonnie's shouts, the catacomb was so quiet that he almost believed Chester might hear his thudding heartbeats. He finally decided to run straight to Bonnie rather than pursuing Chester. If he could warn her quietly, they might manage to slip away before Chester saw him.

As he began to run, he heard a shrill scream that climbed in pitch to a hypersonic crescendo. It echoed several times up and down the long passage.

Bonnie had turned around, and a tall limber figure was silhouetted by her headlamp.

Todd switched off his own headlamp but kept running toward them with the heavy fuel bottle upraised behind his head.

The silhouette swung one long arm from left to right between himself and Bonnie. A fountain of blood spurted from her neck, splattering the wall beside her and trickling down to the floor in a broad swath of crimson. The warm fluid gave off steam in the frigid air and melted the delicate spicules of frost on the wall, creating a smooth spot.

Bonnie's next scream came out as a whining splutter.

She fell to her knees, clasping her throat so that the blood ran down her arms and chest.

Todd kept running.

The next time he looked up, Bonnie lay on her back in a pool of blood. Chester was wiping his knife on her leg.

Todd looked back down to watch where he was going, and suddenly the long corridor went completely dark.

He stopped running, fumbled for his headlamp, and switched it on. A merciful glow surrounded him with rainbow sparkles from the overgrown frost crystals, and Todd realized what had happened. Chester had taken Bonnie's headlamp and fled into a side passage.

He ran on to Bonnie.

She was as pale as blank copy paper but still twitching and moving her lips. Her frightened eyes turned toward

Todd as he knelt beside her, and he saw a glimmer of recognition in them. He recoiled but listened when she tried to talk and part of her voice came from the bubbling incision that ran across her throat.

"I think I know now . . . why they killed your parents . . . but not you," she said. "It was the slime."

She closed her eyes.

"The slime?" Todd whispered. "What do you mean?"

"Chester used it too," she whispered. "All over him. They should have killed him, but . . . they thought . . . he was one of them."

Todd shook her arm. "I still don't understand."

She did not respond.

He waited a second or two, then shook her again. She was still taking shallow breaths. Every time she exhaled, bloody foam bubbled up from the slit in her throat.

Todd concluded that Bonnie was not going to return to consciousness.

He followed Chester's footprints into one of the side passages. This could not be the route Chester had used to sneak up on Bonnie, because his prints went in only one direction. Since the killer was no longer following a trail, he apparently knew where he was going. And so did Todd.

If this passage continued straight ahead, it was a shortcut to the fork Rica had taken.

# CHAPTER 39

# Sleepers

Chester's tracks joined up with Rica's at the next intersection. Then the trail entered an upward spiral. After another crossroads, the air grew warmer and the sparkling frost crystals gave way to smooth walls that glistened with wetness.

I must be getting close to the surface, Todd thought.

The top of the spiral opened into a large room with a low ceiling supported by a forest of thick columns. The floor was flat, level, and covered by an inch or two of standing water. Animal parts protruded up through the water like rice plants growing in a paddy. Todd saw many whole fish and legs from seals. He took one grotesque planting to be a penguin that had been skinned and stuffed headfirst into a hole in the floor.

Todd thought he recognized the creepy shadow cast on the still water by another object. He stepped around the ice column between him and the object and confirmed that it was a man's hand. The pudgy forearm had apparently been severed at the elbow and embedded in the ice so that the hand appeared to be reaching up from a shallow grave, grasping at the air. Todd imagined he would faint if the fingers moved, but there wasn't much chance of that—they were bloated with gas and colored asphalt-gray with black fingernails.

A series of quick splashes came from behind him.

Todd whirled toward the noise but saw nothing. Then he looked down. Ripples were expanding on the water from a point behind the nearest ice column.

He started to lunge away from the column, but his reaction came too late. A glassy cephid arm shot out and snared his wrist, restraining him as firmly as a handcuff. This was the first time they had actually grabbed him, he realized. Whatever charm had protected him and Sophie in the past, it must have worn off.

He clubbed at the arm with the red steel fuel bottle, but the slender tendril just absorbed the blows like a bungee cord until another arm shot out and grabbed his free wrist.

The second cephid arm had come from a column on his opposite side. When it retracted, his own arms were stretched out in opposite directions as if he were being crucified. Todd twisted and jerked, too scared to yell. He dropped the fuel bottle. The cephid arms stretched a little, but they maintained enough tension to pin him in place. Meanwhile, an army of transparent cephids quietly emerged from behind the columns and slinked through the water toward him.

"Todd! Is that you?"

It was Rica's voice.

She sounded so far away that she could not have heard his struggles, which had produced no noise except some splashing. That meant she had heard something else, Todd thought.

Or someone.

Alone in the dark catacombs, Rica had started spending as much time looking over her shoulder as she did watching where she was going.

Until now.

Now she had to watch her step, because one trip or slip could send her plunging . . . who knew how far.

After traversing the hatchery—the low room full of submerged egg holes stuffed with animal parts—she had gone down a long, winding, wet corridor that opened into a room so huge she could not see the walls, ceiling, or floor. Before her was a narrow footbridge that arched upward and disappeared in the dark void about a hundred feet away. It took all of her courage to step out onto the steep, rounded, dripping-wet arch.

About ten feet out on the bridge, she realized that the chamber's bottom was visible after all. It was barely close enough to reflect her lamplight, at least a hundred fifty feet below her. She squatted and leaned to look down, holding her light out over the abyss. The bottom of the chamber was strangely lumpy and swirly, like a colossal bowl of whipped butter. It reflected rainbow shimmers of oily iridescence, unlike any other iceform she had seen on the Floe.

The corner of her vision caught movement, and she swung her headlamp beam toward it. Smack in the bright spot at the center of the beam, a large cephid eye was blinking and squinting up at her. A split second after she realized what she was looking at, the stalk retracted and the eyeball blooped down into the iridescent morass.

Rica snapped off her headlamp and jumped to her feet, windmilling her arms for balance. A rush of blood pressure pounded in her temples. Despite the temptation to gasp for air, she held her breath and listened in the absolute darkness for gurgles or slithers.

So this is where they sleep! She'd figured they couldn't spend *all* of their time swimming or hunting.

The bottom of the chamber was apparently a mass of inert cephids intertwined in the oily water. Her headlamp beam had roused at least one of them. She could only hope that it would go back to sleep rather than alerting the others or climbing up the wall to investigate.

She squatted again, afraid of falling, trying not to groan

from the pain. Now what? She could not continue climbing across the arch of wet ice in total darkness, but she didn't dare turn her headlamp back on.

"Rica! Help!"

It was Todd. The distant cry had come from the passage behind her.

Forcing herself to move slowly, she took tiny steps until it felt like she had turned all the way around. She touched the bridge with her hands to confirm that it was sloping downward in front of her. Still crouching, she took more baby steps until the slope flattened out, then reached her hand into the darkness to feel for the wall.

Instead of the cold ice she had expected, her fingers touched something soft, warm, and stubbly.

Rica flicked on her headlamp, barely managing to stifle a scream. It took her a few seconds to realize that the ghastly apparition standing before her was even human. His skin and eyes had been grotesquely mauled by the cold dry air inside the Floe. Prolonged subdermal bleeding from his broken nose had distended and discolored his features. He looked like a corpse resurrected from the dead after moderate decomposition.

After her initial shock and revulsion, Rica felt a fleeting burst of relief that Chester Wimbledon was still alive, because it meant she was not responsible for an innocent man's death. But as she watched his pained features twist into a menacing snarl, her relief was replaced by fear.

"Hello, *girl*."

Before she could reply, his bony right hand shot out toward her, open-palmed, aiming for her nose.

Despite her injuries and numbing exhaustion, Rica's training kicked in. She ducked, and Chester's palm slammed into the wet wall.

He followed with a left jab that plowed into her right breast. She twisted around and kicked his right calf. Half of her inch-long crampon spikes plunged into his flesh to the hilt. She expected him to fall or at least bellow in pain, but he just glanced down at the steel teeth biting into his leg and then looked at her with a tobacco-stained grin.

"Morphine," he said. "I've been shooting up day and night for *this*." He pointed a finger that was shaking with rage at his lopsided, frostbitten nose.

Todd expected a third cephid arm to wrap his throat from behind at any moment and twist off his head. Or maybe one of the claw-beaks would eviscerate him.

He was bewildered when the gurgling brutes began probing his gloves with their beakless arm tips as if trying to shake hands with him. Looking at the gloves, he realized that their palms were soaked with Bonnie's blood. He had supported himself on his hands while kneeling beside her to listen.

He unclenched his fists, and a cephid pulled off his right glove. Another one snatched it away, and they began fighting over the prize. The cephid arm holding his right wrist let go.

He reached over and pulled off his left glove, and they released his left wrist as well. A small cephid popped the bloody glove into its open maw. The others began using their closed claw-beaks to club its mantle above its retracted eyes.

None of them appeared to notice Todd anymore.

Now he understood what Bonnie's last words had meant. As smart as the cephids seemed, they had apparently mistaken him and Sophie and Chester for members of their own species because the three humans had been smeared with slime from a dead cephid. They obviously recognized prey by smell, and it seemed the scent of mammalian blood could override the slime masquerade, at least after the actual slime had been washed away and its lingering odor had dwindled for several days.

He picked up the fuel bottle, dodged through the slimy throng, and bolted in the direction Rica's voice had come from.

*     *     *

When Todd arrived at the huge chamber, what he saw atop the arching footbridge crossing its center enraged and terrified him. Rage won out, and he began to climb.

Rica was prone on her back with Chester straddling her hips, beating her head against the ice. In his black fleece outfit, Chester looked like a manifested phantom made of pure darkness.

Todd silently crept up behind the escaped killer and raised the red fuel bottle above his head, gripping its cap in the crook of his strongest finger. He leaned back and swung the weapon down with all his might. It thunked against the back of Chester's head and bounced upward with a dent in its side.

Chester collapsed onto Rica without a sound.

The impact had broken the plastic ring cap of the fuel bottle. When the ring fell apart, Todd tried to catch the bottle but couldn't get a grip on it. The heavy red bottle bounced off the arch and tumbled into the blackness below. Todd heard it splash into water.

The splashing continued.

At first he thought it was just echoes bouncing around the vast chamber. Then he realized that the splashes were getting louder.

"Rica?"

She moaned and lifted one arm.

"Rica! Something's down there!"

The air was alive with echoing splashes. Todd could also hear slithers, gurgles, and the same bubble-wrap-popping that he had heard when the cephids overtook Joan. This time there were so many pops that they blended together into a continuous tone like the shots from Paz's minigun.

He started to shove Chester off the arch.

"Wait!" Rica moaned. She grabbed one of Chester's arms as she sat up and dragged his limp body back onto the arch so that he was draped across it, facedown.

"Come on, Rica, dump him," Todd hissed.

"No, if he's alive, we need him."

"What for?"

"To guide us through the tunnels."

The splashes had mostly stopped, but the pops and wet slithers were steadily growing louder. Todd could see iridescent glimmers of movement all over the distant walls.

Rica stumbled to her feet. "Let's go," she groaned.

Todd grabbed Chester's ankles and dragged the unconscious killer behind him as he ran down the slippery arch.

# CHAPTER 40

## Escape

"Coming up on the fork," Rica yelled.

"Bear left," Chester said in his nasal lisp.

"Are you sure that tunnel's big enough?"

"Yes, but slow down!"

It was three hours until dawn, and Rica was taking the curves at full throttle, relying on the gentle slope between the sparkling tunnel's floor and walls to tilt the ALV inward like a car going around a racetrack. Chester sat on the floor beside her, bound but not gagged, giving directions. Jory held the gun they had found on Chester, aiming at the killer's groin to ensure his cooperation. They had also confiscated Chester's headlamp. If he got away from them in the Floe's catacombs, he wouldn't get far.

They had to shout over the reverberating echoes of the roaring engine and grinding tracks. The wind outside was even louder—the ALV almost filled the tunnel, so the air rushing backward toward the vacuum left behind the speeding machine had to travel much faster than the ALV itself. It sounded to Rica like flying in the hold of a C-130 with the cargo ramp down. Now and then the wind shrieked like an old locomotive's steam whistle.

After failing to find the children, or an entrance suitable

for the ALV, Cliff and Jory had returned to the vehicle, as
had Todd and Rica with Chester in tow. They'd found Paz
and Sophie sleeping peacefully, still snuggled together. Todd
had told the others about finding the datalink machine in
Chester's hideout, so they all knew that the failed entrepre-
neur had deliberately postponed a rescue. When Rica threatened his misshapen nose with a hammer, he had not
hesitated to lead them to the largest entrance he knew of,
and then to the lowest level of the catacombs.

Chester told her to stop when they reached a dome-
shaped room the size of a small gymnasium. Rica counted
eight dark tunnel entrances in the walls. "Where do these
branches lead?"

"They all end at big pits full of dead animals," Chester
said. His bloodshot eyes radiated despair as well as hate, but
Rica still did not trust him.

"It'll be easier to defend ourselves at one of those dead
ends," she said, "but we'll need a sentry at the entrance to
watch for cephids while we work."

"I'll stay," Jory whispered. He had become almost completely unable to talk due to his inflamed vocal cords. "As
long as I'm guarding Wimbledon, I can't help you build the
bomb anyway."

Rica nodded. "Fire one shot if you have any trouble."

Jory marched Chester out of the troop cabin at gunpoint.

Rica backed the ALV into one of the tunnels, parked near
the end, and directed the construction of a pyramid with the
crates of octanitrocubane staggered so that she had room to
insert a detonator cap into each of them with a lead azide
primary charge and a cyclonite secondary charge. She
showed Cliff and Todd how to help her wire the detonator
caps so that all of the blocks in the pyramid would explode
at once. Todd called out the time every ten minutes to help
them pace themselves.

Jory held the pistol under his jacket to keep it warm, sitting on the frosty floor of the huge hub-dome. Chester's bro-

ken nose whistled with each foggy breath. Jory finally kicked his leg. "Stop it! I won't be able to hear if anything sneaks up on us."

Chester responded with a pitiful moan.

"What I don't get is how you stole all that stuff from our camp without getting caught," Jory said. He kicked Chester's leg again. "Well?"

"The hole under the Globemaster," Chester wheezed. "I used it during the night after the cephids attacked the planes. The next night, I snuck into your camp under the fog before the cephids came out."

It must have also been before I turned on the sonar scanner, Jory thought.

Slumped against the wall, Jory felt himself beginning to relax for the first time since leaving Hawaii. There was no longer any reason to panic. They had retrieved the datalink machine and requested a rescue by sea. Wondering if any of the lower tunnels had been exposed when Rica blasted off the Floe's stern promontory, they had also driven to the southern end of the labyrinth and found an opening that appeared to be a perfect escape route. It was big enough to drive out through and just a few yards above sea level.

Most important, they were safe from the cephids now, if the slime trick really worked. On Todd's recommendation, Rica had found a cephid pack in the tunnels, run one down with the ALV, and smeared its reeking exudate all over the six surviving humans.

"Many animals recognize each other by smell," Cliff had said, "or use odor to identify their social group. It may seem crazy to us that they can't tell we aren't cephids just by looking at us, but that's the way instinct and brains interact— unless instinct tells the brain to perform a certain task, its potential ability remains untapped."

Jory still had doubts, but he knew the cephids had proven themselves stupid enough to eat a knife just because it was covered with human blood.

He yawned deeply. He'd never felt so sleepy.

A short while later, Jory yanked his head up and opened his eyes, alarmed by a snuffling sound. He looked around but saw no cephids. Chester's head was slumped over. The prisoner appeared to be asleep but not snoring. Jory concluded that he must have made the sound himself.

He thought about calling for help, but if Cliff, Rica, and Todd could still work after what they'd been through, the least he could do was stay awake to guard Chester and watch out for cephids.

Jory stretched and leaned back against the wall again, briefly closing his raw eyes to give them a rest from the frigid air. His tests with the DNA sequencer while retrieving the explosives had provided final proof that the cephids were of this Earth, but if they *had* been extraterrestrials, he mused, what would their spaceship have looked like?

Jory woke feeling pain on the left side of his face. Someone had slapped his cheek. He turned to look forward and saw Chester squatting in front of him, grinning.

The rope they had used to bind Chester's hands lay on the ice. Beside it was Jory's pocketknife. Chester was wearing Jory's headlamp and aiming the pistol at Jory's head.

"No!" Jory yelled as Chester pulled the trigger.

A gunshot echoed through the catacombs.

Rica dashed to the front of the ALV. "Jory?" she yelled.

There was no answer.

"We'd better go see," Cliff said.

Rica nodded. "Todd, you stay here with Sophie and Paz. We'll be back as soon as we can."

They ran to the mouth of the tunnel and found Jory slumped against the wall. Blood was trickling down from a small hole between his eyes, dripping from the tip of his nose. On the wall behind his head was a vermilion corona the size of a truck tire.

Cliff heard a slithering sound behind him and whirled around. More slithers and sloshing echoed from the access tunnel that had brought them down to the hub chamber. He and Rica panned their headlamps all around the dome. Chester appeared to be long gone, but now the cephids were coming.

"Were they drawn by the blood?" Rica whispered.

"Maybe, but they got here so fast. They probably heard the shot and came down to—"

A tremendously loud gunshot resounded in the dome, echoing many times. Cliff thought it had come from one of the side tunnels right in front of them. He flicked his headlamp off. Rica's remained on, shining from behind him. He had just enough time to wonder why she had not doused her headlamp as well before he heard her groan and felt her fall against his legs, knocking him off balance. As he tumbled forward, another shot rang out, and he felt something pluck at the top of his parka hood.

"Rica! No!" he yelled as he landed on the ice.

# CHAPTER 41

# Blood

She was on her side, curled backward. Her long slender back was arched in a way that he had not seen since the cephid on the Floe's western wall had tried to pull her apart. Her headlamp was aimed upward, making the high ceiling sparkle.

In the reflected light, he could see that her face was contorted with agony. Her lips were pulled back and her eyes were squeezed shut. Her right boot kicked at the ice with its crampon points, slowly spinning her body around. Her left leg dragged behind, leaving a broad streak of blood on the frost.

She was clawing at her shoulder rather than her wounded leg. Cliff wondered if the second shot—the one meant for him—had hit her upper body. Then he realized she was trying to take off her backpack. He helped her, glancing around, still unable to spot the shooter.

Cephids were pouring into the hub chamber.

Rica's eyes opened. They were red with rage. Her breath came in short gasps between clenched teeth.

Another shot rang out. Cliff saw chips explode from the wall where the bullet had impacted. At the same time, he and Rica were pelted hard by drops of cold water. The bullet must have passed through a cephid, he thought. That meant the cephids were now between them and Chester.

Rica unzipped her pack and pulled out one of the explosive fish they had retrieved from the demolished igloo camp. She reached into the fish's mouth and retrieved the hand grenade—Cliff assumed she didn't want the cephids to interfere with her aim this time. She sat up with a groan, released the grenade's spoon, and hurled the grenade toward the side tunnel on the other side of the cephid pack.

A beakless arm shot up from one of the creatures and grabbed the live grenade in midair. The cephid was only a few yards from Cliff and Rica, well within the grenade's wounding blast radius. Its comrades swarmed toward it, reaching to steal the prize, which they had apparently mistaken for food because it was still covered with fish juice. One of them snatched the grenade, then pitched over on the floor and used its arms to drag itself away from the rest of the pack, which immediately gave chase. It headed for the entrance of the side tunnel, away from Cliff and Rica, swallowing the grenade as it slithered along.

The grenade exploded.

The concussion knocked the breath from Cliff's lungs, and a few bite-size chunks of cephid meat slammed into his back hard enough to bruise. When he was finally able to inhale, the air was thick with an oily mist that tasted bitter and rotten. His ears hurt, and all he could hear was a pulsating hiss that he knew was not a real sound.

The floor still felt solid, but there was no way for him to sense whether the ceiling was cracking from the blast. Rica had finally doused her headlamp, so they were surrounded by total darkness. Cliff realized he was effectively deaf and blind in a room that contained at least twenty man-eating cephids and one cold-blooded killer.

He had to help Rica.

She was moving around beside him. He heard fabric being cut and knew his ears were recovering. "What are you doing?" he whispered.

"My leg," she groaned. He could hear her quavering breaths now. "Flesh wound, I think . . . lot of blood, though . . . tying on one of my shoulder straps."

"Are you hit anywhere else?"

"Don't think so. You?"

"No."

"We have to keep him away from the kids."

"How?" Cliff asked.

"I don't know. Can you get back to the ALV in the dark?"

"Yes, but . . . can you even walk?"

"I'll *run* if I have to," Rica whispered. "Go finish the bomb the way I showed you. Let Todd help. I'll try to take care of Wimbledon."

Cliff ran toward the ALV, holding out his hands in case he blundered into a wall. At least the other cephids were still preoccupied, fighting over the scattered remains of their comrades. He could hear wet slaps and slithers and sounds of puncturing and grinding all around him, along with splats of liquid dripping from the ceiling.

Rica got up on her feet, a task that took more effort than she once would have thought she could muster. At least the wound could have been a lot worse, she thought. The bullet had passed just beneath the skin on the outside of her left thigh. If it had impacted two inches to her right, it would have shattered her femur, possibly causing her to bleed to death in minutes. The wound *was* bleeding freely, but not fast enough for shock to be an immediate danger.

She tried taking a step. Her lacerated quadriceps quivered and ached but bore her weight.

She knew the cephids would soon finish scavenging. Then they would follow the smell of blood until it led them to her. If she was going to confront Chester, it had to be soon. But first she had to determine for certain which of the eight radiating passages he was hiding in.

She stood with another bare grenade, ready to release the spoon, and shouted his name.

There was no response.

"I know where you are!" she yelled. "I'm coming to get you!"

A peal of strained laughter came from dead ahead. "I nicked you, didn't I?" His voice was still thick and nasal from his swollen face.

*Now* she knew where he was, unless the echoes had deceived her. She flicked on her headlamp just long enough to glance around the crystalline vault, then turned it back off and stepped sideways in case Chester took another shot at her. Keeping her gaze locked in the direction of his hiding place, she released the grenade's spoon and hurled it through the darkness.

She heard a few cephids race into the tunnel after the grenade. They sounded like they were still fighting over it when it blasted a few of them into greasy paste on the walls.

Rica stood on her good leg, wondering if her rapid pulse was all from exertion and fear or partly from blood loss. She could feel chunks of blood already frozen solid in her clothing. She pulled out another grenade and flicked on her headlamp again.

Chester was standing directly in front of her with the pistol in his right hand. His right side and the gun were covered with bluish glop and tiny bits of transparent cephid flesh. Apparently her last grenade had barely missed him.

Rica flicked her light back off and turned to run, but the twisting motion tore something in her punctured leg. She collapsed with a grunt of pain, dropping the grenade as her chin slammed down on the sharp frost. She tried to get up but fell again, then crawled toward the nearest wall. Her damaged quadriceps jerked with involuntary spasms but would not flex at her command.

Slow footsteps approached behind her, crampons crunching the frost. Then a light came on, projecting her kneeling shadow in front of her.

"I knew what you were doing the first time you turned on your light, *girl*. Did you think I'm as dumb as you are?"

Rica pulled herself forward by digging her short fingernails into the frost. She also managed to grip the ice with the
crampon points on the inside of her good foot. Her wounded
leg dragged behind, quivering.

"I think I'd rather have you facing me," Chester said.

Determined not to oblige him, Rica kept her left cheek to
the frosty wall as she hopped to a standing position by relo-
cating the crampon points of her good foot an inch at a time.

Chester grabbed her arm and spun her around, then
jumped back with the gun aimed at her chest. "Come on, I
want to see in your eyes how sorry you are that you left me
locked in that fucking cage."

"I wonder . . ." Rica panted. A grunt of pain escaped her
as she hopped to keep her balance. When she caught her
breath, she said, "I wonder when you'll get tired of waiting."

"Bitch!" He raised the gun until it was pointed at her
face.

His headlamp partially blinded her, but she could make
out the throng of cephids behind him. Two of them were
scraping their tooth-studded radulas across the walls to lick
up the remains of their obliterated comrades, but the rest just
stood there with their eye stalks extended, as if they were an
audience at a play. If they smelled the blood from her bullet
wound, they gave no indication.

Despite her pain and fear and exhaustion and rage, Rica
got an idea.

The longer she delayed, the better her chances were. She
tried desperately to think of a way to stall. Despite her dry
mouth, she finally found words. "You know, Wimbledon, it
takes a special kind of man to shoot an unarmed woman
point-blank."

Chester began to squeeze the trigger, baring his tobacco-
stained teeth.

"Why don't you just beat me to death?" she asked. "You
saved your ammo when you caught up with Bonnie."

Chester pulled the trigger.

Rica almost fainted when she heard the click, but she

knew what it meant. The gun had jammed, no doubt gummed up by a sliver of flesh from one of the cephids she had blown apart.

With a snarl of frustration, Chester drew back the slime-coated pistol and poked at its slide with his other hand.

As soon as he looked down, Rica made her move.

She leaped straight upward and kicked with her good leg. It was a high uppercut kick, designed to break an opponent's neck by impacting his chin with the ball of the foot and snapping his head backward. Under ideal conditions in a martial arts gym, she had once scored seventeen consecutive kills against a computerized dummy with this move.

The kick she delivered now was the strongest of her life, but her aim was off. Instead of a solid impact against Chester's chin, all she felt was a weak tug as her boot sole grazed his right jaw. Nevertheless, he screamed as if gored by a bull, and she could see why. Her crampon points had flayed his face from chin to temple, leaving parallel flaps of skin that reminded her of gills except for the blood gushing from them.

When Rica came back down from her leap, her wounded leg buckled, and she fell straight down on her tailbone. The abrupt compression of her injured spine caused a sensation as if all of her vertebrae had collided and shattered. She fell over sideways and jerked in agony, repeatedly kicking the floor.

Chester tried to stomp her left hand with his crampon spikes, but she managed to pull it aside. Meanwhile, she reached down and untied the severed backpack strap stanching the flow of blood from her leg.

Holding his butchered face, he went for her calf. Rica dodged his spikes again, and in the same motion of her good right leg, she kicked out sideways and folded his knees.

He slammed down on his back with a loud "Oof!"

While he was stunned by the fall, she sat up and began

whipping him with the blood-soaked pack strap, slinging it up and down as fast as she could, lashing him in a different place each time. Each lick left a broad streak of blood across his filthy clothing and spattered him all over with fine droplets.

Chester started laughing. Rica was relieved that he seemed to have no idea what she was doing. He apparently thought she was trying to physically hurt him with the padded strap, that she was feebly attempting to resist in the way a feminine caricature might.

His guffaws abruptly ceased when the cephids closed in, drawn by the atomized blood in the air.

Rica dropped the strap and scrambled back to the wall, then crawled along it away from the cephids. Unlike Chester, she'd been keeping an eye on them, making sure she still had an escape route. She had plenty of blood on her as well, although less than a tenth of the gore that now covered Chester from head to toe.

Chester jumped to his feet and twisted back and forth in a limber crouch, staring at the closing throng. "What's wrong with you?" he bellowed.

He bolted to the right, but two cephids intertwined their arms across his path.

He dashed back to the left and was headed off again.

Rica watched for any signs that the cephids had noticed her too, but they all seemed intent on the game of trapping Chester.

Now surrounded on all sides, Chester boldly stepped up to the nearest cephid and slapped one of its extended eyeballs. The cephid lurched and retracted the eye but did not break formation. Chester swung at the other eye, but it dodged his blow and he lost his balance. He bounced off the cephid's rubbery barrel-body and landed on the floor.

Looking up, Chester raised his long bony arms above his face in a vain attempt to ward off the tangle of glassy tendrils that was descending toward him like a net. "Girl! Help! Please help!"

Rica watched as the cephid arms twined around him from end to end and lifted him above his attackers. He screamed and kicked with the fury of a netted shark, but the sucker-clad arms stretched like rubber bands until he had exhausted himself and was able to do nothing but blubber a prayer for mercy.

One of the cephids opened its radula and ingested Chester's head. Another one engulfed his feet. His long limber arms briefly resumed thrashing about, beating spastically at his own chest and sides, then hung limply from his bony shoulders.

His headlamp was the room's only source of illumination. It remained on inside the cephid that had eaten his upper half, lighting up the transparent monster like a jack-o'-lantern. As the blood from Chester's ground-up face diffused through the cephid's clear tissues, the light escaping from its body turned from white to pink to crimson. Eventually it glinted on the huge frost crystals so that the hub chamber looked to Rica like a gigantic geode lined with rubies.

The two cephids that were eating Chester ignored the clubbing from the closed claw-beaks of their jealous comrades. They raced each other as they swallowed their prey, shuffling around counterclockwise like boxers in a ring. Their voraciousness was well matched—the probing tips of their radulas came together at about Chester's waist. When they began to gouge each other with their teeth, both cephids reached down and back with all of their arms, grabbed the floor with their suction cups, and pulled in opposite directions.

Neither monster won the tug-of-war.

Chester came apart in the middle. His spine disengaged from his pelvis and his abdomen ripped open with a sound like tearing sheets. His viscera spilled onto the floor in a steaming heap, which a third cephid moved in to scavenge.

Staring at the ragged edges of Chester's two halves, Rica

finally understood what had happened to Sergeant Gavril. Two fighting cephids had pulled him apart. They had probably left his upper half behind only because the rising sun had forced them to retreat before they could eat it.

# CHAPTER 42

# Bomb

"Cliff, you're not going to stay behind to detonate the octanitro," Rica said.

He looked glumly at the ten-foot-high pyramid of black explosives. "You said *someone* would have to stand here and touch a wire to a battery pole if we're going to—"

"No! I thought of another way when Todd clobbered Chester with the bottle of stove fuel. I can make a crude timer out of the stove. There are more fuel bottles on the ALV."

"Will it be reliable?"

"Yes, just not very precise."

"Here they come again!" Todd yelled.

Rica hopped around the ALV and threw her last baited grenade to hold off the cephids at the mouth of the tunnel. After the explosion, the ringing in her ears sounded different than it had after the previous blasts. As her ears recovered, it resolved into the sound of a waterfall, and it was accompanied by a faint vibration.

Cliff was listening too. "That's not good," he said.

Rica nodded. "Sounds like that last one cracked the hull. If the sea is pouring in, it might flood these tunnels before we can get out."

"I don't see any water," Todd said.

"Yeah, keep working," Rica said.

Todd replaced the screw cap in a fuel bottle with a pressurizing valve. While he pumped the valve's thumb plunger, Rica set up the tiny camp stove, which consisted only of a burner with three steel legs. At her request, Cliff fetched an empty MP-5N submachine gun, then gouged a pile of ice chips from the wall with the toe points of his crampons.

The heavy steel submachine gun would become one side of Rica's makeshift detonation switch. She connected it to the negative battery pole by twisting a naked wire around the ring site at the end of its short barrel. The other side of the switch was the sheet of thick aluminum foil that had come with the stove. It was meant to be set on edge, forming a cylinder around the stove, to protect the flame from wind. Rica spread it out flat on a rubber mat beside the stove.

Rica tested her crude timer with the switch hooked up to the current meter from her demolition kit instead of the bomb. She put the pot on the stove and filled it with ice chunks, then leaned the gun against the pot and removed the chunks one by one until the pot was so light that the weight of the gun shoved it off the stove. When the gun landed on the aluminum foil, the needle of her current meter jumped.

Now she knew the switch would work. She also knew roughly how much water would remain in the pot when it became light enough to drop the gun, if she left it boiling with the gun leaning against it at precisely the same angle.

"That contraption gives me the willies," Cliff whispered.

"Me too," Rica said. "It will definitely detonate the octanitro. The only question is whether it will give us enough time to get out first."

"What if the cephids come in here and mess it up?" Todd asked.

Rica frowned and glanced past the ALV. Only three cephids remained in the pack that had come down to the hub chamber. All three were trudging down the dead-end corridor toward them. The smallest one looked like it weighed less than a hundred pounds. The biggest one was the size of a horse.

She knew now that they were just animals, amazingly smart for sea creatures but not smart enough to know what the bomb was. And these cephids couldn't be hungry—they were all grotesquely bloated with the ingested remains of their comrades. But the curious brutes were apt to consider the jury-rigged timer an irresistible toy.

She saw a flicker of movement on the floor behind the cephids. She refocused her gaze. Water was pouring along the tunnel, about to overtake the cephids.

She turned and looked up at the pyramid of explosive blocks. "Todd, could you climb to the top without pulling out any of the wires?"

"I could try," he said. "Why?"

"Because I know I can't with this leg," she said. "And you're not as heavy as Cliff."

Todd picked his way up the pyramid.

The cephids trudged closer.

Cliff wrinkled his nose. "The stink has changed."

Rica sniffed. "Smells like a sewage leak."

"It's like the flood that Sophie and I were caught in," Todd said.

He had reached the top of the pyramid. She handed the switch and timer apparatus up to him, then gave instructions while he reassembled it on the pinnacle block. She gave him a small piece of duct tape from the roll they'd recovered from Chester's hideout. He used it to lightly attach the gun barrel to the pot, just to make sure the Floe's gentle north-south wobble didn't shake the gun loose and make it fall prematurely.

"The cephids could reach up there," Cliff observed.

"Let's hope they don't," Rica said.

The reeking effluent abruptly surged out from under the ALV, flowing around their boots and the explosives. The empty carcass pit at the end of the tunnel began to fill with the murky liquid. "And we need to put the timer as high up as possible in case this whole tunnel floods," she added.

"Todd, you'd better hurry," Cliff said.

"Almost done," Todd said. He opened the gas flow, lit the burner with Chester's gilded cigarette lighter, adjusted the flame to low, and began descending backward.

Rica twisted together two wires that completed the circuit between the switch and the bomb. Now, if anything disturbed the timer before they could get off the Floe, the result would be one of two disasters: either the bomb would be disabled, or it would detonate immediately.

They scrambled onto the ALV, Rica in the driver's seat.

"Those cephids are going to screw up the timer," Cliff said.

"No, they won't." Rica shifted into gear and stomped the throttle. The ALV responded with a roaring blast of acceleration. "Hang on!"

The three approaching cephids halted, blinking in the headlights with their eye stalks fully extended. They were obviously contemplating the thirty tons of aluminum and steel bearing down on them, shrieking with torque and belching exhaust. Then they tucked in their eyes and executed a quick about-face, flailing their glassy arms above their headless barrel-bodies. Rotating their eyes inside their bodies to look backward, they realized that waddling on their flippers would not save them from the ALV's spinning tracks, and they all dived forward, stretching their arms out to grasp the floor and pull themselves along as if they were swimming.

The medium-size cephid made it out of the tunnel, but the other two fell behind, splashing frantically in the inch-deep flood. The biggest one was too heavy for speed. The smallest one's arms were too short.

Rica swerved left until the ALV scraped the wall, aiming for the horse-size cephid with the vehicle's broad right track. The struggling creature disappeared beneath her field of view. A split second later she heard a loud pop followed by a splash when its mantle cavity ruptured and sprayed out hundreds of gallons of seawater. Its claw-beaks hammered furiously on the antimine armor beneath the troop cabin as the metal track shoes pulped its fat body.

"One down, two to go!" Rica yelled, her forehead bouncing against the periscope.

The small cephid looked back, saw its comrade's demise, and shot an arm straight upward like the tongue of a frog catching a fly. It hoisted itself up and clung to the ceiling as the ALV zoomed past beneath it.

Rica slammed on the brakes.

Cliff glanced at his wristwatch. "What are you doing? The timer—"

Rica shoved the gear shift into reverse and floored it.

When she could see the trembling upside-down cephid blinking in her high beams, she pushed in the clutch and hit the brake again. "Cliff! Go raise the drilling boom until it touches the tunnel ceiling."

He swung around the ladder and up through the roof hatch. A few seconds later, she heard the hydraulic hoist and felt a small jolt. "Go!" he yelled as he slid back down the ladder.

Rica drove forward. She could feel the boom scraping the ceiling, gouging out chunks of ice that rained down on the aluminum roof like hail. The small cephid began swinging like an orangutan toward the mouth of the tunnel, but the ALV caught up to it. After the boom knocked it loose, Rica threw the vehicle into reverse and backed over it, then waited for Cliff to return the boom to its stowed position.

When the ALV sped out into the flooding hub chamber, Rica saw that the water was falling from a network of narrow cracks in the dome-shaped ceiling. The murky effluent was plunging down in thin sheets that reminded her of translucent shower curtains. The curtains of water seemed to partition the vast room into polygonal segments.

"Looks like the ceiling is about to collapse," she said. "One of the live animal pits must be right above us."

"You think there's enough water up there to fill up this level?" Todd asked.

Rica shrugged. "If there is, and the roof comes down, it'll pour into the ALV's snorkel and trap us down here. If it doesn't crush us first."

She caught a glimpse of the medium-size cephid splashing through the curtains of falling water. Apparently it had gotten lost in the maze of cascades but had just found its way, because it disappeared up the main access tunnel a second after she spotted it.

She was about to pursue the cephid when it came slithering back out of the tunnel. It swam across the floor toward the ALV, moving at least as fast as it had when it was trying to get away from her.

"What the hell?" she whispered.

"What?" said Cliff and Todd, who could not see out.

Rica let the ALV sit still. Two crisscrossing curtains of sewage were falling on its roof, drumming and splashing.

When the cephid waded through the last cascade separating it from the ALV's high snout, it flashed its aqua-blue light belts and took off toward a side passage. Rica engaged the clutch, floored the throttle, and ran it down.

She was about to drive into the main access tunnel when she felt a tremor and heard a deep *gulp-boom* that repeated three times.

"Ah, fuck," Cliff whispered.

Something was moving in the shadowed interior of the access tunnel. Rica peered into the periscope. Swirling shimmers of oily iridescence began to dance in her headlights, coming closer. She thought it must be an army of cephids marching in tight formation. Then she realized that it was one solid mass of flesh. The slimy transparent bolus was plugging the entire tunnel.

Cliff shook her shoulder. "Hey, what's going on?"

When it reached the hub chamber, the quivering pulp began to grow out of the tunnel like a chewing-gum bubble.

It surged outward in rhythmic spurts. Rica wondered if it would expand to fill the whole hub chamber.

"It . . . it . . ." she stammered.

Finally some definition began to take shape within the glistening mountain of protoplasm. She saw a curving row of suction cups that ranged from the size of a teacup at one end to the size of a garbage can lid at the other. At the smaller end of the suction cups was a ghostly hint of the smooth, curved, cutting edge of a claw-beak that was big enough to engulf her entire body.

The whole mass of transparent flesh abruptly disgorged from the tunnel and adopted its natural shape, separating into a body and arms and standing up to tower over the ALV. It had unusually thick arms, a missing flipper, a fat and vertically wrinkled barrel-body with a ten-foot gash along one side . . .

"The king cephid is out there, isn't it?" Cliff whispered.

Rica nodded.

Falling water drummed on the roof.

She watched the titanic beast for several seconds. It just stood in front of the headlights, hulking over the ALV. It glowered down with its eye stalks extended, blinking in the deluge.

Rica glanced at her wristwatch and eased herself out of the driver's seat. "Todd, hand me the chain saw."

*"You're going out?"* Cliff hissed.

"It's blocking the exit," she said. "If we ram it, it's bound to attack the ALV—probably tear it apart. Even if we kill it, it'll still block the tunnel. Either way, we won't stand a chance."

"Oh, and you *will*?"

"Maybe," Rica said, breathing fast. "Maybe I can get it to step aside long enough for us to get away." She took the saw from Todd.

"Let's just wait," Todd said. "Maybe it'll go away on its own."

Rica wiped sweat from her forehead and glanced at her

watch again. "I figure we have about fifteen minutes before the bomb goes off. That might not be enough time to get out of the Floe, even if we left right now."

She headed for the rear of the reverberating cabin.

Cliff grabbed her shoulder. "Rica, you can't go out there by yourself, wounded and unarmed!"

She twisted out of his grasp and limped around to face him. "I'm a U.S. Marine," she spat. "Don't you ever try to tell me what I can't do!"

She stepped back and yanked the starter cord. The saw roared to life, belching blue smoke in Cliff's face. She held the long saw bar away from the nearest objects and gunned the engine. The chain's twisted fangs spun smoothly through the air as if reaching for something to cut.

"Tell me I look unarmed to you," she yelled over the reverberating din. "Now open that goddamn door for me."

Cliff stepped to the troop door.

"Rica, please don't go," Todd said.

She looked at him apologetically, her jaws clenched. "I have to, Todd. We're out of time."

She turned to Cliff, nostrils flaring, lips flexed into a hard ring. "If it gets me, and you have a clear path to the access tunnel, you know what to do, right?"

He nodded.

She turned back to the door. "This is what it's all about," she said. Then she took three deep breaths and said, "Open it."

# CHAPTER 43

# Last Stand

Rica limped as fast as she could, half dragging her wounded leg. She headed for the side of the flooding chamber opposite the king cephid, hoping to draw its attention away from the ALV. She had to dive through several of the thin curtains of putrid water. Her chain saw sputtered but kept running. The icy water on the floor was up to her ankles. It poured into her boots as she splashed along.

She reached the wall and turned around, blinking away the effluent draining down her forehead. The ALV's headlights were reflecting and refracting in the maze of thin cascades, turning the hub chamber into a confusing funhouse full of dancing wraiths. She could barely make out the king cephid through the tumbling deluge.

"Hey, asshole!" she screamed. "Remember me?"

Her voice apparently carried through the partitions of plummeting sewage—the king cephid's eye stalks whipped around in her direction. It took one limping step toward her, shaking the floor.

She wondered what the vibrations from the flood and the monster's movement were doing to her precarious timer apparatus. One hard jolt could dislodge the tiny curl of tape between the submachine gun and the pot of ice chunks it was leaning against. Actually, it was probably a pot of boiling water by now, she realized. Anyhow, if the gun fell, it would land on the aluminum foil and the bomb would detonate.

The ALV's engine revved. Rica presumed Cliff was at the controls, prepared to pick her up as soon as the king cephid moved aside.

The beast charged. It swayed back and forth as it lurched across the hub chamber on its remaining three flippers, sending shock waves through the ice. The shaking dislodged a small chunk from the ceiling. When it fell, it was followed by a torrent of murky water. The cascade doubled the roar of the flood, and the water level on the floor seemed to start rising twice as fast.

Rica fought the temptation to flee into one of the side passages. Instead, she raised the chain saw above her head, triggered it up to ten thousand rpm, and screamed, "Come on, you ugly-ass motherfucker!"

The ALV roared and lurched forward into the access tunnel. For a panicky moment, Rica thought Cliff was already leaving without her. Then he stopped with the rear half of the long vehicle sticking out of the tunnel. She realized he had just moved forward to secure their escape route. Now it was up to her to make her way back to the ALV.

She tried to run along the wall, intending to circle around the hub chamber. With her wounded leg and back injury, she only managed to stumble forward. She was directly opposite the ALV when the king cephid cut her off.

One of the beakless arms shot out and wrapped around her legs faster than she could react. The arm constricted, pressing her knees together, and lifted her into the air. Her upper body teetered as she fought to remain upright. She hung on to the saw despite the pain in her legs and back.

Now there could be no doubt that the blood on her leg had nullified her slime masquerade. Or maybe the king cephid was smarter than his comrades.

The arm positioned her under one of the thin cascades.

She held the saw motor away from the waterfall, gasping and sputtering as the tumbling icewater pummeled her head.

She revved the saw's motor and swung its gleaming chrome bar at the cephid's massive arm. A segment of the arm stretched downward, deforming into a horseshoe shape so that the saw's whirring teeth missed it entirely. She tried swinging the saw faster in the opposite direction, but again the treelike arm dodged the blow.

The king cephid lifted her higher, terribly high, almost to the apex of the leaking dome. She wondered if it intended to smash her against the roof or drop her. Either action would have finished the battle instantly.

The monster's conical radula emerged and opened. The four tonguelike lobes curled back, stretching viscous tendrils of saliva. Rica noticed that the tips of the tongues were shriveled and half of their teeth were missing.

The arm lowered her over the open maw, tilting her forward. She resisted bending at the waist, somehow supporting the weight of her upper body and the chain saw with her injured back muscles.

There's no way the fucker can dodge the saw if he eats me, she thought.

One of the giant claw-beaks emerged through a murky waterfall beside her and began to open. Rica swung the saw, triggering it to full speed. The steel teeth rattled against the beak's smooth surface, making the saw's handle jerk like a recoiling machine gun.

The beak opened wide and snapped down on the chrome saw bar. The toothed sprocket chain broke and whipped away through the icy deluge, barely missing Rica's face. Still gripping the bent bar, the beak yanked the saw from her hands and hurled it away. The heavy tool tumbled end-over-end until it disappeared in the shadows.

Rica's back gave out, and her torso flopped forward. She closed her eyes as her face descended toward the quivering radula. At least I died fighting, she thought.

"Hey! Put down my girl, you slimy, stinking, overgrown ball-sack!"

Upside down, she saw Paz Rodriguez standing on the ladder beneath the ALV's roof hatch. His head and shoulders were protruding above the open portal. He tilted his pale head and smiled at her, waving with the three remaining fingers of his left hand—all of his bandages were gone.

He must be delirious, Rica thought.

Paz reached down and lifted something through the hatch with his good arm. He dropped the heavy object on the ALV's roof and shoved it away from him. It was white with red splotches, a rectangular solid about the size of a small microwave oven. When water dripped on it and the red splotches began to run, Rica realized that the object was the minigun battery wrapped in Paz's bloody bandages.

The king cephid stretched out one of its beakless arms to investigate the offering. The arm's suction cups wriggled independently, sniffing at the gore. Paz had turned the bandages inside out to make sure the blood was fresh and abundant.

The king cephid picked up the battery, dropped it over the center of its maw, warped the four radula lobes shut around it, and retracted the indigestible appetizer into its gullet, all the while keeping Rica—its main course—held high above it.

Paz steadied his good arm on the ALV's roof and squinted his left eye shut behind his Colt .45, which Rica knew contained only one bullet.

Please don't miss, she thought.

Paz took his time aiming at the battery as it worked its way down through the cephid's transparent gut. There was one sheet of falling water between them. Paz was trembling all over from the exertion of climbing the ladder in his barely conscious state. Blood was running down his mutilated arm.

He fired.

The pistol kicked upward, emitting a muzzle flash and a loud report.

For a moment, there was nothing. The king cephid reopened its radula lobes and resumed lowering Rica. Then it dropped her. She landed headfirst, gashing her left cheek on one of the thin triangular teeth.

She rolled over and sat up, wiping diluted blood and a sticky gob of saliva from her face.

Why weren't the sofa-size tongues closing around her? She could feel them twitching. The teeth were jabbing her rear end, which was sitting in a puddle of ice-cold sewage that had collected in the depression between the peeled-back lobes.

She felt herself rotating and looked out beyond the petals of the putrid, dagger-studded flower. The king cephid was gliding across the flooded floor, circling around the hub chamber and spinning like a ballerina. Curtains of icy water swept over Rica, one after another.

The monster began jumping up and down—a few inches at first, then higher than a foot—sending splashes up the walls. The cephid's bizarre seizure flung Rica up in the air as if she were bouncing on a trampoline. The higher she flew, the more painfully the teeth jabbed her when she splashed back down.

She grabbed one of the sticky radula lobes and heaved herself over the side. It was like falling out of an apple tree, which she had done twice. She seemed to bounce off several rubbery arms before the final plunge of at least ten feet.

The fall would have finished her if the floor had been dry, but the flood was now at least three feet deep. She splashed down face-first but instinctively held her breath. Her training kicked in the instant she hit bottom. By the time she bobbed to the surface, she was swimming flat-out toward the ALV. Now her leg wound hardly mattered, and even her twisted back barely slowed her swift American crawl.

Behind her, the transparent leviathan continued its strange dance, bouncing and spinning faster until centrifugal force extended its heavy arms straight outward from its wrinkled body. Its eyes popped in and out, and thick white foam bubbled up from its maw. Its claw-beaks slammed against the wall as they swung around, dislodging chunks of ice.

Rica saw a pair of human legs surging through the flood in front of her. It was Cliff. He was wading out to help her. She grabbed his belt and hoisted herself erect.

The king cephid's huge intestine was jerking and twisting like a wounded snake within its transparent body. Rica wondered how the organ could move so independently—surely it was anchored to the abdominal wall. Then she saw that the intestine had been separated into two parts. Between them, amid a cloud of bubbles, she saw a dark rectangular object that could only be the minigun's punctured battery.

Cliff dragged her toward the open troop door. "Come on," he said, "it's headed this way." She was shivering wildly and felt suddenly weak as she slogged through the icy flood.

Paz waved down at them from the roof hatch.

Rica yelled, "Get down from there, Rodriguez!"

The spinning leviathan bumped into the ALV and paused in its dance.

Rica had never felt so helpless, and never would again, as she did when the king cephid reached down three of its four beakless arms and wrapped Paz's body from chin to ankles. Her brother Marine met her gaze for a split second. She clearly saw the look of grief, pain, and terror on his boyish face. Then the arms jerked him upward into the air.

She yelled his name but got no reply. The king cephid lifted him toward the dripping ceiling above its open radula lobes.

And crushed him.

Rica saw the glassy arms that encircled his chest abruptly constrict as his rib cage imploded. "No!" she screamed, so hard that something seemed to tear apart in her throat.

The king cephid began to engulf Paz feetfirst.

A few seconds later, the titanic beast fell over on its side. The crash generated a wave that splashed up the walls, surged into the ALV, and nearly knocked Cliff and Rica off their feet. She saw a cascade of white froth gush from the monster's bottom end. The foam piled up in a delta and began to float away on the choppy flood.

The king cephid's arms barely twitched, but its radula lobes kept working, dragging Paz in deeper. His blood had already given the giant intestine an opaque crimson color down to the perforation where battery acid had corroded the organ in two.

Finally the radula stopped moving. Only Paz's head and arms remained outside the cephid. Rica waded to him and bent over his face, shielding it from the dripping water. He blinked—once, twice—then his lips moved. She leaned her ear close to his mouth, but no words came out.

His face went slack.

Rica closed his eyes, then hung her head and sobbed, letting the icy drips from the ceiling land on her twisted back. She had not genuflected in years, so it felt strange making the sign of the cross now, but she tried. Then she kissed Paz's wet forehead and whispered in his ear.

"Brother . . . live on."

# CHAPTER 44

# Collapse

Rica drove. They headed for the Floe's stern at full throttle, recklessly surging through the tight passages. "I'm surprised the bomb hasn't gone off already," she yelled.

"Maybe another pack of cephids came down and messed up the timer," Todd said. "Or the flood shorted it out."

"We're pretty far away by now," Cliff said. "Maybe it did go off but we couldn't hear the blast."

"I doubt that," Rica said. She let the ALV tilt up sideways to take a sharp bend at full speed.

For the next ten minutes no one spoke. Rica kept her eyes glued to the periscope, concentrating on remembering the circuitous route to the opening they had found on the Floe's stern. Todd comforted Sophie. Cliff repeatedly checked his watch. Finally he slammed his palm against a wall and hung his head. "Goddamn it! Nothing's going to stop the Floe now. I can't believe it didn't work."

Rica said nothing. Demolishing the Floe had been her responsibility. After so much sacrifice, she could hardly believe the mission had failed.

Without warning something hit the ALV from behind with enough force to break her grip on the figure-eight steering control. The impact ground her back into her seat, flinging back her head. Only her headrest prevented the blow from snapping her neck.

When she bounced forward, her breasts smashed into the steering control and her left temple banged against the periscope. She could feel the pain but felt strangely detached from it, as if she had already endured so much that her brain had decided to start ignoring it.

Cliff lay on his side, wrapped around the forward frame of the door to the driver's box. He wasn't moving.

She could hear Sophie screaming back in the troop cabin, then Todd's footsteps. Her foot had slipped off the gas, and the engine had died. The ALV was eerily motionless. Todd came forward with his sister in his arms and knelt by Cliff, who was groaning and trying to push himself up.

"What happened?" Todd asked.

"Shock wave," Rica said. "Listen."

A mostly subaudible rumble was growing louder. It seemed to come from all around. After a few seconds, it became so loud that Todd put his palms over Sophie's ears.

The ALV began to shake.

Rica restarted the engine, shifted into gear, and floored the throttle. "Here we go!"

Cliff was sitting up, holding his head. Todd hunkered down beside him, bracing Sophie against his chest.

The shaking grew worse until the springy driver's seat was bouncing Rica up and down. "We should be almost there!" she yelled.

"What?" Cliff shouted, cupping a hand to one ear.

The vibration of the periscope and her eyes turned Rica's view field into a sequence of dancing images that flashed by too fast for her to make sense of them. She kept the throttle at maximum, even though she couldn't see where she was going. If she remembered correctly, there were no more intersections before the exit, so she could rely on the curvature of the tunnel to guide the ALV. When the vehicle tilted up on the right, she steered left. When it tilted up on the left, she steered right.

Small chunks of ice were falling from the walls and ceiling. The air was full of ice dust that glittered in the headlights, sparkling with rainbow colors.

Rica caught a glimpse of something new ahead—angular shapes and shadows. A split second later she realized that a segment of the roof must have collapsed.

She slammed on the brakes. The ALV skidded, swinging left and right. "Hang on!" she yelled.

The vehicle ground to a halt a few feet short of the blockade. The jumble of broken ice chunks completely filled the tunnel. "Goddamn it!" Rica screamed.

"What's wrong?" Cliff yelled. He was kneeling beside her to put his mouth close to her ear.

"Cave-in," she shouted.

"Should we go back?"

"To where?" she asked. "The last intersection was five minutes ago. The Floe's not going to last that long."

"How close are we?" he asked.

"To the rubble?"

"To the exit."

"Should be dead ahead," she said.

He glanced at his watch. "Turn off your lights."

She doused the headlights. As her eyes adjusted to the darkness, she could see several bright pinpoints in front of the ALV. A narrow ray of light projected toward her from each point, illuminating swirling motes of ice dust.

She looked into Cliff's frightened eyes.

"Sunlight?" he guessed.

She nodded.

Sunlight shining through the rubble meant the exit was close. It also meant the barricade was not very thick.

They both glanced at Todd, who was preoccupied with trying to comfort Sophie. Then Cliff leaned forward and kissed her on the lips. "Do it," he said.

She slammed the transmission into reverse and stomped the throttle.

"What are we doing?" Todd yelled.

"I'm going to try to punch through," Rica shouted. "It's our only chance."

The ALV accelerated in reverse, bouncing off the walls. The tremor was now so vigorous that she could hardly maintain her grip on the steering control.

Todd scooted his back against the front wall of the troop cabin, clutching Sophie to his chest. He grabbed a sleeping pad to place behind his head and shouted, "Don't worry, Rica! Everything will be all right. We've done this before."

After backing up a hundred yards or so, she slammed on the brakes and shifted to first before the ALV stopped skidding. The vehicle continued backward, slowing as the tracks spun against the ice. Finally its movement reversed direction. The rumble had become so loud that Rica could not hear the roaring engine or the grinding tracks, but she could feel the ALV's maddeningly sluggish acceleration. Through the periscope, she could see cracks propagating along all sides of the passage.

The barricade zoomed closer until it abruptly expanded beyond the perimeter of her view field. Rica jerked away from the periscope and threw her forearms up in front of her face. "Semper Fi!" she yelled.

Semper Fidelis was the Latin motto of the U.S. Marine Corps. It meant *Always Faithful*.

The southern end of the Floe was a wet white wall that gleamed in the morning sun. The wall was randomly polka-dotted with dark round holes. Ranging from a few feet to several yards in diameter, they would have all appeared as tiny as pinpoints to an observer who was floating far enough away on the calm blue sea to take in the whole vast wall at a glance.

When all else was still tranquil at this end of the collapsing ice slab, one of these thousands of holes erupted. It was one of the largest holes, and one of the lowest above sea level. The white fragments and dust that spewed out of it sparkled with rainbow colors in the bright sunshine and then splashed down into the ocean.

Along with the last of the frozen debris, the dark opening disgorged a machine. The machine was rectangular, the size of a dump truck except not as tall. Its rear half was white and its front half was gray. Its tank tracks spun in the air, throwing off more bits of ice, until the vehicle's broad chisel-snout plunged into the sea. The parted waves clapped back together, launching a fountain of white spray a hundred feet high. Then the machine bobbed back to the surface and floated on the calm North Pacific.

Less than a minute later, all of the thousands of holes in the vast white wall simultaneously coughed out plumes of dust and debris, like windows blown out of a building by an indoor explosion. Then the whole honeycomb began to descend, compressed by its own weight, squeezing out jets of wind and airborne debris from the collapsing tunnels. The ice cracked and crumbled, falling from the wall in fragments of all shapes. The tumbling chunks ranged in size from particles borne aloft on the sea breeze to gargantuan segments the size of shopping malls that were riddled with tunnels on all sides.

In front of the rolling bergs and thundering splashes, the relatively miniscule amphibious vehicle sped away from the destruction, leaving a narrow wake of froth behind its powerful water jets.

Rica held Sophie and let Todd look back through the periscope.

"Holy cow!" he said.

"Is it over yet?" Cliff asked.

"Almost," Todd said, "but a bunch of huge waves are coming this way. Everybody hang on."

The passing swells were gentle but thrilling, making the passengers feel weightless when the low-floating ALV sank into the troughs.

"I can't . . . believe it," Rica stammered. "I can't believe we actually made it." Tears were streaming down her cheeks as she handed the baby back to Todd.

She motioned for Cliff to pass her a canteen.

"You're pale," he said as she poured water into her parched mouth. Her hand shook so much that half of the water spilled on her chest.

"Dizzy too," she said. "I've lost at least a pint. Hey, Todd, I haven't heard Sophie cough—is she okay?"

"She'll be fine once she forgets all of this," Todd said. "I wish *I* could forget, but I never will."

"Do you think we got all the cephids?" Rica asked. She was thinking of Gavril and Paz and Joan and all of the other good people who had been lost on this colossal clusterfuck of a mission, as Gunny would have put it.

"Only time will tell," Cliff said with a morose sigh.

"What's wrong," Rica asked, "besides the obvious. Do you miss Dr. Price?"

"Yes. He was the best friend I ever had. But I was also thinking . . . never mind, it's silly after so many people have been killed."

"What? I want to know."

"Well, I was hoping to bring back a cephid carcass, or at least some organs, but we lost everything. I even lost the egg I collected during the dive. We don't have a single specimen to study."

Rica laid her head back with a wry smile. "Which means we don't have a shred of evidence that the cephids exist. We didn't even take pictures. We're going to have a ball at the debriefing."

Cliff laughed sarcastically. "That might be the worst part yet." Looking into the periscope, he said, "There's nothing left now but little bergs."

Cliff turned his head to look at Rica, then swished aside the greasy hair hanging in his face and squinted again into the periscope. He reached for Rica's hand.

She took another drink and began to nod off. Her tears would not stop flowing, even though she was dehydrated

and so emotionally depleted that she felt numb on the inside.
She wondered whether the tears were from grief, pain, relief, hope, or just exhaustion. Maybe it was a combination of
all those feelings, and more.

Rica briefly woke when the Osprey landed like a helicopter beside the seaside runway at the Kaneohe Bay Marine Corps Base in Hawaii. She saw the crimson glow of
sunset seeping into the cabin, and she caught her breath. For
a moment her heart pounded like an air hammer, still slow
from sleep but hard enough to hurt. Her gaze darted in all directions, looking for a passing blue shadow or shimmers of
oily liquid glass. Her ears were alert for gurgles and slithers.
Then she remembered where she was and that there was no
longer a rational reason to fear the approaching darkness.
Still, she couldn't help the feeling of dread resurrected by
the vibrating passenger cabin and the setting sun.

"Solid ground at last," Cliff said. He had been asleep too,
and was still holding her hand. He reached up and plucked
at a tuft of her coal-black hair as if lamenting its shortness.
"So, do you think your dad will be impressed now?"

She thought about that as the Osprey's two huge propellers spun down and white vehicles bristling with antennae converged on the tilt-rotor craft from all sides. Two of
them were ambulances with their emergency lights dis-
creetly turned off.

"Nope, not a chance," she said in a hoarse whisper.
"Even if I could tell him—which of course I can't, because
they'll make us keep this whole disaster a secret until the
end of time. But you know what? *I don't care.* Being a soldier is not about proving something personal. It's about getting a dangerous job done—the most dangerous and most
important job there is—and surviving to do it again when
it's necessary."

"Are you going to reenlist?"

"Damn right," Rica groaned. "Soon as I get out of the
hospital." She lay her bruised and lacerated head back

against the seat. "I feel like I've been through about six consecutive plane crashes, but you know what I figured out a little while ago?"

"What?" Cliff asked.

She slowly turned toward him with a weak but wicked grin and whispered, "No matter why I enlisted, *I was born for this shit.*"

Cliff shuddered and rolled his eyes. "I guess the rest of us are lucky that somebody is."

Rica swallowed and closed her eyes, holding her throbbing leg wound. "A week ago, I was actually thinking about going to college," she said, "but I don't think I'd care for the stress of taking tests all the time."

Cliff stared at her curiously until he saw one corner of her mouth curl upward. Then he realized it was a joke and chuckled.

"What about you?" she asked. "Are you going to keep working so hard? I think you've earned a break."

"That probably depends on whether I can get funding for an expedition to look for the natural habitat of the cephids," he said.

She opened one eye. "You serious? I wouldn't mind facing combat again, but not with the cephids." Despite his fatigue, she could see embers of curiosity smoldering in Cliff's eyes. "You *are* serious. You're crazier than I am."

He lifted her bruised right hand and kissed the back of it. "We'll see," he said.

# ZERØ

A NOVEL OF TECHNOLOGY V. NATURE

# HOUR

T H E

C O U N T D O W N

B E G I N S .

ONYX

# BENJAMIN
# E. MILLER